Westerville Public Library

written by local author

LOST SOULS RECOVERED

ERIC WALKER

Torchflame Books
Durham, NC

Copyright © 2022 Eric Walker

Lost Souls Recovered
Eric Walker
edubbiey@aol.com

Published 2022, by Torchflame Books
an Imprint of Light Messages Publishing
www.lightmessages.com
Durham, NC 27713 USA
SAN: 920-9298

Paperback ISBN: 978-1-61153-474-0
Hardcover ISBN: 978-1-61153-496-2
E-book ISBN: 978-1-61153-475-7
Library of Congress Control Number: 2022915250

ALL RIGHTS RESERVED
No part of this publication may be reproduced, stored in a retrieval system, or transmitted in any form or by any means, electronic, mechanical, photocopying, recording, scanning, or otherwise, except as permitted under Section 107 or 108 of the 1976 International Copyright Act, without the prior written permission except in brief quotations embodied in critical articles and reviews.

This is a work of fiction. All characters, organizations, and events portrayed in this novel are either products of the author's imagination or are used fictitiously.

To my parents
who encouraged me to write my story.

All that I am, my mother made me.
—John Quincy Adams

1

SPRING, 1887

Even with the War a little more than two decades in the past, John was a virtual slave, chained to the people who'd once legally owned his mother. At seventeen, and his youth pulling at him to go, to explore, to find a woman, he hankered to break the chain and go elsewhere—anywhere that wasn't Richmond—but thoughts of leaving his saintly mother kept the chain in place.

His mother would die of a broken heart if he told her about what Madame Laura Billingsly had made him do a few years back. Laura had figured he wouldn't tell a soul, surely not his mother, and certainly not Monsieur Tyrone Billingsly. Laura had been right.

He hated the suffocating mental cage Madame Billingsly caused him to live in; she had taken away his freedom to even tell a secret to his mother. As much as he wanted to mute the voices in his head telling him to kill Madame Billingsly, the voices lingered.

He stood one spring evening in the butler's pantry and poured imported sherry into two teardrop sherry glasses as he had done so many times. He could pour exactly three ounces of sherry into each glass with his eyes closed without spilling a drop.

John was a lean, five foot, eleven inches tall. He had short, wavy, raven-black hair, russet copper-tinted eyes, a mahogany-colored face, full lips, and a slightly bent nose that sat atop a strong jaw.

Tyrone Billingsly demanded that John be turned out in fine clothes when he worked in the house or when he took Billingsly to town. So this evening he wore the usual attire—a white shirt with a stiff, standing collar; a black vest that closed almost at the throat, thereby almost covering his tie; a short, black waist jacket that exposed his shirt cuffs; black breeches; and black-laced shoes.

It was almost dinner time at the Billingslys' mansion, also known as *Billingsly*.

Torrential rain had enveloped Richmond for five consecutive days. The crop fields, cleared by former slave labor, had turned into bogs.

Laura stood in front of the oversized roundel dining room window, her right hand pressed against it. She felt the window vibrate as the hail and rain pelted it. She looked at the leaden sky and wondered if the window, and all the windows in her mansion, would protect her and her expensive furnishings from the relentless barrage of water sent from above.

She saw in the reflection when Tyrone sat at the dining table; then she drew the heavy, ornate blue-velvet curtains and joined him at the other end. Just the two of them.

The Billingsly estate was large—both the house and the three hundred acres of surrounding land. The house was an eight thousand square foot, twenty-five room Greek Revival house, characterized by Dorian pillars that wrapped around it. Intricate wrought iron gates connected the pillars on the second-floor portico. The long entranceway leading to the front of *Billingsly* was adorned with live oak trees that were arranged symmetrically on each side. Sprawling gardens and landscaping contained twenty-four flower beds and twenty different kinds of trees. Seemingly endless walkways formed a maze. A heavily adorned pergola stood at the rear of the massive botanical garden.

Laura had been known to lose herself in the gardens after an argument with her husband.

When the last of the Billingsly children had moved out several years ago, Tyrone Billingsly had decided to reduce his kitchen staff, expecting that he and Laura could get by with one cook. Laura had protested, believing that her society friends would whisper that something was wrong with the Billingslys, that they were depleting their money. Tyrone had won that battle, but Laura knew when to keep her powder dry and when to strike with a full-frontal assault.

Her husband had felt it many times before, as had Sam, John, Ann, and anyone else in her line of fire.

Sam, the Billingslys' longtime cook, had prepared one of Laura's favorite dishes for the evening: lobster cutlet, a pastry shell filled with a timbale of black grouse in a chestnut purée, spring lamb, and johnnycake.

The Billingslys often had a bracer before their meal. Today was no different. The sherry aperitif would be served at six-thirty as was their custom when Tyrone was in town. And maraschino cherry sorbet would be served at the end of the meal to refresh the palate.

John's stomach gurgled and his hands felt heavy as he prepared to serve dinner to the Billingslys. He closed his eyes and took a deep breath to exorcise all images of what Laura had done to him a few years ago and to slow his heart rate as much as he could. He stood ramrod straight, picked up the salver that held the Billingslys' sherry aperitif, and walked gingerly into the dining room. He surveyed the dining table setup, hoping, praying, that he had set the table pieces to Madame Billingsly's satisfaction. She was persnickety and the icy matron of the house. Everything was in place, and John's heartbeat returned to its normal rhythm.

A thunderclap startled him, causing him to stop in his tracks. Horrible images of Laura resurfaced. His heartbeat quickened again, and his mouth went dry, anticipating some kind of rebuke from her, his perfect table setup notwithstanding.

A corner of the ornate Persian rug on which the dining table sat was curled up. John failed to notice it, tripped, and spilled the drink on the Ice Queen.

She shot him a three-second basilisk stare, then screamed: "You stupid idiot!"

As she used her white, monogrammed linen napkin in an effort to dry the amber stain from the lace on her pink satin polonaise, John said, "I'm sorry, Madame Billingsly."

She raised her head from her dress, and John suffered through the same stare that could stop a charging bull in his tracks. He thought he had gotten used to Madame Billingsly's obloquies, but this time they stung hard, penetrating the fortress he'd erected around himself to deflect her fusillade of contemptuous sniping. She had managed, though, to intensify his hatred for her.

"Laura, it was an accident," Tyrone said.

Laura rose up from her chair in a huff, paused to steady herself from John's mishap, and hurried over to look in the Louis XV gilt-framed mirror, which hung above the Louis XV-styled birch sideboard. She turned and eyed Tyrone.

John watched the amber-colored stain on her dress expand in size.

She stormed out of the dining room and ran up the garish, sweeping, walnut-paneled staircase, hurried to the master bedroom, and slammed the door.

Tyrone took in a mouthful of grouse, then suddenly dropped his fork.

The clank from the fork startled John, who was cleaning the table of the wreckage from the spilled sherry. John looked into Tyrone's stoic gaze. "I'm sorry, sir. I didn't see the carpet was out of place."

Tyrone looked at the rug and nodded.

—m—

Laura stood in front of the cheval in her bedroom and removed her corset with the assistance of her servant, Emmaline, or Auntie Em, as Laura's children referred to her. Laura was a petite woman with Victorian-pale skin and long flaxen-colored hair, which she often kept in a stylish chignon netted in black velvet. She was fastidious about her coiffure and had an on-call coiffeuse. Although she'd had a curvilinear shape that had caused men to ogle when she was younger, she'd begun to fill out after the last of her four children moved out. She allowed her expensive clothes to camouflage her amorphous shape.

Tyrone opened the stately oak bedroom door and walked in. Laura was in the walk-in closet where she had stockpiled her expensive and haute attire. *Godey's Lady's Book*, *Harper's Bazaar*, and *The Delineator* kept her abreast of the latest fashions. Her wardrobe was replete with the finest silks, wools, and cottons. She had dresses for each occasion—day, afternoon, evening, and formal. Her clothes were needed for the bon ton who visited her. When robed in her togs, she exuded authority that exceeded her physical stature.

After making Tyrone wait for a sufficient amount of time, she walked out of the closet. "His behavior was most unacceptable. I want that sprat out of here. I don't trust him." Arms folded, she looked at Tyrone through narrow eyes, waiting for him to spill out the right answer.

"My dear, it was an accident."

She tightened her folded arms, as if to wait for the right answer.

Tyrone stood his ground. "For God's sake, just let it go. That boy does fine work around here. Besides, I owe it to Ann to keep him here. And if I were to dismiss him, who'd serve you as well as that boy? He's smart; he does what he's told."

Her anger flared hot, she drew herself up even more stiffly and shouted a harsh retort. "I don't give a damn." She paused to let Tyrone feel her words.

He shook his head but said nothing.

She continued: "Stop defending that insolent boy; I mean it."

She turned around to see Emmaline holding her black pelisse with both arms outstretched, mutely asking if she would like to try it on. Laura liked wearing her haute attire, even if for a moment.

Although Laura didn't care if Emmaline heard her use disparaging language when referring to a Negro, Emmaline managed to escape such degrading remarks. Even after the War, Laura still considered Emmaline her property, for which she deserved some protection.

Although the irony was not lost on Tyrone, he didn't say anything; he had learned to live with it.

Laura loathed that Tyrone had always been so paternalistic with his slaves and the ones who were his present workers. She thought he was too nice for his own good, failing to understand the immutable law of nature that separated the gentry from the untouchables, the mudsills.

John's shift finally ended, giving him a reprieve from Laura's painful disdain. He changed into his tattered togs, placing his work attire in a wardrobe reserved for the house servants. He stepped out the back door and quickly felt the driving rain on his face. He returned to the house and retrieved a mackintosh from the servants' closet and donned it.

He cut through the Billingslys' soggy, wooded botanical garden in the back of the estate, jumped a small wooden fence, and with anger fueling him, he sprinted a quarter of a mile to get home.

2

SPRING, 1887

Ann hung damp clothes on a rope line in the open room of the slave cabin she shared with John; it was a cabin along with others in the area that was built by slave labor a few years before the Billingsly's slaves would have a place to live. When her body cooperated, doing the laundry was her job, as well as sweeping the floor, cooking, and washing the dishes. Her hovel was small, but it was hers, and she did what she could to keep it tidy.

She was a stout forty-nine-year-old with grape-colored skin and dark brown, recessed eyes. Tufts of unruly black hair dangled from her blue-and-white checkered madras tignon.

When not working at the Billingsly estate, John's job had grown into hunting for food and doing whatever Ann needed him to do when her body failed her.

As she wrapped John's trousers around the rope line, she winced at the stabbing pain in her back. She toddled to the wall and put her right hand on it to steady her balance. The pain began to subside after she took in three deep breaths. She knew the routine: Stop and breathe deeply. It often worked, as it did this time.

The front door flung open, and she turned slowly. John stood in the doorway, huffing, his clothes rain-soaked, his ego bruised. Ann had seen this expression before, an expression she knew could bring trouble to her son.

"Something wrong?" she asked. She pointed to one of the mismatched kitchen table chairs for John to sit.

John was too angry to sit. He wiped the rivulets of water that dripped from his hair onto his forehead.

"You listen to what your mama say. Now sit," Ann insisted.

His mother was all he had in the world, so he dared not argue with her. He removed the mackintosh.

Ann wrapped a quilt around him. After John's measured descent to the chair, Ann said, "Now, tell me what's on your mind, son."

He was restless, moving his legs up and down in rapid fashion, and he made fists subconsciously. "I'm not working for Madame Billingsly again."

He told her about the accident with the sherry just ninety minutes earlier.

Ann was quiet as John droned on about Laura. Her mind wandered off to the time and effort she'd expended to convince Master Billingsly to hire John to work in his house. She had worked hard to convince her former owner that John was ready to graduate from the field to the house. In one entreaty, Ann had said, "My boy's ready; he'll do you proud, Massa," as Ann continued to call him, even after slavery was abolished over two decades ago.

She had been an exceptional nurse to the Billingsly children before she'd developed debilitating arthritis in her back, which later forced her to stop working for the Billingslys as a house servant. Tyrone gratefully remembered that Ann had once stayed by his youngest son's side for thirty-six hours, never leaving him—except for a few comfort breaks--until his fever broke. Despite Laura's protest, Tyrone, in appreciation for Ann's exemplary servitude, allowed Ann to remain in the cabin following the War, and he allowed her to feed from his trough of crops after she was no longer able to work.

Billingsly had worried that John was too young at fourteen and a half to do housework, but he'd give him a try. John turned out to be a quick study and was soon able to master the chores of a house servant, or garçon, as Laura frequently called him in a dismissive manner.

Ann had wept with delight when she'd first seen John dressed in something other than the rags he wore when working in the field and even in church.

John's future was now staring Ann in the face again. "John, my precious son, listen to me. It's a good job for a boy like you to work in that house. Could benefit you later someday," Ann said while rubbing his cheeks with both hands.

John's anger was still strong. "Mama, you washed their clothes ... nursed their children. You took care of them from head to toe. Same for that house. You even prayed and took care of Madame Billingsly when she was real sick. It's too painful to even think about."

Ann reached across the table and held John's right hand. In a notch above a whisper, she said, "I remember when the mistress came down with the sweats. Yeah, we prayed. Massa said the prayers saved her life."

John hated that Ann referred to Billingsly as Massa and his wife as Mistress. As he grew older, he fumed silently every time he heard his mother utter those godforsaken words. She was still tied to the past, he wasn't. She was born a slave, had been married, and had twin daughters before John's birth. John was born five years after slavery had been abolished. John's whole life lay ahead of him, one not fettered to the evils of slavery. "I like Monsieur Billingsly; he's done right by me," John said. "He knew of my interest in wanting to read and write, and from time to time he or his pastor would help me with that. He said I was a fast learner."

Ann saw to it that John attended school in a nearby barn during the Reconstruction era where money from the government paid for the salaries of the teachers and meager school supplies. "You are a smart boy. You learned things from that school in the '70s. And you learned things from the pastor."

"The mistress done good things for my boy, too. You learned French words from her," she said, recalling the times he'd talked to her in French. She was also pleased that her son spoke English well. "Son, you talk like you got years of school; you learned that from the mistress; you once told me she often corrected your English."

John nodded to acknowledge there were some nice things about her, but not many. She just rubbed his emotions raw. The rape under the elm tree surfaced, and he flinched and said reflexively, "Madame Billingsly's not fit to be in this world."

Ann's eyes widened slightly, and John decided to dial back his angry thoughts about Madame Billingsly. She nodded her head slightly to acknowledge that she understood her son's complaint. John was no longer her little boy. He was in the first flush of manhood, becoming more independent, like a bird testing his wings to fly the coop. Many boys his age in the neighborhood had already flown the coop; it was just a matter of time.

"Son, you becoming a man. Some day you be on your own. You handsome and smart."

Ann paused.

"What's wrong, Mama?"

She worried about his future in a world of ever-lurking danger for colored folk. She hoped that his future would run opposite of the heart-wrenching hardships she had experienced as a slave. I want my boy to always do the right thing. I teach you that…"

Ann paused again and looked at John. "I wish your sisters could see my boy."

Ann and her husband, Moses, had had twin daughters—Mollie and Sara. Ann had loved being a mother and doted on her children and, for that matter, all of the children in a neighborhood full of slave children. If a child's trousers or socks needed to be darned, Ann found a way to do it. If a hungry child needed something in his belly, she found a way to allay the child's hunger. She could never be faulted for an overabundance of care for her family and others in her slave community.

She, Moses, and her girls were going to be okay, she had allowed herself to think, even though Walter Windsor could easily sever her family. It didn't matter that Windsor had allowed Ann and Moses to marry. They were chattel, and Virginia didn't recognize chattel marriages. Echoing the words of the white preacher who officiated at their marriage ceremony, they vowed to stay together "'til death or distance do us part." Ann and Moses knew what *distance* meant and worked tirelessly for Windsor to show him that they were faithful servants, that there would never be a need to break up their family.

Their tireless work meant nothing to a man who was desperate for hard currency. As the War drew nigh, with the air laden with talk about dividing the country and South Carolina, the first state on the brink of secession, Windsor sold Moses to a Kentucky plantation owner, causing Ann to become distraught following the separation from her husband. She wondered whether the end of her time on earth was near. But she knew that she had to plod on; she was left to raise her twin daughters without the steady hand of their father, the same steady hand that had plowed Windsor's fields for years.

Less than a year after the War started, Windsor sold Ann to Tyrone Billingsly. She was content to work for Billingsly, who did not beat her, unlike Windsor and his henchmen.

Ann and her young daughters lived in one of the clusters of slave cabins that Billingsly had built for his slaves near *Billingsly*, the name of Tyrone and Laura Billingsly's estate. It was officially known as *Billingsly Manor*, but most people called it *Billingsly*. If there was ever such thing as a benevolent slave owner, Tyrone Billingsly came close to meeting the definition. But even Billingsly had adhered to the philosophical underpinnings of slavery.

The spiritual life of slaves, like many things in their world, was a contested space. White Christian slave owners vacillated between their hope that religion would make their slaves docile and obedient and their fear that the central tenet of their religion—equality before God—would encourage slaves to rise up against their oppressors. Tyrone Billingsly tried to find the religious center of gravity for his slaves. He allowed his slaves to worship, hoping that they'd be appreciative of his generosity and strive to be efficient workers. He was careful, though, to retain a white preacher to lead the worship to make sure that the slaves understood the *correct* version of the Bible.

Things went from bad to worse for Ann after her eight-year-old twin daughters died of cholera a couple of years after the War ended, causing her to suffer from deep malaise. When not working at *Billingsly*, tending to laundry and cleaning duties, she was pretty much immured in her cabin.

In the midst of her malaise, she fell victim to a gang of marauding white men who raped her. She had no strength to fight her scrofulous assailants, allowing herself to fill her head with the thought that she would soon be in a heaven with Moses and her twin daughters, a place where no one could harm her anymore. She survived the attack and later blamed herself, just like she blamed herself when Windsor was drunk and beat her just because he could. When she told Tyrone Billingsly about the rape, he vowed to catch the men who did it, but it was never his priority.

Ann's soul, which had been rended immediately after her two daughters died, began to repair itself with new life inside of her. John Moses, her new son, gave her a renewed life and a reason to live and allowed her to escape a hell of death and savagery that had ravaged her body, mind, and soul for so long. She didn't know how or if it would come to pass, but she'd often pray, as she held him snuggly in her arms as an infant or held his hand as he got older, that another world awaited him, a world of freedom, independence, and respect. She'd tell him time and again that he was a special boy that God had put inside of her, so he could grow to right the sinking ship of so many Negroes. That was her dream, but all she really wanted was for him to have a better life than she had.

Even as a little boy, John knew that he didn't like Richmond because he had seen —as far as his young mind could comprehend— how it had broken his mother. He felt the urge to run away, but he didn't know where he'd run because all he knew was a neighborhood of Negroes who lived in slave cabins.

To settle the mind of her eight-year-old son, she'd take him to an oasis of freedom to let him free his mind of worriment about the long tribulations of his mother. She was nearly fifty, and John, who was just eight, told Ann that he was the man of the house as a way of letting her know she'd be all right with him around. Too much for a young boy, so Ann figured he could free his mind from the strictures and daily hardship of being a Negro in 1878 by having him spend time at Blue Pond.

Ann carried the bamboo fishing pole and bait jar, and he'd carry the red pail to put bluegill, crappie, and other panfish in. She had not only taught him how to fish, she'd also shepherd him through the trees, bends, and turns to get to and from the pond. As he got older, he'd mastered the route and no longer needed to clutch onto his mother's coattails.

With the freedom to go to the pond by himself as he got a bit older, John did so on a torrid August afternoon that baked everything in its path. He'd find himself going to the pond frequently as it was a form of succor for John, a place to go for the son of a former slave to think about his future. There just had to be a bigger life somewhere else that awaited him. He knew he and his mother depended on each other as they knew no other family in the world. He knew he'd have to leave Richmond soon to live a bigger life, he just didn't know when that time would come. He didn't even know where he'd find a bigger life—just that whatever else lay beyond Richmond had to be better.

John had the large pond to himself; it was high noon and torrid for other bathers. He took off his moccasins and waded in the water, mindlessly scraping the bottom of the pond with his feet and using his hands to move spidery white lilies out of his way. Dark shadows moving around in the water captured his attention.

He sat down in the shoal area, using both hands to anchor himself against the bottom as the water settled just beneath his chin. He plunged his head in the water to get a closer look at the tadpoles, opened his eyes, and was now immersed in their world, one he didn't understand. A tadpole swam to John, close enough to tickle his nose. John reached out to grab the tadpole, but it swam off where he saw it hide under a rock. John came up for air, balancing himself with both hands, and thinking about the world in which the tadpoles lived.

He submerged his head several times, just long enough to satisfy himself that the tadpoles believed he was a friendly face, someone to look after them. Unable to winnow out the error of his logic in his young mind, he decided that the tadpoles needed to be free, so he removed as many rocks around him as he could and then tossed them ashore. With his guiding hand, the tadpoles would have a life of freedom that he envied. Although not yet ten years old, he already knew that his destiny was predetermined by the color of his skin. It didn't matter that he was one-half Negro and one-half white—he looked like a Negro and that would be enough for the white populace to deny him the true freedom his people sought, his mother often told him. But that never stopped Ann from praying that her son could contribute to a different outcome.

During his many subsequent visits to Blue Pond, he retrieved rocks from the pond and placed them under the limbs of a sycamore tree. One day, he decided to use his cache of rocks by throwing them across the pond. He was throwing away the yoke of tyranny for the tadpoles and perhaps for himself someday. Each rock he threw landed in the water, never quite reaching the far shore.

After weeks of trying, his efforts paid off. He had perfected his pitch and was able to send the rocks sailing to land about 100 feet on the other side of the pond. The tadpoles would thank him someday. His voice pitched high with excitement, he boasted to his mother about his conquest, proud of what he'd done.

He continued to go to his oasis and throw rocks across Blue Pond. Not only could he throw rocks across it, but he also honed his skills to be able to hit a silver maple tree ten feet from the edge of the pond. The multiple nicks in the tree bark bore testament to his accuracy.

On one windy day, one of John's rocks went astray and struck a little Negro girl in the head. He had been at the pond for a few hours, frolicking with tadpoles and tossing rocks, and was not aware of the girl's presence until he heard her piercing screams. They rang like his mother's wailing screams, reminding John of his mother. John knew what had happened. He ran over to the girl. She was about a foot shorter than John, and he saw right away that she was bleeding on the right side of her head.

"Didn't mean to do it, it was an accident," he said, looking at her, not sure what to do.

The little girl continued to wail, knocking his hand away as he tried to console her. Although he wasn't sure, John believed that he had seen the girl, who had two long, familiar-looking pigtails, in church, along with her mother. His brain quickly confirmed that she was indeed the little girl who attended church with her mother, and that she always wore the same dress.

"I know you," John said in an effort to calm her. "I've seen you in church with your mother. I'm John. What's your name?"

She said nothing as she looked up to John's eyes that were welling with tears.

John's anxiety level increased when the blood failed to abate after a few minutes, dripping from the little girl's chocolate-colored right hand onto her threadbare yellow cotton dress at a steady rate. Each drip of blood rang loud in his head, searing his mind, which was riddled with terror. He panicked and ran the mile to get home, hoping that as each stride put a distance between him and his victim, he'd forget about it and so would she.

The girl told her mother about the incident, and the mother stopped by Ann's cabin a few hours later to apprise her of the incident. Ann thanked her and gave her some corn pone and told her she would see her in church. Ann knew how she would have to handle it.

"John, come here," Ann said while he was outside talking to a neighbor from the adjacent slave cabin. "Suppose that was a white girl you'd hit. We'd be in a heap of trouble."

John looked down at the dirt lot outside their cabin.

"Look at me, son," she said, raising his chin with her right hand.

"But Mama, it was an accident. I didn't see her."

She stroked his head as she held it tight against her chest.

"Is she okay, Mama?"

"Think so."

Ann wouldn't whip him for his errant behavior. She never did, as she was imbued with incredible compassion. She knew what it was like to be whipped. The cicatricial marks on her back bore testament to the many lashes she'd received as a slave on Walter Windsor's plantation.

John looked down and made S shapes with his right foot in the dirt. He looked up at Ann and said, "I hate this place."

3
SPRING, 1887

Regardless of his anger, John reported to work the next day after his contretemps with the sherry.

He heard Tyrone's slow footfall coming in his direction as he mopped the Italianate white marble floor in the foyer.

Billingsly cleared his throat. John cocked his head and looked up at the patriarch of *Billingsly*.

John stood up and faced him.

Billingsly put his right hand on John's left shoulder and looked in John's eyes, which were set under long, thick black lashes. John had mostly seen Billingsly's eyes soft, but they sometimes turned opaque when he had a fight with his wife or when he was involved in a business dispute. Billingsly rubbed the stud in his left shirt cuff with his right thumb.

John had seen that foreboding gesture before.

As much as Laura protested about John's behavior, she knew Tyrone was right about one thing: John was a hard worker; he did what he was told. Rather than fire him, she'd exact her revenge in another manner. Laura had demanded that John work in the field for a few months, but Tyrone negotiated a shorter sentence. "I'm going to need you to help Edmund take care of the tobacco field; it'll be just for a couple of weeks."

Despite Laura's flammable temper, John had come to recognize his mother's wisdom regarding the advantages of working inside *Billingsly* as long as he could compartmentalize his hatred from Madame Billingsly. Working there was a desideratum—it made him smarter, which he'd figured as a teenager on the edge of manhood would someday be a serviceable quality. He hated doing back-breaking tobacco work. It was pure drudgery from beginning to end—he'd envied the mules he'd used to work the land because of the respite they got during the day when he'd have to put tobacco leaves in the barn for curing and grading. He thought about asking why he'd been relegated back to doing that kind of work but decided against it. He knew the answer.

In the end, John's sentence working in the field went from a couple of weeks to one month. He figured that Madame Billingsly had somehow stuck it to him again. But he was relieved his sentence ended on time as Monsieur Billingsly had promised, and he returned to *Billingsly*.

Billingsly, of Scots-Irish ancestry, was rangy and had a high, slanted forehead and craggy face. He had deep-set gray eyes with a hint of blue, like the sea in a northern latitude, and they could be soft or hard as the situation demanded. He wore clothes from the finest tailors in London. Where he could be jaunty, beguiling, and patient, Laura was regularly shrewish, spiteful, and bumptious.

Wealth had always surrounded Tyrone Billingsly. His father was a wealthy businessman and his mother a wealthy heiress. Billingsly's father had paid for Tyrone's Oxford University education, but he hadn't asked his father for much money after college, although his father lavished him with it and assorted valuables from time to time.

His fortune derived largely from the foundry business. Though his loyalty to the South was a given, he'd often take the train to Northern states to meet with businessmen who were interested in doing business with him—but that was before South Carolina became the first state to secede from the Union. At that time, money was money, and he did not discriminate against business outside of the South—he'd need lots of it to maintain the lifestyle of his wife.

Before Billingsly's climb to the top in the business world stopped, Richmond's Tredegar Iron Works had been one of Billingsly's biggest customers, supplying it with iron ore and metal materials used to make iron. Tredegar had been the South's largest major antebellum rolling mill, at one time fabricating cannons and gun carriages for the United States government.

Once the War started, Tredegar became a vital ingredient to the South's winning the War; it was the industrial heart of the Confederacy. With sky-high demand for iron to build ships to protect Richmond from Union forces, Billingsly worked feverishly to supply Tredegar with his materials, and his finances swelled in return. And like his father, he'd see to it that his wife and children benefited from the spoils of his wealth. When Tyrone's children were young, he'd taken them and his wife to Paris and other European cities about once every two years. His wealth allowed him to build *Billingsly*, where dozens of slaves worked at the height of Billingsly's empire.

It was not all work for a man of Billingsly's stature—he had other interests. To indulge his passion, and partly to liberate himself from Laura's suffocating carping, Billingsly bred Cleveland Bay horses. He'd been introduced to them by an Englishman who'd told him about their versatility. He later became the chairman of the 1884 Upperville Colt and Horse Show in Virginia where Cleveland Bay horses were showcased. The horses were reddish-brown with small white spots on their foreheads. They were sure-footed, had a strong back and hindquarters, and limbs with plenty of bone, allowing them to move with ground-covering power. He kept a stable of them, selling many to stagecoach businesses, which had a large presence in Richmond.

Richmond had been good to Tyrone. The city was a bottomland along the James River, with fecund soil that produced crops such as tobacco, all kinds of leafy green vegetables, corn, and soybeans for the Billingslys. Although several fruit trees dotted the landscape, Billingsly's prized trees were always peach and apple trees. Billingsly's expansive farmland, which seemingly stretched to the horizon, fed his family, his horses, his farm animals, and workers and their families.

Like many businesses in the Confederacy following the War, Tredegar would later fall into financial trouble, which caused Billingsly's fortunes to suffer. He had to shut down his major shop, which in turn caused him to cut back on household discretionary spending, which rang discordantly with Laura.

Laura never understood. Her rightful place was at the top of the Richmond bon ton. She had been lectured from birth on the stringent social graces of a privileged people. Although Billingsly told her that trade across the Atlantic had come to a halt as a result of the War and the defeat of the Confederacy, Laura searched for any business that could sell her things to which she had been accustomed. She didn't find much, but whatever she found she'd purchase in Billingsly's name, which was enough to cause Billingsly to curse her. He told her that they could lose *Billingsly* one day. Laura dismissed such an unthinkable notion, and blithely went about her life, assured that Tyrone would see that she'd never fall from atop her bon ton perch.

Billingsly would soon lose more money. A fire destroyed one of his smaller foundry shops, and the other shops suffered from poor management. He endeavored to stave off his hungry creditors by using one loan to satisfy another. But even as a man who had been chosen as Richmond's businessman of the year, he had become unworthy of credit.

By 1887, Tyrone simply went through the motions of working; his mind was elsewhere, and he accomplished little. He made the trip home to *Billingsly* one evening and removed his white starched shirt as he stood in front of the oval mirror, attached to the mahogany dresser in the master bedroom. He stared in the mirror as though he didn't recognize the person staring back; his mounting financial crisis had aged him, and his face was even craggier.

Without preamble, Tyrone said to Laura as he sat next to her on the bed, "They're after me, the damn banks."

She had known that something was wrong from the moment he walked into the room. She had already begun to cry. She was angry that her husband was failing her, failing to live up to the standards that she believed were predetermined for her at birth. "Why, *why* is this happening?" Laura said while crying on her husband's chest, pounding it softly with her right hand.

John was in Billingsly's second-floor private study, which was adjacent to the cavernous bedroom. The books that filled the shelves in the room included such topics as literature, botany, history, animal husbandry, and finance. In moments when he took a break from cleaning, he sometimes removed a book from the shelf. He'd stroke its spine, then he'd open it. He'd quickly write down a few words he didn't know and look up the words at home in a dictionary Tyrone had given him.

John had just finished scrubbing the oak wood floor. As he prepared to retire for the evening, he overheard Tyrone say in a raised but sober voice, "Listen to me, Laura."

Laura ignored him.

"I said listen to me," he repeated in the same tone.

Laura screamed, "Why did you let this happen? You have ruined me! Tell me what reason do I have to live?"

John had heard them argue before, but this argument seemed different, an ominous-sounding one. He edged closer to the door in the study to listen.

Although Tyrone was used to Laura's self-entitled attitude, her words rankled him this time more than usual. He was the one who'd made the money, who'd afforded Laura an extravagant lifestyle. All he wanted from her was a little understanding and appreciation of what he was going through. At the nadir of financial downfall, he could not even count on her for emotional support to get him through the mess that had befallen him.

It's something we must face. He steadied himself for what he needed to say, something that would knock Laura off her deep foundational Richmond roots. "Laura, we may need to leave here soon ... for our safety. The banks will harass us, and we can't count on the law to protect us."

The house that had been paid for was in hock. The banks wanted their money, and Tyrone could no longer keep up with payments, even when he had borrowed from a loan shark, who had warned Tyrone he had missed a few payments.

She sighed deeply, and her body shook with spasms.

Tredegar had made a slight comeback after the War, but its fortunes didn't last long. Tyrone blamed everything on the War. "Ever since we lost the War, our fortunes have suffered," Tyrone continued. "Tredegar, one of my biggest customers, has not been the same since the economy went sour in seventy-three. The one thing

I know well is the iron and metals business. It's moving south now, where steel is being made. We need to follow it."

Laura hated talk about the War. "That damn war. It's ruined everything. Those Union bastards burned our beautiful city."

Tyrone looked into Laura's misty, cerulean eyes. He wanted to correct her, to tell her that the Confederate government authorized the burning of buildings, which resulted in considerable damage to Richmond's business district. He dared not tell Laura that he'd actually thanked Union soldiers for extinguishing fires in the business district. He knew it wasn't the time to be correct, and certainly not the time to tell her that he'd ever said a nice word about Union soldiers.

Laura had a positive thought. She managed a flicker of a smile. "But we can bring back Richmond, make it more glorious than ever, Tyrone. You're savvy enough to make it happen."

At Tyrone's look of resignation, Laura ramped up her entreaty. "I can never leave this place, Tyrone. I've lived in Richmond all my life. My daddy, granddaddy, and great-granddaddy were born and raised in this city. I can breathe no other air but Richmond's."

Tyrone looked out of the large bedroom window and stared at a grove of elm trees in the back yard. He wished he had told her at once instead of letting things drip out. He just had to say it. "The Old Security Bank has called in a loan; they're close to getting the deed to this house. They'll be coming soon. We need to take our things and leave."

Laura sobbed again. She longed to turn back the clock to rewrite the War's end.

Tyrone's relief at having told her something he had known for some time that was inevitable lifted a heavy weight from his heart and mind.

He walked to the five-foot-by-three-foot oil on canvas portrait of Papa Billingsly, Tyrone's father, that hung on the wall opposite their massive four-poster mahogany, white cotton, canopy-framed bed. The portrait dominated the room. He had hung it there, so he could see the slender-nosed, portly, bearded white man with his hand in his waistcoat, like Napoleon, every time he walked out of the bedroom.

He thought his father had been a wise man and still hoped to learn from him even though he was dead. He stroked the ornately carved oak frame for a few seconds, then gently removed the portrait from the wall, exposing the family safe. He opened the safe and retrieved a thick wad of money wrapped in a white band.

"We'll use this money," he said, showing it to Laura. "We'll find a new life somewhere else. I'll start another business. We have enough money to last a while."

Laura went numb. She sat on a bergère and stared blankly out of the window.

Tyrone sat on the bed and leaned over and rubbed Laura's right thigh, trying to console his grief-stricken wife. She turned her torso away from him, erecting a wall between them.

Unable to console her, he got up, closed the safe door, put the portrait of his father back in place. He moved a few steps back and peered into his father's gray eyes. As if his father spoke to him, he suddenly remembered two whiskey flasks that Papa Billingsly had given him before he died.

When Tyrone and his six siblings were young, Papa Billingsly would hide treasure around his vast estate. He'd give the children clues to use to search for the coveted prize—whether it was gold and silver coins or just trinkets; the children were always ready for this sporting game. Tyrone recalled that Papa Billingsly read books about lost treasure and had gone on a few expeditions off the Barbary Coast to look for treasure.

So, it was not a surprise to Tyrone when Papa Billingsly told him years ago that he buried the gold and silver coins and bars on the grounds of *Billingsly* while Tyrone and the family vacationed in France.

"Can never go wrong with gold," his father had said ever since Tyrone had been a young boy.

Tyrone had kept the flasks hidden in his study for years, seldom thinking about them, as he had always had more than enough money to take care of his business and to satisfy Laura.

"Laura, Papa left me—left us—something very valuable, which may help sustain us for a good while. It could help restore some of our wealth," he said as a dig at his creditors. "We'll need it after we leave here."

John listened, pressed up against the doorjamb in the study.

"So where is this stuff, this *valuable* stuff?"

"Don't know exactly where, but Papa said the clues to finding it are on the whiskey flasks Pa gave me."

"Why didn't you ever tell me about this, Tyrone?"

"I don't rightly know, Laura, but I'm telling you now. I'll get some men, and we'll start digging after I return from a business trip in a few days' time."

"Where are these flasks?"

"In the oak cabinet in my study."

"Jesus," John whispered, looking at the cabinet.

Laura's life was with Tyrone; without him, she'd cease to exist. She needed to cling to any hope that she'd see her wealth again someday. "Tyrone, you've got to promise me this is going to work out. I just need to hear you say it."

Tyrone nodded. "We'll be fine, dear. I'm going to take care of you, just like I have always done."

Tyrone threw his arms around Laura and hugged her, hoping to offer her a small measure of comfort, but instead he felt her disdain with her cold embrace. The businessman who had always walked and acted with great confidence was faltering in his wife's eyes. He needed to reassure her in some way. "Come with me."

John heard Tyrone and Laura walk out of their bedroom. He looked through the door frame and saw them holding hands, walking to the other side of the house. As they stepped to the far side of the mansion, John stepped quietly in an open area and saw Billingsly open the French doors that led to the balcony. John stepped closer to the French doors to listen to their conversation.

Tyrone and Laura stood on the balcony, holding hands, just like they had done so many times before when they lorded over *Billingsly* watching their subjects come to them in supplication.

He looked into her sullen eyes. "I've been reduced in circumstance, but it's just temporary."

"What is it that is so valuable about the flasks?"

"Papa said he buried valuable items on our land." Tyrone figured he knew that a lot of gold lay buried on his property somewhere but decided not to tell Laura. It would be a wonderful surprise for her soon. "Don't know rightly what it is, but I'm thankful for his deed." With a less than confident tone, he let the words blow out: "We'll use the flasks to keep *Billingsly*, now and forever."

John didn't know what fortunes the flasks contained, but he knew he wanted them. It would be just a matter of time before he'd go after the flasks.

4
SPRING, 1887

Laura had not been the same since Tyrone told her about his financial difficulty a few days ago. The news had hit her hard in the one place where she could seek refuge: the knowledge that she would always have wealth and *Billingsly*.

She gasped for air as she reflexively woke up after her heart stopped beating for a few seconds. She sat up in bed and felt a gush of blood coursing through her arteries as if the racing blood were making up for lost time. Her entire body trembled. She covered her heart with her shaky right hand in an effort to stop the trembling.

As she continued to sit up in bed, her heart soon returned to its normal rhythm, assuring her that she was going to survive—at least for the moment, she thought. She scooted to the edge of the bed, allowing her legs to dangle about five inches from the floor, then slid off the bed and stood up and let her turquoise chemise fall to her ankles. She put on her white Egyptian-combed cotton housecoat that hung on the poster hook near the leather-framed headboard and took her first tentative steps to the window.

The late morning sun glistened in her somnolent eyes. She squinted a few times to adjust to the blast of sunlight. She knuckled dried rheum that had caked in the corners of her eyes, then moved slightly to the right, allowing a large Empress tree to filter out most of the penetrating sunbeams, giving her a clearer view of her grand botanical gardens, a place she sometimes relied upon to console her when needed.

Tyrone had left two days ago to meet with businessmen who were interested in purchasing his foundry business, and Laura had been in a daze since, sleeping late, eating little, crying a lot, and wondering whether the flasks would be the deus ex machina she prayed for.

She toddled down the grand staircase, holding onto the balustrade to steady her shaky descent, still not fully awake. As she reached the bottom, the Russian grandfather clock in the corner of the foyer chimed loudly, announcing high noon. She touched her heart again with her right hand to make sure it was still beating. Satisfied that she could go on, she ambled to her favorite room, mindlessly touching the dining room table and adjusting some of the sterling silver on the tabletop. Dust-moted rays of light that shone through the slit of the heavy velvet drapes caught her attention.

Laura was proud of her opulent dining room, the showcase of the Billingslys' home. The red oak wood floor held many pieces of the Billingslys' prized European imported furniture, including the Victorian dining table, the centerpiece of the room. The table was made of the finest birch, and had dramatic arches and double pedestals, which featured carved leaf and rosette feet. The ten camelback chairs completed the ensemble. Laura's sterling silver brought the table to life. She loved exhibiting many of her table wares for her society friends. The table couldn't be too crowded for her. The more garish, the better. Her wealth had to stand out. The Tiffany pitcher, which her father had given her, dated back to the Revolutionary War, and had paneled sides and an embossed design with shells, scrolls, and flowers; it was the crown jewel of all her sterling silver.

"How you doing, Madame?" Sam asked as he walked in the dining room to set the table for Laura's lunch. Sam was tall but reduced somewhat by age. He was balding, a seventy-year-old with a narrow nose, thin lips, sun-dried, leathery, tawny hands that were still quick enough to play the violin that he used to torment Laura.

She stared at him blankly.

"Can I get something for you?"

"Finish up and take the day off, Sam."

"But, Madame, I got work to do here."

"Do as I say! Finish up and leave."

Sam nodded and bowed slightly. "Yes, Madame. As you wish."

"Return tomorrow."

Sam took Laura's tart manner in stride. He had Tyrone on his side. Tyrone's decision to keep Sam as part of the help had been an easy one. Sam was more than a cook; he was skilled at playing the violin, often entertaining the Billingslys' guests in the garden and in the lavish dining room. He looked forward to playing the violin at a Billingsly ball; it was his way of sharpening his claws to exact revenge on the virago of Richmond; unlike Emmaline, her prized possession, Sam, like John and all the other servants, felt the vibrations of Laura's excoriations countless times. As with John, Laura would on a whim curse Sam, pouring gasoline on his weakened heart.

As Sam well knew before the War, three small glasses of imported bourbon were all that was needed for Laura to fall under the spell of Sam's violin. Once she hit her limit, Sam's revenge meter jumped to full. Laura, a Presbyterian, loved to kick up her heels, and Sam was quick to oblige her. The degree to which Laura had scolded him over a period of time matched how much control he'd exercised over Laura's dance movements. The harsher she scolded him, the more he'd torment her by playing the violin at a fast tempo.

Although she tried, it was always impossible for her to keep pace with Sam's faster tempos. The knockout punch usually didn't take long. After a few minutes of trying to keep pace with Sam's beat, the effects of the alcohol were quick to show: She'd get dizzy and fall. One time, she hit her head on a table, which made Sam feel bad, and he second-guessed his puppetry game. But with the next scolding that came soon enough, Sam's bad feelings were quick to evaporate. He'd figured he would just bide his time and would strike again at the next party, though celebrations slowed to a trickle once the War started.

Laura returned her attention to the sunlight and the dancing dust particles, trapped in the beams. She moseyed in front of the beams and stood there as if hoping they would take her to some ethereal place, a place far away from the maw of the hell she was afraid of living in. *Billingsly* was about to go under because of the traitors up north. Even Tyrone's disclosure about the flasks and the wad of money did little to soothe her suffocating heart. Although the wad of money in the safe was real, she couldn't bring herself to believe the flasks would reverse the impending financial doom.

"Madame, here some fresh cut flowers I put in a vase," Sam said as she stood in front of the sunbeams.

She turned around, looking at the riot of fresh multicolored tulips. "Thank you, Sam. Put them on the table."

"Yes, Madame."

She looked back. "Sam, give me the purple tulip."

She took a long smell of it, closing her eyes while stroking the wet stem with her left hand.

"Good day, Madame," Sam said, bowing his head. "Oh, Madame, there is some chicory coffee on the stove for you. I'm leaving now."

Laura had initially rejected drinking chicory—too ersatz—demanding that Tyrone, anyone really, turn back the clock before the War, so she could savor her fresh-brewed black coffee. As the War dragged on, she faced the harsh reality that the Confederate states just could not gain access to her favorite coffee beans. So even though she succumbed to an inferior product, drinking chicory was her way of taking a piercing stab at the North, her own personal way of remembering the savagery of the North and its ill-mannered people.

She took a sip of her chicory coffee, then strolled to her botanical gardens out back of the house. She ambled across the Kentucky bluegrass, allowing her bare feet to feel comforted by the soft blades of grass. Two quarreling mockingbirds, perched on an elm bough, caught her attention. She craned her neck to look at the birds, which were too busy fussing with each other to notice her. They were ignoring her, just like Tyrone, like the wealthy women of Richmond. Just as she wished that the sunbeams in the dining room could cart her away from her misery, she now wished she could be as free as the mockingbirds, to fly away, to wash away her living nightmare.

It was time to feed her misery by escaping into a bottle of bourbon. She removed the bottle from the cabinet in the butler's pantry and took a long pull. Drips of bourbon fell from her mouth onto her robe. She wiped her mouth with the back of her left hand and then took an even longer pull.

Before long, she lay sozzled in bed, collapsed from the weight of her heavy mind and a liver full of liquor.

Several days had elapsed since John had left *Billingsly* with a wide smile on his face after learning about the coded flasks. There could be no more smiling. Over the next several days, John vacillated about stealing the flasks. It was a grave decision. Stealing the flasks was fraught with danger; his life would likely be imperiled, and he'd never see his mother again. She'd die all over again, and his heart would surely crush from what he did to her.

While his heart and mind ached over the dreadful consequences of stealing the flasks, he breathed deeply in an effort to expunge them from his mind. His thoughts would then pivot to finding another life. He couldn't stand the life that had been handed to him, one in which he'd been dependent upon white men like Billingsly to give him and his mother the leftover dross that fell from Billingsly's pocket, his house. He still clung to seeking a bigger life somewhere, and the flasks could help him with that life, he thought. But inevitably, thoughts about his mother crept back into his mind; he couldn't escape the thought of what would happen to his mother if he stole the flasks.

The prospect of hitting the jackpot with the flasks ultimately proved too much to dismiss. He decided to take his mother with him, and they'd travel somewhere with the flasks. He didn't know where. He didn't even know if his mother with her weakened back would be up to leaving Richmond.

Billingsly's desk, the floor, and his leather chair could be shined only so many times. The longer he stayed in the study, the more he was mesmerized by the cabinet; it taunted him every hour, every minute, every second. It had become too much. The only way to exorcise the spell was to break in while Billingsly was still out of town.

As he left the study carrying a bucket of water, he saw Madame Billingsly at the foot of the staircase. She waited until he'd come down before she started her ascent.

It was six o'clock and he had finished working. "Goodnight, Madame Billingsly," John said as he reached the bottom.

She said nothing.

John walked into the kitchen, where he saw Sam writing something on the back of an envelope.

"What're you doing?" John asked.

"Trying to think of the groceries needed here."

John took a few steps toward Sam. "Let me see it," he said with an outstretched right arm.

Most of the words were misspelled. He knew his mother had made an effort to improve her education through self-study and asking questions of John. John thought of helping Sam improve his vocabulary and writing, but he didn't have time. He didn't even know how much longer he'd even be alive.

"I'll go to market and get the groceries, Sam. When do you need them?"

"No rush on it. Whenever you have a bit of time."

Sam thanked him and told him to give his regards to Ann.

John's mind continued to whirl about his planned break-in. He knew Emmaline would be in Maryland visiting her daughter for two weeks. As he watched Sam limp around the kitchen, he thought of an alibi for Sam. Whatever went down with the plan to steal the flasks, Sam would not be around if he took time off from work. "Sam, you ought to take some time off. Seems you don't miss a day of work. Monsieur Billingsly has said it's fine; that's what you once told me."

"Yeah, son. Reckon you right." Pointing to his right leg, he said, "This here leg ain't getting no better. And I ain't breathing like I should. Something wrong. I'll take them days I got coming."

Sam walked out of the kitchen on gimpy legs and went home.

John quickly doffed his work clothes and donned his tattered clothes that were kept in the servants' quarter.

John sat on the back steps mulling his next move. His head began to spin, his heart raced madly, his hands trembled violently, and his stomach made gurgling noises. He stood up, took a few steps forward, and lowered his head to allow the contents of his stomach to gush out of his mouth.

He sat down, lowered his head, and asked God to understand what he was about to do. He promised God that he'd do the right thing later.

Time needed to pass before he could act. John would have to wait for Madame Billingsly's signal. She almost always had a glass of cognac before going to bed, no matter the hour. As was her habit, she'd placed the empty snifter on the marble top parlor table outside her bedroom just before going to bed.

He meandered through the Billingslys' botanical gardens before settling on a small bench near the pergola at the back of the gardens. He curled up on the bench in a fetal position and dozed off. About three hours later, he awoke to a late-night light drizzle.

He gathered his nerves, took a deep breath, and walked stealthily up the long staircase. As he climbed each step, the thought about how Madame Billingsly loved cognac, how he'd seen her caress the snifter and circle the rim with her right index finger, and how she'd become somnolent after her last sip. He hoped that she had surrendered to the glowing liquid amber that he had poured so often for her. After reaching the landing, John observed the empty snifter and smiled.

It was time to act.

He scurried into the study, careful to tiptoe and avoid the squeaky floor panel near the cabinet. He tugged on the door to the oak cabinet; it was locked. He'd never thought it would be easy.

He tiptoed to the corner of the room away from the cabinet and opened the center drawer in Mr. Billingsly's large walnut desk, hoping to find the key to the lock. He saw a pocket watch and a band of keys, too many to count. Trying each key to unlock the cabinet door would consume too much time, time which would gnaw at his nerves. He looked in the other drawers, shuffling paper in his quest for a key that would unlock the cabinet. Nothing. He put the watch in his front pocket.

The voices returned to his head, his mother's, his own. He saw an apparition of Tyrone Billingsly in the room with him. He swallowed hard, forcing the bile back down his throat, wincing at its brackish taste. He'd have to act soon, or he'd slowly lose his nerve.

He sat in Billingsly's black leather swivel chair, spinning it fast, as if that would help him think of the answer for how to claim his prize. It simply made him dizzy, and he stopped.

As he rose from the chair, his right hand accidentally knocked over a book that sat on the corner of the desk. He reached out with both hands to catch it, but he could only deflect it, causing a softer landing. He quickly picked up the book and put it on the desk.

His mahogany face swelled with panic, fearful that the commotion might have awakened Laura. John stood in place, frozen, waiting to see if his plan for a bigger life were about to be ruined.

A minute later, Laura's door squeaked open, and John's heart began to pound. The bile in his throat, having not quite gone away, reappeared, forcing him to swallow again. He skulked behind Billingsly's oak desk and positioned himself to be able to peek though the opening of the door to the study.

She walked in the study, the .22-caliber rifle pressed up against her right side, just as her husband had taught her in one of the shooting lessons he'd given her many years before.

She walked over to the window and looked at the first-quarter moon. A barn owl perched in a live oak tree hooted, and she caught the barn owl's iridescent yellow eyes staring at her. Satisfied that the noise may have come from the owl, or perhaps some foraging nocturnal animal, she closed the jalousie and returned to her bedroom.

A deep sigh of relief spilled out of John on her departure. It was a close shave, too close, one that could have left John wounded or dead. John had to act that night, or he'd never act.

He wanted it over and decided to move tantivy to capture the flasks. Quick action was called for, something in the form of a heavy, blunt tool to break into the cabinet. But before he could claim his prize, he decided to rehearse his plan. He opened the jalousie, then the window, leaned over the ledge, and measured the distance to the ground. He debated whether he should jump out the window. It would be better to jump out the window *after* he claimed his prize.

If he jumped now and broke his leg, he'd never claim it. The decision was made for him.

He closed the door to the study, sidled to Laura's bedroom door, and listened for sounds of sleep. After fifteen seconds, he heard a loud snore. Relieved, he crept down the long staircase and then slipped out the back door.

He spied a kerosene lantern sitting on the back porch. He lit it, then looked up and saw the Big Dipper in the sky and smiled as he recalled that Ann loved gazing at the stars at night. The smile evaporated as his thoughts quickly turned to how his mother would die all over again if she found out what he had done. He had to find a way to make it work.

He walked to the front of *Billingsly*. Seeing the grove of live oak trees, he recalled how he had climbed some of them as a child, how he could see the Billingslys' vast estate. He put down the lantern and ran to a live oak and sprang from the trunk with his right leg, able to go high enough to grab a thick bough.

Reaching the top of the live oak, he took in the vast estate. The garage that once housed barouches, cabriolets, and other vehicles, came into view first. Pictures of Tyrone Billingsly, perhaps in his heyday, surrounded by his vehicles hung throughout *Billingsly*. Many of his vehicles had fallen into disrepair, like the garage that housed them. His eyes then fell upon the crop and grazing fields, recognizable by the twenty-foot watch tower that stood in the middle of the fields. His mother had told him about how the overseer would use it periodically to check on the slaves. Just a few years ago, several oxen, mules, dairy and beef cattle occupied the fields. Most were now gone as a result of Billingsly's declining finances. He turned his head slightly to the left and saw the tobacco-curing house off in the distance. Billingsly had hired help on a seasonal basis to help with his tobacco crops. John figured he and Edmund would be the last people to work in the curing house. The clapboards had warped badly, and it was only a matter of time before it caved in, John thought. The horse stable was next to the curing house. It was Billingsly's pride and joy. Where Laura loved her botanical gardens, Billingsly, as John knew, spent a lot of time tending to his Cleveland Bay horses. He had sold most of his Bays, keeping three. Finally, his eyes landed on the tool shed; that's where he'd head first.

As he said goodbye to the estate and began his descent, he heard a soft growl, which stopped him. The growl turned into rapid barks. The dog looked up at John and down the path of the driveway several times. After two minutes, the dog tired of John and chased a raccoon.

He had spent too much time in the tree. His patience grew thin; it was time to act, yet again.

He pulled on the door to the tool shed, but it was locked. The bile at the back of his throat would not leave him alone. He swallowed hard, wishing he could have a dipper of water.

He canvassed the tool shed, looking for an entrance. The window held promise, but it was stuck. But with some pressure, he forced it open. He leaned over the sill and put the lantern on the floor. He climbed into the shed and walked around, holding the lantern high. A few field mice scampered in front of him, startling him, which caused him to stumble backward. His heart raced. He took two deep breaths and regained his composure. Moving closer to an array of tools, he espied what he was after.

There it was, mixed in with some garden tools. He placed the lantern on the uneven dirt floor, and the lantern tipped over. Quickly, he grabbed the heavy sledgehammer and tossed it out the window. As he followed after it, a protruding nail dug into his right thigh and ripped off a part of his denim trousers. The pain stopped him in place; he groaned with a closed mouth as he teetered on the ledge with nearly half his body out the window. With a slight effort, he pushed himself forward, tucked his head in, and somersaulted to the ground.

Blood oozed out of the two-inch nail scrape on his upper right thigh; he applied pressure to his thigh with both hands to staunch the bleeding. He shook his right leg a few times to make sure it worked, and then ran in place for a few seconds. Satisfied that he could go on, he retraced his steps to the house.

As he walked across the foyer, he lamented his thoughtless act of leaving the lantern in the shed.

He crept up the sweeping staircase, careful not to bang the sledgehammer against the balustrade. The sconce light outside of Laura's bedroom allowed him to see that her snifter was still in place. He opened the door to the study, then closed it. He quickly turned on a paraffin lamp that was on a stand. He was one step closer to claiming his prize.

Intrusive thoughts invaded his head. He sat in the corner of the study thinking about his saintly mother—thoughts about her were never far removed from his mind. He wondered how many times would he need to strike the hasp with the sledgehammer? What would he do if Laura awoke from the violent noise? If necessary, he wondered if he could kill Madame Billingsly if she tried to impede him from stealing the flasks. He hoped it would never come to that. His mind continued to be racked with doubt, which expanded as he got closer to his theft operation. Then he speculated that if the flasks were not there his operation would be for naught; he'd be captured and hanged from one of the Billingsly's trees.

He stood up, took a deep breath, and walked to the cabinet. He took one practice swing. The next swing hit its mark. He crushed the hasp, knocking it to the floor. He opened the oak cabinet door, then grabbed the only box on the bottom shelf in plain sight.

As bile percolated in his esophagus, he opened the pine box and saw the flasks with engravings on them. He swallowed hard to tamp down the percolation. He covered the box, then kissed it with that same feeling of satisfaction that he felt when wrapped in his mother's arms as a young boy. He scurried to the open window, leaned over the ledge, wincing when the small wound pressed up against the ledge, and tossed the box to the ground below, hoping the soft Kentucky bluegrass would soften the blow and protect the coveted prize he had worked so hard to obtain.

John placed his left leg over the ledge.

"Stop right there, coon!"

He turned around and saw her pointing a rifle at him.

"Don't you think my husband would be disappointed in you?"

John didn't answer.

She moved the rifle to her right, motioning John to move away from the window. He complied.

John didn't know what to say at first. He thought of his mother. "Madame Billingsly, me and Mama been good to your family," he said, hoping to avoid execution.

"That gives you no right to steal from my house."

John watched her tapping the trigger with her finger. "Sorry, Madame Billingsly," he mumbled.

She ordered John to move to the hallway, where she retrieved her long, dark cloak from the hall closet and put it on slowly, careful to keep her aim on the mass of John's chest, an easy target. John thought her putting that on was a bad omen, perhaps her disguise. He wondered whether she was going to keep him alive, so her husband could see her quarry, like a proud pointer with a game bird in his mouth, whipping his tail feverishly as the owner petted his head.

John's mind stopped racing on its own accord, as it was overcome with the crushing and mind-numbing fear that his tormentor was going to kill him like a rabid dog.

"Look at me!" she shouted with such ferocity that her words reverberated in John's head and stomach. He forced himself to halt the trickle of urine that was ready to drip.

John willed his head up in her direction. As quickly as his mind stopped racing, a bolt of adrenaline zipped through him, and he balled his hands into tight fists.

He was much taller and bigger than she was; he could overpower her. The adrenaline dissipated with as much force as it had arrived, leaving his brain in control again. No matter how fast he was, he knew he wasn't as fast as the bullet that would zip through the barrel in the rifle, killing him instantly.

"I'm so sorry. I don't know what I was thinking. Please don't tell my mama," he said, his voice quavering. "If you kill me, please don't tell her. If you tell her, you'd be killing two people."

"I should shoot you right now, but I want you alive so I can hear you explain to my husband what you did. He'll finally see why I never trusted you. I knew sooner or later you would slip up."

Trust rang in John's head. He saw no hope for his life; it was over. Laura had him trapped and cornered with no way out. But he decided not to go down without saying something to the Ice Queen about *trust*. He squeaked, "You say you never trusted me. Monsieur Billingsly trusted you not to touch me. You made me do something that wasn't right."

"What are you talking about, boy?" she asked, the rifle aimed steady at his chest.

When he was a stripling a couple of years back, she stripped him of his innocence. "After you kill me, tell Monsieur Billingsly what you made me do to you."

Laura's eyes went blank. Still holding a firm aim, she repeated, "What are you talking about, you spineless cur?"

"Madame Billingsly, you know what you did. You asked me to dig a hole for a rosebush and you came out with that nightgown …"

As her eyes remained blank, John gazed down at his crotch. "You shouldn't have done that."

He'd be dead soon, but she had given him the opportunity to confront her about the rape. He had confronted her about it and given her a visual she'd not soon forget, he thought. But as much as he wanted to enjoy her abject humiliation, he couldn't because he knew she would have the last word. And the last word would no doubt have something to do with his mother.

She'd done it to strike back at Tyrone. Although she'd never confirmed her husband's dalliances, the persistent rumors of Tyrone's affairs were all the confirmation she'd needed, along with her mother-in-law's warning about the Billingsly men.

Shortly after Laura and Tyrone were married, Laura had complained to her mother-in-law about her husband's rumored assignations. Her mother-in-law told her that there was a wicked strain encoded in Billingsly men to "stray," to sometimes even cross the color line to satisfy their lusts. "You may not like it, but you'll grow to tolerate it. My Edward has done it, as did his father, and right on up and down the line." She'd paused, then offered a bit of solace. "The Billingsly men come from a long line of patriots; they're well respected and they take care of their families."

Laura decided to strike when her husband was away. She started drinking early to work up her nerve to do something so taboo. After the cognac had dissolved her inhibitions, she found John cleaning the pantry. She instructed him to dig a hole in the backyard to plant a rosebush. As John dug the hole, Laura stumbled outside wearing a silk robe on top of a gauzy chemise. She took a swill of cognac and tossed the snifter to the ground. She sat under an elm tree and called John, snapping, "Get over here!"

Her robe was partially open and only the gauzy nightgown covered her breasts.

He looked at her with gobsmacked eyes. While averting her glassy eyes, he reached down to help her stand to her feet, but she grabbed him and forced him down.

"Madame Billingsly, please, don't ..."

"You love your mama, don't you?" she asked, slurring her words.

John nodded and understood the implication.

"Then do what you slaves do best."

Although she was intoxicated, he couldn't challenge her; that'd make matters worse. His eyes welled with tears as she touched his nether region.

After listening to John's account of the assault, the raging fire in her eyes resumed. She said, "You are a filthy liar and a bastard. I hate you. You've just signed your death warrant."

The condemnations no longer hurt John at this point. He figured she was lashing out at him to deny the truth.

"After I kill you, I'm going after your mama. I'm going to burn down that rat hole she lives in."

She motioned with the rifle for John to walk down the stairs. She poked him in the back with the rifle as he went down, letting him know she was fully in charge.

Halfway down the staircase, she caught her right foot in the hem of her floor-length chemise, and she jabbed the barrel of the rifle into John's upper back, then the two tumbled down the stairs, ricocheting off the wall and balustrade. Both lay motionless about a foot apart on the white marble floor in the foyer.

John came to after a few minutes, staring at the leg of the Victorian chaise lounge chair. He raised himself off the floor with his elbows and turned and looked at Madame Billingsly. With his mouth agape, he shook his head at seeing her lying motionless on the floor. He snapped up from the floor and debated whether to flee.

A dram of guilt overcame him. "Madame Billingsly, are you alright?" He repeated it. No response. He shook her. No response.

Fearing the worst, he grabbed the rifle and darted out of the front door. Just as fast, he pivoted and returned to the house, knelt down beside her, closed her eyes, straightened and pulled her chemise to her feet, and said he was sorry for what happened. His teacher and tormentor, the woman who had a heart as hostile and inhospitable as the desert, was dead. And he had a part in it.

He darted out of the house and made his way to the side, where he saw the barn owl's penetrating eyes again, watching his every move. The bile resurfaced. He swallowed hard, squinted hard, then looked at the owl again, which hoo'd a few times as though he were decrying John's deed.

John ignored the owl, picked up the flasks, and ran home under a quiet moonlit night.

5

SPRING, 1887

Ann had made it a habit of not going to sleep until John had returned home from work or wherever else he'd been. Tonight was no different.

She sat at the wonky kitchen table looking through a magnifying glass, struggling to read bits and pieces of last week's *Richmond Dispatch* under the lantern's dim light. Although she could only read the simplest of words, she delighted in asking others the meaning of a certain word. As she finished scratching out m-u-n-i-c-i-p-a-l on crumpled foolscap, she heard footsteps at the front door.

No sooner had John opened the door, Ann said in a soft voice, "It's late, John; where have you been, son?"

"Nowhere, Mama; just out."

Ann looked at the pine box in John's left hand. "What's in that box you holding?"

"Just some fishing tackle."

He was getting irritated with the questions, but he knew he'd have to remain calm, despite his whirling mind and aching stomach.

"Okay, son." She looked at the rifle John held in the other hand. "Where'd you get the rifle?"

He was ready with another concocted answer. "Old Man Wilkins gave it to me. He said it was for my birthday. Told me to shoot some rabbits with it."

She looked at him askance, and John was troubled by it. He didn't like lying to his mother, but there was no choice.

She touched his forehead, which was dappled with beads of sweat. "Son, you ... your head's warm."

Another question and more irritation. He didn't answer.

Noticing an odor on his mouth, she sniffed twice. "What's that smell?"

He ignored the question again. He still had the nasty taste of bile lodged in the back of his mouth.

Her eyes drifted downward, stopping at the hole in his pants.

He realized what she was looking at. He sat down at the kitchen table as the weight of her questions and eyes was too much to bear.

Ann put a lantern on the kitchen table, then poured him a dipper of water, hoping it would erase the foul odor emanating from John's mouth.

He had rehearsed it on his run home from *Billingsly*. He had now sawed off the chains that bound him to Richmond. It had to be said: "Mama, you told me that I'm a man and that I'll be moving on soon. That *soon* is *here*."

"I know, son," she said quickly, failing to grasp what John meant by *here*. We can talk about it tomorrow. It's late; go to bed. I'll fix you a nice breakfast in the morning. I'll make your favorite—fried apples."

John couldn't wait until the morning to talk about it. Nothing could change his mind. The sooner he left the better. He had to escape Monsieur Billingsly, who'd have lots of questions for John, as Billingsly knew John had wide access to the mansion while he worked there. "Ma, it's not safe here for me. I need to leave."

He'd never told her about ever feeling his safety was in jeopardy. He had to get to the bottom of it. "Tell your mama what's the problem, son."

His departure time was set; Tyrone was scheduled to return to *Billingsly* in two days from his business trip. "Just trust me, Mama. It's best that I leave."

Given John's age, Ann suspected that John's departure had been coming; that didn't mean she was prepared to accept it. She emitted a cry for help from the Lord, as she often did when in pain.

She felt the familiar twisting and harsh pang in her stomach. John failed to ease her mind as to the reason he felt he needed to flee. She'd be prepared to accept it if she had more notice and they had talked about it over time. She was losing her family once more, and she had no control over it. She thought of how she had sobbed for weeks after Moses had been sold to a slave owner in Kentucky, how she had lost her will to live after losing her twin daughters.

"Where will you go?" she asked haltingly, her voice cracking.

Although he had imagined this day would arrive in one form or another, he never developed a plan. "Just go; don't know where," he said with a bewildered look on his face.

"Son, can't you wait a few days?"

His dark and foreboding eyes spoke for him. He was leaving, and his mother couldn't talk him out of it, not for a week, not for a day.

As John had done no planning, Ann thought of something to help with his impending departure from the only place he called home.

Douglas popped in her mind. Douglas had once told Ann that he wanted to move to Alabama to live with an older half brother. He was a handyman around town, someone who had demonstrated exceptional carpentry skills. He was a few years older than John. He'd helped build the tiny addition to Ann's cabin that had later served as John's bedroom. She allowed herself to believe, along with her prayers, that Douglas's maturity would help them in their travels. Like Moses in the Bible, Douglas would shepherd John to some promised land.

"Douglas been talking about leaving Richmond to go to Alabama. Maybe you can go with him. Your Mama would like that."

John nodded to acknowledge that his mother was scared and that she had just offered a good piece of maternal advice.

"If you make it to Alabama, try to find Cousin Riley."

"Who's Cousin Riley?"

"I saw Cousin Riley a few times on old man Windsor's plantation. My mama called him Cousin Riley. Don't know why we called him Cousin Riley. I just figure we related somehow. Heard he was sold down the river years ago." She paused, then added, "Last I heard, he's somewhere near a place called Mount Hope. "If you find him, son, that be good for you; maybe we share his blood. You hang on to that hope."

"I wish I could have met your mama. Tell me her name again."

"Esther. She was a quilter; they say the best one in all of Richmond. She made that quilt you use to stay warm at night. I wished she had lived long enough to see my handsome boy."

John smiled and the darkness that lived in his eyes and heart began to dissipate.

Ann gave more information about John's grandmother. "I remember Mama telling me not to upset the white man. She didn't want the white man to sell us like they sold Cousin Riley. I remember Mama saying she heard he ended up in Mount Hope after being sold to another slave owner."

"When was he sold to another slave owner, Mama?"

"Don't know. Thinking sometime before the fighting started."

John had no siblings, and no cousins, aunts, or uncles that he knew of. This Cousin Riley was an unknown putative familial bond. Ann was his sole family. The possibility of finding someone who was related to him, of seeing someone else who had some of his blood, excited him. "Describe him, Mama?"

"Can't recall too much about him. He's years ahead of me. I do remember Mama telling me that he has a long, nasty scar on his right cheek. Mama said Windsor cut him with his fishing knife because Cousin Riley sassed him."

"You never told me these things."

"Lots of things I ain't told you. Some things just too painful for a child to hear."

"Mama, I'm not a child."

Ann protested. "You my child."

Early the next day John and Douglas sealed the deal—they were going to Alabama, everything be damned; they'd leave around dusk to get a head start on Billingsly and his hounds that John thought would be sure to follow.

Ann hated to see John leave; he'd just turned seventeen, young enough to need his mother's protection and advice, yet old enough to start his own life, his own family, like she did at a young age. She was sixteen and Moses was twenty-one when they jumped the broom on Windsor's plantation.

After John had finished the breakfast Ann made for him, she kissed him on the right cheek, then squeezed him tightly.

John went to his room and sat on his bed. He adjusted the light in the lantern on a stand, then put his head in his hands. His heart was laden with guilt from the wreckage he had left behind at *Billingsly*, but he knew there could be no turning back. Whatever lay in front of him was worth the risk of staying alive. He was ready to test his wings, even given the circumstances, and hoped his mother's abiding love would keep him going.

He broke his contemplative mood by packing his haversack with a few clothes, Billingsly's pocket watch, and sundry things he thought he'd need for his uncertain trek. Ann had told him she'd give him some of his favorite victuals for the trek. After a half hour of packing, a small, blue-gray mouse crept warily up to John's feet and began sniffing his brown brogans. John picked up the mouse with his right hand and stared at it, feeling the mouse's heartbeat, wondering if he were old enough to leave his mother. He raised the mouse to his nose, able to feel the vibrissa tickle his nose and hear the faint whistle of his breath as he looked in the mouse's coal-black, beady eyes, hoping for confirmation that he was doing the right thing by leaving Richmond.

He bent down and shook his hand to dislodge the mouse; it settled on the dirt-stained pinewood floor. The mouse continued to sniff at John's feet even as John walked around his eight-by-ten-foot bedroom. John knelt down on his knees and cupped his left hand, and the mouse settled comfortably in his warm hand. It was best for the mouse to move on, just like him. He set his new friend loose in a large crop field several yards from the cabin, hoping that the mouse, like himself, would be able to survive a new life.

He returned to his bedroom and removed the flasks from the pine box, shoved the box under the bed, and put the flasks inside his haversack. He rubbed his hands across the brocade of his grandmother's green-and-white, floral-patterned quilt, which had kept him warm for so many nights, as though he were trying to caress his grandmother's spirit, asking her if the course he was about to set out on was the right one. He shook his head several times; he had to leave.

Standing up, he hefted his haversack over his right shoulder feeling its weight, wondering whether he could carry the freight on a long and uncertain journey. He abruptly took the haversack from his bag and tossed it on the bed, lifted the flap, and retrieved the flasks from one of its pockets.

The engravings were enigmatic to him. As if to make them appear more discernible, he traced his right hand over one of them. They meant nothing to him. He had claimed his prize at great sacrifice only to have no understanding of its value. He espied a small muslin poke sack in the corner of his room and placed the flasks in it. He pulled the hemp strings tight and put the poke sack in his haversack.

With the .22-caliber rifle in his hand, he stood in the door frame watching Ann rock in a rickety rocking chair.

As if she heard him standing behind him, Ann said, "Son, something on your mind?"

He stepped quietly in front of Ann. "Ma, don't be afraid to use this," he said with his left arm outstretched, the rifle a foot away from her.

Ann had no use for such a weapon. "I ain't never shot nothing. Don't plan to start."

"Okay, Mama, but it'll be in the cockloft in case you ever need it."

He worried about his mother, who had always taken care of him, his sisters, the Billingslys, people of all stripes, caring little for herself, asking little in return. She was all magnolia and no steel. It made sense why she couldn't harm anyone.

Ann stopped rocking. She struggled to get up. John helped her stand, and she led him to the front porch where John helped her sit. She patted the warped floorboard for John to sit next to her.

It was a warm and still May night, a propitious time to leave. Douglas would be coming soon. And Billingsly would soon return home to discover his dead wife; he'd return with questions for John and Sam and anyone else who could possibly shed light on Laura's death.

"Mama, what's my name?" he asked, looking with his head down while he tapped a loose plank with his left foot.

Before she could respond, John pointed to the meteor shower racing across the sky.

"Beautiful, like my son's heart."

Bile percolated in John's esophagus when he heard his mother's praise.

After the shower grew faint, Ann rested her head on John's shoulder and said, "Your name John Moses."

"No, Mama, I mean my last name. Don't I need one?"

Ann paused. She thought of the Windsor name, the surname of the man who'd owned her as chattel. "Reckon you do, son. I was told they attached Windsor to my name. Then Billingsly got on there, too. You want Billingsly?"

"Never will I take that name!"

"What if I need to find you some day? Someone'll need to know your name."

John scratched his head; he was stumped. He conceded that his mother had a point, so he decided to accept it for now. "Okay, Mama, for now."

"Good, son. That make your Mama happy. Maybe you change it later."

"You'll know, Mama."

She wagged her narrow, right index finger at him. "That be right by me, son, but don't you dare mess with John Moses. Them my names I gave you."

"No, Mama, I won't touch John Moses." He paused then said, "I'll make it back someday for you to tell me about Moses. I know he's not my pa. I just want to know why he was so special to you, that's all."

Ann wiped the tears with the back of her weathered hands. "Yes, someday."

Ann tried to rise from her seat on the porch, but the arthritis in her back forced her back down. John stood up and helped lift her to her feet. "That's my boy—handsome and strong." She stopped in place, held her back with both hands as to try to settle the throbbing pain. Satisfied that the pain had diminished, she grabbed John's hand, and they toddled slowly inside their cedar log hovel.

John kissed his mother on the cheek. She threw both arms around him, and hugged him for about two minutes, squeezing him tight.

"Let me look at your face," she said as she pushed away from the embrace, only to see fear in her son's eyes. She straightened his galluses, then tucked his shirt in his trousers and retied his twine rope belt.

She sat in her rocking chair and began singing:

> *Steal away, steal away*
> *Steal Away to Jesus!*
> *Steal away, Steal Away home*
> *I ain't got long to stay here*
>
> *My Lord, He calls me*
> *He calls me by the thunder*
> *The trumpet sounds within-a my soul*
> *I ain't got long to stay here*
>
> *Green trees are bending*
> *Po' sinner stand a-trembling*
> *The trumpet sounds within-a my soul*
> *I ain't got long to stay here.*

"Mama, you're singing that song again."

Ann replied, "I know. It's a song I first started singing years back when I was a slave."

"But Mama, you are not a slave anymore."

"I know, son. Your Mama was happy when Father Abraham gave us freedom."

It was a somber song to John, just one more thing that made him detest slavery, a life he never experienced, but saw wreckage from every day. "You've been singing it a lot, Mama."

"I started singing it more after your sisters left."

"But I'm not dead, Mama."

"I know, you as lively as ever. But you the only family I got left now, and you going away, far away, to find a better life somewhere."

"I'll come back for you, Mama," he said, desperate to tell her about how he'd try to return to look for the fortune buried on the Billingslys' property somewhere. He'd make it all right for her someday. She'd have a better house, better clothes, good food to eat, and more. But the thought quickly became too distasteful. He knew how Ann felt about the Billingslys.

"Lord willing, I'll be here waiting."

But she knew she couldn't count on it. So many dangers lurked ahead of him, she figured. She was left with the heavy hope that she raised him well and he would do well for himself someday, somewhere. She didn't have much of anything to give to John to take with him but her counsel, which she'd giving him since he was old enough to understand it.

"Son, you remember when you was younger, we walked to the polls so our people could vote? Pastor Jeremiah told us that it's our duty to vote. Kept saying we citizens of this country. You was about ten years old, I reckon."

"Yeah, I remember. It was cold when we walked all that way; my feet got cold. I remember when we got there some fools called us nasty names."

She knew he may not be able to foresee the future per se, but she hoped he'd find a way to help enable it. "Wherever you call home someday, I want you to vote, son. We free now, and you got the right to vote. Teach your children and grandchildren to vote. We need to be counted. Make your voice heard; do something in the community for your people." Ann had more instructions for her son. "You gonna see a lot of things on your trip down south—good and bad. Just trust in the Lord; he'll see fit to get you there."

She then thought of the times that she'd been belittled by slave owners and other people who crossed her way. Her son had to handle things differently than how she'd handled them; she wanted her son not to allow people to run over him. "No one can make you feel less than a man if you don't allow it."

She realized she wanted something from her sole remaining offspring, something that she no longer had, a family. "Son, it's just me, you, and the Lord now. When you leave, I will cling to the Lord; he won't abandon me. Someday, and you'll know when, you find a good woman and have lots of children, you hear me?"

"I'd want someone like you."

Ann allowed her lips to form a slight smile.

Ann rarely smiled. Laugh lines found no place on her face. It was like the nerves surrounding her mouth were frayed, preventing her from smiling or laughing.

"Mama, why don't you smile more often?"

"Not much to smile about."

She wanted him to remember her history because it was his, too. "I told you a lot about our family, the life I had before you came along. Don't you ever forget these things. Carry them with you. They make you a better man. To remember where you came from is a part of where you going, son. You hear me?"

John nodded several times.

Then, for the first time that John could recall, Ann flashed him an enormous smile, revealing a mouth beset with a slight overbite and crooked teeth. He closed his eyes like a camera shutter to imprint his mother's smile in his brain, an image he'd hope would last a lifetime. But he knew that beneath Ann's smile lay a long rip current of despair.

He stared at the strands of Ann's hair that hung from her ubiquitous tignon. It came to him in an instant. He decided to take a piece of his mother with him on his long journey. "Mama, I want a piece of your hair to take with me."

Ann felt her hair, moving her left hand around her head, feeling the strands of hair not covered by the tignon.

She smiled again, but this one was not so wide. John returned the smile.

She went to her bedroom and used her sewing scissors and cut off a small piece of her hair from the back of her head. She opened a small drawer and removed a rusty locket that someone had once given her. She opened it and placed her hair in it.

"Here," she said, handing John the rusty locket holding her hair in it.

John smiled and put it in his pocket.

John knew Ann would soon find out about Laura; he debated with himself yet again whether to tell her what happened.

"Mama, even in this mean world we live in, I never killed anyone in my life. Had no reason to."

Ann narrowed her eyes in bewilderment, then gave John another piece of counsel. "Bible say to guard your heart. Do that."

She reached over and grabbed John's left hand and prayed as he sat on his bed next to her.

Her soul was in retreat once again, and her heart sank with the heavy burden of losing yet another member of her family. Her head was hangdog, and her eyes welled with tears as she continued to sit on the bed.

But before John and Douglas would flee, John had scouted *Billingsly* to see if there was evidence that anyone had been there. Each step toward *Billingsly* had increased his dread; the bile that rose in this throat could not be stifled, and he vomited the rabbit stew, corn pone, and biscuits Ann had made for him. The area around *Billingsly* was eerily quiet except for the horses and cattle that moved about. He saw a farmhand in the distance who was milking a cow. John had never seen him inside of *Billingsly*, so he dismissed the thought that a farmhand knew something about the mistress of *Billingsly* lying lifeless on the floor. John had thought for a fleeting moment about returning to the scene of the crime to move the body to a less conspicuous location or even placing her in the comforts of her king-sized bed. But he knew he would not be able to stomach looking at her again, all caused by his theft.

As he turned to return to his slave cabin to prepare to leave in a few hours, he heard the clacking of hooves off in the distance. He panned the area and descried a stagecoach cruising toward *Billingsly*.

Damn.

He sprinted home, collected his things and Douglas, and began running quickly to escape his executioner. Ann wasn't there and he couldn't say goodbye for the last time.

Damn.

6

SPRING, 1887

Tyrone knew that his money ship had been out of kilter for some time. A fresh start was needed. So, he plodded on by selling his businesses to satisfy his hungry creditors and by signing over the deed to his house, along with title to his 300 acres of land, to The Old Security Bank. He'd find and use the buried gold to pay off The Old Security Bank to get back his beloved *Billingsly*. He was a Billingsly, and Billingsly men knew how to will themselves to come out on top with luck or no luck; there could be no other way.

As the stagecoach proceeded along the path bordered by live oak trees leading to *Billingsly* at around three o'clock in the afternoon in late May, the clouds began to part, giving way to blue skies. The stagecoach driver followed the dirt path and stopped several feet from the sprawling porch. As the driver placed Billingsly's portmanteau on the floor of the foyer, Billingsly smiled broadly as he looked at *Billingsly*. Laura deserved something special. He'd take her to Paris and Rome after he unearthed the valuables buried on his land. He didn't know the worth of the valuables, but he knew his father and his father was generous with his wealth.

Billingsly tipped the driver and bounded up the steps with eyes full of mirth, excited to tell Laura that they wouldn't have to leave *Billingsly* and that she'd get a much-deserved European vacation.

No sooner had he loosened his cravat as he walked in than he looked near the staircase and saw Laura lying on the floor. He ran to her and knelt beside her, shaking her. "Laura, Laura! My dear God, what has happened?"

Eyes that were bright just a few seconds ago were now full of mist and pain. The clues of her condition were staring him in the face; they were too obvious for him to ignore: Her eyelids covered her eyes, her pallid face was lifeless, and her body was stiff.

He stood up and looked at the grand staircase, guessing that she'd fallen and tumbled down the steps. The two broken spindles to the balustrade confirmed the idea. The shock of finding his wife dead collapsed him on the floor, and he began to sob.

Reflexively, he lifted Laura enough to hold her head against his chest. He caressed and stroked her head like a little girl would do with a doll. Feeling a knot on the back of her head, he screamed, "John, Sam, anybody. Help."

No response.

He thought about lying next to Laura in bed, telling her about his vacation plans for her, which he imagined would spring her to life. But he first needed to alert someone about Laura's death. He stood up and carried her body upstairs, periodically resting her against the wall to gain a better grasp, recalling the days when he was younger and had no trouble carrying a much lighter Laura to bed.

On the way to the bedroom, he felt a breeze coming from his study.

He then walked to the grand bedroom and gently put her down on the left side of the bed and arranged her clothes and body as to make it appear she was asleep.

He then took heavy steps to the study to close the window.

The damage was on stark display. A metal hasp was on the floor, and shards of wood lay scattered. Laura's imported French bibelots, which had been on a shelf, were now shattered as they lay on the floor. The cabinet that contained his father's gift to him and Laura was caved in. His face went flush with rage and cordlike veins throbbed at his temples when he realized what probably happened.

He dreaded looking in the cabinet, afraid that the box containing his father's flasks was gone, as would be any plans to use the buried treasure to restore his wealth, or at least some of it. He kicked shattered pieces of wood out of his path, then bent down to look at the bottom shelf. Empty. His head swelled with thunderous pain. He wanted to go to his bedroom and lie next to Laura and fall asleep, just like Laura. But he couldn't move much; the pain intensified with his every move. He chose to sit at his desk and will the pain away.

At the first sign that his headache had begun to subside, he stood up and took two steps and stopped. The pain was still there, but it had leveled out. He took two more steps. The pain was subsiding. As he walked out of his study, the sledgehammer that had crushed his cabinet, and now his heart, came into view as it rested against the wall near the door. He picked it up and turned the wooden handle. His initials were etched along the bottom of the handle.

Filled with rage, he threw the sledgehammer against the wall of the study, oblivious to the huge hole in the wall he made.

As much as they could be his best laid plans, they were now ruined. He bit his bottom lip and uttered with quiet ferocity, "I'm going to kill the son of a bitch who did this to me!"

But he'd first have to figure out who killed his wife, stole the flasks, stole *Billingsly*.

He rounded up a courier and sent him for the chief of police, a person he knew well. But he'd start his own investigation for now.

He unlocked the rifle cabinet, which was in a room near the kitchen, and grabbed a .22-caliber rifle. Although he thought the killer was probably long gone by now, he was trigger-happy, ready to kill anyone who possessed the slightest suspicion. He loaded it with two cartridges, then hied to the tool shed to look for evidence of an intruder.

The door lock to the tool shed was in place.

As he walked away from the shed contemplating what he'd do next, he caught a whiff of kerosene that stopped him in his tracks. He sniffed like a hound until he stopped at the open window to the shed, convinced that the smell emanated from there.

He blew the lock open with his rifle and flung open the door to the shed.

He picked up the lantern and walked over to the window, wondering if that was how the killer had gotten into the shed. A piece of cloth attached to a rusty nail caught his attention. He took it off the nail and examined it after he exited the shed. It was a small piece of blue denim cloth that had been torn from someone's trousers, he thought. The reddish color on the cloth had saturated most of the cloth. He rubbed it with his right thumb and index finger—it was blood.

Once back inside the house, he put the piece of cloth in a small muslin bag for safekeeping.

While waiting for the chief of police, he put out hay for his remaining horses to eat, then rode his favorite Cleveland Bay into the paddock while thinking of how'd he exact revenge on the bastard who had shattered his life. The killer couldn't just die a simple death; he'd have to be hanged, drawn, and quartered. He owed as much to Laura.

As his thoughts turned to who killed Laura, he spotted the chief of police proceeding down the driveway atop a roan horse. "Chief," Billingsly shouted, "I'm over here."

The chief waved and directed his horse to the paddock.

Billingsly and the chief dismounted in unison. Billingsly closed the gate to the paddock and shook the chief's hand.

"I came as fast as I could, Mr. Billingsly. Is something wrong?"

"Yes, Chief, something is wrong. Someone killed Laura."

"My God! Where is she?"

"Come with me. I'll take you to her."

The chief tied his horse to a nearby hitching post and climbed the steps to *Billingsly* with Tyrone.

In the foyer, the chief said, "Okay, tell me what you know."

As Tyrone told the chief about what he knew and when he discovered Laura's lifeless body on the floor, the chief removed a tobacco can from his breast pocket and inserted a wad of tobacco on the right side of his cheek. The chief had an extended paunch that strained the buttons to his shirt, a bulbous nose, a drifting right eye, and long, untamed salt-and-pepper hair.

"I see," the chief said. "Anything else you care to add?"

Tyrone had to report that his wife had been killed. But he didn't have to offer a reason. To do so would mean he'd have to tell the chief about the gold hidden on his property. He envisioned the ghoulish site of men digging up his land, looking for gold like forty-niners.

"Nothing I can think of, Chief."

"Where is she, Mr. Billingsly?"

"Upstairs in bed ... " Billingsly said with a trailing voice, mindful that the door to his study was open.

Tobacco juice spilled from the chief's mouth, which caused him to use his shirt sleeve to remove the juice from his lips. "Let me take a look at her."

Billingsly decided to walk alongside the wall and in tandem with the chief to obscure the chief's vision of the study. Billingsly, with his long legs, found himself moving ahead of the chief, whose stubby legs and heavy weight caused him to climb slowly up the long, winding staircase. Billingsly slowed down to allow to the chief to catch up. As they reached the top of the staircase, Billingsly blocked the entrance to his study and pointed in the direction of where the body lay. He quickly closed the door to the study and caught up with the chief in the bedroom.

The chief looked over Laura, looking for signs of blood. He didn't see any. Except for the slight bluish cast of her face, she looked like she was sleeping on her oversized bed. "You sure you have nothing else to add?" the chief asked.

"No, Chief."

"Well, I only ask because I don't have much to go on. All I know is she fell down the stairs. Could've been an accident."

"Damn you, Chief. It was no accident."

The chief widened his eyes at Tyrone's harsh tone. "How do you know it wasn't an accident?"

"Laura's never fallen before."

"Was she depressed about anything, Mr. Billingsly? Word around town is you're not in the best of financial health."

Tyrone's eyes darkened and he felt as though the chief had punched him in the gut with the force of a prize fighter. He had been good to the police department, giving money for uniforms and weapons. Yet the chief failed to show proper respect and deference.

Tyrone softened his disdain for the chief's line of questioning. He lowered his voice and tone and said, "I just don't think it was an accident."

The chief turned around and began to exit the bedroom when he noticed the gargantuan portrait on the wall. "Who's this?" the chief asked, standing two feet from the portrait.

"That's my father, Edward."

"That's a big portrait; he must have been a hell of a man."

Tyrone nodded.

Tyrone escorted the chief out of the house. As the chief was about to descend the porch steps, he turned to Tyrone and said, "The coroner will be here in short order."

"Thank you," Tyrone said.

"If there's something you have forgotten to tell me, I'll listen."

Tyrone felt another punch to the stomach. He held his tongue and emitted a tight smile.

After a couple of hours at *Billingsly*, the chief mounted his horse and waved goodbye.

Laura's body would be taken to the morgue several hours later, and he made arrangements to notify his children of their mother's death. He then drank copious amounts of bourbon until he passed out on the kitchen floor.

After his hangover slackened, he looked in the mirror as he dressed; his face looked craggier than usual, worn by the death of his wife.

A few hours later, he went to see Ann and John. Ann had been good to his family, and he wanted her to know. He knew John had access to the mansion and thought John might know something. At this point, he'd cling to anything John could offer. He'd check with Sam later to see what he knew.

Ann opened the door. "Massa, this a surprise to see you here at this hour."

Billingsly was silent, working up the nerve to tell Ann about Laura.

"Why you have that long look on your face? Come in, Massa?"

Billingsly stepped inside. "Ann, something terrible has happened."

Ann braced her stomach with both hands as she waited for Billingsly to divulge the bad news.

"Someone killed Laura while I was out of town," he said, straining to maintain his composure.

Ann's body went limp. Tyrone grabbed her by her left arm as she was falling to the floor, weakened by Tyrone's heavy words and an immediate sinking feeling that John may have had something to do with it; it fit with his need to leave so fast. He helped her take a few steps to a chair where she sat.

"Where'd you find her, Massa?"

"On the floor of the foyer, lying there like she just went to sleep," he said as his shaky voice trailed off. He coughed to remove the catch in his throat, then continued: "She did not deserve to meet her demise that way. Where is John? I'd like to talk to the boy."

Ann was silent, not knowing what to say.

She began sobbing and her body heaved.

Billingsly grabbed her by the shoulders and shook her. "Ann, where is the boy? Tell me."

Ann didn't like lying to Billingsly, but her first instinct was to protect her son. "Don't know, Massa. He said something about looking for a job because the missus said he was no longer needed." She paused, then said, "Mentioned something about going elsewhere to hunt for work."

"You suppose John knows anything about this?"

She recalled that John had fulminated about how Madame Billingsly wasn't fit to be in the world. It began to make some sense. But then she recalled that John told her that he'd never killed anyone. She breathed a sigh of relief. "No, Massa. I can't imagine my boy would know anything."

"You're sure?"

"Yes, Massa. My boy would never do nothing like that."

"I know that Laura rode him hard."

"My boy got too much respect for you, Massa. You taught him a lot. I look at his manners, the way he talk, and thank you for helping him. No, he could never hurt you like that."

"Mind if I look around?"

Ann had no choice but to assent. Although he asked permission, he was going to do what he wanted. She nodded her head.

He looked in John's small room, which held a mattress on a rickety pinewood bed frame. Billingsly looked behind the bedroom door and saw a tattered shirt attached to a hook. He sniffed the shirt; it was suffused with John's body odor. He folded it and put in the pocket of his frock coat—he figured he'd study it for possible clues.

Billingsly walked to the front door and turned around. He reached into his pants pocket and pulled out the bag with a bit of denim cloth that he removed from a nail in his tool shed. He walked over to the lantern that sat on the rickety kitchen table.

"This is all I got to go on," he said, holding the denim cloth near the light for Ann to see.

He gauged Ann's reaction. She looked confused as she squinted to understand what he was showing her. "It may lead nowhere, but it's something for now."

"What is it, Massa? What's that red stuff on it?"

"That's blood. I found this in my tool shed. The bastard cut himself on a nail while climbing out of the window in the shed. It's a piece of denim to someone's trousers; looks like it was torn when the bastard snagged his pants on the nail on the window ledge." He hesitated, then allowed himself to think revenge had taken its own course. "Maybe the bastard bled to death somewhere." He paused. "If you hear something, you must tell me."

"Yes, Massa."

Billingsly walked to the door of the cabin he had built for Ann and walked down the crooked steps. He donned his hat and hopped in his barouche and drove off. He'd see to it to talk to Sam and Emmaline to ascertain if they knew anything.

―∞―

Within a week after Laura's death, Billingsly had buried his wife in her family's plot in Richmond, a city she'd known she'd be buried in someday, just like a long line of her ancestors. He used the week to sell his property, including his prized Cleveland Bays. The Old Security Bank would put *Billingsly* on the market for sale.

Since he didn't tell the chief of police all he knew, there would be no official police investigation. As a last act to find out who killed

Laura, Billingsly hired two bounty hunters to find John to talk to him. Sam had told Billingsly that John had encouraged him to take some time off work that Laura had promised him. This news raised Billingsly's dander. Emmaline knew nothing.

He asked the bounty hunters to send word to him in Birmingham, where he'd soon move, of what they learned from John. They had orders to kill John if they had the slightest indication that John knew something about Laura's death.

Without Laura and the flasks, the world he knew in Richmond had finally collapsed on him.

He had one bit of fortune: he had maintained contact with James Sloss, the owner of Sloss Furnace in Birmingham. Both had an interest in Cleveland Bay horses and had first met a few years ago at the Upperville Colt Show where Sloss encouraged Billingsly to work for him. Billingsly had begged off, telling Sloss that his wife would never leave Richmond.

Within a few weeks after his creditors had hounded him, he sent Sloss a telegram asking if he still needed an executive to work in his steel business. Sloss replied by telegram: "We can use a talent of your caliber. Come on down to Birmingham where you belong."

When Sloss learned of Billingsly's plight, he told Billingsly a move to Birmingham would be good for him, a chance to start anew, to leave behind the wreckage in Richmond.

Billingsly agreed.

7

SPRING, 1887

Fannie opened the front door of her house and screamed in soprano: "Caroline, Tilla, y'all come on in; time for supper."

Although she didn't see her daughters, she suspected they'd heard her; they knew what time supper was usually served on church Sunday.

"Pony Hawkins," she yelled to her husband who sat in the living room reading the paper, "The front door is a bit loose. I want it fixed today."

Tilla rushed in and sat at the maplewood kitchen table, exhausted from playing tag with a few colored and white girls. She wore a white pinafore that covered her mauve-colored dress, which she'd worn to church earlier in the day.

The smell of warm corn pone, cow peas, and poke greens wafted in the air, igniting Tilla's olfactory nerves. She sniffed a few times to taste the air. With a fork in one hand and a knife in the other, she leaned back in the chair and swung her legs back and forth, ready to eat.

Fannie hovered over the stove, stirring the cowpeas on a coal stove. Tilla dropped her fork on the table. Fannie turned to Tilla and looked at her with reproving eyes. Tilla quickly averted her eyes and looked down. But she recovered quickly as Fannie turned around to resume stirring the cow peas.

"Ma, I hope I can cook like you someday. You can cook anything and make it taste real good. Pa said you cook like Grandma Jane."

A smile grew on Fannie's face. Her daughter knew when to turn on the charm with words and eyes that were as bright as the noonday sun. Tilla was a popular eleven-year-old girl, who possessed an effervescent personality that attracted children and adults alike. Her smooth skin was a shade darker than her quadroon father's pale skin. She'd inherited high cheekbones and straight auburn hair from her mother, Frances, or Fannie as she was called, who was a Griffe, a commixture of Creek Indian and Negro ancestry. The census counted them as mulatto, but there was no mistaking that they were Negro for all intents and purposes. They identified as Negro and attended the one community venue that established their identity—the Negro church.

Fannie put down the wooden ladle and turned around to look at Tilla. As she wiped her hands on her green-and-white checked apron, she said, "Honey, supper's almost ready; be ready in ten minutes. Where's your sister? She know what time we eat on Sunday."

The Hawkins family had strived to live the respectable life their church taught them. Every Sunday after church, they put aside their chores. And as usual on church Sunday, Fannie had covered the dining table with her favorite damask tablecloth and put her finest china on top. For years, as best they could, the Hawkins family had made a habit of eating a meal together on their day off from work, Fannie from the usual household chores, and Pony from his carpentry business.

To spice up things a tad, Fannie and Pony's family and friends often joined the Hawkinses for dinner. Tilla liked listening to grown folk conversation, especially talk about slavery. She enjoyed listening to Taz, a colored man who frequented all the groggeries in town. Although Pony had told him to avoid drinking before eating dinner with the family, Taz didn't always abide. But because he made Tilla laugh, and sometimes Caroline, Pony excused Taz's slip. When worked up, Taz regaled the Hawkins family with tales of how he survived plantation life as a slave. He'd show them a dance he did for the slave master's family: He'd suddenly fall to the floor and get up limping, a way of getting out of his back-breaking slave work. He'd tell the Hawkins family that the slave master never caught on to him because he was careful to execute his plan at the right moment.

Pony slipped into a groggery every once in a while; one of them is where he met Taz. He didn't go there for the firewater that contributed to the general liveliness in the inn, but for fellowship with the men he knew. After witnessing his father's pitiful descent into alcoholism, he didn't need the church to tell him he had to be abstemious. He was a businessman, and he thought it helped his business if he mixed with the people periodically.

But today it would be just the four of them eating together on church Sunday.

"I saw her last at Troublesome Creek," Tilla said. "That's been some time."

The Hawkinses lived in Mount Hope, a wisp of a town nestled in northeastern Alabama in between the slightly larger towns of Moulton and Russellville. The locals said Mount Hope got its name from the pioneer days when settlers, cutting through canebrake for days, stopped when they came upon a creek that was "swollen with rains," which somebody named a troublesome problem. Some pioneers crossed the creek and set up their homes, and the others remained behind. The locals also said that this represented the first split of many for the Mount Hope community.

Despite its name, the creek held something for both the younger and older children. The babbling creek held the younger children's attention, who were told that the creek contained the ghosts of dead Confederate soldiers. They liked to play by taking turns walking on an old, fallen bur oak log that stretched across the narrowest part of the creek, fearful of falling into the clutches of dead Confederate soldiers. Among the older children, it was the place to find other young people, to see and be seen. For those who wished not to be seen, there were always the many hollows that the older children occupied to explore the anatomy of the opposite sex. It was a place that did not respect a color line; it was as though the children didn't care about the grown-up talk about race. There would be plenty of time for talk of race, but for now it would have to wait. It was a place where adults did not wander, and the children knew it. It was as if a gatekeeper checked everyone's age at the gate, allowing only age-appropriate children to pass through.

Pony walked in from the front porch holding a folded newspaper. "Go get your sister," he said, in a rich baritone voice. "Let's not keep your mama waiting much longer." He said this as much for Fannie's benefit as his—he was hungry, too, all the more so after looking in the tall pot of poke greens.

Tilla didn't look forward to a return trip to Troublesome Creek. She was knackered and hungry. She rose slowly from her chair and shuffled to the door.

"Wait, baby." Fannie handed Tilla three corn pones. Tilla ate one and put the others in her pinafore pocket. "Now drink this." She handed Tilla a mug of water.

Off Tilla went to look for her sister Caroline, who was three years older. Caroline was nearly a head taller than Tilla, and she'd inherited her mother's Indian-brown skin and her frizzy jet black hair, perhaps from an ancestor down the line somewhere.

Tilla was gregarious and loquacious, but Caroline was introverted and diffident. Tilla liked people and studied them to find a way to make them bend her way, but Caroline avoided people, afraid they'd discover her odd behavior and recurrent and intrusive, obsessive and compulsive thoughts that often left her immured in her bedroom. She'd count the poplar floorboards in her bedroom every day to make sure the number stayed constant. If the number from the previous day was off, she'd count again until the number matched. But even when the number matched, she wouldn't leave her room until her two pillows sat up against the headboard at the right height.

Pony and Fannie took Caroline's diffidence as something she would grow out of. She just needed to meet more people, they thought. And because she was ripening into the age when boys would come calling, she'd eventually break out of her shell. They were never aware of her world that kept her isolated.

They told themselves that they loved Caroline and Tilla equally. But to Caroline, it was like suckling puppies maneuvering to latch onto one of their mother's teats in order to sate their hunger, and Caroline got pushed aside.

Tilla and Caroline had settled into their chores, each taking on more responsibility with age. Tilla usually prepared the table for meals, washed the dishes, swept the floor, and did other sundry menial chores asked of her. Caroline usually scrubbed the floors, washed and ironed clothes, helped with the cooking, milked the cows, and sometimes wrung a chicken's neck.

Caroline never complained about her chores, not so much because Fannie told her that Tilla would acquire some of her chores as Tilla got older, but because that was her nature. Complaining would invite questions, and questions meant more talking, which she wasn't good at.

Pony couldn't wait on his daughters to return before eating. Fannie set his plate in front of him as he sat down to eat. Fannie was every bit the cook as her mother, Jane. Pony had tasted Jane's cooking as a young boy and fell in love with it. Without Jane, there'd be no Fannie in Pony's life.

Pony first met Jane when he was a teenage farmhand. Jane smelled him before Pony had said his first word. Jane put the shirt she was washing back in her bucket of water, put down the washing board, and turned around on the bench to acknowledge who was behind her. "Hi, mister," she said.

"It's a bit cooler where you are," the slender-framed boy said.

She nodded. "This here shade tree good to me," she said, looking at the elm tree's expansive branches that blocked out the sun.

"You been singing for some time now," the skinny boy said. "I never heard songs like that."

"They slave songs," Jane said. She studied him to determine his age and color. She had seen many men like him: they'd have a hint of a colored person whether in the hair texture, skin color, the shape of the nose or lips. But often it was not enough to prevent them from passing as white. Sometimes folk like Jane just had a feeling what race such a person claimed.

The skinny boy nodded and offered his age: "I'm sixteen."

"I reckon you be about nine when they say Lincoln said we free." She paused. "Why you talking to me?" she asked gently.

"When I take a break from working on the barn to get water, I hear your songs, pretty as a nightingale. You pretty, too."

Jane was middle-aged, but she accepted the compliment. "Mighty nice of you to say."

"You sing all the time?"

"Sing when I'm happy, sing when I'm sad. Tell you the truth, not many happy days. Not much changed since the War ended."

He shook his head, barely noticeably. Jane couldn't tell if the shake was because she said too much or because that was his way of commiserating with her.

He used his shirt to wipe sweat from his brow. A new subject was called for. His eyes landed on hers. "I ain't seen a colored person with your eyes."

Her small cornflower-blue eyes contrasted with her reddish-brown skin, long, black feathery hair, and full lips. Though she had some features of the Creek, she was classified as a Negro, and had been a slave.

She smiled weakly, not sure whether a response was required.

"My name's Pony. What's yours?"

"Jane," she said as she looked past him and saw a white man looking in their direction.

Pony turned around. "He's another worker; he wants me to get back to work."

"How you get that name?" she asked.

"Mother said I liked ponies as a little boy."

Jane continued to study his features as his race confused her. He looked white but there was a hint of color in him, she thought. The gray eyes, curly brown hair, and slightly reddish skin confounded her.

"Why're you looking at me like that?" he asked.

Her look turned sheepish. But she wanted to know. "Where'd you get that curly hair?"

He had seen the stares before and had heard it before. "My pa said his grandmother had colored blood."

"Mr. Pony, I best return to work. I don't want Mr. Childs or the missus after me."

"Who?"

"Mr. Childs is the owner of all this land. That barn you building is for him. I stayed on with him here in Mount Hope after the War."

"Bye, Miss Jane," Pony said. He ran back to the task of helping build Mr. Childs's barn.

Jane sat on the same bench the next day washing clothes, wearing the same long skirt and ratty blouse. And with his next break, Pony walked over to the singing chickadee.

She smelled him. "You back again," Jane said.

Rivulets of sweat began to sting his eyes, causing him to use the tail of his musty cotton shirt to wipe his clammy face, hoping the already sweat-soaked shirt would work better to slow down the rivulets than his sweaty hands. "My pa told me the colored people are good people."

Looking at Pony's slender frame, Jane said, "Seem you can stand a good meal. Why don't you stop by my home? Me and Fannie will cook a good meal for you."

"Gee, thanks. I love to eat," he said, rubbing his flat belly. "I'll be there after we finish throwing up the barn." He paused. "Tell me where you live."

Jane told him, and he said, "Be there in a couple of hours."

He paused, then asked: "Who's Fannie?"

"She my fourteen-year-old daughter."

"I see. You have a family?"

"Two grown boys; they done moved on. Got two girls at home with me. My husband died a few years back."

Fannie had worn a long, gray dress that that hugged her slender frame at the waist. She and her younger sister had set the table.

"Come in," Jane said, hearing a knock at the door.

"Good evening, Miss Jane," Pony said. "I came with an empty stomach."

Jane tilted her had back and laughed. "Good, we got plenty."

Pony returned several more times for dinner, and with each visit he took more and more of a liking to Fannie.

Within in two years' time, they were married; she was sixteen and he was eighteen. Jane had seen something in the skinny boy, and believed he'd do right for Fannie, so she happily assented to the marriage by signing her name with an X for approval on the marriage license.

As Tilla opened the front door to go to retrieve her sister, Pony told her to take Jughead with her for company. Jughead was Caroline's find. Caroline adopted the black-and-white border collie when he walked up to her one day—a day she had had an accurate floorboard count—while she sat in a pasture under a Spanish moss tree, contemplating her hollow place in the world. As was the course, Jughead would lick her hands and face, then snuggle in her lap.

But Caroline later began to ignore Jughead as she developed recurrent and intrusive thoughts about harming him; ignoring him was her way of saving his life. As Caroline deprived Jughead of affection and attention, he soon found it in Tilla, who rubbed his belly and took him for walks.

Tilla yelled in a drawn-out voice: "Jughead, Jughead." He finished his business against an old tree stump and sprinted in the direction of the waves that carried Tilla's voice. He wagged his tail feverishly, ready to please.

They made it to Troublesome Creek thirty minutes later. Tilla saw a colored boy walking on the bur oak log that crossed the shoals of the creek. After a few steps on the log, he jumped in the air to prove he could land squarely on the log without falling into the water. Tilla stopped to watch, entranced. He did it again. He landed on the log, put his arms in the air, turned slightly to the spectators on land behind him, and cocked his head to the side as to say it was easy, nothing to it. As he turned to face forward, he failed to see the notch in the log. He lost his balance and fell in the warm water and went under.

After about forty seconds of being under water, the children's faces sagged, wondering whether he had drowned. Suddenly, he burst through the water, his arms flailing, pretending to escape from hands of a Confederate soldier.

A little white girl shouted: "Andy, stop playing like that. It's not funny."

"C'mon, boy," Tilla hollered. Jughead had held off long enough. Hunger pangs gnawed him, and he sniffed the corn pone in Tilla's pinafore pocket. "Okay, boy, let's share." She broke off a piece and Jughead quickly snatched it from her open hand. "We gotta find Caroline so we can go home to eat."

She asked the children who were congregated in a small group if they had seen Caroline. They didn't recognize the name. Even Tilla's description of her sister was of no help.

Tilla stumbled upon a colored girl who knew Caroline. She told Tilla that she had seen Caroline earlier at Troublesome Creek, but she had left.

"Did you talk to her?" Tilla asked.

"Yeah, I did. She looked sad. She mentioned something about 'going away.'"

"Did she say where?"

The girl shook her head.

Tilla and Jughead continued to search for Caroline all around Troublesome Creek. Tilla walked in several hallows calling out Caroline's name; the only thing Tilla heard was the echo of her own voice.

The sun begun to set and Tilla and Jughead headed home. Caroline was probably already at home, Tilla thought.

"Where's Caroline?" Pony asked.

"Don't know, Pa. I thought she'd be here. Me and Jughead didn't see her."

Fannie walked around town calling Caroline's name every day for three weeks, hoping she'd hear her mother's cry, like a cub animal recognizes her mother's call. The search continued but was less frequent. But the pain was still present. She blamed herself for her daughter's disappearance; she bottled her grief by withdrawing inside herself.

Pony feared that Fannie's melancholy could lead to the disintegration of his family. He coveted an intact family, unlike his family that unraveled when he was young. His father Charles sympathized with the Southern poor coloreds and whites and yeoman farmers who forged an alliance with the Northern Republicans as a strike against the planter aristocracy they so resented. He put his hat in the political ring and ran for a seat in the Alabama legislature but took a drubbing at the polls. He just couldn't overcome the scalawag label that his opponent pinned on him. Pony witnessed his father become a defeated man after the wretched political race. Charles drank himself into oblivion, eventually dying of a broken heart.

8
SPRING, 1887

Richmond lay a fortnight behind.

The hard biscuits and smoked bacon that Ann had packed for them were gone within the first three days of leaving Richmond. It was John's idea to keep plodding south at breakneck pace for fear of Billingsly or hired men giving chase. They sopped up water from streams along the way, and even caught a couple of thin trout in one of the streams.

Wayworn and famished for food, drink, and sleep, they wended along on adrenaline and the naked reality of putting as much distance between them and Richmond as quickly as possible.

While the fear of being nabbed by Billingsly began to slake a bit as they covered more ground, their adrenaline began to evaporate as they walked along in a thatch of pine trees, each step harder than the next. Suddenly, they dropped to the carpeted forest floor together, unable to will their tired bodies to keep moving forward. It was a good place as any to rest and recuperate.

The warm spring temperature dropped with the sun; periodic nippy breezes ripped through the forest. Douglas removed a gray wool blanket from his haversack and wrapped it around himself and fell to the carpeted forest floor. He was asleep inside of ten seconds and snoring within thirty.

When John had packed his haversack, he'd never thought about bedding; he was focused more on just getting away from Richmond. Looking at Douglas wrapped snugly in the wool blanket caused John to think of his grandmother's quilt.

But thinking of his grandmother's quilt led to thoughts about his poor mother and whether he had put her life in jeopardy. He knew Billingsly would have questions, and he wondered what she'd tell Billingsly, what she'd tell the law. He was sure both had been to visit. He closed his eyes to erase any thoughts of Billingsly. His legs were nerveless and ready to collapse; he removed the flasks from the poke sack that was inside of the haversack and stuffed it with duff. He then put the flasks in his haversack, put the duff pillow under his head, and curled up in a fetal position to conserve body heat.

Ten hours later, Douglas's eyes, glued shut with dried rheum, popped open. He rolled over onto his back, sticking his arms out of his blanket, and stretched them to shake off the stiffness in his muscles. He leaned over and shoved John, who was in a deep sleep and didn't respond. Douglas shoved harder, turning John over onto his stomach.

John moaned.

"Wake up, sleepyhead," Douglas said.

John sat up slowly, happy to see daylight, though concerned by the fog that hung in the air.

The sun was almost at its zenith, and the fog was burning off, just in time to search to sate their hunger pangs.

Something caught Douglas's attention. "What's that over there?" he asked, pointing to a grayish, weather-beaten wood building in the distance.

An elm tree obscured part of the building, blocking John's view. "Where?"

"Down yonder," Douglas said, standing closer to John while pointing at it.

Douglas packed his haversack, slung it over his shoulder, took his first steps out of the protective covering of the forest, and eased cautiously into a fallow field, headed for the building.

John was hesitant to follow, like a cub afraid to leave the safety of his den to follow his mother on unfamiliar terrain. Douglas widened the gap between him and John, and soon Douglas was three hundred feet in front of him, obscured by the swales and bushes that dotted the field.

John felt the gulf between them grow like a weed. He removed the pocket watch from his haversack and looked at the time. Panic set in as he realized that for the first time since they'd left Richmond a few days ago, Douglas was no longer within eyesight or even a loud whisper. He put his haversack on his shoulder and decided to act. Like the frightened cub, John left the safety of his den, running as fast as his still half-asleep body would allow.

A large reddish-brown doe crossed his path and stopped, training her saucer-plate eyes on John, who was paralyzed in his tracks. The doe snorted and stomped her forelegs, trying to persuade John to move. She was protecting her fawn that John hadn't seen sleeping in tall timothy. John caught his breath and walked laterally and slowly away from the deer to show her he meant no harm.

As he widened the gap between him and the doe, the doe lowered her head and resumed chewing the timothy. He descried a large beech tree about forty yards in front of him, which he hurried to. He took off his haversack and slid down against the tree. He sat under the tree, tossing rocks in front of him, wondering if he'd be left to fend for himself in a world that was unfamiliar to him. He retrieved the pocket watch again from the haversack and figured nearly an hour had passed since Douglas had gone out ahead of him. It seemed longer. No sight of Douglas. No sound of him.

He decided to move again. He stood up, found his next target, another beech tree ahead of him, and slogged to it. After reaching the base of the tree, he fell hard to the ground, having no strength to bend down to sit.

Ann's unforgettable smile that he captured as time had drawn nigh for him to flee Richmond popped into his thoughts. He wanted to touch her, to have her hug him. The guilt at this moment ravaged his mind. He'd come clean and tell Billingsly about Laura and the flasks and hope for mercy. He regretted his decision to leave Richmond, and now he'd give an eyetooth to return to the place he'd despised for so long, all to ease his mother's pain.

He removed his ragged cotton shirt, exposing ribs that poked like ladder rungs through drum-taut skin. While sitting up against the tree, his strength left his body and he slumped sideways. Madame

Billingsly was dead because of him. His actions were sure to devastate Monsieur Billingsly once he learned about his wife. And he had left his precious mother back in Richmond under a false pretense. He had killed one person and knocked the heart and souls out of two.

To join the carnage he left behind, he struggled to cover his torso with his shirt as though it were a shroud. He moved his hands across patches of dirt and grass as though he were touching his final resting spot. Douglas had failed him by leaving him to fend for himself. He had no strength to look for him. Each hunger pang increased in intensity and his mind had loosened such that he dreamt of dying to get away from the hell on earth he had created. If he was lucky, he'd die in that spot, and someone would find him and dig up dirt and throw his guilt-laden body in a hellhole he felt he deserved.

9
SPRING, 1887

A splotchy, red-faced man knocked on the cabin door in rapid succession.

No answer. He knocked harder, but still no answer.

His companion, a wraith-looking man with unfriendly eyes and a pustulate complexion, spit out a wad of tobacco juice on the porch and said, "Suppose them slaves are here?"

"Don't know, but we'll find out," said the red-faced man. He took two steps back, then kicked open the door. He picked up his black slouch hat that had fallen off with the kick and walked in with his sidekick.

Old newspapers, a pencil, and scraps of foolscap were on the kitchen table. A few clothes hung from a rope line. Wicker baskets were scattered around. The beginnings of a quilt were on a molded and broken-down settee. The wraith looked in John's bedroom. He stooped down and looked under the bed. Too dark to see, he moved his arms back and forth until he felt something. He removed a small pine box from under the bed.

The wraith walked out of the bedroom into the main room. "Hey, Caleb," he said with a smirk, "look here." He paused. "Mr. Billingsly said something about a pine box."

"Yep, look to see if there's some writing on it," Caleb said.

The wraith blew wood dust from the bottom of the pine box. He brushed the remaining dust with his right hand. With a clear view of the stenciling, he said, "It say property of Edward Billingsly."

As they continued their search, Ann walked to her cabin on a quite warm Friday morning carrying a basket of wild berries. She dropped the basket and her jaw dropped upon seeing the open door; she raised her cotton dress above her boots with both hands and hurried up the steps and through the front door as fast as her arthritic back would allow. She feared Billingsly or his henchman had been there and left John's body to rot inside. A pall of doom suffused her, and this time would be her last on earth, she thought.

Her eyes met the wraith's, then fell to the pine box in the wraith's hand.

"You probably wondering what this is?" the wraith asked.

Ann said nothing.

"We talking to you!" Caleb said.

"Get out of my house!" Ann screamed.

The wraith smirked. "This wench must not know who she talking to."

Her anger escalated and her voice reached a crescendo, "Get out my damn house!"

Caleb closed the door, then grabbed Ann by the right arm and flung her to the floor. "We here on business."

Pain exploded in her back. She was stuck to the floor; she tried but couldn't push herself up straight.

Caleb became impatient. "Get your ass up."

She couldn't move. Caleb grabbed her left arm and yanked her up, forcing her to sit in a chair. Using his left arm, he swiped everything off the kitchen table and slammed the pine box on the table.

Ann flinched.

"We want some answers," Caleb said.

Ann closed her eyes, hoping it all was a bad dream.

The wraith removed a pocketknife from his breast pocket. He moved toward Ann with the knife in sight. He grabbed her chin with has left hand and squeezed tight, forcing Ann's eyes to pry open.

"Where'd this box come from?" Caleb asked.

She shook her head. Her mind was going to a familiar place—the time she lost her husband, her twin daughters, the rape. She mustered, "Don't know."

"Where's your boy?" the wraith asked.

She was even quieter, saying in a whisper, "Don't know."

The wraith yanked the clothes off the clothesline and cut the rope with his pocketknife.

"Stand up," the wraith demanded.

She crept up, grimacing as she rose.

With his narrow right hand, the wraith pulled on Ann's dress at the neckline, forcing the buttons to pop off. He used his knife to rip the bottom part of the dress. He inserted his hands into the tear and pulled hard until she was naked, except for her run-down black boots.

A smile lit the wraith's face. "Get over by that wall," he said, pointing to the back wall.

Ann inched her way to it.

Caleb sat at the kitchen table. "Now, unless you tell us what we need to know, you gonna get whipped."

Ann was silent. Her face folded into a blank expression, one that she had spent all her life shaping; one where laughter and happiness was halted; one where hope did not often take refuge.

The wraith looked at Ann's scarred back and shook his head. She flinched with the first lashing. The second lashing forced open her mouth; she screamed and collapsed to the floor.

"Shut up!" the wraith said.

Her screams quickly dissolved into a whimper.

Caleb said, "I'll make the bitch talk."

He walked over to her and unfastened his pants and they fell to the floor. As she lay on the floor with her head resting against the wall, she saw a pair of dark eyes from outside of the back of her cabin that peered in a small opening.

The dark-eyed person was carrying a dead rabbit by the scruff of the neck; he dropped his kill, cocked his shotgun, and lumbered up the stairs. A floorboard near the door squeaked. He froze.

Talking within Ann's cabin resumed, and the dark-eyed man relaxed a bit.

Caleb pulled Ann's legs until she lay on her back. He put one knee on the floor, then the other. The wraith looked on.

The door banged open, and the barrel of the shotgun quickly found Caleb's wide body.

"Get off her," growled Herbert, the dark-eyed man. He drew his face inward by pursing his lips and making his eyes small. "Now!"

Ann had known Herbert since they'd both been slaves. He'd brought Ann and John food, often something he had killed or trapped, on occasion. He was one of the many people who'd found a way to repay Ann for the things she'd done for others.

Caleb stood up and pulled up his pants.

"No funny business," Herbert said. Herbert removed his bowler hat and tossed it on the table. He was a large man both in height and girth, and he possessed a swarthy complexion; had short, matted black hair, and hands large enough to strangle a bear.

The wraith moved toward Herbert.

"You move again, and I'll shoot you between the eyes."

The wraith stopped.

Herbert picked up Ann's tattered dress and tossed it to her. She caught it and covered herself. "You alright?" he asked her.

She nodded with her eyes closed.

He looked at the intruders. "We going for a walk." Looking at Ann, Herbert said, "Won't be gone long."

The henchmen walked ahead of Herbert as they exited the cabin. Herbert told them he'd shoot them if they looked back or made any furtive movements. As a few small children were frolicking in the distance, Herbert kept the rifle at his side so as not to raise suspicion.

As they walked toward the back of the cabin and out of sight of anyone else, Herbert trained the shotgun on Caleb and the wraith as the henchmen continued to walk several paces ahead of him into a small, wooded area that Herbert knew well; it was one of his favorite places to hunt.

After reaching a bluff, Caleb turned around and yelled, "What the hell you think you doing?"

"Y'all going to join the fishes," Herbert said. "Maybe they like them some white meat." He paused, then shouted, "Jump!"

The wraith looked over the bluff. His mouth resembled a shallow grave as he gasped out, "That may be a hundred feet down."

A buckshot whizzed passed him. "Next one will hit one of you. If the other run, I track him down and kill him." Herbert made a slow circle with his thick neck as to say he was deadly serious. "I said jump, you crackers."

The wraith jumped first. Then Caleb. Herbert walked to the edge and saw ripples from the splash. He waited for five minutes, looking for signs they had survived the crash landing. He saw none.

Herbert returned to Ann's hovel and found her in her bed. Her empty eyes landed on him. "Ann," he said, "they won't be bothering you no more."

Ann said nothing.

He sat on the floor next to the bed. He scratched his head. "Can I get you something?" he asked.

She shook her head and moved his hand away from his head so she could scratch it. She was doing what came natural to her, taking care of people. After five minutes, he stood and told her he'd return the next day to check on her.

She whispered, "No, don't go." She moved over to the edge of the bed and patted it for Herbert to sit.

He complied.

She unbuttoned the top button of his shirt, then the next. Herbert said nothing as he looked into her eyes that were slowly regaining life. He pulled back when she unfastened a third button, but she simply lay back on the old quilt and smiled softly. The afternoon shadows deepened as they lay there, finding solace in each other's arms. Ann allowed hope inside her mind again; she had found a kindred connection with the giant man that saved her life.

10
SPRING, 1887

A raven pecked at the ground near John's feet.

It cawed, and another raven dropped from the sky and walked toward John as if looking for signs of life. John's face was devoid of pain and worry as he lay covered in his shroud.

John's arms started moving again, grazing the ground.

The ravens jumped back, startled. They flew away.

John felt a round object. He squeezed it, feeling moisture in his hand.

He picked it up and looked at it, but his vision refused to allow him to decipher what he was holding; it was as if he were trying to focus while being submerged in a vat of milk. He sniffed it. That sense wasn't working, either. He took a small bite of the wizened peach, then another, and another, until he stripped off every piece of fiber that was attached to the pit. His dark eyes grew lighter.

After a while, he stood up against the tree. As he regained a modicum of strength, he realized that he had the capacity to dread again. He thought about his mother and reached in a pocket and took out the rusty locket that contained a few strands of her hair. He cleared his throat to prepare himself to say something: "I'm sorry I left, Mama—"

Douglas tapped him on the shoulder.

A bolt of anger shot through John seeing Douglas chew on a luscious peach.

"Why'd you do that?" John asked.

Douglas didn't answer as he was still gnawing on the peach. He retrieved another peach from his back pocket and started chomping through that one, too, with a satisfied and relieved look on his round, cinnamon-colored face.

John wanted food and demanded an answer: "Where'd you get that?"

"There's a peach tree behind that building," he said, pointing to the old, weather-beaten clapboard building.

John picked up his haversack and willed himself in the direction of the building where he saw a grove of peach trees several feet behind the building. He wolfed down nine peaches, but as he started his tenth, he felt the onset of nausea from devouring the lashing of peaches so fast. He ate it anyway; after his ordeal, it was no time to waste food.

"You going to be all right, fella?" Douglas asked. "You can't be a baby out here. You gotta find a way to be strong," he said pointing to John's heart. Otherwise, you ain't gonna last." He paused then continued, "Your mama trusted me to go with you on this here trip south. You can turn around and go home—you be by yourself because I'm keep going."

While John lay in his trance-like state under the beech tree, he'd imagined himself back in Richmond, his mother smiling, knowing that he was still working for the Billingslys.

But now that he regained his faculty, he knew that while his fate on the road to Alabama was uncertain, he also knew that his fate in Richmond would end in one way: with him dead.

"Wonder what's in there?" John asked, pointing to the ramshackle building.

John sniffed the air. "I smell smoke; think it's coming from there," he said pointing.

Their eyes met as if they had hatched the same plan.

They stepped out of the peach grove and stopped near the perimeter, searching and listening for anyone who could bring them harm. Seeing and hearing nothing, they collected their nerves and dashed to the building, and John quickly opened the lopsided door.

Douglas spied a sack of grain and used it to prop open the door to allow a skosh of daylight into the windowless building.

Different sizes of slabs of cured hog meat hung from hooks that were attached to overhead beams. The smoke emanating from the hickory wood in a makeshift fireplace was just about exhausted. Douglas had once worked in a slaughterhouse and knew at once the fortune that had just befallen them.

No one could see them in the smokehouse, but they couldn't see if anyone was coming in their direction. Quick action was needed to allay deepening anxiety. John spotted a small red wagon in the back. "Let's use this wagon to carry the meat. We gotta get out of here."

Douglas donned a black leather apron that sat on the large butcher's table.

"Hurry up!" John whispered.

Douglas grabbed a slab of meat with both arms, allowing it to rest on his torso, then slowly and gently put it in the wagon as though he were putting a baby in a crib. After filling the wagon with five giant-size slabs of ribs and bacon, he told John, "Grab that skillet, that cleaver, and the bowie knife on the table."

"Yeah, boss," John said as to acknowledge Douglas's leadership role in this instance.

"Give me the cleaver," Douglas said as he pulled the meat wagon toward the door.

John put on his haversack, stepped outside of the smokehouse, and ran to the safety of the grove of peach trees; he'd act as a sentry. He paced back and forth in between the trees, looking for someone who could impede the theft operation. He called to Douglas, who appeared in the door frame gripping the handle of the wagon with one hand and the meat cleaver in the other.

John held up his right hand with palm facing forward, signaling Douglas to wait for his command to leave. Nervously, John glanced around a few more times to make sure there were no signs of possible danger. Satisfied it was safe for Douglas to move, he nodded and waved rapidly.

Douglas caught the signal and pulled the wagon, heavy with fresh slabs of meat, as best he could. John waved again, this time with added emphasis; he stomped his right foot to tell Douglas to pick up the pace, and just as Douglas did, the handle on the wagon twisted in his hand. The top slab of meat fell onto the ground, and the wagon righted itself with a twist of the handle by Douglas.

Although he had expended a lot of energy by the time he reached the peach grove, there wasn't time to rest. They were too close to the crime scene and needed to move on. They took turns pulling the wagon, stopping about two miles away, surrounded by switch grass, redwood pine, and assorted maple trees.

They rested before setting up a kitchen. John collected branches and brush to use for fire to cook. Douglas made a makeshift rack to place the skillet on. When the meat that Douglas had selected was cooked, John's eyes grew brighter with each chew of the smoked ribs and bacon.

With their bellies full again, the decision whether to move on or get rest was made for them. They'd set up camp by their kitchen and hoped that no one would trail after them. And even if they did, they'd decided to either beg for mercy or find a way to kill anyone who dared stop them on their ultimate destination.

Patches of moonlight peeked in between the canopy of trees. They sat with their backs resting against elm trees about eight feet opposite each other.

John did not have many contemporary friends in the slave cabin neighborhood. He spent most of his time working for the Billingslys; hunting; improving his reading, writing, and language by reading books his school and others had given him and the dictionary Monsieur Billingsly had given him; and talking to the pastor who believed John was a fast learner. He tended to be a loner and enmeshed himself in solitary activity, like wading in Blue Pond, or fishing and hunting.

John gazed at Douglas's face, studying it as though he was determining whether Douglas was a friend or foe. In reality, he was neither—he was a companion that Ann had asked to shepherd her boy to Mount Hope. Perhaps that would change later, John thought, but for now he'd just have to trust his companion.

With each step away from Richmond, John was learning more about his companion: he knew Douglas liked to crack his knuckles; he knew Douglas snored; he knew Douglas liked to laugh when he farted. But he really didn't know much about what kind of man he was.

Determined to get to know Douglas a little better, he'd decided to listen to the rhythm of his words, judge the veracity of his stories, and observe the movement of his body, at least as much as his seventeen-year-old mind would allow.

Douglas removed his gray socks and black brogans. He looked at his swollen feet and began to massage them with his hands to relieve the pain. He was not muscular in build but stood on oak tree legs that powered the rest of his body. He was about a head taller than John, not counting his tall mop of uneven and thin, curly black hair.

John stood up and moseyed a few feet from where he would sleep, pulled down his dark brown corduroy pants, and drained his bladder. As he pulled up his drawers and pants, he smelled an unpleasant odor that he thought was coming from his groin area. He scratched himself with his left hand, then lifted that hand to his nose, not wanting to believe he'd identified the source of the odor. "Whew!" he said, shaking his head.

Douglas watched, laughing. He reached inside his haversack, retrieved a tin container, and tossed it to John.

"What's this?"

"It's for the problem you having with your privates," Douglas said, still laughing.

John opened the container and took a whiff of the white powdery substance. He arched his eyebrows.

"Just take a little bit and put it down there."

John's eyebrows stayed raised.

"It's crotch powder. You'll smell a lot better."

John tossed the powder to Douglas and plunked down where he'd sleep. The light from the moon shined on John's smooth, unblemished, youthful face. The sclerotic coating of John's eyes was as white as fresh fallen snow, but there was a fear that resided in his eyes that revealed a scared young man who was on the road many miles away from his mother, traveling with some stranger, someone he hardly knew.

It was high time for him to know the inside of Douglas. "Mama mentioned something about how you needed to leave Richmond; something about you wanting to go to Alabama. Is that true?"

"Yeah. I got people there."

John detected there was more to Douglas's answer. "But why leave Richmond?"

Douglas told John that he had been born in the middle of the War, as far as he knew. His mother's sister later told him that his mother died just after giving birth to him, which he was told later was the day Lincoln freed the slaves. He knew nothing about his father. His aunt raised him until she died when he was nine years old, whereupon he was bounced from house to house, staying with people who were willing to care for him as a lodger. And now he was bouncing around again, this time with John. Douglas had had to fend for himself since he was nine years old.

Back in Richmond, Douglas had just purchased a few pieces of fruit from a huckster who'd set up his pushcart on a street corner. With his bag of fruit in his hand, he turned around and accidentally bumped into a young white girl behind him. The girl stumbled backward, losing her balance, but didn't fall. Douglas told her he was sorry, apologizing profusely while looking around to see what danger he'd brought to himself. He saw no one who would report him. He thought he'd escaped danger, only to learn that the girl's father heard about it because a white man who had seen Douglas around town had witnessed it.

The girl's father was furious that his daughter didn't tell him about the *assault*. Although the girl had no interest in being embroiled in a legal proceeding, her father wanted to see that the colored boy understood the gravity of his transgression. Douglas was arrested on assault charges. He was released from custody and expected to appear at his trial, but he figured there was no need to wait for something that was sure to go against him; a jail stint would crimp his plans to go to Alabama.

Douglas's situation was not new to colored men. The South had formed the cult of sacred Southern womanhood and with the end of slavery and the beginning of Negro freedom, Southern whites had intensified their belief in the fixed formula that required the affirmation that Southern womanhood had to be protected against colored men. Thus, any colored man who mocked the formula by looking at, gesturing to, or touching a white woman often risked a trial with a foregone jury verdict. If for some reason the justice system didn't work as intended, then justice for the accused colored man was often left to the offended white man.

"Man, that's some story. No wonder you needed to leave," John said.

"Ann said something about you may be in trouble with the boss man," Douglas said, referring to Billingsly. "That true?"

John's heart skipped a beat and he heard strange sounds stirring in his belly. He wondered what his mother really knew. He bowed his head and sent out a silent message: "Mama, if you can hear me, know that I didn't kill her."

Since Douglas had shed some light on his travails, John figured it was his turn. Perhaps it'd serve as a bonding moment to trust each other. Or if fate saw otherwise, Douglas would use it against him at some point. He rolled the dice and opened up to Douglas, telling him that he needed to flee because Monsieur Billingsly would surely sic his henchman and hounds on him for killing Madame Billingsly, the virago of Richmond who had tormented him.

"Did you?" Douglas pressed.

"No. I'm not crazy. She fell down the stairs in her house."

"What'd you mean?"

"I was walking down the steps in front of her, and she accidentally fell on top of me."

Douglas guffawed. "You touched a white woman?"

Douglas's crack caused John to picture Madame Billingsly partially clothed under the elm tree where she used her position of authority to compel John to touch her. A pensive look took hold of his face.

"Something wrong?" Douglas asked.

He couldn't tell Douglas about what happened under the elm tree. "No," he said, shaking his head.

John emitted a big yawn. Douglas didn't ask any more questions.

They soon fell asleep, rose at dawn, packed their haversacks with an abundant supply of peaches and smoked bacon, and trudged south.

Although Richmond faded into the distance with each step, thoughts of Ann and the Billingslys stayed parked in John's mind, one beset growing shame and guilt.

11

SPRING, 1887

The morning heat gave an indication that the day would ripen into broiling heat.

Ned Sawyer walked out of the front door of his tannery, lit a corncob pipe, and took his first long draw of the day. As he was wont to do at ten o'clock each workday morning, he'd take a break from the smell of the tannins to read the newspaper.

With the pipe dangling from his thin lips, he reached into his breast pocket and retrieved the newspaper. With his head low as he read, he sauntered to a bench located twenty feet from the front door of his tannery.

He removed the pipe from his mouth and emitted a harrumph.

As he didn't get a response, he tapped John on the shoulder as John sat slumped on the bench, asleep next to Douglas, who was also asleep.

John popped up from the bench and peered at Sawyer with saggy eyes. Sawyer had small, soft eyes, an aquiline nose, and a thick white horseshoe mustache.

John reached for his haversack on the ground, then awakened Douglas, who rose slowly.

This was their first encounter with a white man, or anyone for that matter, since they'd set out on their trek from Richmond several weeks ago.

Their first instinct was to run. But their legs were too wayworn. They had made it to Raleigh, North Carolina, overcoming oppressive heat and fitful snatches of sleep. But it wasn't easy. Their food supply didn't last long. Instead of pacing themselves with their meat and peaches, they had eaten much of it within a few days after they had removed the meat from the smokehouse. Other than the squirrel that Douglas trapped and skinned with his bowie knife, they ate timothy like ruminants. John later slowed their trek when he was down for about eighteen hours after being bitten by a recluse spider. Douglas fed him clay dirt in effort to ease the pain and to speed his recovery.

Sawyer spoke first. "This is my tannery," he said, pointing to the large wooden sign—SAWYER TANNERY—affixed to the front of the building. "You boys looking for work?"

John's stomach gurgled, and his head roiled with pain as he pondered whether to keep moving or talk to a potential benefactor. He thought he had come too close to death at least twice on his uncertain and increasingly dangerous trek—when he covered himself with a shroud under an elm tree several weeks ago, and when he was bitten by the spider. If death hadn't claimed him yet, perhaps he had gained a reprieve of sorts. Although he did a lot of things by himself, he generally liked people, liked studying them as he acquired more knowledge and wisdom. He had Douglas, but he was famished for more human contact.

But Douglas, who was itinerant by nature, did not need much human contact to survive. As he had been entrusted by Ann to shepherd John to Alabama, he said, "We just traveling through, sir."

"You boys not from here?"

Before Douglas could find an answer, Sawyer saw Rick, one of his workers, come out of the tannery. Sawyer waved Rick over to him. Rick had soft eyes, but John would have to warm up to him a little before determining whether danger potentially lurked underneath.

John and Douglas stood silent as Rick strode to Sawyer. Rick was a lanky colored man with russet-colored skin, dark brown hair, and waffle-sized ears. A black tanner's apron covered his blue overalls.

Sawyer pressed his mustache with his left hand. "Rick, show these boys around our operation," Sawyer ordered.

"I was on my way to pick up some lunch, Boss."

"That can wait," Sawyer snapped.

Douglas interjected. "That won't be necessary. We best be moving on."

Sawyer looked skyward and found the rising sun. "In this heat? Where you boys going?"

"Like I said, sir, just traveling though," Douglas said.

John stepped slightly in front of Douglas. "Maybe we can stay a while longer," John said as his stern eyes locked with Douglas's nonplussed eyes.

Rick slung his head forward and John followed in tow. Douglas, still nonplussed, hesitated before joining them. It was the first time either had seen the inside of a manufacturing company. Rick explained Sawyer's operations from beginning to end: workers were needed to unload the hides coming in by rail, to peel the bark from hemlock to release the tannin properties, to organize and treat the hide with lime to loosen the hair, to put the hide in a scrub house and later a drying room.

After the twenty-minute tour of the tannery, Rick stopped and leaned against a rail. "Boys, this is what we do."

John curled his nose at the smell of the tannin.

Rick said, "You'll get used to that smell." He paused, then added: "We turn this stuff"—he pointed to a pile of rawhide, "into something people want—bags, clothes, shoes, you name it. If you want the job, you boys will do most of the lifting and sorting. It's hard work, but you boys're young; you'll catch on quick. I'll help you along the way. Sawyer'll pay you a decent wage. And as you can tell, he don't mind hiring colored folk."

Cogs in John's head turned. His mind was addled with a mixture of possible good fortune and the need to continue on to Alabama. While they were a good distance from Richmond—and thus Billingsly—he couldn't quite shake the feeling of hearing Billingsly's menacing footsteps behind him. But a respite from the hostile world John and Douglas had witnessed on their trek, along with a chance to make some money, would be good, John thought.

Just as John nodded slightly, Rick then asked presumptuously, "Can you start tomorrow?"

Douglas resumed his leading role and spoke first for the duo. He had given in to John by touring the tannery, but he was now listening to his internal clock. "We don't live here; we don't have a place to stay. All we have in the world is what's on our backs."

"How long you boys been on the road?" Rick asked.

"Early May," Douglas said.

"It's now the middle of June. No doubt you boys need a break," Rick said.

John and Douglas locked eyes again.

Douglas caved. They needed food in their bellies.

"Y'all stay with me and my wife. But first, let's go get you something to eat."

—⚜—

Even during the four short weeks Douglas and John toiled in Sawyer's windowless tannery, the tannery blew through working men; the men came and went. The work was drudgery—constantly picking up and walking with heavy loads. Douglas and John didn't quit because of the work as much as because they knew it was time to move on, to get to Alabama before the shadows from the sun grew longer.

They were pleased to have acquired a bit of money from Sawyer's tannery. They bought denim pants and flannel shirts in anticipation of the cooler weather that was soon to come. John bought a blanket for his bedding. Their faces sparkled with tremendous elation when Rick gave them two large beige leather knapsacks he made especially for them, each embroidered with their name on the flap.

Carrie cooked a feast the night before Douglas and John were set to go on the road again. Carrie and Rick lived in a middling, two-story, seven-room white clapboard house. Rick was a hunter, and the walls of the house were adorned with animal parts from some of his catches—an elk's head with palmate antlers on one wall in the dining room, a moose's head on the wall of the living room, a black bear skin attached to the wall in the living room. He once had many more heads and skins and other animal body parts in his house, but Carrie made him get rid of some of them, telling him that she wanted to live in a house, not in the woods.

Dinner was almost ready. Rick sat in his favorite oversized tattered sofa chair and Douglas and John sat on an equally tattered Queen Anne sofa in the living room while Carrie prepared dinner.

Carrie walked to the opening between the dining room and the living room. She was a petite woman with an hourglass figure, smooth caramel-colored skin, and whiskey-colored eyes. She wore a chic red and white tignon that mostly covered her thick black hair, and was dressed in green form-fitting dress that was covered by a long white percale apron. "You boys're hungry, I bet," Carrie said revealing straight bone-colored teeth as she smiled.

Rick rose and strode to the dinner table. Douglas and John quickly followed.

John surveyed the fixings—venison, trotters, green beans, sweet potatoes, rabbit salad, pemmican.

As Douglas and John sat still, Rick said, "You boys, don't be shy. Dig in."

Carrie interjected, "Someone gonna need to bless this here food."

After an awkward pause, John spoke. He spoke at length, first thanking Rick and Carrie for putting up with two strangers. As his mother had instilled in him since he was a moppet, he gave thanks to the Lord for being alive and the good fortune that had befallen them by meeting Rick and Carrie. He ended by saying, "And please, Lord, bless this banquet Miss Carrie prepared."

Carrie emitted a slight smile, and said, "John, you sure have a way with words."

After Douglas had gulped his tea, Rick said, "Honey, can't you see Douglas needs some more tea?"

Carrie went to the kitchen and returned with a carafe of cinnamon tea, which she poured for Douglas and John.

"Thank you, Miss Carrie. Rick's a lucky man to have someone like you," John said.

"Don't I know it," Rick said while smacking on rabbit salad.

"Maybe I'll find someone like you one day," John said his eyes fixed on Carrie's eyes. Carrie smiled again, reached over and gently squeezed John's hand with a tender touch, reminding him of his mother's warm caresses.

"Ain't you sweet. I wish both you boys well. If y'all come by this way again, y'all come by and see us, you hear?"

Their bellies were swollen, and they could eat no more. Carrie gathered the dishes and piled them in the kitchen sink and tended to the business of cleaning up. The men returned to their seats in the living room and Rick provided a discourse on hunting and trapping, something he'd figured could prove useful on the long trek ahead of Douglas and John.

Douglas told Rick that they'd leave first thing tomorrow morning. "You'll leave first thing after you eat breakfast," Rick said correcting Douglas. Douglas and John smiled, happy to know that Rick had taken care of them.

"Why're you heading to Alabama?" Rick asked as he sucked his teeth trying to remove the fibrous venison that was lodged there.

"We both got family there," Douglas said.

"Do you know the way to Alabama?" John asked.

"I don't know the way to Alabama. Never been. Just know that it's west of Atlanta. If you pass through Atlanta on your way to Alabama, try to stop by to see my cousin. He's a professor of some kind at Atlanta University. His name is Thomas Bodie. Tell him Cousin Rick sent you his way. He'll take care of you."

"Do you know how to get to Atlanta?" Douglas asked.

Rick had gone there a few years ago to see his cousin receive a literary award for his writings dealing with Black economics. Rick told them which routes to take, to generally travel in a southwesterly direction. Rick drew up his body laden with food, walked to the mantle above the hearth, and picked up a compass. "Here," Rick said handing Douglas a compass, "this should come in handy to get you to Atlanta."

Carrie finished washing the dishes, cleaning the kitchen and dining room, and put large plates of food on the dining table. "You boys come here," she said, interrupting their conversation with Rick. "You're going to need to take some food with you. We got plenty."

Quite a spread lay before them. They looked at red and green apples, carrots, peaches, smoked bacon and ham, pemmican, soda bread, pocket soup ... "Take what you want. Use this wax paper," she said pointing, "to wrap some of your food."

"Thank you, Miss Carrie," John said.

"You boys're welcome. Now you boys go to bed now. You'll need your rest before heading out tomorrow."

"See you boys tomorrow morning at breakfast," Rick said as Douglas and John climbed the steps to the guest bedroom.

12
SUMMER, 1887

Legs now logy, each step was harder than the next after slogging for days in a dizzying maze of tall pine trees. They finally exited the maze, and open daylight awaited them where they soon stopped and fell down behind a thicket of brambles. The whinny of horses caught their attention. Douglas parted a section of brambles and peered ahead. John sat on the grass Indian-style and tilted his head back, and drank spring water from one of Billingsly's flasks. Douglas looked at John and whispered, "Hey, John, come here."

A short, stocky, middle-aged colored man dressed in a black jacket and pants alighted from the driver's seat of an ornately designed stagecoach powered by four large bay-colored horses and parked in front of a tavern.

The driver went into the tavern. John and Douglas looked for someone else to emerge from the stagecoach. After five minutes, the colored man pushed open the tavern door and returned to the stagecoach, opened the right door, and nodded. He extended his gloved right hand, which a well-proportioned, thirty-something-year-old woman used to balance herself as she stepped down from the stagecoach. She propped open her parasol and waited for the rest of her family. Her husband, although tall and straight, appeared much older; he had white hair and a well-lined face. He stepped down next, followed by three young children. The woman rested her parasol on her left shoulder, securing it with her left hand while she straightened her husband's string tie. The husband bent down and pecked her on the lips, then led the way to the tavern.

Douglas moved his hands from the brambles. His eyes glistened and he grew a puckish grin. "Our ride out of here is staring us in the face."

"What do you mean, our ride?"

"We gonna steal it to take us along. Seems to me we got a long ways to go; we can stand some help."

Douglas took in a deep breath and told John his plan. After three minutes or so, Douglas said, "Got it?"

"No."

"Man," Douglas said, making his eyes small and dark, "we need to do this."

"*We* need to do this? You want me to do everything in the plan."

Douglas studied John's sprig face for a few seconds. "They'll trust you."

John shook his head and said, "No, no, too risky, boss man."

"Look," Douglas said and put his hand on John's right shoulder, "we won't get many chances like this."

Damn, John thought. Putting more distance between Richmond and therefore Billingsly, could not be ignored. John nodded, head bowed and eyes closed. He trotted to the tavern, a way of getting on with the plan before he lost his nerve. Standing at the entrance, he breathed in deeply and exhaled, then grabbed the large brass door handle and opened the heavy oak wood door where he was greeted rudely by the hostess at the door.

"No pickaninnies allowed in here," she said bluntly. "Remove yourself."

John wondered if the stagecoach driver had gotten the same treatment. He ignored her, turning his head where he saw the stagecoach driver's passengers eating dinner near the window in sight of the stagecoach.

John needed more time to plan the heist. Turning his attention to the fussy hostess he needed to temporize: "I'm just here to see if you have a room for my boss."

She frowned, clenched her teeth, and snarled, "Get out of here now."

John observed the husband from the coach lifting his head and looking in their direction.

The hostess nodded at the husband, turned to John with a scowl, and said, "You're disturbing the senator and his family."

Holding firm, John said, "My boss sent me here. He's needs to know if you have rooms for family he's got coming to town. He told me to tell the pretty girl at the door that he will leave a big tip."

She allowed herself a brief, tepid smile. "When does your boss need the rooms?"

"Next Wednesday."

As she flicked her hand waving him out, she said, "That's five days away. Come back in two days' time." The driver walked toward the tavern door, carrying a large, gray canvas valise. John held open the door for the driver to enter the tavern. He heard the husband call out in a stentorian voice, "Malcolm, take our bags to our room; we're coming now."

A good sign, John thought. He rushed to Douglas still ensconced in the bramble hideaway and reported that the family and the driver were probably out of sight of the stagecoach.

"We must be sure. Go over there and look in the window to see if you see any sign of them," Douglas commanded.

John looked at Douglas askance. But wanting to get the heist over with, he scurried to the large window with *Henry's Tavern* stenciled on it. Not seeing them, he darted back to the bramble hideaway and gave Douglas his scouting report.

John was surprised to see a foreboding look in Douglas's eyes.

John felt the hesitation, but would have none of it "Let's go," he said, grabbing Douglas's left arm. Douglas didn't move.

"What's wrong, man?" he asked. "It was your idea to steal the stagecoach."

"We don't know how to drive that thing," Douglas said. "If we can't get it moving right away, we gonna be in trouble."

John looked through an opening in the brambles and saw the black points on the horses' manes, tails, and lower legs. One more thing was needed. "I'll be right back," John said. He scurried to the horses to confirm what he believed he'd seen on the horses' foreheads—white, star-shaped spots. He had his proof.

Confident that he could handle the Cleveland Bays, John said, "Let me handle this."

They walked to the stagecoach, trying not to hurry or bring attention to themselves. Douglas opened the door, tossed their new leather haversacks inside, jumped in, and curled up on the floor. John climbed on top and sat in the driver's seat. He closed his eyes and caught a glimpse of himself driving a Billingsly barouche, commanding a Cleveland Bay all the while.

"Giddy-up," he said and snapped the reins. The horses didn't move their legs; only bobbed their heads and nickered. "Giddy-up," he repeated as he snapped the reins again. Still no movement. He felt the sour tang of bile at the back of his throat. His heart rate picked up.

He called to Douglas and asked him to retrieve some carrots from his haversack. Douglas pounded the floor with his left hand, as though he were upset that he had to open his eyes. He passed the carrots to John through an opening in the coach. John jumped down from his perch and shoved the carrots in the horses' mouths.

"Got any more?" he called as loud as he dared to Douglas.

"Just apples."

"Give them to me."

"No, we gonna need them later."

John's anxiety grew as he looked around for signs of danger. Nothing, but something could arrive soon. "Look, Douglas, we gotta get a move on. Give them to me." Douglas handed John the apples. "Thank you," John said, relieved.

The horses quickly devoured the apples. He rubbed the two lead horses on their foreheads, looking them in the eyes, to let them know he was in charge. He climbed back to his perch.

As the driver walked out of the tavern to retrieve more of the family's luggage, he saw John sitting in his seat. "Hey, you! Get down from there," he said, running on stubby legs.

Douglas lifted himself slightly off the floor to see if he could see the driver. He couldn't, and returned to the floor, curling up to make himself smaller.

"I was just playing. I mean no harm, sir," John said, sounding sheepish.

As John climbed down, the driver opened the left door to retrieve luggage. Douglas kicked him hard in the stomach, which sent him to the ground and knocked the wind out of him.

John climbed back into the driver's seat. "Giddy-up!" he screamed as he snapped the reins.

The horses moved slowly at first, then began to trot. The driver looked on helplessly, trying to catch his breath as his stagecoach began to disappear.

Sunset was a few hours away, as good a time as any to stop the stagecoach. They'd need daylight to cover more ground for their getaway. "Hey, wake up," he said, tapping Douglas on the leg.

Douglas sat upright. "Where we be?"

"The compass is pointing south."

"I gotta hand it to you. I didn't think you could do it. You got some pretty good skills," Douglas said, laughing.

John smiled, acknowledging there were good things he learned working for the Billingslys. His familiarity with Cleveland Bay horses had paid off.

Douglas rifled through the portmanteau in the stagecoach. He found a pistol, a wad of cash, clothes, and two full bottles of Jack Daniel's. As he held a bottle, he knew it was time to ditch the stagecoach; it would be no match for people on horseback who'd come after them. He put the Jack Daniel's and two men's pullover shirts into his haversack. He put the money in his pocket and gave John the rest. He threw his haversack over his back.

"Someone's probably after us. We need to ditch this thing. Let's go."

"No, I'm not leaving them."

"Leaving what?

apron. He was taller, wiser, and had begun to find his own voice, which, as much as he didn't like it, was attributable in some way to working for the Billingslys. Where he once was shy as a younger boy, he now found his quest to live a bigger life impelling him to take more risks with his young life.

As John donned his clothes, Douglas saw a man on horseback coming in their direction. Douglas sat on Thunder ready to go. "C'mon," Douglas hissed. "Look like we got company."

John tied his haversack to his horse's saddle and mounted Lightning.

"Stop right there!" the man shouted. The man moved in front of them, brandishing a rifle in his right hand. He sat tall on his cinnamon-colored horse, whose coat almost matched the color of the man's reddish-orange skin. He tilted his black Stetson back on his head, revealing a long scar on his forehead.

"What you boys got in those bags?" the man asked, looking at the haversacks attached to Lightning and Thunder's saddles.

"We just traveling through," Douglas said.

"Where?"

"Don't rightly know," John offered.

The man kicked his horse with his cordovan boots; the horse edged closer to Douglas and John. "Ain't you boys got a home?"

"No," Douglas said.

The man decided to test Douglas and John, to see how they'd act under pressure. "How about if I shoot you right now? Maybe no one will hear the rifle shot out here in the wilderness."

John was confident enough about his riding skills that he thought about kicking Lightning into a gallop, but he knew Douglas was far less confident, and he just couldn't leave him in a lurch.

The man ordered John to dismount and to show him the contents of his haversack. "Careful, one false move and your friend dies." He pointed his rifle at Douglas.

The poke sack was on top in the haversack. John dug below the poke sack that held Billingsly's flasks, trying to avoid letting the bandit see it. He felt his shirt, and pulled it to the top, causing the poke sack to fall out of the haversack and onto the ground.

"What's in that white bag?"

"Just a whiskey container," John said.

"Show it to me." As John opened the haversack, the bandit said, "Careful," while keeping aim at Douglas's chest. John held it up for the man to see. "Okay, now toss it to me." John complied. The bandit caught it, looked at it, admiring the etching on the front. He put it in his vest pocket. "What else is in that bag?"

"Just another whiskey container."

"Take it out and toss it to me."

John removed the other flask and allowed it to fall to the ground.

"Pick it up, boy, and toss it here," the bandit demanded, annoyed.

As John bent down to pick it up, he grabbed a dollop of sand in his right hand, swung his right arm back, dropped the flask to his feet, and aimed the sand at the bandit's horse's nose and eyes.

The horse snorted in the sand and reared high and violently off his front legs.

The bandit fired off a shot at John with one hand as he tried to control the horse with the other. The bullet whistled near John's head.

The bandit did his best to hold on, but fell off to a hard landing, hitting his head on a nearby boulder. He lay on the sandy ground in agonizing pain, grimacing.

John saw that the bandit's rifle was a few feet away from where he'd landed. He walked up to the man, who was moaning low, and his eyes were flickering like a burning candle trying to give one last burst of fire.

John picked up the rifle by the long barrel and swung it hard into the lake. He bent down and retrieved the flask from the bandit's vest pocket, saying, "I think this belongs to me." As he stood up, he saw the bandit's Stetson a few feet away on its side. He stepped over the bandit, picked up the hat with his left hand, and dusted it off with his right. He stepped back over the man and looked the bandit in the face, whose eyes were still flickering, and donned his new hat, which fit as if made for him.

John turned to walk to Lightning, but the bandit reached out and grabbed John's left leg. John shook his leg from the bandit's feeble grip, turned and looked at him, shook his head as to say he wished it all could have been avoided. He picked up the other flask from the ground and restored the flasks to his haversack.

"John," Douglas said, "check his pants, jacket, and saddle to see if there is something we can use."

John complied and extracted some bills and coins and a couple of pewter mugs. They figured he must have been a bandit roaming around looking for the next victim.

John threw himself on top of Lightning, leaned forward, and stroked the bridge of Lightning's nose, which caused Lightning to nicker.

John sat confidently atop Lightning wearing his new chapeau, a blade of grass protruding from his lips as though he had just defeated the enemy in battle. He looked over at Douglas and nodded, kicked Lightning with his heels, and said, "Let's go."

13

SUMMER, 1887

The woods finally thinned and a commercial center appeared. They sat astride their stolen Cleveland Bays, staring at people moving around. The town was bustling with activity. All seemed so ordered: colored and whites walked the same streets, and people waited their turn to purchase goods from the abundant pushcart vendors.

Douglas jumped off his horse first, followed by John. They tied their horses to a hitching post near a sweet gum tree and sat under the tree's wide canopy. The shade of the pine trees in the woods was good while it lasted, but for the last hour, they had lost that cover and had ridden exposed to the open sun, sucking them dry. They were parched; their mouths felt like they were eating cotton. The last of the water-filled apples Rick had given them had been sacrificed to get the Bays moving.

The Bays drank from a lake, or a creek here and there, and chewed on vegetation here and there; they were ready to go for another few hours before needing to refuel. But not John or Douglas.

John stood up and panned his surroundings. He locked onto a toddler boy drinking from a cup of water. He thought about his mother's smile, and he smiled back at her.

"Be right back," he said to Douglas. "I need to wet my tongue. Don't wander too far. We don't know no one around here."

While standing at the water fountain for whites only, John removed a flask from the poke sack and used a narrow dipper to fill the flask with water. He put the cap on the flask, then filled the other flask. As he put the flasks back in the poke sack, a dog barked. He dropped the poke sack to the ground.

A well-fed brindled canine snarled at John in a low rumble. John maintained eye contact with the predator, worried he'd soon sink his teeth in the fleshy part of his legs.

A man behind the dog bellowed, "Boy, you can't read?!"

John raised his eyes and saw a short white man who was dressed like a country squire; he wore a brown Norfolk jacket and short baggy breaches. The predator growled as if to tell John not to look away from him. The county squire gave a quick tug of the leash, and the canine calmed down a bit. The squire pointed to the WHITES ONLY sign above the cooler.

"Sorry, sir," John said, tipping his Stetson to the squire. He picked up his poke sack and skedaddled to the sweet gum tree, happy that the squire was only a Billingsly ghost.

As John approached the tree, Douglas was looking in the direction of a buxom, walnut-colored woman dressed in a dark green empire waist dress that hung just above the ground. She was strolling, as though looking for a target. Douglas stood against the tree, his back resting against the trunk, right leg firmly planted on the ground, and the sole of his left foot resting against the trunk just below his buttocks.

"Hi, good looking," he said, smiling broadly, revealing long, gapped front teeth. He was ready to make nice.

She returned the smile, then looked at John drinking his water. She winked at him and batted her eyes at him, but it was Douglas's more mature face that demanded her attention.

"Hi, yourself, handsome. What's your name?" the harlot asked as she stood about a foot away from him, well within range for Douglas to smell her mingled scents of tantalizing perfume.

Douglas's eyes were as dreamy as his mind. "Whatever you want it to be," he said softly.

She inched closer, close enough for him to see the scales on her rouge-colored full lips. She stood tall and confidentially emitted an urbane smile as though she possessed a grand delightful secret. "Know what I'm thinking?" she said.

Douglas was distracted by looking at her high-rise bosom.

"How abouts I call you *Lucky?*" she said, stroking Douglas's lips with the underside of her left index finger.

"That'll be right by me."

She jiggled her jugs for him and said unctuously, "You wanna play? I know a place we can go."

"Go?"

She moved closer to Douglas, pinning him up against the sweet gum tree, then whispered "You know." She grabbed his crotch, an effort to give him a bit of an appetizer before the main course. Her tongue scraped Douglas's left earlobe. She said, "Got anything for me?"

Douglas felt the moisture on his ear and the warmth of her breath. "Like what?"

"A girl needs something to help pay her obligations," she said.

"I can't offer you no money."

She refused to give up. "How abouts your friend?" she said, looking at John who was smiling and looking strikingly handsome in his trophy hat.

"He's with me, and I know he got nothing."

She looked at Douglas in his soft, dreamy eyes, able to see her reflection. Her mouth moved closer to his. As he closed his eyes anticipating a kiss, she grabbed the bulge in his pants with her right hand, then squeezed hard, digging her fingernails into flesh; Douglas hollered and winced. As he bent over in pain, she flounced away and sashayed off to another target.

John laughed at the sight of Douglas massaging his genitals. He was relieved Douglas did not give her any of their lucre, which he knew they'd need to last awhile for the long, arduous trek ahead.

"Be on the lookout for women like her, pretty and all. They can mess you up," Douglas said, sounding winded as though he'd been punched in the stomach.

"Here," John said handing Douglas the other flask that he had filled with water.

Douglas removed the cap from the sterling silver flask, took a swill of water, and another, and another, until all the water was gone.

No sooner had they stopped in town than two omens had greeted them. After John's encounter with Billingsly's ghost, and Douglas's painful experience, it was time to move on.

Onward to Alabama.

14
SUMMER, 1887

The sun's brilliant rays were at their peak at high noon, but abundant heat didn't stop the shoppers who abounded in the streets, bargaining with hucksters selling a spread of fruits and vegetables, pastries, bread, and other edible sundries. They had made it to Greenville, South Carolina, a few weeks after their brief stay in Charlotte. As John dismounted Lightning, he observed a colored man draped in tattered overalls sitting atop three pallets next to a wagon topped with fruits and vegetables. He and Douglas scurried over to him carrying their haversacks. Douglas surveyed the people milling about. John quickly surveyed the produce, settling on a bushel of peaches, hoping they'd taste as scrumptious as the peaches he had weeks ago in the peach orchard.

The man was carving a piece of wood with a carving knife. As he knocked shavings from the wood, he looked up at John.

"How much for the peaches?" John asked.

He looked at John and Douglas for a few seconds, then said, "For you boys, fifteen cents a bushel."

John dug deep in his trousers and fingered his money to separate one bill from the others. He handed the pushcart vendor a one-dollar bill. The pushcart vendor held the dollar bill to the sky, stretching it as though to make sure it was real.

The vendor was walnut brown, with shoulders and chest whose girth came from lifting, pushing, and pulling heavy objects. He had short, coarse black hair, a broad nose, full lips, and a jowly jaw. "I'm

Kelly," he told them. Giving the dollar back to John, Kelly said, "You keep this."

Accepting the return of his dollar bill, John said, "Thanks, sir. I'm John."

"I'm Douglas."

"You boys from this way?"

"No, we from Richmond," Douglas said.

"Greenville's a mighty long way from Richmond. What'll y'all doing in Greenville?"

"We're on our way to Alabama," John said.

"We just got here minutes ago," Douglas said.

They had set out from Richmond in early May and had made it to Greenville, South Carolina, in late July. Rick had told them that where they found plank roads, they should consider using them because they generally offered a more direct route south, and they'd see more signs pointing them in the right direction. These roads were also close to commercial centers and railroad tracks were not too far off.

When they were not riding atop the stolen Cleveland Bay horses, they found themselves taking Rick's advice, walking along the plank roads where available, which were close to merchants that offered rooms for colored only. They stayed in rooms in small townships a little longer than desired because Douglas sprained his ankle when he tripped over a step as he turned his head to look at a buxom, young colored woman. After a few days, John insisted they move on because he did not want to raise suspicion that they had money.

They'd also used their lucre to buy used clothing and shoes; they'd discarded the tattered and odiferous clothing they had worn weeks at a time to lighten the load of their haversacks. They even exchanged their pewter mugs and Billingsly's pocket watch when they hitched a ride for several miles on the back of a horse wagon.

They had so far survived by the grace of God, fortunate happenstances, and the sheer will to drive their young bodies as far as their young bodies would take them.

After several minutes of chatting with Kelly, John heard their Bays whinny. He pivoted and pointed to the hitching post where they had tied Lightning and Thunder; two men were atop their Bays pressing them to gallop at full speed.

"Damn, they done stole our horses!" Douglas exclaimed.

After the risky operation of stealing the Bays from the senator, John settled on the belief they wouldn't be able to hang on to the horses forever. He just wanted to get to Mount Hope before the weather turned cold, assuming there'd be no other unforeseen long stops. His bigger life was waiting on him.

Where you boys going before the sun go down?"

"Don't rightly know," Douglas said.

Kelly looked at Douglas and John. "You carrying everything you own on your backs in them bags, I suppose."

Hesitant to reveal more than necessary at this point, John said, "Yeah, it's not much."

Looking at Douglas and John, Kelly said, "Your eyes be tired. Seems to me you can stand a wash of clothes ... and a bath. Tell you what. Me and Emily got a bath you can use. Won't y'all come with me? You can stay with us 'til you rested to get going on your way."

"Who's Emily?" John asked.

"Emily's my little girl. She ten by my count."

As Kelly picked up his pine wood stand to place on his wagon, Douglas said, "Let me help you with that."

"No, you boys help put the bushels and bags on the wagon."

It took John and Douglas about an hour to load the wagon.

Kelly walked around it to ensure his cargo was secure. Satisfied things were in place with the rope he used to secure the cargo, he said, "You boys, hop on."

Douglas threw his haversack on top of the cargo, but John kept his close to his side.

Kelly snapped the reins and his mules began to pull the cargo. Douglas and John lay back on their backs and inhaled the bread and pastry.

"John, we got food here to last us a while. We can fill our bags and go," Douglas said.

John was getting tired of running. Billingsly and his henchman could not possibly catch him—they were just too far away, he thought. He needed to entertain thoughts from time to time about his mother, and dream, as he had done so many times before, that he had made the right decision and that she'd survive like she had always done. Slowing his trek to Mount Hope would give him time to fuel his mind and body. Ignoring Douglas's suggestion that they pilfer and run, John closed his eyes and thought of Ann as Kelly's wagon bounced along a dirt road.

He opened his dreamy eyes upon hearing Kelly singing.

"What are you singing?" John asked.

"It's the *Jim Crack Corn* song. Don't you know it?"

"No," John said. "You know it, Doug?"

"Never heard it."

"You boys'll know the song by the time we reach home. Just listen."

> When I was young, I used to wait
> On Massa and hand him the plate;
> Pass down the bottle when he get dry,
> And brush away the blue tail fly.
>
> Jimmy crack corn, I don't care,
> Jimmy crack corn and I don't care,
> Jimmy crack corn and I don't care,
> Old Massa gone away.
>
> And when he ride in the afternoon,
> I follow with a hickory broom;
> The pony being very shy,
> When bitten by the blue tail fly.
>
> Jimmy crack corn and I don't care,
> Jimmy crack corn and I don't care,
> Jimmy crack corn and I don't care,
> Old Massa gone away.
>
> One day he rode around the farm,
> The flies so numerous they did swarm;
> One chance to bite him on the thigh,
> The devil take that blue tail fly.

Jimmy crack corn and I don't care,
Jimmy crack corn and I don't care,
Jimmy crack corn and I don't care,
Old Massa gone away.

The pony run, he jump and pitch,
And tumble Massa in the ditch
He died, and the jury wondered why
The verdict was the blue tail fly.

Jim crack corn — I don't care,
Jim crack corn — I don't care,
Jim crack corn — I don't care,
Old Massa gone away.

They buried him beneath the sycamore tree,
His epitaph there for all to see,
"Beneath this stone I'm forced to lie,
The victim of a blue-tailed fly."

Jimmy crack corn and I don't care,
Jimmy crack corn and I don't care,
Jimmy crack corn and I don't care,
Old Massa gone away.

After three passes of the song, Kelly said, "Okay, boys, all together now."

Douglas and John joined in.

John and Douglas slept in an attic room with a low ceiling caused by eaves that slanted sharply. John woke first several hours later, with the Jim Crack Corn jingle stuck in his head. John felt moisture on his face. He raised up a bit, opened his eyes, and saw a tabby's lustrous eyes. He pushed the tabby away, telling it to go elsewhere. No sooner than the tabby strolled off, John was awakened by the cock-a-doodle-doo of an annoying rooster. It was dawn. He stood up in his blue drawers and looked out the small window.

He recognized Kelly's brawny build and complexion, and figured the young girl near him was Emily.

"Doug, wake up," John said, while rocking him.

Douglas groaned.

"C'mon, Doug. Didn't you hear the rooster? We gotta get up."

As John donned his trousers, he looked in the place where he'd put his haversack. "Doug," he said in a panicked voice, "where's my bag? I put it right there," He pointed to a corner. "I see the rifle but not my bag."

"I don't know. Where's mine?"

Douglas fell back to sleep.

John walked out of the back door of Kelly's house and into an expansive orchard, one that seemed to stretch as far as the eye could see. He spotted Kelly and ran to him. He breathed in heavily and said, "Mr. Kelly, have you seen our bags? They're missing."

"They're not missing. They're sitting on the floor by the stove. You okay, son?"

John turned and ran to the house. He flung open the door and looked to the left, where he saw the two haversacks resting on the poplar floor. He opened his bag. It was stuffed with peaches, apples, and muscadines. He put his haversack onto the kitchen table and removed the fruit. A smilet surfaced when he saw the white poke sack. A bigger smile emerged when he removed the two whiskey flasks. "Thank you, Jesus," John whispered.

"John, over here," Kelly said, waving his right arm high in the air as John walked out the back door again.

Emily was sitting in a small chair several feet away under a shade tree eating a biscuit. "Emily," Kelly hollered, "come from over there and greet John."

She ran to her father, followed by a small piebald mongrel dog. John moved closer to Emily to formally introduce himself, at which point the dog growled and showed his small canine fangs.

"Go on, pet him," Kelly said.

John was hesitant, but sensed the dog was harmless after he wagged his tail feverishly and extended his head to John to be petted. John leaned over and scratched the dog on the head, who then licked John's hand. As John stopped scratching him, the dog whimpered, begging for more. John complied.

"What's his name?" John asked Kelly, who was snapping apples off the branches.

"Dog," replied Kelly.

"Yeah, the dog. What's his name?" John asked again.

Kelly repeated, "Dog." John looked puzzled. "John, my boy, he's just some dog that come this way every so often. I feed him, so he come by knowing I'll give him something. Dog don't seem to belong to nobody. I don't really know where he goes after getting a bite from me."

With his heart overruling his mind, John said, "He belongs to me."

A half hour later, Douglas donned his clothes for the day and joined everyone else outside. Looking in the direction of the bath, Douglas said, "Mr. Kelly, you mind if I take a bath over there?"

"Emily," Kelly yelled.

"I'm right behind you, Pa."

"Oh, sweetie, your pa didn't see you. See to it that these boys have soap, wash rags, and towels."

Tall for her age, Emily was giddy at being around two young men. She giggled as she looked at Douglas's bare chest. When Kelly turned away, Douglas twitched his pectoral muscles rhythmically. Emily covered her mouth as she giggled again. Douglas cracked a toothy smile, and Emily ran off to get the things needed for the bath.

The outdoor bath consisted of large oak boards that were bound together to form a wall for privacy. A large barrel of water was hoisted up high that the bather used by pulling on a string to pour the water over himself.

John entered the shower first, doffed his clothes, and threw them on top of the wall. He pulled lightly on the rope as he stood under the barrel waiting for the first splash. With another gentle tug, he was thoroughly wet. He stooped down and picked up powdered soap and began to lather his body.

Douglas tossed a brush into the bath. "What's this?" John asked.

"You gonna need it; that rag you have ain't gonna do the job."

After twenty minutes, Douglas screamed, "Hurry up." He added: "I need some of that water." John ignored Douglas and continued singing his now favorite ditty—"Jimmy Crack Corn."

They sat on folding wood chairs on Kelly's wide, covered front porch, having just eaten dinner on their third day of staying with Kelly. The sky was dark and the moon shone radiantly. The weather was humid and the breezes were few, but no one complained.

John looked around and asked, "Man, you're out here by yourself. Are you lonesome out here?"

"Nah, me and Emily got friends. People come now and then to pick fruit. We got our church. People get any wrongheaded notion, I got rifles and revolvers. My little girl's a crack shot with the rifle. The Lord's gonna take care of me and Emily on His own terms." Looking at Emily sitting to his right, Kelly asked, "Right, baby girl?"

"Right, Papa."

"Mr. Kelly, I never asked, but where is the lady around here?" Douglas asked.

"My wife passed on a few years ago. Just me and my baby girl, now. Maybe I find someone. A girl need help with girl things; know what I mean?"

"Reckon so, Mr. Kelly," Douglas said.

"You boys want some more lemonade?" Kelly asked.

Without waiting for an answer, Kelly instructed Emily to fetch some lemonade.

"Mr. Kelly, you've been carving since you sat down. What're you making?" John asked.

"Gigs. This one almost finished," he said as he was finishing shaping the third of four tines.

"What's that?" John asked.

Kelly made a few more shavings on his project, then held it up for Douglas and John to see.

"Me and Emily like to eat frog legs. We catch frogs with this."

After watching Kelly shape the wood with a carving knife, John asked to try.

Pointing to the other three tines, Kelly instructed John to shape the last tine like the other three. Kelly handed John the carving knife and watched John carve. After a few minutes, Kelly said, "That's pretty good, son," admiring what John had carved. "You a natural, keep it up. It'll get easier and soon you'll be doing it with your eyes closed. Carve lots of things with a good knife; good hobby for you, son."

Emily returned and handed one mug of lemonade to Douglas and one to John.

"Thank you," Douglas said as he winked at Emily. She covered her mouth and giggled.

The conversation shifted to Douglas and John's upcoming trek. Kelly agreed with Douglas that it'd be best if Douglas and John went through Atlanta on the way to Alabama. "There're a lot of colored folk down there in Atlanta," Kelly told Douglas and John.

"Maybe we meet some there as nice as you," John said.

"There're a lot of good people in the world. You just gotta find them," Kelly said.

"Thanks for everything, Mr. Kelly," John said. "We'll never forget you."

"Okay, boys, I know y'all best be moving on. So listen closely."

Douglas and John put the empty mugs on the floor as Kelly told them how to hop a freight train that left Greenville the next day at eight o'clock in the morning. "I think it go near Atlanta. The station an hour walk from here. You boys go on and rest your heads; you got a long day 'head of you."

—∞—

"Douglas!" Emily yelled, "Papa say y'all come to breakfast."

"Douglas, you hear that? Your girlfriend's calling."

Douglas tossed his pillow at John. "The little girl's got some taste," Douglas said.

"Yep, *some*," he said.

After filling themselves with ham, biscuits, and fried apples, Douglas and John finished packing and met Kelly and Emily on the front porch.

"Remember what I told you about the train. Be careful. Plenty people out there mean to do you harm."

Douglas and John nodded.

Kelly extended his right hand, and said, "You boys take this."

"What is it?" John asked.

"Something to make you feel good when you need it." He handed Douglas two bottles of Jack Daniel's. "Someone gave them to me for a favor and I never had use for them."

As they walked away, Kelly said, "Hey, John, you forgetting something?"

John turned around and said, "No, Mr. Kelly."

Kelly emitted a crack whistle and Dog ran to him. "It seems Dog wants to go with you," Kelly said.

John walked back to Kelly. "Come here, boy," John said as he clapped his hands twice.

"What you gonna call him, John?" Kelly asked.

"Dog."

"Nah, that's not much of a name. Give him a good name."

"His name's Greenville," Douglas interjected.

"There, it be settled; Greenville it be," Kelly said.

"I like it, but it's too big for him. How about Greeny?" John said.

The piercing sound of the train whistle quickened their pace. Greeny, sensing the need to hurry, stayed a few steps ahead. As they approached the tracks, they discovered that the train was moving slowly. They were about a quarter mile away.

Douglas and John stopped. Gloom filled their eyes as the train chugged farther from them. Greeny turned around and walked to John, where he wagged his tail and lifted his head to be petted. John ignored him.

Greeny barked and Douglas and John looked in the direction of the train. It had stopped for some unknown reason.

"Let's go!" Douglas said. They ran toward the boxcar, but were slowed by the weight of their haversacks. They were less than a quarter mile from the caboose, but it might as well have been five miles. As they slackened their pace, the boxcar started moving again.

Douglas and John stooped over with their hands on their thighs, breathing heavily from exhaustion. As they looked up, the gloom had returned to their eyes. Greeny seemed to sense their despair. Unburdened by weight, Greeny sprinted on his short legs and caught up with the slowly moving train.

As fortune would have it, the boxcar stopped again. Greeny barked and Douglas and John ran to catch up with him. They scoured the train looking for a suitable car to get in. "Let's look in car twenty-one," Douglas said as he looked at the white number on one of the box cars near the caboose.

John leaned over the opening and saw several cows looking back at him. He turned around and said to Douglas, "We'll need to share space with cows."

Douglas and John threw their haversacks into the boxcar. John picked up Greeny and put him on board. Douglas hopped on first, then John.

John touched his belly with both hands. He knew what he had to do, which he did not want to do in the boxcar even though he smelled the scat from the cattle. Cattle had no decency, and even in this moment, he'd show a modicum of it. Hoping the train would delay a few moments more, he jumped off the train and ran to an area densely populated with magnolia trees and juniper shrubs and emptied his bowels. Greeny alighted the car and tagged along with his new best friend. As John was finishing, the train started moving.

"John! John! We're moving," Douglas yelled as he stood on the edge of the car's opening, leaning outside the car, holding onto a bar attached to the train.

Greeny quickly caught up to the moving train. As John ran full stride toward the train, he suddenly realized that he'd have to toss Greeny inside the car. He needed Greeny to jump up to his chest as he ran so he could carry him. "Greeny, come here," John hollered. Greeny barked and bounced up and down several times in place on his front legs. "C'mon, Greeny. Come here, boy," John said, hoping the dog would figure out what he wanted.

The caboose passed Greeny. John's face with flushed with dread. "Dog! Dog, come here," John shouted hoping the reversion to the

Greenville's original name would make him run to him. Whether Greeny responded to his original name or whether he sensed that John was in distress, he sprinted to John as fast as his little legs would carry him. John ran toward Greeny, patting his chest repeatedly, hoping that Greeny would jump to his chest allowing him to catch Greeny so he wouldn't have to break stride. Greeny, running with equal determination, hit his mark. Douglas stood near the ledge, ordering John to throw Greeny to him.

"Move back a little," John shouted, panting almost uncontrollably.

John counted on Douglas to make the catch. As John struggled to keep pace with the train, he tossed Greeny in the air where he seemed to hang for an eternity.

"Got him!" Douglas yelled when Greeny landed safely in Douglas's chest and arms. The velocity of the throw knocked Douglas back onto the straw-covered floor. John breathed deeply, then sprinted several yards and jumped with all his might on board the train.

All were exhausted and soon fell asleep. Greeny snuggled in John's arms. John woke after several hours to find a cow staring him in the eyes.

The train rolled along for hours. Movement was good. Douglas reached in his haversack and began to nosh on an apple from Kelly's farm. John found a peach in his bag and joined Douglas for lunch. Greeny isolated himself in a corner gnawing on a pork chop that Douglas gave him.

The cattle made a stink in the car, but John and Douglas trained themselves to ignore it. Douglas needed a jolt to fully wake up. He reached into his bag and felt the familiar neck of the Jack Daniel's whiskey bottle. "I'd like to meet you someday, Mr. Daniels," Douglas said, holding the bottle at arm's length at eye level. He took a swig and immediately crinkled his nose and face. Douglas looked at John, who was staring forlornly out the door. "What's wrong with you?"

John shrugged. "I was thinking about leaving my mama by herself back there in Richmond."

Douglas screwed on the top to the whiskey flask. "Maybe you send for her once you get to wherever you going in Alabama."

John did what he could to ease the pain of missing his mother by doing what he often did—thinking of and holding onto her counsel and her many other admirable qualities. "My mama ain't got a bad bone in her body. She's good to everybody, treats everybody fairly." John sensed he had seen her for the last time; he held the hope that Billingsly would keep his promise to take care of her.

"Yeah, I know, John. She did right by me," he imagined Billingsly telling him.

John closed his eyes and went to sleep.

Hours later, John opened his eyes. Douglas was counting the bullets in the revolver he'd glommed from the stagecoach. He stood up and pointed the gun at one of the cows.

"What're you doing?" John asked.

"This here baby will help keep the peace."

The train began to slow appreciably, and Douglas was thrown into a wall. The gun fell to the floor and slid out of the door opening. "Damn!" Douglas snapped.

John went to the open boxcar door to see where it landed. No sight of it.

Thirty seconds later the boxcar was at a full stop. "We need to find that gun; we gonna need it," Douglas said.

"Doug, it's too dark. You won't be able to find it."

Seconds later, hearing footfalls, Douglas whispered, "Shh. We got company."

He was older, bigger, and more powerful that John, so he'd be the one to confront danger first if necessary; he ordered John and Greeny to go to the nearby corner while he investigated.

Douglas jumped off the boxcar and sidled alongside it. As he moved stealthily in the direction of the ambient noise, he was startled by the luminescent eyes of a raccoon pointing at him like a bird dog on a quail hunt. The raccoon blinked first and returned to foraging. Douglas took a few more tentative steps forward when he spotted men on horses holding lanterns and brandishing rifles and ordering conductor and locomotive engineer to alight from the engine.

Trains were favorite targets of brigands because they were known to carry sacks of payroll money.

"What you hauling?" Douglas heard a brigand call out from astride his horse.

"Just some lumber and cattle," the conductor answered.

The brigand brandished a Remington .36 caliber revolver, and said, "Mind if I take a look?"

The conductor alighted from the train followed by the locomotive engineer; the brigand said to the conductor, "Careful there, old man; don't be stupid. I'll blast you right through the head you think about doing anything foolish." Douglas stooped down and ran to hide behind a long and high line of boulders.

John picked up Greeny and held him snugly and edged closer to the back of the car, standing directly behind a mature heifer, whose tail swished Greeny in the face. Greeny didn't seem to mind, merely extending his left paw in a weak effort to deflect the swishing tail.

As the night marauders approached the locomotive, one of them jumped off his horse and strode to the open door where John, Douglas, and Greeny had decamped alongside the cattle.

Douglas' stomach gurgled as he observed the bandit tiptoe toward the open door.

John felt the bile rising and swallowed hard to force it back down. Greeny met John's eyes and knew to keep still.

The bandit held up his lantern as he leaned against the boxcar and peered inside the open door. The bearded man turned his head slowly as he tapped his rifle on the floor of the boxcar. Greeny emitted a whimper and John covered Greeny's mouth and looked at him with reproving eyes. The bandit put his rifle on the floor and jumped up and sat of the edge of the door opening.

Douglas's attention was now focused on the bandit inside the locomotive. He soon saw the bandit jump down from the locomotive and wave for the conductor and locomotive engineer to return to the locomotive, having failed to find any money.

The locomotive engineer restarted the train and heavy plumes of black smoke poured from the top exhaust.

The bandit remained perched on the floor at the opening to the box car. As the box car began to creep along, Greeny yelped, and the bandit turned around and fired his rifle in the direction of the sound. As he cocked his rifle again, John dropped Greeny and rushed the bandit as he was now standing. John punched the bandit in his overstuffed belly with his left hand, then in the throat with his right hand, causing the bandit to drop the rifle and fall to the floor disoriented. John used the butt of the rifle to strike the bandit in the head in an effort to send him to sleep for good.

As John began to roll the bandit out of the opening of the box car, Douglas yelled, "John, watch out, the man on the horse got a rifle."

As John dropped the bandit to the ground below, he jumped off the slowly moving boxcar and aimed the rifle at the charging bandit as the bandit held aim at John.

John fired first, hitting the bandit squarely in the head, causing the bandit to drop from atop his steed. With one bandit likely dead and the other for sure dead, John ran and caught up with the boxcar as it gained a bit more speed. He tossed the rifle inside and jumped in. Douglas soon followed. Greeny wagged his tail feverishly to thank his companions for saving his life.

John and Douglas decided that they'd disembark in the morning or with the next stop, whichever occurred first.

It was a little after dawn, and John awoke to Greeny licking his face. Douglas was sitting up against the wall sipping Jack Daniel's.

The train slowed to a stop. No time to waste. John and Douglas quickly grabbed their haversacks; Douglas picked up the rifle and jumped out first, followed by John and Greeny.

15
SUMMER, 1887

Two days later after disembarking from the boxcar, they were still walking through a forest. No matter how far they walked, the trees looked the same. Two days in the woods was taking its toll. It was like being locked up in a cabin for two days without seeing daylight. John hoped the curtain would lift soon, and they'd be out of the woods.

John removed the compass from his pocket once again and waited for it to settle down. It pointed south. "This way," he said, eyes following the arrow's direction.

The curtain lifted.

Thin clouds of gray smoke filtered through the trees. John sniffed a few times, recognizing the smell of brushwood and kerosene.

"Doug, look over there," John said, pointing. A fire was raging off in the distance. They moved in the direction of the leaping fire, curious more than anything else. As they got closer to it, they heard a gaggle of people; they slackened their pace, but Greeny decided to gad about. John went after him.

"John," Douglas whispered, "let him go."

As they inched toward the fire, it became clear the fire was devouring a house about fifty yards away. They saw a short and paunchy white man dressed in black suit and gray Confederate kepi standing on a platform next to a tall, wide red oak tree, speaking to a throng of whites and a few Negroes.

As the crowd milled about, Douglas and John sneaked closer for a better view that allowed them to see a colored man sitting atop a piebald horse with a rope around his neck and his hands tied to the back.

They were too far away to hear the speaker. John, anxious to learn what the speaker was saying, spied another red oak tree and ran to it. Douglas quickly followed.

They could see that the paunchy man had a book in his left hand, which he used to punctuate the air as he spoke. The white attendees moved and swayed to the man's words.

"I reckon he's a preacher of some sort," Douglas said.

As John and Douglas moved a bit closer, the man's words rang in their ears.

"This man is a troublemaker, an agitator of the first degree. He's been writing that darkies deserve equal treatment and all that crazy stuff. Probably thinks it's okay for coons to marry white women! He had a coon baby with a white woman, is what they say."

The preacher removed a pint of whiskey from his front pants pocket, uncorked it, and took a sip. He returned the whiskey to his pocket. "These coons think that traitor Lincoln freed them. They need to know this is still here a white man's country. Always will be." He pointed to the colored man on the nag facing imminent demise, and said, "This here coon needs to understand that." Pointing to the few colored men in the crowd, he said, "You coons need to understand that."

Greeny returned from his frolic and sniffed at John's feet. John picked him up and scratched his head, a tonic that worked to calm him.

"For you coons out there, let this be a reminder that this can happen to you if you get too uppity. White privilege and power's here to stay." He paused to let the words resonate. Then speaking as though he just had a personal conversation with God where God told him whites are the favored people: "It's ordained by God and that's the way it's got to be."

John and Douglas, from the blind of the red oak tree, had an up close, in-real-time seat to the prevalent attitude held by the majority of Southern whites. The preacher typified the belief that Southern whites would not let the official end of slavery prevent them from asserting their dominance over coloreds; they would find a way to *redeem* the South.

President Rutherford B. Hayes fulfilled his promise to remove federal troops from the South, thereby ending the troops' ten-plus years in Southern states. The second blow to Negro advancement came in 1883 when the United States Supreme Court held in an 8-to-1 decision that the 1875 Civil Rights Act—which was passed by Congress and signed by President Ulysses S. Grant to end discrimination against Negroes—to be unconstitutional. The clock was turning counterclockwise for Negroes, and men like the preacher would see to it that it continued to turn that way.

After the preacher finished his diatribe on the perils of race-mixing and the superiority of the white race, he walked to the edge of the makeshift pine-board platform, bent down, and handed a skinny young white boy the book he held, instructing him to put it in the breast pocket of the man that was condemned to death for nothing more than his speech. The boy's father picked him up and held up his son high enough so the boy could put the book in the man's pocket.

The boy opened the jacket, exposing the waistcoat. The boy looked into the colored man's eyes for two long seconds. The boy blinked first, knowing that he'd just stared into the desolate eyes of a dead man, something the boy's father was happy to see his son witness at a young age.

John and Douglas looked at each other off and on—they knew what they were about to witness.

Douglas cursed the preacher as his eyes raged with fire.

John held the rifle by his side and contemplated putting a bullet between the preacher's eyes. He could do it, he thought. He had killed the bandit at the lake and the two bandits that stopped the boxcar several weeks ago. But he knew in this instance that if he pulled the trigger, he'd be caught and would soon face the same fate as the man about to be executed. His dream of a bigger life would end, and he'd never see his mother again.

Damn.

The preacher jumped off the platform and walked to the victim's horse. He bent down and picked up a sharp-edged rock from the ground with his right hand, positioning it so the sharp edge faced outward. He slapped the horse on the rump with his right hand and let loose a scream: "Giddy-up!" The horse raised his forelegs and leaped forward into a full gallop, not stopping until it was over a hundred yards away.

The people dispersed only after the preacher stayed long enough to ensure the noose had suffocated the life out of the man he'd ordered hanged.

Two colored men remained behind several minutes after the crowd had dispersed. A tall, spindly man sawed through the rope with his pocketknife while the other held the dead man's limp body. They gently lowered the dead man to the ground.

John and Douglas walked out in the open. Greeny followed. The two colored men said a prayer for the dead. Despite hearing so much about lynchings that fed the flames of neighborhood talk of "an eye for an eye" back in Richmond, John had never witnessed one. He pulled on the thick, coarse twine rope with both hands, feeling and testing its strength, wondering why a rope so thick that it could easily strangle a thick-necked ox was necessary to kill a human being.

John's eyes burned with hate as he turned and looked at the fire, which had begun to lose its intensity, revealing a small ramshackle house; it remained a mystery to him. He asked Douglas what he thought had caused it; Douglas told him he didn't know.

The spindly elderly man overheard John's question and told him that the whites were burning down houses of coloreds as a warning to stay in their miserable place and not to agitate the white man.

As the two colored men walked away, Douglas yelled, "Hey, can you tell us how to get to Atlanta?"

The spindly man turned around and waited for Douglas and John to come to him. "Y'all not that far. By train, about an hour. By foot, several hours, half a day."

"What kind of train?" Douglas asked.

"It's a passenger train," he said.

John smiled and asked, "No cows on it?"

"The one I know for people," the elderly man said.

"Good," Douglas said, rolling his eyes at John.

"If you take the train, you boys best know your place," the other, and noticeably younger, colored man said.

"Place?" John said.

"Yeah, find a place in the back, or tell someone you are some white person's servant," the younger colored man said.

"You boys got fare?" the older man asked.

Douglas nodded. "How do we catch this train?"

After listening carefully to the directions, Douglas and John thanked the men for their kindness. The two men left, walking in the direction of the fire.

Douglas and John sat the deceased's limp body up against the red oak tree from which he'd been hanged, John wondering if that tree had been used for other lynchings.

"What did that white man put in his pocket?" John asked.

Douglas leaned over and removed it from the dead man's tight breast pocket.

"What is it?" John demanded to know.

Douglas handed to John.

John held it up—the Holy Bible. He opened it and the well-worn crease opened the Bible to page 1,241. His eyes were immediately directed to the words circled in red contained in Titus 2:9—*"Exhort servants to be obedient unto their masters, and to please them well in all things; not answering again."*

John ripped that page from the Bible and put it in his pants pocket. It was time for them to move on. As they walked away, they turned around to look at the man under the tree. He looked like he was taking a nap, his head cast down.

16
FALL, 1887

As Douglas, John, and Greeny disembarked at the Union Depot, they saw the haze and felt the ever-present heat. The autumnal equinox had just occurred, easing Atlanta out of the summer, but tropical winds from the Gulf kept the air hot and humid.

Brick-and-mortar and wooden buildings choked the blocks along the dirt streets. Traffic hummed with streams of coaches, phaetons, cabriolets, broughams, gigs, and barouches, all indications of a commercial area. They were in the heart of Atlanta.

The street sign said PEACHTREE. They headed north.

Greeny lagged behind as Douglas and John ambled along Peachtree Street. When they reached the intersection of Peachtree and Wheat Streets, John looked behind him. Greeny was lying along the side of the street, his head resting on his forelegs. He whimpered. John handed Douglas his haversack and walked back to Greeny, picked him up, and sat down on the walk in front of an old building on the corner of the intersection, his back resting against the building as he scratched Greeny's head. "What's wrong, boy? Tired? I'll get you something to eat soon. But for now, I need to know if you can walk with us." He touched his nose to Greeny's nose.

John stood up, holding Greeny in both arms, and walked to Douglas, carrying his twenty-five-pound freight.

"What's wrong with Greeny?" Douglas asked.

"I reckon he's just hungry; he'll be fine once he gets something in his belly," John said. "Empty out my bag, would you?"

"Why?"

John pointed his head down to Greeny, signaling that he was going to carry Greeny in his haversack. Just as Douglas began to remove John's belongings from the haversack, Greeny became fussy, and writhed in John's arms, demanding to be put down like a toddler wanting to walk and not be held. As John opened his arms to release him, Greeny jumped to the ground and looked at John as if wondering what the fuss had been about. John shook his head and put his belongings back in his haversack, thinking that perhaps Greeny was homesick, but was now feeling better. Greeny now led Douglas and John as they headed east on Wheat Street.

The signs above the entrances announced their business—Kellogg Clothier's, Carlson's Barbershop, Bandar Shoes, Wheat Street Baptist Church, Wilson's General Store, and on and on.

The wafting smell of pork ribs pulled John and Douglas to the intersection of Wheat Street and Younge Street. They stood at the corner inhaling hickory smoke, unable to ascertain its precise location; then a middle-aged man walked out from an alley.

"Where can we get some of those ribs we smelling?" Douglas asked the man.

"Right there," the man said, pointing to a small, two-story brick building with a lopsided roof called Granny's Barbeque Ribs.

A man was standing at a pit turning over a hefty slab of ribs when John, Douglas, and Greeny walked in.

"What can I getcha?" the man asked.

John and Douglas sat at the wooden counter, exhausted. Greeny settled to the floor and nuzzled John's feet.

"Be all right if we sit here?" Douglas asked.

The man nodded and moved slabs of ribs around. He turned around and looked at Douglas and John with one eye. His right eyelid hung over his right eye like a closed curtain. "What yous boys want?"

"We're trying to get to Alabama," John said. "But we'd like to know if we can get some fixings?"

The man put both hands on the plank board that served as a counter and looked over Douglas and John with his one eye. "You boys're going to need to fatten up before moving on to Alabama. Yous gonna need some fat reserves, like them bears that hibernate."

John's stomach gurgled, as his hunger was palpable.

The one-eyed cook heard the whirling sounds coming from John's stomach. "You boys hold on a little longer; got two plates coming your way," he said, while tending to several husks of corn on the pit. The one-eyed man sat down on the other side of the counter facing Douglas and John.

"Can yous boys wash dishes?" Douglas and John nodded in unison. "Then, yous got a job. Nothing's free 'round here."

"What time do you open up?" John asked.

The cook told them that the restaurant was open from five o'clock in the afternoon until two o'clock in the morning, most of his business occurring during the late hours when patrons from the local dives found their way to line their stomachs in between drinking shots of whiskey.

"Yous boys go to the washroom and wash up," the cook said, pointing the way, "and I'll have your grub ready when you get back."

"Thanks, sir," John said with appreciation. John looked at the ribs on the pit, smelling the intense aroma of the honey-whiskey sauce, then spied a sign above the pit that said—GRANNY'S. "Where's Granny?" John asked.

The one-eyed man guffawed. "Granny's been cooking them ribs, started hours ago."

"Is she here? Can we meet her?"

"Yous looking at her," Granny said, extending his long arms and revealing a wry smile and mild laugh lines on a fawn-colored faced that looked well lived in.

With a bewildered countenance, John asked, "You're Granny?"

"Since when does a granny wear a wide mustache?" Douglas asked, looking at Granny's salt-and-pepper mustache that touched the bottom of his nose and almost covered his lips.

Granny chuckled. He told them that he'd named his restaurant after his grandmother who was known for her mouth-watering ribs. "My granny got me started. She always told me the secret was in the honey-whiskey sauce. If yous boys learn the secret, yous boys keep that sauce a secret, hear?"

Douglas and John returned refreshed to the plank board counter where they saw the ribs and corn waiting for them on their plates. Greeny had obeyed John's command to stay put.

"Don't yous boys want a knife and fork?" Granny asked as John and Douglas wasted no time in separating their slabs with their hands. Douglas and John sawed through the sinewy ribs. Granny grabbed a pan of cornbread and put it next to them. John broke off a piece of meat and tossed it in Greeny's waiting mouth. "Go 'head and give that dog some more food," Granny said to a surprised John, who was happy that Greeny did not have to hide anymore.

Douglas bent over, grabbed his bag, and put it on the counter. He retrieved the flask John had let him keep with him. John figured it was better to separate the flasks – that way, if something happened to one, he'd perhaps have the remaining one. And he began to wonder more and more if he'd ever return to Richmond to find the answer that lay engraved on the flasks.

Douglas took a swallow of Jack Daniel's. Granny nodded when Douglas asked if he wanted some. He removed the bottle from his bag and poured the last of it into a glass for her.

Granny took a swig. "This some good whiskey. Where'd you get it?"

Greeny whimpered. John looked down as Greeny rubbed his nose against John's left foot. He licked John's sauce-laden left hand as John rubbed his head with his other hand.

"Leave me alone!" a woman shouted, looking back as she entered the front door to Granny's joint.

"Who yous talking to, Sally?" Granny asked.

"That boy I been mentioning want to get with me."

Granny reached under the counter, retrieved an old rifle, and held it up. "Yous tell that boy your papa got something for him."

"Papa, no need to shoot him. He knows better to put a hand on me," Sally said, patting her left hip as she slinked away, capturing Douglas and John's attention.

"Yous boys get her out of your sights, now. Baby girl just turned sixteen."

She looked older, wearing a dress that accentuated her hips. Granny didn't seem to mind Sally's attire; it was good for business.

Douglas turned to Granny and nodded.

"John," Granny said, "I see I gotta keep an eye on you."

"C'mon, Granny. I suspect you know how to use that rifle."

"That's right."

John laughed.

"I could stand some help around here. Yous boys can clean, help bring in the meat. How long y'all plan to stay?"

"Long enough to get to know Sally," John said to himself.

"Couple of weeks, maybe," Douglas said. "We can stand some rest from walking."

"Y'all can sleep in the attic on the upper level. Not much space, but it'll do."

Just over three weeks after arriving at Granny's, the heat still gripped Atlanta. But the heat didn't stop a bustle of people—colored and white—from crowding the stores and vendor carts on a Friday mid-afternoon. Men looking for a leisurely time filled that time gazing at women, and many women wore alluring attire to attract men's eyes.

Sally, despite her age, welcomed the attention of male admirers as she walked down Wheat Street with John at her side. John wore a tattered cotton shirt and weather-beaten tan corduroy pants held up by galluses; Sally wore what she often wore when not working, a neat tight dress that magnified her curves and a jaunty, wide-brimmed green straw hat.

After walking two blocks and witnessing both colored and white men stare and whistle at Sally, John spied a sycamore tree and ambled to it. She sat first, then John.

"You sure gather lots of attention," John said.

"Don't hurt to look, right?" she asked and batted her eyes, a technique that seemed well practiced. "You don't look, or do you?"

"Sally, you're a pretty girl...."

His eyes locked on Sally's eyes that were as open and inviting as her effervescent personality; they then drifted to her button nose, ruby-colored lips, then her ample bosom. She caught John gazing at her bust, which caused her to lean forward exposing more cleavage.

John had proven to be a fast study when it came to reading and writing, and he absorbed the world around him in an intuitive way that impelled him to want to live a bigger life. He didn't seem to have time to be intimate with anyone, or at least the desire, after what Madame Billingsly had done to him when he was fourteen.

But the Madame Billingsly nightmare occurred a few years ago, and he wondered whether he should try it with Sally, especially since his hormones were clashing hard with his mind.

"Oh, so you do look."

"Okay, of course I look," he said. Deflecting his thoughts about having sex with her, he said, "But that's all I do. Granny's rifle saw to that."

She smiled lightly with closed lips. "Pa go after men who I don't like and I tell him I don't like."

"Your pa is a good man. I don't know what to do after working for him for about three weeks. Douglas's telling me we need to move on. Maybe I stay here, not go on to Alabama. Maybe Doug can go on without me." He began to imagine a life spending time with Sally.

"Give me your hand," she said. John extended his right hand and she held it with her left hazelnut-colored hand. "What's tearing you apart?" She squeezed his hand as to reassure him he could open up to her. "You can tell me."

"I'm tired of running. I just want a place to call home.... "

"Go on," she said prompted after a minute of John's silence.

"I promised my mama I would go to Mount Hope, Alabama, and find Cousin Riley. I have no idea who he is or where he is."

Sally nodded. "What's your mama's name?"

"Ann."

"What's she like?"

"Everyone likes her. That's because she cared for everyone. I just hope I can see her again someday."

Sally nodded again.

"Truth be told, Sally, I like you. I've been thinking of asking Granny...."

She cut him off. "You don't have to ask my pa nothing. I like you ..."

When she didn't complete her thought, John filled in the space and said with a chipper smile, "You do?"

She laughed, then paused to allow her voice to ready itself for a serious tone. "But, I can't let you do it."

"Do what?"

"Stay here, be with me."

"Why, pray tell?" using language that he often heard Monsieur Billingsly say.

She was a coquette and good at it. It was part of her survival technique. She could be that way with others to extract money, but not John. If she were, and he stayed with her, he'd soon crack under the weight of her fast life.

"John," she said, "you a good boy, a smart boy. I see the way you add numbers in your head, the way you use nice language, the way you talk to Pa's customers. You got a special gift. I could only disappoint you."

With inflamed hormones, John said: "No, you wouldn't!"

She removed her hat and lay her head against his chest. "Listen to me. I've been pregnant two times. The first time I lost the baby. Second time I had the baby. The baby's in some orphanage now. I know the streets, you don't. Keep your promise to your mama."

John was silent.

"Say something, John."

John held her head on his chest. "Thank you, Sally."

—⚊—

On the day before they were to depart, Granny had a dinner to thank Douglas and John for working for him. Douglas asked him for directions to Atlanta University. Although he didn't know the directions, he asked one of his customers who knew. The customer drew a map for Granny, who then gave it to Douglas.

They threw their haversacks over their shoulders. As with every departure from a stay more than a day or two, especially when the haversacks were not tied to them, John checked to make sure he had one flask and Douglas had the other.

They had a little lucre left between them and didn't know how much luck they'd have with keeping it. The rifle Douglas carried would run interference if need be to prevent them from being robbed.

Time had come for them to see Professor Bodie, the man they'd learned about during their stay in Raleigh with Rick.

17
FALL, 1887

Six days later, the hand-drawn map landed them on the campus of Atlanta University. The lawns were stiffly manicured. The young men and women who walked along the paths in the grass carried books and walked with erect posture. Marble statues adorned the grounds. Neat brick-and-mortar buildings saturated the area.

As they walked around campus, many students flung quizzical looks at them. John looked at his brogan boots, and the tan corduroy pants and shirt he'd worn for weeks. He looked at Douglas, who'd been wearing the same clothes for weeks, too. All the possessions they owned in the world were in the overstuffed haversacks on their backs. John had convinced Douglas to hide the rifle so as not to frighten the students and staff. They were like fish out of water and knew it.

They stumbled onto a directory next to a pedestal that held up a statute of a Negro man holding a book. John read quietly, "Science Department, Humanities Department, Admissions…"

The University was started in 1865 and chartered two years later as a university with the assistance of the Freedmen's Bureau; its purpose was to provide a college education to male and female Negro students as a means to increase Negro upward mobility.

"Let's try this one," John said, pointing to Admissions. "We need to find Merman Hall on Whitehall Street." He looked at Greeny and said, "Come on."

They walked up the wooden stairs. John pointed a finger at Greeny to tell him to stay put while he and Douglas went inside.

John opened the single massive oak door to the school. Douglas entered first. The Admissions office was to the right, in a long corridor that stretched the length of the building from right to left. Highly polished wood floors continued under doors that led to other offices, and one door that looked wide enough to have an auditorium behind it. A bespectacled Negro man sat at a desk.

"Hello. My name's Dean Lucien Fairbanks. What can I do for you boys?"

John told him that they were looking for a Professor Bodie. After a long period of silence, Fairbanks said, "Well, I'm afraid that's impossible." He paused, then added, "Professor Bodie is no longer here."

"Could you tell us where we can find him, sir?" John asked.

"With the good Lord," Fairbanks said, looking up. "It's been in the newspaper. He was killed; they say he was lynched." He shook his head in disgust and added: "His body was found a few days ago with a Bible in his breast pocket."

John and Douglas were still, eyes bulged and jaws slack.

"You boys look like you just saw a ghost."

"Did the paper say anything about a page missing from the Bible?" John asked.

"Yes. Why are you asking?"

John took page 1,241 from his pocket, unfolded it, and said, "I think this is the missing page."

Dean Fairbanks looked at the Bible page for ten seconds with eyes that didn't blink. "Where'd you get that?"

Douglas and John took turns telling him about how they stumbled upon the preacher in the woods a few weeks ago and how they saw a small boy place the Bible in Professor Bodie's breast pocket.

"But how did you get the missing page?"

"I ripped the page from the Bible because a passage on the page was circled in red," John replied, then handed the paper to Fairbanks. "You can keep it."

"You should talk to the law about this," Fairbanks said, after folding the page and putting it in his shirt pocket.

John wanted no part of it. The last thing he wanted was for his name to be in the paper. Although Billingsly was way in the rear and had been parked there for some time, John couldn't afford to take any chances with Billingsly finding out his whereabouts.

Douglas agreed.

Fairbanks looked at John and Douglas; his eyes settled on John as he asked, "You want to try course work at the University?"

The question stunned John. He could read and write and understood complex sentences, but he had no real education beyond the age of ten. Much of his education was based on his discipline to learn, often done heuristically.

After John did not respond within a few seconds, Fairbanks looked at John and asked, "How old are you, son?"

"Seventeen."

"How much schooling have you had?"

John told him the extent of his education. And Fairbanks in turn told John that many of the students enrolled in the University didn't have a diploma.

John nodded.

The University had benefited from money from the Freedmen's Bureau to help Negroes' educational advancement, and private donations also poured in during Reconstruction. "Look," Fairbanks said, "We want as many of our colored folks to get a college education as can. We have financial assistance and tutors that can help you. You may not finish with a degree, but having this education could help you down the line."

John turned to Douglas and looked at him blankly, as though he was lost in thought. He recalled from time to time that he'd stand in Monsieur Billingsly's study and stroke the spines of the plenitude of books on the shelves. He knew he wanted more knowledge.

"Excuse me, sir," Douglas said, "I need to say something to John."

Douglas told John he should do it—it could help him with the bigger life he had dreamed about. But John's need to find Cousin Riley, who may not even exist, overrode anything else that would abort his mission.

John broke the huddle with Douglas and returned to Fairbanks. "Thank you, sir. That's really kind of you, but we need to be moving on."

Fairbanks didn't press the issue. Looking at John and Douglas, he said, "Where're you going from here?"

"We trying to get to Mount Hope, Alabama," Douglas said. "Heard of it?"

"Can't say that I have. But I know it's a ways to the Alabama border. How're you getting there?"

Douglas marched in place, then added, "Unless we find another means."

Fairbanks looked at their brogans, then at them. "The weather's turning soon. Your boots look fine. You have socks?"

"Yeah, we have socks," Douglas said.

"Wait here. I'll be right back."

John turned to Douglas and hunched his shoulders as to say he didn't know what Fairbanks was up to.

Fairbanks returned in two minutes. "Here," the man said, handing ten one-dollar bills to John and the same to Douglas.

"Gee, thanks Mr. Fairbanks. Why?"

"Let's just say it's an early Christmas present."

Douglas expressed his gratitude, too. He widened his smile and said, "Thanks."

"Farewell," Fairbanks said.

They collected Greeny and left.

Fairbanks later told the local sheriff about the missing page, deleting John's identification. The sheriff determined it was the missing page that had been ripped from the Bible that was found in Professor Bodie's breast pocket. *The Atlanta Constitution*, under the leadership of publisher Henry Grady, would later publish an article about how the much discussed missing page from the Bible was found:

> Two young colored male itinerants witnessed a Negro man's execution in Shelby Woods by a gang of outlaws.

They only found out that they had witnessed Professor Bodie's lynching later when they went to Atlanta University to talk to him upon the suggestion of a friend in Raleigh, NC. At Atlanta University, they encountered Dean Lucien Fairbanks who told them that Professor Bodie was found dead in the woods, that a Bible was found in his breast pocket, and that a page was missing from the Bible. The itinerants told Dean Fairbanks that they had ripped out a page of the Bible because someone had circled in red the verse about how servants must obey their masters—a stale reference to slavery and how the Negro man must understand his place in society.

We understand that it is painful for many Southerners to see their world turn topsy-turvy after the War. Although the War ended over two decades ago, too often the ghosts of the War are resurrected through vile, ritual forms. We believe Atlanta begs for a new South, one that endeavors to treat our neighbors kindly. The denizens of Atlanta, of the South, must not lick their wounds from the War by attacking the colored man. As the War fades into the past, the new South must strive to be first in industry, first in citizenship, and first in humanity. We should all try to hasten the day to bring these worthy goals to fruition.

The *Constitution* received a lot of hate mail, but Grady didn't care. His mission was to help build a new South, in part by convincing the North to invest financially in the South.

18
DECEMBER, 1887

They had lost track of time on the next stage of their trek. All they knew was it was December, and they were cold. It tuned out December would experience low temperatures in the teens for the last two weeks of the month. Newspaper articles advised citizens to avoid going out in the cold weather to avoid possible heart attacks and frostbite.

A white passerby told them they could try to seek shelter from Father Murphy. "He's got that YMCA in Birmingham," they were told.

Tucked into the Jones Valley, the YMCA facility was a three-story, English revival-style, auburn-colored brick building with contrasting trim, a stepped parapet, and a shallow Gothic archway framing the heavy oak front door.

Douglas studied the building and asked through teeth chattering from the cold and the vicious wind, "Suppose this it?"

"One way to find out," John said.

John pulled on the massive door, but the wind made is slow to open. Douglas stuck his foot in the doorway, allowing John to grab the door above the handle. John pulled hard. Greeny scrambled in first, followed by Douglas, then John.

About two dozen men and boys were gathered around a fireplace dancing with flames and heat, listening with rapt attention as a white man read aloud passages from Charles Dickens's *A Christmas Carol.* The man spied the new arrivals and motioned with his right hand for them to sit with the others. Douglas and John sat on small wood chairs, and Greeny dropped to the floor, nestling in between John's legs. Greeny had a straight line of sight to the orange flames shooting from the splintered logs. He furrowed his brow each time a log popped from the fireplace.

John removed his wool mittens, put them in his coat, then rubbed his hands together to create some much needed heat. He turned to Douglas and said with his eyes pointed at the reader, "That must be Father Murphy?"

"Yeah, that's him," someone whispered. "Shhh."

Satisfied that his hands had warmed up after several minutes of rubbing, John turned slightly in his chair. A few people had formed a line, the beginning of which led to a cider tank with steam erupting from its top.

When Murphy stopped reading, John stood up and walked around to the back of his chair where Greeny had already slithered out. As he often did when he wanted Greeny to stay put, he held out his right forefinger to tell Greeny not to move. Greeny whimpered softly and slithered back into position.

John walked to the back of the line and Douglas followed. They had a wider view of the lobby. Most of the people were white, with a scattering of colored. They had the same look—despair in their eyes and tattered clothes on their backs.

Just as it was Douglas's turn to scoop the piping hot cider into his glass, Murphy said with a thick Irish brogue, "Be careful with that; it's hot. Don't want no accidents here the day before Christmas."

Douglas nodded, then took a sip of cider.

"Did Jack Frost bite your tongue?"

"Who's Jack Frost?"

Murphy emitted a hearty chuckle.

Murphy was a middling handsome Irish American with titian hair, a dimpled chin, a long angular face made more dramatic with heavy eyebrows, and oversized emerald-green eyes.

Murphy had first settled in Charleston after coming to the United States as part of the third wave of immigrants out of Ireland. He had been a priest in Dublin. He heard that men were needed to work in the railroad and iron and steel businesses in Birmingham, so he packed his few belongings and moved there, a city that erupted out of an abandoned forest in the 1870s. It was a city within five miles of three main ingredients that served as the bedrock of Birmingham's early development: iron, iron ore, and limestone. It wasn't long before the entire US economy was surging with industrial fervor, generating a ravenous appetite for Alabama's precious iron ore.

Murphy was lucky to be a lottery winner, which allowed him to work for one of Birmingham's giant industries—Sloss Furnace—making iron, but after he injured his right foot while working at Sloss, he could no longer do the heavy labor.

Two years later Murphy found a job running the YMCA. He knew first-hand the deep poverty in Ireland. His mother had taken in strangers in their slum home, and the memory of that, coupled with his devotion to his faith, made him ideally suited to run the YMCA. He commonly wore a black shirt with a white clerical collar and black pants.

"I run this place," he said while Douglas blew into his cup of piping hot cider. "Just call me Father Murphy. Ya got a religion?"

"No, sir."

"Well, we'll have to do something about that." Murphy turned to John. "How about you? You got a religion?"

"Yes, sir, my mama saw to it," John said.

"Good, but we'll need to work on this one," Murphy said, placing his hand on Douglas's shoulder.

John moved two steps away to check on Greeny.

"I saw the mutt," Murphy said. "He made some kind of noise each time the logs popped. What's his name?"

"Greeny," John said.

"You looking for a place to stay?"

Douglas told Murphy that he and John had trekked from Richmond and needed a place to stay for a few days.

"Yer welcome to stay here, but to do so requires ya work."

"Whatever you need," Douglas said.

"Atta boy," Murphy said. "This is the season for us to have a cracking good time. But we all will be working very hard soon."

Like he did for all new arrivals, Murphy told Douglas and John about his rules, ones that were in keeping with the YMCA's mission: to develop young men's Christian character of high standards. Murphy's brand of Christianity differed widely from the perverse idea of Christianity that had been suffused in the South for so long: He rejected the notion that God considered Negroes to be inferior to whites.

Murphy turned serious. "You must obey the rules. They're simple. Rule number one: I already told you about. You must work. Rule number two: No alcohol. Rule number three: No fighting. Rule number four: No smoking. Rule number five ..." He turned and looked at Greeny still resting under the chair. "No pets."

John stood motionless. Eyes that had begun to be enlivened a bit, turned dark. "Douglas and Greeny are the only family I got in the world. And it's cold outside."

"The dog can lie next to the steam vent in the back of the building to keep warm. You'll just have to check on him from time to time."

"If Greeny must go, then I go."

John walked over to his chair, sat down, and tightened the matted strings of his black brogans, picked up his haversack, put on his moldering linsey-woolsey coat, and headed to the front door with Greeny in tow.

He turned to Murphy, who looked nonplussed. Douglas recalled what Murphy had read about Ebenezer Scrooge. "Don't be like Scrooge on Christmas Eve."

Murphy appreciated the irony and relented. "I see ya was paying attention."

John opened the door and a gush of icy wind whooshed through the lobby. Murphy shouted, "C'mere, laddie! Greeny can stay." John and Greeny reversed course, and John ran to Murphy and hugged him, nearly knocking him over.

Murphy put two fingers from each hand and whistled loudly, piercing all conversations. The clatter stopped. "Dinner'll be ready in five minutes," he announced.

Every year the moguls of Birmingham expiated their excesses by delivering a bountiful supply of food and clothes to the YMCA during the Christmas season. They would eat more than the leftover watery stew called slumgullion. Recalling the menu as best he could, Murphy said, "We're having wigs, trotters, jugged hare, sweet potatoes, marrow pudding, soda bread, collard greens.... Tonight, we eat like kings."

"Hooray!" someone yelled.

The men and boys ran to the dining area and sat at picnic-style wooden tables. John was not put off that Murphy demanded that Greeny could not enter the dining area. He told Greeny to lie by the fire and he would retrieve him after he ate. "Don't worry, boy. I'll bring you something back," he said as he massaged Greeny's head.

After feasting on Christmas Eve dinner, Douglas and John were weighed down with bellies full of food. Feeling logy, Douglas asked Murphy where they'd sleep.

"There's a room on the second floor for ya boys. Take two-oh-two. There should be two more bedrolls in there. Already two guys in there—Ian and Jeffrey. There's a lantern near the bottom of the steps. Use it to help you find the room."

"Okay, thanks, Father Murphy," Douglas said.

"Good night, Father Murphy," John added.

The door was open. Douglas walked in first, followed by John, then Greeny. Two white men sat on the floor with their backs resting up against the wall next to a lantern. The room was spartan in appearance—only a small table and a dresser kept the room from being completely bare. Douglas put the lantern he had carried in on the small table near a window that admitted phosphorus light from the moon.

Looking at their roommates for the time being, Douglas said, "I'm Doug. This here is John. And that there be our dog, Greeny."

Silence.

John then asked which one was Ian and which one was Jeffrey.

No response other than a death stare from both men.

Greeny moved to the other guests and began to sniff them. The taller and heavier guest, who was carving an apple with a pocketknife, pushed Greeny away, causing him to whimper.

John didn't want any trouble. "Greeny," John said, "over here." Greeny complied.

As Douglas and John put down their bedrolls, the man holding the pocketknife said, "We ain't rooming with no slaves."

The other companion piped in: "Yeah, you heard what Jeffrey said."

Douglas turned, and snapped, "Then leave."

"You a stupid somma bitch," Jeffrey said.

Douglas ignored the comment.

After realizing he had killed two men before, John knew he could fight and kill again anyone who meant to cause him harm—if he didn't find Cousin Riley, at least he'd fulfill half the promise he made to Ann by making it to Mount Hope. In this instance, he'd be prepared to fight if it came to it, but for the moment he just wanted a place to rest and let his Christmas Eve meal digest. He nestled himself in his bedroll. Greeny fell to the floor near John's feet.

—※—

It was midnight. Christmas had arrived and so had the pealing of church bells. Ian and Jeffrey stood together and walked slowly and in a determined manner toward Douglas and John. Greeny lifted his head and growled.

Jeffrey rushed Douglas and then Ian jumped on John.

Douglas used his left arm to block the knife aimed at his chest. He grabbed his attacker's shirt with both hands and pulled him to the floor and began hitting him in the face.

The attacker managed to get up as Douglas relaxed his hold, only for the attacker to rush Douglas, who then used his right leg to kick the attacker in the stomach, sending him flying against the wall, where he slumped to the floor breathing heavy. Douglas grabbed the pocketknife, folded it, and placed it in his trouser pocket.

John had quickly thrown Ian, the smaller man, to the floor and stood ready to do more harm. John inched toward Jeffrey with clenched fists, but Douglas extended his arm and held John in place.

John was impressed with Douglas's ability to fight, especially to fight someone who probably weighted significantly more than

Douglas; where John would have to move to avoid getting in the bear's arms, he knew Douglas's height and strength would allow him to outpower and outlast the bear. Responding to the hullabaloo, Murphy rushed into the room holding a lantern while shouting, "What the hell is going on?"

Silence.

Murphy raised his voice. "I asked, what the hell is going on?"

Douglas told Murphy that he and John were only defending themselves when they were attacked.

Murphy looked at the Ian and Jeffrey. "Ian, Jeffrey, say something."

They'd started working together at Pratt Mining in Birmingham where they made coke. Jeffrey's drunken diatribes against colored workers got him fired. Ian left Pratt out of loyalty to his best friend. They had trouble finding jobs elsewhere and had become vagrants, staying at Murphy's YMCA periodically.

"Ian, Jeff, I want you out of here right now. I gave ya a chance to explain things, but ya said nothing. You know the rules around here, no fighting, eh?"

"If we go, the slaves should go."

Murphy cheeks turned ruddy. "Enough blather. I say who stays and who goes around here. Grab your things. Start stepping before I call the gardai."

"We being kicked out on Christmas Day?" Ian asked.

Murphy nodded.

Murphy walked with them down the stairs to the lobby. He told them to wait in the anteroom off to the side of the lobby while he walked to the closet.

"Here," he said, handing them each a bag.

"What's this?" Jeffrey asked.

"Merry Christmas," Murphy said. Each bag contained a blanket, wool pants, and a dreadnought. "I can't let you boys stay tonight, but you can come by later today for Christmas dinner."

"But we ain't got no place to go," Jeffrey whined.

They were weak young men and Murphy had reached the end of the line with them. Murphy's steely eyes pointed in the direction of the door.

An hour after Murphy entered the room and had sent Jeffrey and Ian packing, Greeny used his nose to nudge John on the leg.

Half-dazed, John said, "What it is, boy?" Greeny continued to nudge. "You hungry?" John got up and walked over to his haversack that was on the table and retrieved a bit of pork sausage. He threw it on the floor. Greeny ignored it.

The commotion woke Douglas. "I think he wanna go pee," Douglas said quietly.

John hated the thought of going outside in the frigid weather in the dark.

"Unless you want a foul-smelling room, I'd suggest you take him outside now."

John sat in a corner and donned his socks and brogans. He stood and put on his coat. Greeny was waiting by the door. A glimmering light from a gaslight from outside a large window in the lobby aided them as they walked down the stairs. John unlocked the front door and Greeny burst out, happy to feel the brisk, cold air. John looked up at the clear sky and saw the Big Dipper. He thought of his mother and wondered how she'd spend Christmas Day. He hoped Billingsly would be as generous with gifts as he had been in the past.

John jogged around the corner. Greeny was at the other corner doing his business on a strip of grass. After Greeny finished, he walked in the direction of the steamed air, which he thought was coming from a vent.

"Greeny, let's go," John snapped.

Greeny ignored him and soon disappeared. John resumed his jog on the lightly snow-covered sidewalk to retrieve his pet. As he was halfway to the other corner a sudden gust of wind knocked him over. He bounced up, furious with Greeny for delaying his return to warmer quarters.

As he turned the corner, he saw Greeny sniffing at what appeared to be two rolls of blankets. As John inched closer, he realized it was two people sleeping on top of the steam grate. Just as John reached down to touch one, his tormentors rose quickly.

Seeing John, Jeffrey said, "Well, look what we got here."

Before John could say anything, Jeffrey rushed him and pinned him against the wall of the YMCA with his right forearm pressed firmly on John's neck, choking him. He leaned forward within an inch of John and blew stale breath in John's face. "I oughta kill you right now," he said as he wielded his pocketknife.

Greeny charged after Jeffrey, who kicked Greeny in the muzzle with such force that he flew a foot into the air. Greeny was dazed, in apparent distress, and he hobbled a few feet before collapsing in the street. Within minutes a wound opened, and blood streamed from Greeny's mouth and nose.

"Go ahead, Jeff," Ian said. Jeffrey hit John in the stomach five times with his fist; the last blow sent John slumping to the ground.

"Get up!" Jeffrey snarled.

John was disoriented, his strength sapped.

Jeffrery qucikly grabbed John by the lapels of his coat and lifted him up against the wall. Fear roiled in John's eyes as Jeffrey thrust him against the wall, each time harder than the last. A wound opened at the back of John's head, and blood oozed out. Jeffrey took his pocketknife and held it horizontally against John's jugular.

Adrenaline shot through Jeffrey's body. Like a wild animal that has his prey in a death grip around the neck, Jeffrey was ready for the coup de grâce: He slid the knife across John's neck, opening a superficial wound to give John a taste of a slow death.

"Jeff, we can't kill him. We don't want to face no murder charge."

"Ain't no jury going to convict us of killing this coon," Jeffrey shot back. He spat in John's face and let him fall to the ground next to the steam vent.

At seven a.m. on Christmas Day, Douglas, still snug in his bedroll, called out: "John?"

No answer.

A little louder: "John!"

He used his arms to sit upright. There was nowhere for John and Greeny to hide in the room. He raised both arms high in the air and stretched mightily to convince himself he was fully awake. He donned his shoes and went down the steps to the lobby.

Murphy sat at an old Knabe upright piano near the fireplace playing "Jingle Bells." As Douglas moved toward the music, Murphy said, "Okay, all together now ... *Jingle Bells, Jingle Bells* ..." His chorus of about ten people joined in. Douglas sat on a chair near the piano, swiveling his head to look for John and Greeny.

The music stopped a few minutes later. Murphy saw Douglas. He picked up a cup of chicory and took a swig, then walked the few feet to Douglas and sat down next to him. "Merry Christmas. This is the day Christ was born. Ya know, He died for our sins and because of that we live to celebrate his life."

Worriment filled Douglas's eyes. "That's real good," Douglas said.

"Something wrong?" Murphy asked.

"Have you seen John?"

"Probably in the chow line getting his fill of rashers and bangers—sausage and bacon to you—and eggnog."

Douglas nodded. "Yeah."

"Go get your fill."

Twenty minutes later Douglas had his fill and returned to the lobby where he saw Murphy talking to a patrolman near the front door. It was Birmingham Patrolman Bernie Ahern, someone whose beat included the YMCA. They were both immigrants from Ireland and loved swapping stories from back home.

"What can I do for ya, Bernie?"

Ahern asked Murphy if he knew there was a colored boy passed out on the steam grate at the back of the building. "Probably some drunk," Murphy said.

"He may be dead. Take a look for me," Ahern requested.

Murphy agreed and wished the patrolman and his family a Merry Christmas.

"Will do."

"Can I get you a cup of chicory?" Murphy asked.

"No thank ya. Already had some."

"Yer a good Irishman, a good American," Murphy told him.

Murphy lifted his linsey-woolsey shirt from the antlers on a mounted stag's head, donned it, and walked with Ahern to the back of the building.

A shoeless and coatless body lay prostrate on the grate. Murphy moved closer. "Dear God, that laddie is John. He came yesterday with Douglas."

Ahern strained and groaned as he picked John up. He was out of shape, with a belly that lopped over all sides of his waistband. He struggled to carry John inside through a side door. Ahern breathed heavily as Murphy led him to a room that had a bed. Ahern placed John on a hard, thin mattress.

Murphy removed John's socks and felt his pallid feet; they were icy cold. He wrapped John in a woolen blanket to conserve what heat John's body still held.

John's right leg twitched. Murphy looked at John's face and noticed his pallid lips, nose, and ears. A trail of dried blood ran from his nose to his pullover cotton shirt. Looking into John's eyes for the first time, Murphy felt dread. But there was hope, as John blinked periodically.

Ahern said, "Looks like he was roughed up, eh? Any idea how this happened?"

"No."

"Did he have any enemies that ya know?" Ahern asked.

"Maybe. He and Douglas had a fight with Ian Dunst and Jeff Reynolds a few hours earlier today."

"Jeff Reynolds. Huh. I arrested him a while ago after he banjaxed property owned by Pratt Mills. He's a real yob. Why're ya so concerned about this colored boy?"

"This boy has no family, except for his dog and his friend Douglas. He needs a helping hand."

Ahern removed his hat and a forelock of unruly hair, gray and thin, fell over his forehead. He swept it back with his right hand. "Suppose so. Get him some medical attention. Don't hesitate to call on the gardai if you need us."

Murphy sent for medical help, which arrived the day after Christmas. In the meantime, John slept on a small bed covered with blankets. He ate nothing and only took a few sips of hot cider from time to time.

A colored physician attended to John the day after Christmas. He told Murphy that John's toes were frostbitten and that he needed to convalesce for a few more days.

As John recovered over the next few days, Douglas told him that Greeny had died. John's heart sank. His sisters were gone, his mother was just in a reserved placed in his heart, as he didn't know whether he'd ever see her again—so for now, she was also lost. And now he lost Greeny, another family member. The only family he had left was Douglas.

When Douglas asked Murphy whether their short-term roommates had had anything to do with John's near demise, Murphy was silent, but his expression told the answer. A sharp pain grabbed Douglas's body like an alligator's jaws. He was ready to kill.

19

DECEMBER, 1888

The days of John's convalescence from being left for dead in the back of the YMCA turned into weeks, and the weeks into months. Not only was the frostbite on John's feet slow to heal, a recent infection in his lungs brought him close to death; the doctor listened to John's lungs and thought there could possibly be a form of death rattle, which extended John's bedrest. At the advice of the doctor, Father Murphy placed John in a room by himself to reduce human contact as much as possible. The doctor told Father Murphy that if John were to survive the infection, it would be attributable to his age and answered prayers.

When not attending to John, Douglas busied himself with routine janitorial duties, cooking, and doing whatever Father Murphy requested. Like John, he wanted to move on to Alabama, but he could not abandon the one he had come to love as a trusted brother.

As John's infection began to lift, life returned to his body. He'd hold onto Douglas as they walked about the building. With time, his health was restored, except his feet ached on occasion.

On a balmy Tuesday December day, Douglas and John set out beyond town to pick up a package for Father Murphy. Several miles into their journey, they stopped and pulled ham sandwiches from the poke sacks they carried; they took shelter in a ramshackle one-story barn.

No sooner had they settled in on a dirt floor when they heard a man outside of the barn say in a menacing tone, "Get in that building." Douglas and John stuffed their sandwiches in their mouths and scurried behind several bales of rotting hay.

A thirty-something-year-old woman and a young girl walked in, followed by a man pointing a pistol at them. The woman was white, with a round face, long, curly brunette hair, and a thin frame. She had on a shabby, cream-colored floor-length dress. The girl, who appeared to be about six years old, wore a ponytail and was dressed in a yellow faille dress. The man was nattily attired. He had on a stylish blue woolen greatcoat that partially covered his charcoal gray woolen pants. He had thinning brown hair, deep-set cold blue eyes, a Roman nose, a walrus mustache, and a weak chin.

He barked out an order for them to sit in the corner.

"Richard, you don't have to do this," the woman said.

"Shut up, Emma." The woman and the girl started crying. "Make her shut up," he said as he pointed the gun at the girl. Emma reached over and held her tightly, wiping away the tears.

Richard put the gun to his side. "You might as well know. No reason to keep it a secret. You can take the news with you to your grave. You are no longer my wife. I have a new wife, a better-looking wife. Someone who loves me, and not the bottle. Working at Georgia-Pacific Railroad, I can provide a good life for her. But you and the children are in the way of me making this right."

"Richard, please ... you don't have to do this."

"You want me to let you and Irene walk out of here as if nothing happened? Well, it's already happened. Your oldest daughter is at the bottom of a lake. Two more to go."

"You bastard!" Emma screamed. "You mean you killed Mae? Mae and Irene are our kids!"

Richard smirked, but otherwise remained emotionally arid. "Do you have anything else to say before I shoot the both of you?"

John and Douglas remained silent. John looked at Douglas. He hated what he was witnessing—a bully about to shoot and kill his wife and child. Madame Billingsly was a bully, but she had never killed anyone as far as he knew. He spied a pitchfork behind him and tiptoed to it and picked it up. He knew he had to act fast to disable or kill the devil somehow. As he rose slowly to charge the devil who would not see John coming in time to shoot him, a shot rang out and hit Emma between her eyes. The next shot hit Irene in the chest. He put his pistol in his holster, then looked for somewhere to hide the bodies.

John and Douglas remained crouching behind the hay bales, realizing the pitchfork was useless to them. They listened as Richard began to drag Irene's body to the bales of hay.

Noise from outside the barn startled Richard. They heard him drop Irene's body and walk slowly to the door. A strong wind blew it open.

John stood up slightly and peeked over a bale of hay. He saw Richard standing to the side of it with his pistol cocked, waiting for someone to enter.

Richard looked out the door, put his gun behind his back, and stepped outside.

"What're you boys doing out here?"

"We playing tag," one of them said.

"There's a storm coming this way. You boys go on home."

John and Douglas stood up, not sure what to do. They had failed to stop the double murder. They looked at the dead bodies and the bright-red blood pooling on the floor. Bile rose to John's mouth; he spit out the bad taste.

The two of them looked at each other and then each walked silently to the opposite sides of the door.

When Richard turned and walked back into the barn, John charged him and punched him in the stomach, and Douglas gave him an uppercut when Richard doubled over. Douglas pushed him to the floor; he landed next to his dead wife.

As Richard lay on the floor, he reached for his pistol that had fallen near him. He shot a round at John and Douglas as they darted out of the barn.

Richard got up with his pistol in his hand and strode to the door, took two steps to the left, and saw Douglas and John running.

He rushed back inside of the barn. As he hurried across the floor, he spied a vertical trap door that led to the outside. He opened the door and pushed the bodies through it. He hid the door and blood with hay and dirt.

As John ran alongside Douglas, John felt the weight of being chased by both Billingsly and Richard. It was too much, and he collapsed. Douglas carried him the rest of the way.

Douglas flung open the door as Father Murphy was about to exit. Father Murphy saw the alarm in their eyes and told them to hurry and to sit near the piano. Father Murphy sent for the beat patrolman, who would likely be Ahern, after John and Douglas told him what they witnessed.

Ahern arrived an hour later. After John and Douglas related their story, he asked, "Anything else ya need to tell us?"

They shook their heads.

Ahern looked at Father Murphy and said, "Thanks for calling me on this one. It could be a big one."

Father Murphy looked at Ahern. A year later and his belly still spilled over his waistband and his face was more deeply etched. "How much longer before ya give it up?" he asked.

"Soon. The knees're about to give out."

The police soon found Emma and Irene's bodies under the barn. The oldest daughter's body was found in a nearby lake. The police later went to Georgia Pacific and asked to speak to a man who fit the description Douglas and John gave them. The Birmingham police arrested Richard Hawes and charged him with triple murder, and he was placed in cell in the jail house.

The *Birmingham Age-Herald* was all over the story. RICHARD HAWES ACCUSED OF TRIPLE MURDER, screamed the front-page headline, and pictures of the bodies told their own chilling story.

Matthew Trowbridge, the Jefferson County prosecutor, faced a racially based dilemma, like so many things in the South were. His case depended on the testimony of two colored men. It was considered generally established that a colored person should not testify against a white person in court. If Douglas and John were permitted to testify against Hawes, the social contract between colored and white could begin to unravel.

The Birmingham citizenry was appalled at the savagery of the ghastly murders, and they demanded the death penalty, but Hawes's conviction would depend on Douglas and John's testimony—which no one wanted. The *Birmingham Age-Herald* feared for Birmingham's reputation. Crime was already high in the city, and the *Age-Herald* feared that the city would be sullied even more if a crowd were to storm the jail and kill Hawes. It implored Birmingham citizens to let the justice system work.

The story soon grew beyond Birmingham and was reported nationwide, and many Northern newspapers took up the cause for allowing Douglas and John to testify against Hawes.

Trowbridge made up his mind. Hawes had to pay for his crimes. He was going to order Douglas and John to testify, but he knew he'd have to provide them protection.

Father Murphy convinced John and Douglas, at Ahern's behest, that they would be safe in a cell in the same jail where Hawes was locked up. "The gardai will keep ya safe. I promise," he said. "It'll be for a few days. They'll feed ya. I'll come to visit every day. I'll keep ya things here locked up."

Douglas and John had been in their cell for a few days before they were scheduled to testify before a grand jury that had been convened quickly. They had felt safe from the white men in particular that hated them as much as they hated Hawes.

But this day was different. The first of an eventual mob began to trickle in at eight o'clock in the morning despite a steady rain. Within an hour, the rain abated, and the mob swelled to hundreds more people. Many in the crowd swayed rhythmically, stimulated by alcohol and revenge, ready to break into the jail despite the heavy presence of police surrounding it.

Referring to Richard Hawes, Jeffrey Reynolds led the shouts of "Kill the dirty bastard!" Reynolds had secured a position atop a large boulder and ever the lout, had a penchant for finding trouble and was always willing to walk through trouble's door.

Douglas and John felt the frenzied racket from inside their cell. The mob's screams pierced the jail walls and bounced around their heads. Father Murphy had told them that Ahern had said that their presence in the jail would be kept confidential, but they no longer believed it.

A white police officer let it leak that John and Douglas were at the jailhouse.

The crowd's emotions grew to a fever pitch. Sheriff Joseph Smith had given his men orders to defend the jail at all costs. A deputy sheriff on the roof of the jail fired his Lee rifle into the crowd, felling a young man. The riotous crowd lost all semblance of control and broke through the door in seconds. More shots were fired into the crowd, killing more people.

John held Douglas's hand as Douglas said the rosary as taught to him by Father Murphy.

Reynolds was the first inside. Someone inside the jail had leaked to Reynolds where Hawes's cell was. "This way," Reynolds said, pointing the way to Hawes's cell.

Reynolds demanded that the deputy sheriff sitting at the small oak desk give him the key to the cell. The corpulent deputy sheriff put down his sandwich and rose from his chair, walked away from his desk, and pointed with a nod of his head to the key in the right drawer of the desk.

Reynolds unlocked Hawes's cell door. Hawes saw the end coming. Two men held Hawes's arms as Reynolds used his pocketknife to extract Hawes's heart. Soon other men were able to tear off Hawes's limbs. As men went outside holding Hawes's limbs, the crowd erupted with cheers.

Trowbridge later lost his reelection bid. His opponent defeated him, arguing that Trowbridge was unfit for office because he had been willing to let two colored men testify against a white man.

20
SUMMER, 1890

His stomach gurgled throughout his meeting, and he pined for the turkey sandwich and pickle his wife made him for lunch. When the executive meeting ended, he hurried to his office and took the first satisfying bite of his sandwich and sighed as though he had just emptied his bladder. As he sat in his leather chair, he propped his feet on his carved birch desk, opened the *Birmingham Age-Herald,* and popped it to weaken the fold.

He went right to his favorite section, the editorials—always conservative and red hot, just as he liked them. His eyes stopped on the editorial: "*The Leader* is Fomenting Trouble."

The Leader was a newspaper owned by coloreds that promoted the interests of colored people in Birmingham. It had run stories about the need for social equality and the need for companies to hire colored workers. With the recent turmoil about Prosecutor Trowbridge's decision to allow two colored men to testify, *The Leader* endorsed that decision in writing.

After reading a couple of paragraphs, his eyes widened and his mouth was agape. He reread part of the sentence:

> Two colored boys, Douglas James and John Billingsly, twenty-six years old and twenty years old, respectively, both working at the YMCA....

The name and age match, he thought. "My God, can it be?" he mumbled. He read on:

> Birmingham will solve its problems at its own pace. Some colored men now work alongside white men at the

factories ... There is no need for the colored men at The Leader to stir a pot that has just begun to settle.

Billingsly lay the newspaper on his desk, opened his cigar box, and lit a Cuban cigar. He was now an executive with Sloss Furnaces. He had successfully parlayed his experience in the iron business in Richmond into the steel business in Birmingham. Over two years had passed since he'd left Richmond in a blaze of humiliation and heartbreak. But within two years at Sloss, he was firmly established as a top-level executive and much of his wealth had been restored, thereby elevating him to Birmingham's *gens du monde*. He'd married a woman more than two decades younger, which for him meant two more offspring.

He never forgot, though, about that horrible day when he'd returned to *Billingsly* and found his wife's body on the floor near the base of the staircase. His new family and business obligations helped soften the anger of what had happened to Laura, but not eliminate it.

As he sat as his desk, he pulled opened a side drawer and removed the small bag that contained the denim patch he'd collected from the rusty nail in his tool shed those years ago. His gray eyes turned dark as he stared at the bag, wondering if it'd be wise to open it, for fear of the mental anguish sure to follow. Overcoming his fear, he picked up the bag, turned it upside down, and shook it a few times. The patch fell out.

His anger boiled up and he determined he'd go to Father Murphy's YMCA to talk to this *John Billingsly.*

"Good day, Mr. Billingsly," Father Murphy said to Billingsly as they shook hands in the lobby of the YMCA. Billingsly was still tall and erect. He radiated the same confidence he had in Richmond, and he maintained his taste for fine European clothing. He was turned out in a black frock coat lined with red silk jacquard, a navy waistcoat, and black pants, from a bespoke tailor on Savile Row. A pearl gray Gibus hat with a black silk band announced his importance as well as his wealth. Murphy wore his usual black shirt with a clerical collar and black pants.

Billingsly wiped his lips with his tongue, anticipating his encounter with John Billingsly. John is a common name, Billingsly less so. He was convinced this John was his erstwhile servant who held answers to what caused Laura's death. The bounty hunters he had hired never were able to find John. Where they failed, though, he thought he'd succeed, even if by happenstance.

"Yes, I'd say it's a good day. It's springtime, the season of renewal and rebirth."

Several residents milled about the lobby. Billingsly spied two colored men in the lobby cleaning the floor, one of whom was short and whose skin was the color of eggnog, and the other who was about six feet tall, a muscular build, and wore a patch over his left eye. Billingsly quickly dismissed the first one as being John because of the wrong height and skin color.

"Mr. Billingsly? How can I help ya?" Murphy asked.

Billingsly continued to pan the lobby.

"Mr. Billingsly," Murphy repeated. "How may I help ya?"

Billingsly turned to Murphy: "Who's that fella mopping the floor, the one wearing the eye patch?"

"That's Johnny."

Billingsly's heart began to race. He licked his thin lips again. "Where is he from?"

"Don't know."

"What's the boy's last name?"

Although Murphy was getting annoyed with the questions, he had to conceal it. Billingsly and his company were one of the YMCA's biggest benefactors; they donated money and goods to the YMCA, and their donations helped make Christmas a bit merrier.

"Don't know," Murphy said. "I can check my books if you like."

"That won't be necessary. Just ask him to come here."

Murphy hallooed, attracting everyone's attention. "Hey, Johnny, come here."

Johnny put down his mop and walked to Father Murphy and Billingsly.

Johnny was six feet tall on a broad frame with light chocolate-colored skin, dark eyes, and short black hair.

Billingsly eyed Johnny. His nose appeared a bit broader that what he recalled of John's nose. "Yes, boss," Johnny said.

"What's your last name?"

"My name be Johnny Bigsby."

Billingsly got his answer, and nodded slightly at Murphy, signaling that Johnny could return to his duties. "That'll be all," Murphy said to Johnny. Billingsly got to the point. "I'm looking for a colored boy by the name of John Billingsly."

"John's not here at the moment, Mr. Billingsly. Should be back in a few hours."

Billingsly's detective work was making progress. He needed to know more. "Do you know where John's from?"

"He told me he came from Richmond, Virginia."

Billingsly's heart began to race, and he breathed heavily.

Murphy continued: "He's one of my best. Never complains. Works hard."

"I want to offer him a job at Sloss. We at Sloss are making an effort to hire colored men."

Billingsly's point was true but his intent was subterfuge. Sloss *had* begun to hire colored men to work alongside white men. Men at Sloss were hired for their brawn and energy. Color couldn't stand in the way of making money.

"When he returns," Billingsly said, "tell him Sloss Furnace wants to offer him a job. Don't tell him the offer is coming from me. It's to be a surprise. Have him come to Sloss tomorrow at nine o'clock in the morning; he is to go to the hiring department."

"I'll right tell him, Mr. Billingsly."

"Thank you," Billingsly said, nodding slightly to acknowledge Murphy's receptiveness to help.

John read the sign that told him he was on 32nd Street, but he didn't need it to tell him where Sloss Furnace was located. Everyone in town knew about the big complex with tall smokestacks.

The YMCA had been good to him; he had a place to live, food to eat. With Murphy's help and the tutors Murphy hired through in-kind donations to help John and others with reading and writing, John excelled, and Murphy soon asked John to read the newspaper to other residents who could not read. He fell in love with the written word and understood how it could impact people and possibly change lives. He didn't know how much longer he'd stay in Birmingham before moving on to fulfill his saintly mother's desire that he make it to Mount Hope to find Cousin Riley. But for now, he was satisfied to work for Father Murphy, earn a bit of income, and help others read and write, which had included Douglas for a period of time.

John owed Father Murphy everything, so if the man wanted him to work here, he'd do it because he knew that Sloss was one of the YMCA's biggest benefactors.

John walked in the front door of the office side to Sloss Furnaces. He saw a short, white, bearded male who appeared to be someone important. "Excuse me, sir," John said, "I was told to report to the hiring department. Can you tell me the direction?"

Looking askance at John, the bearded man told John where to go.

"Excuse me," John said to a young man sitting at a small desk in the hiring department, "I was told to report here today about a job."

"What's your name?" the young man asked, looking at a paper filled with names.

"John Billingsly."

He spotted John's name and told John where to go.

John climbed up a long marble staircase to the third floor, where he didn't see anyone. He sat down in a wingback chair, waiting for someone to greet him. After twenty minutes of waiting, he thought that perhaps he was in the wrong place. As he began his descent down the marble staircase to return to the hiring department, he heard a voice call his name, a voice that sounded familiar.

He stopped in his tracks, believing that the voice belonged to Monsieur Billingsly, but he figured it couldn't be. He stood still for three seconds, allowing his brain to continue to process the voice. What would be the chances of Monsieur Billingsly working for Sloss Furnaces in Birmingham, he thought? He wondered whether Monsieur Billingsly had asked Murphy about him. If he did, how did

Billingsly know he stayed at the YMCA? John had no answers, but he knew he'd have to turn around to find out if he was dreaming.

John was on the third step from the landing; he turned slowly, staring at the black trousers of the man who called his name. His eyes drifted upward where they met Billingsly's jolly eyes.

He emitted the kind of smile that someone gives an old friend. "John, my boy! It's been a long time. What's it been, a couple of years?"

Billingsly moved away from the steps, causing John to follow the man who exuded confidence. John sat in the same wingback chair, and Billingsly sat in the one next to him. He quivered as he watched Billingsly rub the stud in his left shirt cuff with his right thumb.

"What's wrong, boy?" Billingsly asked.

John's experience in Richmond had taught him that when Billingsly rubbed his stud in his shirt cuff, he was about to deliver unwelcome news. But John would have to wait and see.

"I'm okay, sir."

Billingsly put his right hand on John's left shoulder like he'd often done when John worked for him in Richmond. It has been Billingsly's way of asserting his will with his workers without incurring anger or annoyance. But the touch didn't seem right to John. Too calculated.

"John, I want you to work for me here. You did a good job for me in Richmond, and Father Murphy says you're one of his best workers."

John struggled to determine whether Billingsly was dissembling. "How did you find me, Monsieur Billingsly?"

Billingsly disliked the questions, and shrugged it off. "Ah, that's not important. What's important is that I found you."

John wanted to say something—to really learn how Billingsly found him—but the words just sat on his lips.

"Let's go to the shop," Billingsly said.

John followed Billingsly to one of the furnaces that made the steel that was sold in many states, steel that greatly contributed to the continuing of America's Industrial Revolution.

They stopped and stood about twenty yards from the blast furnace. John looked around the cavernous space for workers. He didn't see anyone. Billingsly turned to his right, walked a few steps, and turned a switch on a console panel. John heard a low rumbling noise—the furnace had been stoked.

John felt the temperature rise. Billingsly stood calmy in his three-piece suit, seemingly impervious to the heat. He put his hand in his left pants' pocket where he felt the bag that contained the denim patch. The anger that he had felt when he'd found his wife on the floor of his mansion back in Richmond began to bubble up, like a volcano that makes noise after years of dormancy.

"John, I'm married, but it's not to Laura. Laura died in Richmond over two years ago." He had been counting the hours for his encounter with John. He had to ask, "Do you know anything about that?"

John was quick to answer, perhaps too quick. "No, Monsieur Billingsly."

Billingsly clamped his hand around the bag of evidence; it felt hot to the touch. He pressed on. Billingsly said, with eyes as harsh as a winter's landscape, "Well, I need to satisfy myself that you don't know anything about what happened to Laura, as well as some property that was stolen from my house, two sterling silver whiskey flasks."

John's stomach gurgled, as if to try to untie the knots that gripped it. He wanted to flee but that would convince Billingsly that he was guilty. And he knew Billingsly knew he stayed at the YMCA. The sour tang of bile began to rise at the back of his throat, just like it did on the night he taken the flasks out of the *Billingsly* mansion—he was tasting his own fear, and he smelled menace in the air.

"Take off your pants, John."

John's face creased with concern. "What?"

Anger darted out of Billingsly's eyes, and a muscle in his jaw quivered. "Just do it!"

John complied and dropped his trousers, revealing his gray woolen union suit.

Billingsly gestured with his right hand, telling John to remove the union suit.

The bile had inched to John's tongue. He squinted and forced it back down, disgusted at its taste. Billingsly moved close to look at John's right thigh. He saw a faint, two-inch scar on John's lower right thigh.

"How'd you get that scar on your right leg?"

"Why are you asking me these questions?"

"I want to know if you know anything about Laura's death and the two flasks that were stolen from me. Now, tell me how that scar got there."

"I don't know," John said in a tone that he immediately regretted.

Billingsly removed the bag from his pocket while John still stood naked before him. Billingsly opened the bag and retrieved the denim patch, careful to watch John for any kind of reaction. John offered none. Billingsly moved closer yet to John, showing him the patch. The scrape mark on the patch was about the same length of the faint scar on John's right thigh.

"Put your clothes on," Billingsly said.

John's mind was a mess of wounds and panic. He pulled up his pants and prayed that someone would walk his way to save him from the same kind of hell he experienced when he'd stared down Laura's .22-caliber rifle three years ago in Richmond.

After putting his clothes on, John stood facing Billingsly. Even though his mind was turning to mush, he managed to string together a bold question: "Monsieur Billingsly, sir, do you want to hire me, or did you call me here to find out what happened to Madame Billingsly?"

Billingsly's eyes turned darker yet, a warning of some sort for sure.

He removed a tattered flannel shirt from a bag he was holding. He was about to rip off another scab. "Do you know what this is?"

A trap, John thought. He shook his head.

"I got this from Ann's cabin the day I talked to Ann about my wife's death."

John's heart sank to his stomach. His face creased with bafflement.

"It's your shirt."

John's heart sank deeper. He wondered how Billingsly got the shirt and what his mother had told him. He knew Ann was loyal to Billingsly but believed that she wouldn't do anything to betray her flesh and blood. The only way to get information from Ann about him, he thought, had been for Billingsly to deceive her.

Billingsly stepped up the pressure. "If you want to see your mother alive again, you must tell me all you know. All I need to do is send a telegram to some folks in Richmond. ..." He couldn't bring himself to finish the sentence because of his conflicting emotions about Ann, the slave who had nursed his children, prayed for Laura, and stayed by her side until she had recovered.

John said nothing. Billingsly grabbed him tightly by the left forearm, forcing John to walk with him near the open furnace, but in an area that was obscured from others who could enter the shop. They both looked into the furnace below.

Billingsly spoke through clenched jaw. "Now, do you want to tell me what happened to Laura? And don't think you're going to get out of here alive without telling me the truth."

Panic poured out of John as hope went overboard. He decided to beg for his life while his head was still above water. "Please don't do this, Monsieur Billingsly."

"You're doing it to yourself." He paused to pursue an angle to get John to consider spitting out the truth. "I really don't need the whiskey flasks or care about them any longer. I just need to know whether you know anything about Laura's death, and if you have knowledge about my whiskey flasks."

John remained tight-lipped. Billingsly pulled him closer to the furnace, which was now making an infernal noise, making more heat. He offered no resistance as he had caused the demise of the virago of Richmond, and he had never offered penance for his sin to anyone. He took a life, and now his turn had come, he thought. It was only just.

A memory of his mother's face jumped to the fore of John's mind, and he remembered her wish that he try to find Cousin Riley in Mount Hope. His brain was working as God wanted it to work, he thought. He couldn't let her down, and for that matter himself, as he still dreamed of a bigger life. He jerked his arm back, hard, causing Billingsly to lose his grip.

John walked backward. Billingsly walked toward him. John's left shoe slipped imperceptibly on some kind of oily substance. All he'd need to do now was to guide Billingsly over the same spot, and hope that Billingsly would lose his balance and he could run. He kept stepping backward.

Thoughts of Madame Billingsly lying dead near the staircase surfaced in his mind again. He contributed to her death. John thought either he was going to die, or it would be Monsieur Billingsly.

John continued to walk backward as though without awareness of the desperate situation he was in.

Without warning, it happened: Billingsly slipped on the spot and fell to the floor, his momentum throwing him onto the ledge and then forcing him to hang over the fire below.

John snapped out of his dreamy state, but his mind swirled in the moment of torment: He could flee from the monster who'd threatened to dump him into that same furnace, or he could try to save the life of the man who'd often tried to protect him from Madame Billingsly's scalding words.

"Grab my right hand, sir," John said as he looked at Billingsly's sepulchral eyes.

"I can't. I'm slipping," replied Billingsly in a labored whisper.

John bent down and grabbed Billingsly's right hand and pulled with all his might. After a long struggle, John pulled the man from his certain death. Billingsly stood up slowly, wiped his coat and pants. He didn't say a word; he just stood there and looked at John with eyes that were being restored to life.

Billingsly stood still even as John walked past him with his eyes trained on Monsieur Billingsly as he left Sloss. John then sprinted to the YMCA, relieved that he'd live to see another day. John knew he had to leave the YMCA and Father Murphy.

—⁂—

A couple of weeks before John went to Sloss to inquire about a job opportunity, Douglas was arrested for stealing a hammer at a hardware store. He pleaded his innocence, but the store owner said he saw Douglas take the hammer. As a condition of his release, Douglas could pay the cost of the hammer and a fine. When Father Murphy learned of Douglas's problem, he told the court that he'd provide the money in about a week. However, within a couple of days after his arrest, Douglas had been convicted and sentenced to one year of hard labor and ordered to serve his sentence at the Pratt Mining Company.

Many colored men in the recent past had been falsely accused and convicted of petty crimes in this same manner and had been "leased" to private industries like Pratt Mining that were desperate for workers. It was a money-making arrangement for Jefferson County and companies getting the prison labor—the county received payment from the company, and the company got cheap labor. The county just asked the company using the prison labor to provide food and health services to the prisoner.

Although the county was to keep records of the prison labor it leased to companies, such records were either incomplete or simply didn't exist. Hundreds of colored men were lost to slave labor across the South. When Father Murphy asked the authorities about Douglas's whereabouts, he was told that Douglas pleaded guilty and was sent away to do some mining work for one year.

Father Murphy told John that he'd do all he could to gain Douglas's return from Pratt. John needed to see his best friend again, but knew his own life was in jeopardy because Billingsly knew where he lived. The man who had shepherded him from Richmond, the man who had protected him, was now gone in a flash. He could only hope he'd get a chance to at least see him to say thank you. But he doubted that would happen; he knew it was time to fulfill his mother's request that he go to Mount Hope to find Cousin Riley. He'd endeavor to fulfill that request—and although he wanted to find a blood relative, he wanted more.

He packed quickly, pouring his possessions into his haversack and a used valise he had purchased. He kept some of the lucre for a rainy day, spending the money he earned working on the things he needed.

But before he left the YMCA, he had made sure to collect both flasks, which he had hidden in a box in a crawl space no one used. He opened the box, stroked the engravings on them, and wondered why he had kept them for so long. Billingsly had finally caught up to him, and therefore the stolen flasks. The flasks had haunted him for all these years; perhaps he'd throw them in a lake, and the pall that enveloped him would be lifted. But because he remained somewhat intrigued about possibly uncovering valuables buried by Papa Billingsly someday, he decided to keep them. He then gathered some things from Douglas's haversack to take with him, as he knew Douglas had a new home.

21
SUMMER, 1890

Since he left Richmond in May of '87 up until now, he and Douglas had wended their way south by foot, stagecoach, the powerful Cleveland Bays, rides with strangers, and by boxcar. He had overcome a near-death experience with the infection in his lungs. And he had thrived working for Father Murphy, who told John he was an excellent worker, a smart young man, and someone who'd be a leader somewhere, someday. He was a bit more urbane, and he intended to use it to move through society in a way he could bend.

He knew time was drawing nigh to move on after an extended stay in Birmingham. The near disaster with Billingsly accelerated his decision, along with the loss of his best friend to a government-sanctioned slave labor prison run by Pratt Mining.

John was assigned a berth in a passenger car with other colored passengers. As the train readied to roll out, John stood on the landing just outside of the car, and waved goodbye to Birmingham, his home for the past two years.

The whistle blew, followed by a shout of "All aboard!"

John made his way over to the remaining open seat. The armrest was broken, and the thin cushion assured him of an uncomfortable train ride. He nodded at the occupant of the seat next to him as he sat down. She was a whey-faced colored lady, probably somewhere between 90- and 100-years-old. She was wrinkled, thin as a crack, and hunched over. Her face folded all over itself, which told a story of a hardscrabble life. Her blue buckram bonnet covered some of her wispy gray-and-white hair. She wore a long white cotton dress and button-up shoes. She alternated between using a fan to cool herself and using a doily to dab the sweat beads that formed at her hairline.

Forty passengers, all colored except for two white men who were assigned there because they smoked, were berthed in John's car. The car floor was peppered with refuse, the upholstery tattered, and the windows speckled with mud.

She adjusted her bonnet, turned to John, and said, "I'm Harriett." Her voice, as soft as a summer breeze, didn't match her crumbling façade.

"Good day, I'm John."

Within minutes, the locomotive was humming along at a nice clip. John closed his eyes and took stock of his life. Nothing could disturb him; not the conversation around him, not the clangorous train wheel noise. He was lost in thought about whether his mother was dead or alive. His mother's megawatt smile still burned brightly in his head, which served as an impetus that kept him moving on his trek to locate Cousin Riley. He wondered about her nightmares and if she still had them; he had witnessed her screams many a night as a boy: screams over the lashings she'd received as a slave; screams over the loss of her husband; screams over the loss of her twin daughters. A heart could only take so much torment before it gave out, he thought. He shuddered when he thought he had added to that torment.

He had drawn a crisis that had spiraled into a tenebrous outcome for his mother, Madame Billingsly, and Monsieur Billingsly. And he figured that if he hadn't stolen the flasks, he wouldn't have killed three bandits.

That led him to think again that maybe he should have jumped in the charnel at Sloss and ended it all. It was he who stole the flasks; if he hadn't, Madame Billingsly would be alive.

"Hey, you, wake up," the white train porter said, nudging John on the shoulder.

No response, as he was praying that Monsieur Billingsly would not continue to chase him. Although Father Murphy knew John's ultimate destiny was Mount Hope, he wondered whether Monsieur Billingsly would squeeze that information out of him. He settled on believing that Monsieur Billingsly and the damn flasks would haunt him for the rest of his life.

"I'm talking to you," the porter said in a louder voice, simultaneously kicking John's right foot.

John whiffed a foul odor from the porter's mouth. His eyelids opened slowly as though he were waking from a long, dreamy nap.

The porter looked at John and Harriett. He wore a lightweight white cotton jacket and black hat. His belly was large, and he had small dark eyes. "One of you gonna have to move."

"Why?" John asked.

"Look, I don't have tell you a damn thing. We got a white man who needs a place to smoke; this is the place for it."

Harriett rose slightly before John put his left hand on her leg, using gentle pressure to force her to sit back in her seat. John said to the rotund porter: "There are no more seats."

"Are you getting cross with me, darkie?"

John ignored the question. "This old lady should stay put." John stood up and took a few steps to the aisle. "He can have my seat."

"I say what seat he can have," the porter huffed with more dragon breath and shot spittle from his mouth. "I want that wench to move."

John's eyes narrowed and a rush of adrenaline flooded through him, making him as strong as an angry lion. One or two more wrong words and he'd pounce on the porter.

Now twenty years old, he had grown to his full height of six feet, one inch. His hair was still raven-black, but it was slightly less wavy than when he was younger. The porter had girth on John, but John was muscular and agile. One punch in the mouth and he knew he'd slay the dragon.

Breathe, he heard his mother say when he was a boy and angry about something. *Breathe, son.* He took two deep breaths, deflating his swollen temper. He had just saved himself a trip to the hoosegow.

"Listen," the porter said with a harsh tone to Harriett.

John looked over the porter's shoulder and the porter followed John's eyes. A white man with a cigar in his mouth tapped the porter on the shoulder and told him he didn't want the seat because he'd refuse to sit next to Harriett. As the porter moved toward the front, the white man extinguished his cigar by pressing it against a petition that separated the cars.

A few minutes later, the porter returned to the colored car and said, looking at John, "You're asking for trouble. I can have you arrested." He panned the car and growled, "That goes for all of you."

Harriett turned to John. "That be a brave thing you did there. Don't go to jail on 'count of me. Why you so angry?"

"I think it's because I wish I could see my mama," John said softly. John looked at Harriett. Words just sat on his lips. She caressed John's left hand with her bony right hand. Her motherly touch proved to be the salve he needed to talk. All thoughts he held in his head on the train earlier gushed out of him like a flood of water racing to find a low point. The flood found its low point twenty-five minutes later.

"Seem like you feel bad 'bout those whiskey bottles you took from ... "

"The Billingslys."

"Yeah, the Billingslys. Don't feel bad. Lots of stuff stole from colored folk. If those bottles make you rich someday, what you gonna do?"

John was no longer vigilant about keeping the flasks close at hand. They were in his haversack in the train storage along with his valise. "Truth is, I don't know whether I'll go back there looking for this fortune. It doesn't belong to me."

"Nonsense," Harriett intoned. "You use it to help the colored people. Help build a school, something like that. Help your mama."

John nodded to acknowledge her point. But the whiskey flasks had begun to lose their appeal. "If I hadn't taken them, Madame Billingsly would be alive; there'd have been no need for me to leave Mama, back in Richmond. I have the flasks, but I'm without Douglas, my best friend. He came with me from Richmond. We ended up staying at the YMCA in Birmingham. Father Murphy told me that he was charged with stealing something from a hardware store. He said he'd raise the money to get Douglas out of jail, but I couldn't stick around.... "

"Why not?"

Ignoring her question, John turned the focus to Harriett, asking, "What about you? Where're you from?"

Although unsure of her age, Harriett recalled the name President Monroe when she was a slave living in Baltimore, Maryland. All ten of her children were born into slavery. Three died young of various diseases. Four of her children traveled north, escaping slavery. She moved several times after they left, so she suspected that they probably would not be able to find her if they tried. She moved to Birmingham shortly after the War to live with her oldest son, who died a year ago. So she decided to move to Cullman to live with her grand-niece and her husband.

As Harriett rambled on with her story, she kept her gnarled hands folded in her lap restfully, as her glistened eyes gazed out the window. As the trained continued to steam to Cullman, Harriett both looked out the window, seeing a vista familiar to many colored folk who toiled on some white man's land. Stretches of cotton, tobacco fields, and orchards dotted the landscape. Colored people working in the fields looked up at the fast-moving train.

John awoke from his nap when he felt the train slow appreciably. He leaned to his right to look out the window, where he could see people standing on the depot platform.

The train stopped.

After a few minutes, the porters exited the train and placed stepstools on the ground for exit doors of the passenger cars. The passengers in the colored car were permitted to exit twenty minutes later. As there was not a stepstool for Harriett to use, John helped her sit down in the doorway. He jumped down to the ground, picked up Harriett, and put her wobbly legs on the ground. Harriett asked John to retrieve her two suitcases from storage. He retrieved them, along with his haversack and valise.

A colored man extended his hand to shake John's hand. "You a brave young man. Thanks for looking after my auntie."

"Oh, it was nothing," John said.

"I'm Troy, I be her nephew," he said as he hugged Harriett.

John watched as Troy helped Harriett board a rockaway. They rode away.

John looked up on the façade of the building and saw the sign: CULLMAN STATION. He put his haversack over his right shoulder and carried his valise in his left hand and walked into the station.

The cavernous station, bustling with people, had a cathedral ceiling, ornate architecture, and paintings on the walls. John spied a bench and sat down. He pulled pemmican from his haversack and began to nosh on it. Two hours ago, he'd been in Birmingham, a place he had called home for two years. He knew its streets and avenues, its buildings, its people. Now he was in a strange city.

He saw a large, black sign with white letters that said: DEPARTURE TIMES. John picked up his bags and walked closer to read the schedule. He read the cities to himself—Birmingham, Atlanta, Nashville, Louisville, Montgomery, Decatur, Mobile, Augusta, Mount Hope.

"Mount Hope, canceled," he muttered.

He walked to a man dressed in a bland gray shirt, shuffling through papers behind a counter. His name tag said "Bartlett Kohl." John asked him what time the next train was leaving for Mount Hope.

"It's not going nowhere today."

John's face sagged.

"Mechanical problems," Kohl said.

"What times does the train leave Mount Hope tomorrow?"

Kohl retrieved a sheet of paper from a drawer. His right index finger rolled down the page. "Aha," he said, "you can catch it next Thursday."

"How far away is it?"

"About fifty-five minutes by train."

"I can't wait that long."

Kohl offered hope, telling John about a new transportation line called an interurban, which had just opened, and that it was about five miles away. Because John hadn't heard of an interurban, Kohl explained that it was somewhat similar to a passenger train except that it ran within and between cities and towns.

"There's an interurban about five miles from here; it opened for business just a month ago. It makes a stop in Mount Hope: it's leaving at seven in the morning."

22

SUMMER, 1890

It was a scene from the Arizona Territory being played out in a small Alabama town. It was an old-fashioned stickup, the robbers looking for targets for easy money from small-town America.

Two robbers had gone from one small town to another hoping they could make a hit and move on quickly to the next town. As they had rehearsed and done with other robberies, one robber would threaten the clerk at a lodging place or at a train station, and the other robber would stand in the back as a customer scouting the customers' movements, and the lead robber would force the clerk at gunpoint to disclose where the money was located.

The lead robber, a young man with severe acne and shaggy blond hair, stood behind a counter pointing a Remington .36 caliber pistol at the woman clerk working for the Cullman Interurban. He told her it was a stickup and then shouted at the ten or so unsuspecting people in the small station to sit on the floor and not to make any sudden movements, and that they'd be shot dead if warranted.

A woman screamed profanities at the robber and the robber screamed back, telling her, as he waved his gun in the air, to shut up. Moments later, John tapped her on the shoulder and shot her a reassuring look with eyes that had grown cold like the eyes Monsieur Billingsly radiated at John at Sloss as he aimed to send John into the inferno. He had by now come to hate robbers and thieves, though he of course had been one back at *Billingsly* and that had caused him a lot of angst and nightmares.

Hearing a lot of commotion, an elderly bowlegged man of about seventy-five, emerged from behind a wall near the ticket counter and saw the robber pointing his pistol at Gretchen, his ticket counter clerk. He told the robber he was in charge and that there was no need for violence. Although the station had opened for business not long ago, the elderly man had been beaten by a robber a few weeks earlier and needed a cane to help him walk. It was then that the elderly man kept a couple of pistols nearby.

The lead robber pistol-whipped the operator on the side of his right jaw and demanded that he go to the safe and open it. At that point, a young lady and her toddler walked into the station, and the lead robber pointed his pistol at her and shouted for her to stand with the other hostages.

On the way to the nearby safe, the operator made a feeble attempt to grab his pistol that was hidden under a newspaper on a shelf under the ticket counter. The lead robber struck him again and told him he'd shoot him and the clerk if he got out of line again.

With the safe open, the robber handed the operator a loot bag, and the operator quickly filled the bag with all the money in the safe.

The second robber had gone unsuspected as an accomplice. He wore a bolero tie and a business suit, and his young face portrayed innocence. He walked to the ticket counter carrying his pistol in his right hand and a bag that contained rope in the other. He tied the clerk's hands behind her back as the lead robber held a pistol steady at the operator's head. Then the owner's hands were bound similarly.

With the clerk and the owner tied up and the loot secured, they were not finished.

Addressing his hostages, he said, "Listen up, we gonna make this quick. Stand up and empty your pockets and bags, take off all jewelry; necklaces, watches....Put everything on the floor."

No one complied.

The young accomplice shot a bullet from his pistol into the ceiling, causing the hostages to face life or death; they began to comply.

The toddler cried and the robber's attention was drawn to him and the mother.

"Psst," John said to the man with the cane in front of him.
Nothing.
"Psst," John said again.
The man turned slightly toward John.
Talking softly, John said, "I'm going to try something. I need you to fall to the floor and pretend you can't breathe."

John had noticed a whiskey bottle in the man's jacket; he removed it and put it in his pants pocket.

"Fall to the floor," John whispered. The man was old, and he wasn't going to fall to the floor on his own. He needed help. John quickly kicked him in the back of the right knee, sending the man to the floor.

"This man needs help," John yelled. "He's not breathing!"

Both robbers walked to John and the man lying prostrate on the floor.

"How 'bouts I put a bullet in him to make sure?" the lead robber said.

"Please," John pleaded, "you don't have to do that."

As the lead man moved closer, John removed the whiskey bottle from his pants pocket and struck the lead robber on the head with it, sending him crashing to the floor. As the young robber lifted his gun to aim it at John, John quickly picked up the lead robber's gun that was surrounded by broken glass and said, "You don't want to do that. Drop it."

Someone yelled, "Shoot the sons of bitches."

John looked down at the man on the floor rubbing the back of his right knee. "Sorry about that."

The man grinned and said, "You wasted a damn good bottle of Jack Daniel's."

With John now in control, the hostages untied the clerk and owner, and the same rope was used by two hostages to tie the robbers' hands.

The police came, the robbers were arrested, the hostages were interviewed, and the police later closed the station, but not before they returned the money to the owner.

John had missed his ride to Mount Hope.

John lay on patches of grass under a shade tree near the station; he used the valise as a pillow, and his haversack stayed tucked at his side. He had dozed off for a couple of hours when the clerk accosted him and woke him by kicking his brogans with her moccasins.

John sat up.

"Hey, you," she said in a throaty German rumble. "That's a brave thing you did."

"Not really. But thank you."

"I'm Gretchen. I was on my way back to check on the doors to the station, and I saw you lying here."

She was a comely twenty-one-year-old, with sand-colored brown hair, which she wore in ringlets. She was petite and had full lips. She wore a blue cotton dress that stopped at mid-calf, revealing nicely shaped calves. She had come to the United States from Germany ten years before.

"You are …?"

"John."

"What are you going to do now?" she asked.

"Don't reckon I know at the moment. I'll catch the interurban tomorrow to Mount Hope. You will be open for business tomorrow?"

"Of course. Have you eaten?"

"No, ma'am."

"Well, a strong man like yourself needs to eat. I can fix you something at my place. I'm a really good cook."

John had been concerned that he could meet the fate of Professor Bodie if a certain white man got the wrong idea. The South was the South, and he had to tread carefully. He didn't want to die before making it to Mount Hope to fulfill his mother's request to find Cousin Riley and to live a bigger life that must be out there somewhere.

He walked alongside Gretchen carrying his haversack on his back and valise in his right hand as they walked a half mile to Gretchen's brick duplex home that she shared with her mother. She told John her mother had recently traveled to Germany to tend to her father. She had told him not to worry walking with her because if anyone had any questions, she'd just say he was her helper. Though the walk to her home was brief, his head remained on a swivel looking for any lurking danger regardless of what she had said.

John sat at a small round kitchen table. Gretchen removed a skillet from the cabinet and retrieved three eggs and one pound of sausage from the ice box.

They dined on omelets, biscuits, and bacon.

John told her about his trip from Richmond, and she told him about life in Germany and why she came to the United States.

"You're right," John said.

"About what?"

He peered into her gray eyes and thanked her for sating his appetite.

She bowed her head as a gesture of appreciation.

The specter of Professor Brodie popped into his head. "I best be moving on."

"Where're you going?"

"Don't know."

"Why don't you stay here tonight, wake up in the morning, and be on your way. You can sleep in my *Bett*. I'll sleep in *Mutter's Bett*."

John felt his neck tighten with the same rope that had sucked the life out of Professor Brodie.

He shook his head no and pounded the small table where they had just eaten. "No," he snapped.

She stood and placed her hand on John's left shoulder. John hunched his shoulders and swayed to remove her hand.

Gretchen was unmoved. "Let's go for a ride to the lake. You can decide later."

The day would be long, so it would be many hours before the interurban would depart to Mount Hope.

Expressing a slight interest, John said, "A ride?"

"It'll be fun. We'll take *Mutter's* carriage. I'll make a meal in case we get hungry later."

John wanted a way to fill the time before catching the interurban the next day. And he didn't want to stay closeted in the house with a white woman. He figured he'd spend most of his time outside as her assistant or driver, return for good night's rest, and walk the half mile to the station in the morning.

He threw caution to the side. "Okay, we'll go for a ride, but," he said, holding up his right forefinger, "I'm the driver." Gretchen placed the food in the back of the hansom, and John assumed the driver's seat. He snapped the reins and the nag moved forward.

She liked colored people because they were the underdogs, and because they felt a pain no other race experienced.

"How old are you?" she asked.

"Mama told me I was born in eighteen-seventy."

"You're two score. I'm two score plus one."

"What's a score?"

"Twenty years."

"Oh … "

"John, you're a tall and handsome man."

John felt obliged to return the compliment. "You're a pretty girl."

"I've known you for a few short hours, and I can tell you are a special colored man, a special man, period."

Ann surfaced in his mind, and he knew that whatever he was or was to become was because of her. And as much as he'd hate to admit it, the Billingslys also played a part.

John did not respond.

She moved to another topic. "Do you read books?"

"Yes," he said, recalling how he had become a strong reader with Father Murphy's help.

She asked another topic that had no connection to the last:, "Have you heard of Frederick Douglass?"

"I can't say that I have."

"He is a famous colored man, born a slave. He married a white woman." She paused, then added: "Love … affairs of the heart should respect no color line."

"What about affairs of the head?"

"See, you are a thinking man. But sometimes it's good to think with the heart. You have *wunderbar* qualities that a girl finds attractive."

They reached Gretchen's destination, a lake which was surrounded by dense trees and shrubbery. John was pleased.

Gretchen alighted from the hansom first. "Let's go for a swim."

John looked around; he didn't see anyone.

"Don't worry, no one will see us," she said.

He wasn't hungry, but he offered a pretext. "No, you go. I'll eat one of the sandwiches now."

She divested her clothes piece by piece. John caught a glimpse of her round bottom. As his eyes moved upward, she turned, and his eyes landed on her small breasts. She smiled at seeing John avert his eyes to avoid her nakedness.

She waded into the water, then turned around to John and said, "C'mon, get in, the water feels *wunderbar*," she said, capering in the water.

John looked at her, but he quickly turned away.

"You're impossible," she said.

As the seconds ticked by in John's mind, he worried that he'd be caught in the presence of a white woman and a naked one at that. No breach of a written law, but certainly a breach of Southern mores.

His anxiety began to lessen slightly as Gretchen finally emerged from the water. She retrieved her clothes and hopped in the hansom where she slowly donned them. "The water was exhilarating," she said. "Next time we swim together."

John was silent, but his eyes were filled with worry.

Nighttime did not come soon enough for John, but it arrived at last. "If you don't mind, I'm going to bed," he said.

"Of course." She pointed to her bedroom.

John soon doffed his shoes, pants, and shirt, leaving on only his union suit. He peeled back the counterpane and climbed into bed.

No sooner had he adjusted the thin pillow for his comfort than Gretchen entered her bedroom to retrieve her camelhair brush. She ambled toward the door, turned around, and said in a coquettish voice, "You must let me know if you need anything."

John smiled and nodded.

Suddenly, she turned around, sauntered closer to John, puckered her full rouge-colored lips, and said, "*Kussen sie mich.*"

The dappled bedroom light enlightened her smile. John's loins throbbed. *You should think with your heart,* she had said to him earlier. John picked her up, and gently sat her on the bed. She doffed her nightshift and slipped under the counterpane. John lifted the counterpane and tossed his union suit to the floor.

As Gretchen stroked John's chest, the spectral image of his nemesis—Madame Billingsly—appeared in front of him, hovering above him like a mythical beast flapping its wings and belching fire. He hated her all over again. Then the spectral image of Professor Brodie surfaced; he had a clear vision of the hanging preacher talking about how Southern white women must be protected from colored men—the white race could not be commingled with Negro blood, thereby diluting the dominant white blood.

Gretchen raised her head and looked into his distressed eyes. "It's okay, I want this," she said.

John didn't move.

"You know, *Mutter* told me to wait for the right man."

She had only known him for a few hours. But he wanted to believe that her motives were sincere.

"Did *Mutter* say anything about the right color?"

"Only to follow my heart."

She batted her eyes a few times in an added effort to inveigle John by breaking open his locked heart.

"You can have a lot of men; you're beautiful. And from what I can tell, head smart, too."

She rolled on top of him cheerfully naked. He felt her warm breasts pressed against his chest.

"I don't think we should ...," his unfinished sentenced died; only a muted disturbance in his head lived on.

After a few minutes, he cast her aside and sat up in bed with a panicked look on his face. His mind boiled with alternatives, schemes, solutions, each more hopeless than the last.

"What's wrong?" she asked.

Although John had come to believe her motives were sincere, that didn't matter. She was a roadblock to his fever to finally getting to Mount Hope.

There'd be no post-coital contentment for him. He rolled over and went to sleep. Gretchen kissed him on the chest, put on her clothes, and went to sleep in her *Mutter's* bedroom.

Gretchen toddled into the kitchen in the morning, where she was surprised to see John dressed and sitting at the kitchen table. His haversack and valise were at his feet.

"*Guten Tag*, John."

"That means ... ?"

"Good morning."

"Same to you."

She massaged his shoulders. "Listen to me. I want you to stay with me. I really like you. We can be like Frederick Douglass."

As he had ruminated all along about his need to move on, he knew that was best for his safety. Above all, he needed to find the life that would satisfy his injured soul. He extended his right hand and touched her right hand. He stood up and faced her. No need to discuss it. "I must be moving on."

"Fie, John! You don't have to leave."

He stood up and looked into her portentous eyes.

Two hours later, John was on board the interurban to Mount Hope.

Standing alongside the interurban, Gretchen shouted her valediction as the car pulled away. "*Auf Wiedersehen!*"

23
SUMMER, 1893

John had settled in Mount Hope but had yet to find Cousin Riley. He had asked around but came up empty. From time to time, he'd think about his mother and the Billingslys, but with his work as a young farmer, thoughts of them appeared less frequently.

He'd kept busy, though, working. He'd started off as a farmhand picking and planting cotton, tobacco, and produce. After over a year's time, he had saved enough money to buy a parcel of farmland and a small house. Operating his farm as a business proved difficult as his prices were low, and he was competing with white farmers who knew the area and whose families had farmed the area for generations.

After getting hold of a pamphlet that promoted the interests of colored farmers, he asked if he could join the group and ended up working for the Lawrence County Colored Farmers Alliance. Its mission was to advocate for better prices and market conditions through the collective actions of individual farmers. The farmer would buy into the Alliance and in return, it would publish a pamphlet letting them know the best prices and places to sell.

In time, John became a spokesman for the Alliance, speaking at meeting halls, talking with farmers, and attending exhibitions and fairs to learn about things such as soil fecundity. He was determined to give the colored farmers of Lawrence County the best advice the Alliance could offer.

One day, after talking to a farmer who had questions about corn prices, he boarded his wonky hansom and looked at the names of the farmers he wanted to talk to within the next hour. About ten minutes into his ride, he pulled the reins and the horse stopped. He looked to the right and saw a vast stretch of land that was filled with soybean and cotton. He spied a man he didn't recognize and as he got closer, he heard the man singing "Steal Away, Jesus."

The song immediately reminded him of his mother, who'd sung it all the time. The lyrics were coming from a tall, hulking man in his forties with apple seed-brown skin, massive arms and legs, and large feet that gave him the ability to do the work of a mule by plowing his field from sunup to sundown.

The singer held a hoe in his large hands. He turned around and stood looking at John. An oversized straw hat sat atop the man's large head to block the sun from his eyes.

John walked closer to the towering singer. "Excuse me," John said. "What's the name of the song?"

"Steal Away, Jesus," the big man answered in a tenor voice that didn't match his girth.

"Yes, I thought so," John said. "It's a wonderful song."

When John asked the towering man if he had an interest in joining the Alliance, he replied that he didn't have a farm and that the land he was working belonged to Mr. Ellis.

"I work his land. He give me a share of the crops. Sometime when he nice, he pay me something."

John knew about Mr. Ellis; he didn't like the mission of the Alliance and aimed to stop its work. If the coloreds worked together, Ellis was concerned they'd try to undercut his prices.

"I just had a word with Mr. Ellis. Seems like he doesn't like what the Alliance is doing."

He spat out tobacco and looked at John and said, "Mr. Ellis all right,"

"Say, what's your name?"

"Jimmy."

"I'm John."

"You from round here?" he asked John.

"I've been here for a few years. We have a hall meeting next Tuesday to discuss wheat prices. Why don't you come?"

After their words dried up, Jimmy returned to moiling the soil, each hack as efficient and economical as the next.

"Jimmy," John said, "next Tuesday. It's on Decatur Street."

Jimmy stopped hoeing. "You go to church?"

"No."

"You seem like a good man. Reverend Owen looking for good men. You come to First Baptist on Sunday; it's two miles from here. I'll think about going to the hall meeting."

Jimmy held open the door as the parishioners walked into First Baptist Church. He was dressed in a mottled white shirt with missing buttons, black trousers that were frayed at the hems, and boots with holes in the sides. John wore a black suit with a white shirt and blue tie. He saluted with his fedora at the door.

The church was a modest-sized, white clapboard building. The sides of the church were stippled with red poppies, and several cropped hedges stood near its front. A sign above the freshly lacquered oak door to the entrance of the building read COME UNTO ME.

Although it had room for over two hundred worshippers, it had begun to burst at the seams, thanks to people like Jimmy who were on the prowl for new recruits. Reverend A. J. Owen had developed a reputation as a fine orator. Once Jimmy brought in new members, Reverend Owen would try to keep them coming with his sermons, which were delivered with a spellbinding, rhythmic cadence.

"Morning, John," Jimmy said. Glory be to God. Glad you could come."

"I'm upholding my end of the bargain."

"Go on in; we starting in five minutes."

John took a seat in a rear pew.

Reverend Owen looked out at the nearly full church. He was a young minister, in his early thirties. He had red-boned skin, hazelnut-colored eyes, and short, black hair that had begun to recede slightly. He was persnickety about his attire. He wore a white shirt with a turnover collar and an ascot tie, a gray jacket, a matching waistcoat, contrasting blue trousers, and white spats adorned his polished, black, laced shoes.

Reverend Owen stood behind the altar and said: "Before we get started ... Tilla, come up here and give the church announcements."

John was in the rear and couldn't see Tilla approach the altar.

Tilla had a lilting and confident voice, a voice that betrayed an above-average education. John moved over to the right slightly to get a better view, which was only from the chest up. She wore a blue bonnet. Shards of sunlight made her look angelic.

Two minutes later, Reverend Owen said, "Thank you, Tilla. You may return to your seat."

John locked onto her as she went to her seat. He could see a quarter of the left side of her face after she sat in a pew full of people. He needed to find out more about her.

He missed a lot of the sermon. He kept stealing surreptitious glances at Tilla. On one occasion, she turned around slightly and caught John's gaze. Embarrassed, he quickly averted his attention elsewhere.

He was relieved when church ended. He was certain to see her close up, he thought.

Jimmy walked in his direction. John stopped him. "Jimmy, who is this Tilla girl?"

"She the daughter of Pony and Fannie Hawkins." Pointing, he added, "That be them there."

"Does she have a man?"

"Word is she seeing Roscoe ... She like them educated types. C'mon, let me introduce you to Reverend Owen."

They stood in line with other parishioners waiting to greet their pastor.

Reverend Owen said, "Good to see you, Jimmy, God bless you." He looked at John and said, "Is this young man with you?"

Jimmy nodded. "This here my new recruit."

"What's your name?"

"John Billingsly."

Reverend Owen shook John's hand. "John, you'll need to come back. I should like to introduce you to everyone when you return."

By the time John finished greeting Reverend Owen, Tilla had vanished.

24

SUMMER, 1893

The drizzly fall evening didn't stop the regulars and a few first-timers from lining up at the back of Riley's shanty to receive their fill of the best-in-town moonshine. The shanty was a single-story puncheon frame constructed from local pine, bound on two sides by covered porches. The shanty unfolded into a thicket of brush and tall pine trees, as good a place as any to conduct moonshine business.

Riley, Jr., or Junior as he was called to distinguish father from son, had learned the business at his father's knee, so when Riley's health deteriorated, Junior made the whiskey, filled the orders, and took the money, and when he saw fit, extended credit to some of their whiskey-imbibing customers. Junior had grown into a powerfully built twenty-five year old. He had caramel-colored skin, cinnamon-colored eyes, and specks of premature gray hair that he kept short.

A flicker of light from a lantern sitting on a table on the back porch, coupled with the moonlight, helped Junior meet the demands of his customers, who were athirst for Riley's brand of whiskey. Those in line brought their own bottles to be filled.

A tall man with a sallow, freckled face was next in line. Junior greeted him: "Mick, how you been?"

Mick was not only a drunk, he was a nosy drunk who had a knack for delivering news before it reached most people. "Question is, how you been? Heard the new sheriff's shutting down all the stills."

"Where'd you hear that?"

"I hear things," Mick said.

Junior handed Mick his refilled bottle, looked into Mick's grainy eyes, and said, "If you hear something a little more definite, let me know."

Mick nodded and smiled, revealing a toothless mouth. He turned away and raised the bottle to his lips.

"Mick, you forgetting something?" Junior asked with a raised eyebrow.

"You know I's good for it, Junior. I pays you when I can."

Mick was one of the customers who had a line of credit, one that was well beyond his means to ever repay. But because of his friendship with Junior's father and because he'd ring the alarm if he heard something about the new sheriff, he walked away with another free bottle of whiskey.

After filling his last bottle at two o'clock in the morning, Junior tidied up and went inside the house and stood in the kitchen doorway, where he saw his father still sitting in a rickety rocking chair with his dog. Sadie, a black-and-sandy-brown, mixed-breed bull terrier, was at his bare feet. The man's feet and ankles were ravaged with arthritis, which anchored him to the rocking chair. His eyebrows, bushy as a mustache, were hopelessly tangled. A jagged and ugly scar that streaked up the left side of his face glowed in the light of the lantern. His long lids rolled up and down his drowsy eyes.

Before Riley's vision began to fail, he amused himself by looking out his front window, counting the birds as they perched themselves on a tree limb in the front yard. He mustered a wee bit of excitement when blue jays cavorted in the tree, as though they were performing just for him. He expressed himself with a mixture of coughs and laughs when they started fussing loudly, reminding him of his arguments with his wife. When night fell, he often fell with it, sometimes well before. If he made it to his bedroom, Junior thanked God, for it seemed to be a miracle for Riley to break away from his mooring and walk just a few feet to bed.

Riley felt Junior's presence in the doorway. "The law catching up, son."

Junior shook his head. "What're you saying, Pa?"

Riley coughed a few times. He caught his breath from the strain of coughing and then said, "I reckon it's time to call it quits. My stuff's the best, but it'll kill you before too long. Don't know why I didn't stop a long time ago."

Junior walked into the small living room and sat on an uneven bench next to his father. He grabbed his father's left hand and felt bone. "Why didn't you? Why didn't you stop, Pa?"

"I knew that stuff made people sick, but the money was too good. The money helped your sisters build homes in Atlanta. But I done paid a price now. Look at me. Can't see. Got a weak bladder. I'm a mess, son." Riley was silent. His lids stopped moving. Just as Junior started to say something, Riley squeezed Junior's hand. "Your mama's been gone at least five years; you been here helping me with the business and taking care of your old man. No more. It's time to let me be. You got a life to live."

"But Pa ... "

"But nothing, Junior. You gotta find a wife and get busy having children."

It sounded like a dying wish to Junior, and he didn't want to hear any more about his father's regrets. "Pa, let me help you to bed."

Riley raised his left arm from the armrest, and Junior stood up and half-lifted his father from the wonky chair to help him to the bed. As he lay there, he told Junior to retrieve a corrugated can that was on the floor of his closet. "Open it."

Junior moved it closer to the lantern to see what it held.

"Don't know how much in there, but should be at least two thousand," Riley said.

Now Junior was sure his pa thought the end was near.

Riley told Junior to use some of the money for his burial; the rest would be his. He paused, then added: "I want Reverend Owen to bury me. I'm probably the biggest sinner in all of Mount Hope, but I know he'll bury me."

Riley remembered some unfinished business that he hoped Junior would work on. Riley told Junior that he'd once promised Cousin Ann that he'd one day return to Richmond to see her.

Junior knew nothing about Ann. He knew that his father's father was "some cracker" who'd worked for Chad Davis, the massa who'd sold Riley down the river. He knew that his mother died young. Beyond that, there was nothing.

His frail health had prevented him from traveling out of Mount Hope, much less traveling to Richmond. He told Junior that he'd probably never know the extent of his family, but perhaps Junior would find the answers someday. He'd be satisfied with that. And that would be his dying wish.

Before his health declined, Riley had been a sporadic member of First Baptist for several years. Junior offered to take him and be his eyes, but he begged off. He was content to bide his time by sitting in his favorite rocker, talking to his dog, and listening to the cantankerous blue jays.

25
SUMMER, 1893

Texas had beckoned. He'd had to meet with members of the Colored Farmers' Alliance there. He'd wanted to put it off, but he had no choice. Important speakers had gone, and he'd had to be there. Aside from making money from his farm crops, he also earned income from speaking fees. He'd been away for two weeks, two Sundays away from First Baptist.

The two weeks had dragged, but he had toughed it out. He couldn't remember her look so much as her voice. It was a voice that could soothe an angry lion, a voice that could make walls crumble down.

Back in town, he sat in a rear pew again, anticipating the sight of the young woman with the mesmerizing voice, but as it turned out, there were no announcements that Sunday; Reverend Owen jumped right into his sermon. John looked where she had sat three Sundays ago; she wasn't there. He then scanned the sanctuary for her but found no sign of her.

As best he could tell, she wasn't in the sanctuary. As he could not purge his mind of thinking of her, and his mind was not on the sermon, he rose and tiptoed out of the building.

The air was warm and still outside, just like inside the church. All open space was splashed with sunlight. He spied a red oak tree and loped to it and sat down with his back resting against it. Soon, he lowered his head and nodded off with his black fedora covering his face.

"Excuse me, shouldn't you be in there?" he heard a woman say.

"No, I'm fine," he mumbled.

"You're sure?" he heard another's woman say. But he knew and felt that voice; it was the voice he'd waited three weeks to hear. He sprang up and adjusted his hat.

"I'm Fannie Hawkins and this is my daughter, Tilla."

He willed himself to look at Fannie, otherwise he was afraid he'd stare rudely at Tilla.

"I'm John."

"Are you a member?" Fannie asked.

"No."

"Well, we gonna need to change that," Fannie said. "C'mon, Tilla, let's go. We're late enough."

Fannie and Tilla pivoted and hurried inside.

His eyes locked in on Tilla until she faded from view. Her body was as exquisite as her voice. If he returned to his seat, he wouldn't listen to the sermon; he'd stare at Tilla. He decided to remain outside to work up the nerve to talk to *Roscoe's woman*. He had not captured his quarry; far from it. Even so, he felt like he was flying through the ether toward the stars.

An hour later, Jimmy opened the door, and Reverend Owen took up a position just outside of it, ready to greet his flock.

The line moved slowly. John continued to collect his nerves and hoped they would stay in place.

Finally, Reverend Owen greeted Fannie by kissing her on the cheek. He did the same to Tilla.

As they walked away from the church, John ran in their direction, carrying his black fedora in his right hand.

"Excuse me," John hollered, "Fannie Hawkins!"

Fannie and Tilla stopped. John continued to run to them. He looked at Fannie first. She wore a strawberry red-colored hat and a long, mauve-colored broomstick dress that was flattering to her trim body.

He turned his eyes to Tilla. He saw now that she was achingly beautiful and taller than he recalled. The light blue, bustled cotton dress hugged her slender frame. Her silky, auburn hair was piled behind her head in a waterfall of curls secured by hair sticks and ribbons. He breathed deeply, then looked into Tilla's eyes and said, "I was wondering if I'd be permitted to talk to you."

"Well," Fannie said as she batted her eyes, "I'm a married woman, but thank you for the idea."

John chuckled. "Not you, Mrs. Hawkins."

Fannie extended her right hand. John raised it slightly and kissed the top of it.

Now that John's nerves were in place, he took note of mother and daughter. It was easy to see where Tilla got her powerful good looks.

As John lowered Fannie's hand, Fannie said, "A man with manners."

"What do you want to talk about?" Tilla asked.

John's nerves started moving again; he shivered as she talked. Fannie stood at Tilla's side.

"I'd like to see you?"

Tilla looked at Fannie. "Ma, do you mind if we talk?"

Fannie moved away to afford John and Tilla a bit of privacy.

"Well," Tilla said, "I suppose we can talk."

"How about Friday? Troublesome Creek has that wide bend near the blacksmith's shop. Meet me at three o'clock?"

Tilla emitted a wide smile and turned to Fannie and said, "We can go now."

Fannie was curious. "What's he want?"

"I suppose to go out."

Fannie stopped, causing Tilla to stop. She looked at Tilla, and said, "Now Tilla, I'm gonna give you a warning. You know you have Roscoe. Don't be a fool."

"Oh, Mother. I won't be a fool. Me and Roscoe will be together."

"Roscoe's going to that fancy school ... "

"Tuskegee."

"Yeah, that's it. Word is John is doing work for the Colored Farmers' Alliance. He's a farmer."

"How do you know so much?"

"Jimmy mentioned it."

Five days after his heart nearly stopped beating when he talked to Tilla at church, they met at Troublesome Creek. She knew she was making the right decision with Roscoe, but nothing was wrong with having a little male company before marriage. John had brought along perch, bread, and wine for a bit of plein air dining.

They sat on a grassy slope. Her posture was erect, John's slightly less so. John looked straight ahead at the creek as he spoke: "Why did you come here?"

She ignored the question. "Eat your food."

John took a bite of bread. "May I have an answer?"

"You said you wanted to talk."

"Yeah, I know, but why did you come?"

"You're new around here. I thought I'd get to know you. I might add that you're good looking."

"Oh, yeah?"

"Yeah ... "

It weighed heavily on his mind, and he needed to say it: "I don't have a college education, much less a high school one...."

"You seem educated enough."

"But not educated like Roscoe."

"That's an impolite thing to say. How do you know about Roscoe?"

"I hear things."

"Look, it's complicated. Feelings are complicated."

"I suppose you're right." He leaned toward her, closed his eyes, and aimed to kiss her on her sienna-colored lips.

She leaned back and turned her head. "What do you think you're doing?"

"Is it because I'm a farmer?"

She curled her lip and shot him an angry look. "The food is gone, and I think I better leave."

He immediately regretted acting like a masher and treating her like a minx. Even when she was angry, no austerity could diminish her lissome form and beauty. He grabbed her arm. "No, don't leave. I'm sorry. That wasn't fair of me. I'm more than a farmer."

Tilla's curled lip stretched into a smile.

He told her about his work with the Alliance and how he had worked to help colored farmers.

She extended her right hand and touched him softly on his right hand, then rubbed his cheek. The wine had begun to take effect. He felt she was receptive. Her touch and her flirtatious eyes made it worth the risk again. He closed his eyes and went straight for her lips. She didn't move. Within two seconds, she moved her lips around his. He untied her bonnet with one hand as his other hand held the back of her head. About twenty seconds later, he released his lips. And two seconds later, they did it all again.

A gaggle of squawking geese flying overhead pierced the slumberous afternoon. They looked skyward.

John looked down from the sky, then Tilla.

Pointing, John asked, "You want to go over to the cave?"

She smiled a puckish grin, and said, "I don't know."

She had sent another mixed and confusing signal, but he'd chance it. John stood and helped Tilla stand. They strolled in the direction of the cave.

26
SUMMER, 1893

The congregation was singing a hymn as John walked in and sat in a back pew. The woman next to him stooped slightly and gently pulled him up with her left hand. The lyrics were unfamiliar to him. Reverend Owen walked down the center aisle clapping as the congregation continued to sing.

Reverend Owen reached the altar, his waving arms stretched high. "You may be seated."

John was relieved at being able to sit.

"Before I get on with my sermon today, I want to introduce to you a young man who was with us a few Sundays ago. John, won't you come to the altar?"

John didn't move. Perhaps there was another John who fit that vague description.

Reverend Owen walked to the back and pointed at him. "Come with me, John."

John pushed himself up from the pew, pressed down his neat black trousers, and strode to the altar, anxious to get it over with.

"John, how about you tell us something about yourself?"

A blur of people stood before him. His words stood still.

He looked in her direction; she sat next to her parents. She said she wouldn't see him again because of Roscoe, and he was trying to force his feelings for her out of his heart.

Someone shouted, "All glory be's to God."

Reverend Owen nodded in a show of support.

"Good morning, I'm John. All glory be to God."

"Amen," someone shouted.

"Where're you from?" Reverend Owen asked.

"Richmond, Virginia."

"You're a long way from home," Reverend Owen said.

While nodding, John said, "Yes, I am."

"Well, John, the church would like for you to consider joining First Baptist. We can use a good man like you." Reverend Owen put his arm around John, adding, "John's being doing some good work for the colored farmers."

Reverend Owen released his hold and John happily returned to his seat.

"Oh, I do want to mention one other thing before moving on. We can stand to use a bit of good news. As you know, Brother Riley Davis departed this earth a few weeks ago. He gave generously to the church. Even though he stopped coming, he made sure to give to the church. The new church we're building is because of Brother Riley. Keep him in prayer."

Riley Davis rang loudly in John's head.

Two hours later, the sermon was over. The woman next to him nudged him. John moved out and joined the other congregants in line to shake Reverend Owen's hand.

A burly man waiting in line touched John on the shoulder and said, "Thank you for what you doing for the colored farmers."

"Oh, you're welcome."

Pony Hawkins got out of line and walked to John and said, "Excuse me." He extended his hand and said, "I'm Pony Hawkins."

John recognized him as the man who sat in the pew next to Tilla in the past.

"We'd like you to join," Pony added.

John studied Pony and saw a hint in his skin color and hair that led him to believe Pony could be a colored man. By the fact that he attended a colored church, John figured Pony was colored and wanted everyone to know it. "It seems to be a good church; good people here," John said.

Reverend Owen extended his hand, waiting for John to grasp it. "John, thanks for coming. Give it some thought."

Riley Davis still hung in John's mind. "Who's Riley Davis?" John asked the reverend.

"He was a member of this church."

"I really need to know more about him. It's important."

"Wait 'til I'm done greeting my people, then we talk."

Within ten minutes, Reverend Owen escorted John to his small office in the back of the church. John looked around. The bookshelf was well stocked. A large picture of Jesus in a wood frame hung on the wall behind the rosewood-surfaced desk. Reverend Owen sat nearly erect in his desk chair across from John with his hands clasped. "What do you want to know about Riley?"

It had been six years since his mother had sent him in search of Cousin Riley. It was a stab in the dark, but he needed to know whether he was close to finding his mother's dream. "My mama told me that if I ever made it to Mount Hope, Alabama, to look for her Cousin Riley," John said as he looked up at the pictures of Jesus with olive skin and frizzy hair. He added: "I don't know a last name."

"Riley was a member of this church for many years. He and his boy used to come. Not so much after Riley's vision and health began to fail."

"What about a wife?" John asked. "Does he have one?"

"She died a few years ago."

"Can you tell me what he did, where he worked?"

"I heard things; not really sure what he did."

"Wonder if there is more than one Riley around here?"

"Probably. Seems to be a common name."

Suddenly John thought of the scar Ann said Riley had on his face. "Mama said he had big scar on his face; came from a fishhook."

Reverend Owen paused and scratched his head with his left index finger and said, "Come to think of it, he did have some kind of scar like that."

John's eyes widened and his heart beat faster.

"You may want to talk to Junior. Maybe he can be of help."

"Who's Junior?"

"Riley's son. He's named after Riley.

"He has a son," John muttered. "What do you know about him?"

"Well, let's see; he called on me when he father's time was near, and I visited Riley, praying with him and for him. He had asked forgiveness for his sins; told him to talk to God about that one. A lot of it was difficult to hear—his voice was weak—but as far as I could make out his dying wish was that I'd pray for safe passage for Junior to make it to see a lady named Ann."

Excitement now rained in John's head as he thought of his mother. Tears welled in his eyes.

Reverend Owen handed John his white handkerchief that he removed from the breast pocket of his brown, light-tweed frock coat. "What's wrong, John?"

John wiped his tears with the handkerchief. "Ann is my mama. I haven't seen her in years."

"Good Lord," Reverend Owen said. "I don't know if Junior left yet. You may want to go to his father's house to see if he's still there." Reverend Owen told John that he too had a connection to Richmond. He had traveled there several years ago to meet with Reverend John Jasper of the Sixth Mount Zion Baptist Church. Large numbers of colored were drawn to Jasper's charismatic ministry. "I was blessed to hear his sermon "De Sun Do Move." But enough of this. Go find Junior." Reverend Owen told John how to get to Riley's house.

Reverend Owen stood and extended his hand to John, who in turn extended his, and they shook hands. John complimented the reverend on his natty attire and told him that the reverend was his sartorial inspiration.

John rode his favorite mixed-breed, cinnamon-colored swaybacked horse to Riley's house. He dismounted and surveyed the surroundings.

He walked up three crooked wooden steps, took four steps on the porch to the door, then pushed open the creaky door, where he was met by a musty smell of a house that lacked sufficient ventilation.

He stood in the mostly barren living room. "Anybody here?" He walked into a small kitchen with an uneven floor. "Anybody here?"

A dirty skillet sat on top of the wood-burning stove. Rat droppings dotted the floor. As John turned around to look out of the kitchen door window, a rat with a long tail charged out of the kitchen at full speed. He stamped the floor to convince the rat he was bigger.

As he turned the white porcelain doorknob to open the back door, the knob came off and thudded to the floor. He stopped in his tracks and listened intently. He heard only the faint pitter-patter of vermin.

A cat meowed. He followed the sound. The cat was resting on a urine-stained, thin mattress in a bedroom. A small dresser and two chairs were in the room. The closet door opened a little wider and another cat moseyed out.

He gave it another try: "Anyone here?"

It was a fragile idea, but he needed to hang onto it: Junior would find Ann in Richmond. And he'd try to get to Richmond in short order to meet Junior and to see his precious mother at long last.

With his head hanging low, he walked to his swayback and retrieved a Granny Smith apple from one of the panniers hanging on its rump. He took three bites and shoved the rest in the horse's mouth.

A whitetail hawk flew about, capturing his attention. Another one came into sight. Then another. He followed them as they flew toward the back of the shanty.

He loped toward the back but quickly slowed to avoid scattered piles of manure. Without warning his heart skipped a beat, and he stopped. When he started again, his steps were slower and guarded, the equivalent of raised eyebrows. Although he didn't meet Cousin Riley before he died, he was floating on a wing and a prayer that he was closing in on something that had eluded him for a long time—a relative who shared his blood.

As he resumed his steps, he felt the vibrations of a dog's growl. John's heart skipped two beats. The canine's bark felt like the roar of a lion; John worried whether he'd live another minute; he was defenseless and didn't want to make the wrong move. The beast roared even louder, and the beast's bristled hair was manifest.

John spied a long, thick tree limb three feet from him. He inched his way to it.

The salivating beast inched closer to John, cutting off his path to safety.

"Hold it right there," a man with a gravelly voice said from behind him.

John's heart thudded again, ready to jump out of his chest. The dog moved to within three feet of John, snout crinkled, long fangs exposed. John thought the animal was going to rip out his heart while it was still racing. The dog stared him down, seemingly waiting for the right moment to attack.

"Keep your arms in the air. Turn around real slow," the man said as he aimed his rifle at John's heart.

Satisfied that John was sufficiently petrified, the dog padded to the man's side and waited for a signal to attack.

John concentrated on the rifle that could snuff out his life faster than the dog.

The rifle was long. The man holding it was shirtless. Except for possessing an older man's steady gaze, the man was young, about John's age. He was compact, with taut abdominal muscles. He had the look of being able to move swiftly and efficiently.

"What're you doing here?" the man asked, swinging his rifle in the air to the right, signaling John to say something or perhaps face serious consequences.

"I'm looking for Riley's son."

"You must not be from around here. What do you want with him?"

Perhaps Reverend Owen's name would make an impression. "Reverend Owen of the First Baptist Church told me I could find Riley's son here," John said with his arms still raised.

"He ain't here. What do you want with him?"

"I wanted to catch him before he went to Richmond. Heard he might be headed that way to see my mama."

"Oh, God," the man said, his mouth gaping in disbelief. After about ten seconds, he said, "Ann's your mama?"

"Yes."

"I'm Junior." Pointing to the beast, he said, "That's Sadie."

Junior put the rifle to his side and signaled with his head that John could put his arms down. John blew out a sigh. Sensing all danger had passed, Sadie wandered off to patrol the house and yard like a disciplined sentry dog.

"Yeah, that's my mama's name."

They sat on the back steps. John told Junior about his promise six years ago to find her Cousin Riley.

"It took you six years to get here?"

John deflected the question. "You're still going to Richmond?"

Junior looked skyward. "I think Pa won't mind if I put it off. I gotta get to know my cousin."

27

SUMMER, 1893

Pony Hawkins saved the money he earned from being a well-known and sought-after carpenter and blacksmith with the hope of using it for educating his daughters, but with Fannie's fragile state due to losing Caroline, he used the money to buy a new home on two acres of farmland. He thought she needed a change of scenery to help repair her heart.

The brick house had a solid foundation: three bedrooms, a living room, large kitchen, a dining room, a small parlor room, and an indoor commode. Fannie kept herself busy by cleaning, cooking, and keeping her new home in pristine condition. Flower beds surrounding the house received daily care, as did her large doll collection.

As the sun worked its way to its peak on a cloudless spring day, Fannie poured water on newly planted red geraniums.

Tilla, having finished washing the dishes, ambled out of the house and greeted her mother.

Tilla wore a long white cotton lisle dress that was buttoned to the neck. Her hair was kept in place by a raspberry-colored straw hat with a green picot ribbon.

With a cheery smile, Tilla said, "Morning, Mother."

"How's my baby?" asked Fannie.

In a dialect she had practiced to add to her charm, Tilla said with flair, "I's do fine."

Fannie put down her pail of water and moved a few steps closer to Tilla, looked into her daughter's eyes, and said, "Please don't leave me, Tilla."

Tilla took Fannie's hand and guided her to the porch, where they sat. "What's wrong, Ma?"

Fannie slightly lifted Tilla's pearl necklace as to adjust it. "You know, I couldn't take it if—"

Tilla didn't wait for Fannie to finish. She knew Fannie was thinking of Caroline. "Ma, I'll always be in your life."

"There are a lot of menfolk ... " Fannie said, "who admire you."

Pony had spoiled Tilla, even more so after Caroline disappeared. He'd bought her modish clothes, let her buy anything she wanted out of the Sears Roebuck mail order catalog, and encouraged her to read books she could get from the new-fangled lending library. She had become accustomed to nice things and expected that her future husband would do the same thing for her. She had graduated from high school at sixteen and knew she'd be expected to marry within a few years.

Tilla still had her eye set on Roscoe Sutherland. Pony liked him, calling him an "up-and-comer." He had completed one year at Tuskegee Institute. His father owned a successful printing shop business.

"Speaking of men, I'm going to see Roscoe."

"He's a good boy. Do you like him?"

She feigned annoyance, saying in an exaggerated tone, "Mother."

After a twenty-minute stroll, she met Roscoe at his parents' house. The house was large for the community and the locals knew it belonged to the Sutherlands, the colored elite of Mount Hope.

As Tilla waited for Roscoe, his younger sister played the piano in the parlor. Tilla sat in a chaise lounge.

Roscoe walked into the parlor. He wore a white starched shirt, blue tie, charcoal pants, and jacket. He was an inch shorter than Tilla and stood on a solid frame. His black hair was closely cropped, and only his oversized ears put a dent in his good looks. His skin was a shade darker than goldenrod. He looked at his sister and moved his head sideways. The music stopped and his sister left the room.

Tilla and Roscoe sat across from each other, very decorous and proper, like a swain paying a call on a maiden.

After a few seconds, he patted the piano bench with his right hand. Tilla smiled, stood, and walked to him.

He looked Tilla in the eyes. "May I just say," he said, "that your eyes remind me of the softest day of summer. I've been writing poetry, all because of you."

Tilla giggled.

He struck a serious note. "Father has asked me about my intentions toward you." After an expectant pause, he continued: "He wants me to run the business someday. Imagine that. I want you to be a part of it."

"What are you saying, Roscoe?"

He fell to one knee and removed a ring from his coat pocket.

Tilla covered her mouth with her left hand.

"I need that hand," Roscoe said.

She extended her left hand to him.

"Will you marry me? Will you be Mrs. Roscoe Sutherland?"

Although she had long hoped for the engagement, she gave pause because her mind drifted to John; he wasn't as educated as Roscoe and didn't have Roscoe's pedigree, but she had felt something when she kissed John. She inhaled deeply and let it out: "Roscoe," she said, "yes, I will."

Roscoe slid the ring on Tilla's long narrow ring finger. He then stood up and kissed her on the lips. "Mr. and Mrs. Percy Sutherland will be delighted to hear the news," he said.

Emitting a smile that betrayed her feelings at the moment, she matched Roscoe's formal tone and said, "I'm sure Mr. and Mrs. Pony Hawkins will also be delighted."

Roscoe chuckled. "Won't you stay for dinner?"

"Of course."

28

SUMMER, 1893

Junior knocked on the door of the tiny, woebegone, wood-framed house that sat upon a rickety foundation. The house teetered a bit during strong winds, but it never fell.

Lillian answered the knock, saying, "Who be there?"

"Morning, Miss Crenshaw," Junior said through the door.

Lillian appeared in a dingy yellow cotton robe. Her hair was held in place by a white tignon. She had elegant cheekbones and skin the color of a copper penny. Junior could see where Goldie had gotten her melon-sized breasts and round backside.

"Morning, Junior. Now, I done told you to call me Lillian. I ain't old enough to be no Miss Crenshaw. Maybe when I gets some grandbabies ..."

She pointed to a rocking chair for Junior to sit. "What you done to my daughter?"

"Where's she?" Junior asked.

"Running errands somewhere."

"I ain't done nothing to her, at least I don't think I have."

"What're your intentions toward her?"

"I like her, that's all."

"And you know all that after two weeks?"

"I just know what I know, Lillian."

"You musta put something on her because she changed, started taking care of herself. I'm going need to go into town. If Goldie not back when I leave, you welcome to stay here. Make yourself at home. We got some chicory, hardtack; find whatever you want."

Twenty minutes after Lillian left, Goldie hadn't returned. Junior rose from his chair, walked around, and blundered into Goldie's room. The room was small but neat. An old cedar dresser and a full-sized bed crowded the room. He opened the top drawer of the dresser. He saw a jumble of things: necklaces, bracelets, broaches, scarves, gloves, the pink-and-white sachet he'd seen her with when he'd first met her. He closed the drawer and opened another where he saw what appeared to be a book. After picking it up, he realized it was a diary.

He thumbed through the pages, wondering whether to read any of it. The diary taunted him to open it. He turned to the last entry. Tears welled in his eyes after reading it. *Junyer make me feel gud. He make me feel spesshal like a lady.*

The front door squeaked open. Junior's heart raced as he quickly returned the diary to the drawer. He collected himself and sat on the bed.

As she turned to enter her bedroom, Junior stood up and said excitedly, "Surprise!"

"Junior," she said with shock in her voice, "what are you doing here?"

While he hugged her, he observed that the part of a scarf over hung the drawer, and the drawer containing the diary was not fully closed. "I came by to see my favorite girl."

"Where's Mama?"

"She said she was going to town, for me to make myself at home."

"In my bedroom?"

Junior ignored the comment.

She held onto him as they swayed back and forth toward the dresser. He picked her up and kissed her about the face while tucking the scarf into one drawer and closing the other.

She went to the kitchen. Junior followed and patted her on the rear each step of the way.

As she stood at the sink, Junior took note of the dress that sagged on her curvy body. He gamboled up to her, grabbed her around the waist, then squeezed tightly; she dropped the plate in her hand, which shattered when it hit the floor.

They laughed.

"You want something to eat?" she asked him. "Place your order."

While stroking his goatee, Junior said, "Hmm, I'd like to order a French kiss. Is that on the menu?"

"My man ask, he shall receive, and more."

Goldie sat on the bed and kicked off her shoes. The undressing ritual had begun. Junior doffed his boots and black wool socks. He unfastened the clips to his overalls allowing the straps to fall to the sides. He pulled down his overalls and stepped out of them. His white union suit went next.

In the excitement of doffing his clothes, he didn't see that Goldie was still dressed.

His spoony behavior slowed upon seeing her sagging eyes.

He moved closer to her as she sat on the bed. "What's wrong?" he asked.

She rubbed her hand on his stomach several times as though she was counting the number of crevices there. She sniffed and her voice cracked, as she said, "It's nothing, Junior."

She asked Junior to unfasten the hook at the top of the back of her dress. He did so while kissing her on the nape of the neck. She slowly shimmied out of her dress. She closed the jalousie and the room darkened. They stood face-to-face. Junior locked in on Goldie's large, whiskey-colored eyes. She reached for the counterpane, but Junior pushed her hand down.

He just wanted to hold her for a moment to feel her soft skin, but she wanted the refuge of the counterpane. Junior continued to stand face-to-face with her. She exhibited a saturnine sexiness that he found appealing.

She didn't want to lose him. She liked the walks to the park, jumping on his back for a piggyback ride, and the other zany things he did to make her laugh. She especially liked cooking for him. She'd have to trust herself and him.

29

FALL, 1893

Both John and Junior had promises to fulfill that were tied to Richmond.

After nearly four years of being in Mount Hope, John had succumbed to his inner demons and pushed full speed ahead to return to Richmond to see his mother. He didn't know if she was living in the same godforsaken cabin, or even if she was alive for that matter, but the trip would be worth it. He'd commit himself to searching far and wide to find her. And he even entertained the thought about stopping near *Billingsly* to offer penance for his misdeeds.

He had done well with his farm and the Lawrence County Colored Alliance. He hated himself for not returning earlier, especially after Billingsly had intimated that Ann could be harmed if he wasn't forthcoming about what happened to Madame Billingsly and the dreadful flasks. Settling in Mount Hope and working in the community had surpassed his need to see his mother. No more; it was time to lift the anchor.

Although he wanted to see more of Goldie, Junior agreed to accompany John to Richmond to see Ann. Junior would be Cousin Riley's stand-in—he'd tell Ann all about his father, what little his father had shared with him about being a slave for Chad Davis.

He and Junior were set to make the trip to Richmond. John had already planned the itinerary. John had his own money, and Junior had money from his father's whiskey still business. They'd reverse the course John had taken from Richmond to Mount Hope as much as possible, only this time they'd spend most of their time on a passenger train seated in the colored-only sections. Along the ride, they'd commiserate and tell each other they were glad they found each other. It was just the two of them and Ann in the world that shared the same blood, as far as John knew.

Dreaming about Richmond, he'd envision Ann's powerful smile when he'd tell her how he first met Junior. He'd envision years of heartache for him and his mother wiped away with their reunion. And he'd tell Ann why he'd left Richmond; he'd promise her he'd return the flasks to the rightful owner.

They'd bought their train tickets and were scheduled to leave the next day, but in the meantime, a night out at the Blind Tiger was in order.

John was never a big carouser. But because he had kept his head down and worked hard, he felt he could relax a little. The more alcohol he imbibed, the more forward his tongue had become, which for him led to several men jumping him and breaking a couple of ribs. He wished Junior had been there; Junior's powerful frame would have either deterred the attackers or made the fight more manageable for John. Instead, he was somewhere entangled with Goldie.

With broken ribs, he was immured in his rented five room abode. He walked little and said little for five days, as he swallowed the price of two tickets.

During his convalescence, Junior and Goldie took food to John and worked to nurse him back to health. To speed up recovery, Junior paid a young woman with an ample bosom and a cheery smile to help John where needed. But they just talked, and she proved to be a good listener. When his mind was not on his farm, the Alliance, or his mother, he'd dream about Tilla and wonder if she was out of his league. But the dreams would quickly vaporize because it was not to be. He was smart and handsome with good skills; he knew he'd find someone else soon. Perhaps that would be in Richmond, where he'd get married and his mother would dote on her grandchildren.

John healed up within two weeks. He purchased tickets for Junior and himself. The day had come for him to leave for Richmond.

He had already said his goodbyes to Reverend Owen, and some of his parishioners. Fannie and Tilla had missed church after Pony died. John asked Reverend Owen to say goodbye to them for him.

His bags lay at the door. As he had always done while traveling, he packed light. He picked them up and walked to the hansom cab he'd retained to take him to the station. He threw his bags in the back of the hansom and climbed aboard. The clouds parted, giving way to sunshine as the driver snapped the reins and his two dobbins lurched forward.

A voiced called out. "John! John Billingsly!"

Nothing was going to stop him from going home to see his mother. Not this time. He ignored the call.

The same voice called out again: "John, it's Tilla. Stop! Won't you stop?"

"Should I stop?" the driver asked.

John hesitated. He had fallen in love with her voice when he'd first heard her speak at church. Though the voice was the same, a voice that had conquered his heart, mind, and soul, the magic was gone. It was better that way; it'd be easier for him to get to Richmond to have his reunion with his mother. An interruption of a few seconds on his long journey ahead couldn't hurt. And he'd now have the chance to tell her goodbye. "Yes, stop."

He turned in his seat. Tilla lifted her hem and ran toward the hansom.

He jumped down and spoke first. "I'm so sorry about what happened to Mr. Hawkins. I wanted to tell you at church, but I haven't seen you."

Eyes that looked like they had cried for weeks couldn't derail her beauty. His eyes drifted from hers and landed on her humdrum calico mutton leg-sleeve dress. Something wasn't right.

"I know. It's been hard on Mother and me." After a pause, she said, "I need to tell you something before you leave." After another pause, she said, "I'm pregnant."

"Well, I think Roscoe will be a good father. You'll have a good life with him. But thanks for telling me. I must be moving on. I'm going to see my mama in Richmond."

"It's not Roscoe's; I never did it with him."

She had cheated on Roscoe. But he didn't care. He was more curious than anything. "Well, who's the father?"

She arched her brow and widened her eyes, waiting for him to figure it out.

He remembered the one encounter they'd had a couple of months ago before she became betrothed to Roscoe. "No," he said, "it can't be. That's impossible."

Touching her stomach with both hands, she said, "This is the impossible ... It's yours."

"Have you told Roscoe?"

"No."

"Why not?"

"Roscoe's not for me. We're no longer together."

"Does Mrs. Hawkins know?"

"No, I thought you should be the first to know."

John's eyes went vacant and a moment of silence ensued.

Richmond beckoned, and he was ready to set foot there again, ready to face his demons. After five years away from her, his mother was the lacuna in his life that he sorely coveted. He pictured her toothy smile in hearing that he had found Cousin Riley's son. He'd move her out of that godforsaken slave cabin and find a new place for them to stay with the money he had saved. He'd find that bigger life back in Richmond. His affiliation with the Colored Farmer's Alliance helped him understand the labor, business, and political aspects of running a farm. Someone would want his skills. Or perhaps he'd start his own business. And he'd come clean and tell her about the flasks. Things were looking up.

He turned and walked to the hansom, climbed aboard, and sat for a few seconds as the driver waited for instruction. He jumped down from the hansom and walked to Tilla, who had not moved.

Tilla spoke after the awkward pause. "Will you come see the baby? Come anytime."

The dobbins nickered, and John looked at them as a way to temporize.

Finally, after ten long seconds, Tilla moved closer to John and said, "John, a girl isn't supposed to say ..."

John turned to Tilla. Feelings for her that he thought he'd drowned at the bottom of his heart rushed to the surface. His heart whooped and ineffable ecstasy washed over him. At long last, he had corralled his maiden beauty.

"A girl needn't say it. Tilla, I love you."

Using both hands, he cupped her face and kissed her deeply.

The driver clapped, and then said, "You go on and get your bags."

30
WINTER 1894

The new church that Riley Davis and Pony Hawkins had helped fund was finished. Reverend Owen sat in his new office.

The Norman Gothic structure was nearly three times as large as the original. The interior was striped horizontally with terra cotta, green, blue, all colors of the rainbow. Little cherubs leaned on their crossed arms looking down from the vaulting, and between them were large cockle shells. The crowning glory was the three medallions in the chancel on either side of the altar; in each was painted the head of an angel with long flowing hair. There were five stained glass windows along both sides of the sanctuary. The transfiguration window showing Peter, James, and John accompanying Jesus to a mountaintop where they see the transfigured Christ converse with Moses and Elijah was Reverend Owen's favorite.

The sanctuary consisted of a simple building on a raised basement with a crenellated bell tower centrally placed on the front façade of the building. Wooden finials decorated the corners of the tower. The church exterior was made of red common brick. Round brick arches, brick corbelling, and brick piers divided the bays of the building that characterized the exterior treatment. The cornice consisted of brick corbelling and a small wooden boxed cornice. Within the sanctuary, there was first floor pew seating and upper balcony pew seating. The clerestory consisted of the choir loft and a large segmental-arched art glass window.

Reverend Owen sat at his desk sans his jacket, something he did rarely. He rolled up his freshly starched shirt sleeves, then sat down.

"Thank you for coming," he said to John and Tilla as they sat across the desk from Reverend Owen.

Tilla held John's hand tightly.

"You been coming to church a few months now and I can tell that you're quite an impressive young man. You're doing a lot of good for the colored farmers. You got your own farm, place to live. You're doing things for this church."

Tilla squeezed a little tighter, and John looked into her eyes that shone with a limpid luster. He took her right hand and with his thumb caressed the tender web between Tilla's thumb and forefinger.

Reverend Owen looked at Tilla, whose face was aglow with the excitement of being a first-time mother. "I understand you've got something in the oven."

Tilla's stomach was still flat, but she rubbed it with her left hand. "Yes," she said letting loose a beatific smile that could melt an iceberg.

Looking at John, Reverend Owen said, "You gonna be getting married, son, and I'm honored that you asked me to marry you."

Tilled interjected, "Mama would have it no other way."

"I've counseled lots of couples on marriage. I'll tell you what I told them. Marriage is about love and respect. John, you must attend to the emotional needs of your wife, and Tilla, you must always give and show respect to your husband."

John's eyes begged for a meaning. Reverend Owen continued: "Think of a bank where you make deposits and withdrawals. When you make a deposit of love, you will be able to withdraw some respect." He turned slightly and looked at Tilla. "And Tilla, when you make a deposit of respect, you can withdraw love. Understand?"

Silence.

"It's simple: you need to speak and know the language of love. There are many, but I'll give you five things I want you to remember. Women liked to be touched. Give your wife hugs; kiss her and slap her on the rear, but not too hard."

John and Tilla laughed in unison.

"Women like gifts. They also like words of affirmation; tell her how she looks to you. Look at her and say, "Honey, you're beautiful."

John was silent.

"Go ahead, say it, John."

John looked adoringly at Tilla's visage, focusing on her lustrous protruding orbs. From the beginning, John had admired Tilla's bewitching blend of brains and beauty and believed he'd claimed a prize that would make even his mother smile.

"Honey, my precious stone, I'm so blessed to have a beautiful and smart woman like you."

"Wow, man, you're a natural." Reverend Owen continued. "I can't stress this one enough—spend quality time together," he said looking at both of them. "The last one is to do acts of service. If she asks you do something, try to do it, John. But Tilla, I say to you, be careful what you ask your man to do."

Tilla nodded.

"Okay, any questions?" Reverend Owen asked.

John and Tilla looked at each other, then shook their heads sideways, almost imperceptibly.

"I'm going to get your marriage license tomorrow," he told the betrothed couple.

He opened a drawer to his desk and retrieved a piece of paper and slid it toward Tilla. "I want both of you to write your names and the year of your birth on this paper."

Tilla moved the paper close to her, then picked up the pencil on the desk and signed her name—*Otilla Hawkins*. She added the date—*1876*. She slid the paper toward John, who gently took the pencil from Tilla. He was struck by Tilla's curlicue penmanship. It was the first time he had seen Tilla's signature. *John Moses Billingsly; 1870.* John slid the paper to Reverend Owen.

"Otilla Hawkins and John Moses Billingsly," Reverend Owen said aloud.

Suddenly, John thought about the Billingslys in Richmond. He didn't want their name attached to his, his wife's, his kids'. "Reverend Owen," he said using his right index finger in a gesture for Reverend Owen to give him the paper, "I need to make a change."

John crossed out Billingsly and wrote *Davis*. John showed the change to Tilla, who evinced her approval by nodding. He then handed the paper to Reverend Owen.

"Why the change, John?"

John explained he decided to adopt the new name to show his kinship to Junior.

"I told my mama that I didn't like the Billingsly name. That's the name we took after slavery ended. Mama told me I could change it so long as I didn't change the names she gave me—*John Moses*."

"Well, let me be the first to call you Mr. Davis."

Reverend Owen looked at Tilla. "And on January tenth, you'll be Mrs. Davis."

John would later have his new surname officially changed at the right time.

Fannie soon forgot about Roscoe. Her husband was gone, and she had to be happy for her daughter. As best she could, she tried to let her daughter's wedding distract her from thoughts of Pony. His killer was never found. Cecil Thornsberry coveted a tract of land that Pony owned; Thornsberry wanted the land to build a general store, as the location would be ideal. When Pony refused to sell the land at a deep discount, Thornsberry hired a gunman to kill Pony. But before he shot Pony, the gunman forced him to sign his name on a fraudulent deed, which Thornsberry later had officially recorded.

Fannie took charge of the wedding, inviting people, doing the cooking along with some women from church, and making the seating arrangements. But inevitably, thoughts of Caroline and Pony surfaced from time to time, as well as the thought that Tilla was leaving her to be with her new husband.

John's emotions ran from euphoria to melancholy. He'd found the woman he'd coveted. The combination of Tilla's smarts, patience, affability, culinary skills, and powerful good looks proved irresistible.

The day before the wedding, John placed his clothes on his bed, making sure all the necessary pieces were accounted for. He could not depend on Tilla's help; she was staying with Goldie. He made a mental note of his matrimonial togs. Black, lightweight, single-breasted, wool frock coat. Check. White cotton, button French-cuff shirt with turned up collar. Check. White ascot tie. Check. Black, lightweight wool, five-silk-covered-button vest edged with black silk grosgrain. Check. Contrasting-striped, black, lightweight wool trousers. Check. Black Oxford shoes. Check. White spats. Check. Black cotton socks. Check. White pocket handkerchief. Check. Watch and watch chain. Check. Silver cuff links. Check.

Satisfied all pieces were accounted for, he sat on the edge of the bed and stared ahead with Richmond, his mother, and Douglas on his mind. Where his impending nuptials brought half his heart to a high, thoughts of his mother and Douglas plunged the other half to a low. He wished his mother could attend the wedding—he cursed himself for not making more of an effort to locate her and bring her to Mount Hope. But he convinced himself his mother would be content to have him married no matter the venue. Douglas of course would have been his best man—the man to whom he owed his life. And as far as John knew about state-sanctioned private prison camps, Douglas had forfeited his life to an abyss of a hellhole.

After a few seconds, he stood and took a few steps to the pine wood chest of drawers in the corner of the bedroom. He opened the top drawer and removed one of the two flasks that he purloined from *Billingsly* seven years ago. He sedately shook the flask. He heard nothing. Yet he removed the cap and turned the flask upside down, shaking it a few times. Empty.

He ambled to the kitchen and removed a bottle of Jack Daniel's from the kitchen cabinet above the wood stove. He removed the cork and slowly filled the flask with the eau-de-vie that he'd somehow hoped would raise his spirits. After taking a swill, he shivered.

He stepped outside to gauge the temperature. It was a balmy day, Tuesday mid-morning; an overcoat was unnecessary. He'd be comfortable in his dark brown wool sack suit and derby.

As he meandered along the dirt road leading him away from his house, he thoughtlessly imbibed from the flask. He hadn't eaten breakfast, and his last bite was around eight o'clock the night before. Before long, the alcohol sluiced straight into his bloodstream. His steps became less sure, and he blundered hither and yon.

Dusk had arrived. All cooking was done. One thing left to be done: Tilla needed to don her wedding dress; she hadn't seen it since she was fitted for it at Bernstein's Haberdashery three weeks ago. Fannie kept it under close watch in a closet.

Fannie removed the long gold dupioni-silk dress with pearl-edged double sleeve flounces in silk and ivory lace. The lightly boned bodice had back lacing. Fannie laid the dress on her bed. Goldie gawked at it.

Tilla quickly doffed her floral, woven, cotton-lined bodice broomstick dress. Goldie helped her put on the bodice. Fannie held the dress gingerly as Tilla stepped in it with her right leg, then her left. Fannie pulled up the dress where it briefly stopped after meeting the curves of Tilla's hips. With a wag of her hips the dress continued its slide up Tilla's torso. She put her left arm in the left sleeve first, followed by the right. Tilla turned around and Goldie fastened the back of the dress near the neck. Tilla walked over to the large oval mirror in Fannie's bedroom and looked at the doppelgänger who stared back at her. She smiled broadly. She then turned ninety degrees showing off her sinuous profile in the agreeable mirror.

"How do I look, Mama?"

A glint appeared in Fannie's eyes. "Dazzling, Babe. Simply dazzling."

The glint quickly disappeared. "What's wrong, Mama?"

Fannie stroked Tilla's left cheek with the back of her hand. "Oh, I wish your father could see his beautiful daughter right now. He'd always told me you would be a beautiful bride someday."

"Papa said that?" Tilla asked.

Fannie nodded.

"Remember when you asked me which day of the week you should get married on?"

"Of course I do."

"It was your father who wanted you to get married on a Wednesday, so that's what I told you."

"But why Wednesday?"

"Your father was a bit superstitious. He wanted you to have lots of kids, and thought getting married on a Wednesday would somehow help. He said getting married on a Monday was for health; Tuesday was for wealth, Wednesday was best of all, Thursday was for losses, Friday was for crosses; Saturday was for no luck at all."

"I never knew that," Tilla said.

"Did you know that, Goldie?" Tilla said.

"Can't say that I did."

"Goldie, please tell me my matron of honor has her dress ready to wear?"

"Girl, you know I do."

It was seven o'clock in the morning and the weather had turned a bit colder.

—⚬—

Junior rapped on John's front door. He was dressed and ready to go, a full five hours before the wedding. He wore a navy-blue coat with covered buttons and matching waistcoat, black trousers, short turnover shirt collar, floppy bow tie, and black high-low boots.

After standing at the door for several minutes, Junior sat down on a small wood bench near the door, believing that John was still in bed. After a few more minutes, he stood up and called John's name several times.

No response.

"John, are you there?" he hollered.

He walked to the back of the house where he was met by two white and brown beagles. "Where's John?" he asked them.

A harsh sounding noise came from the front of the house. Junior moved in the direction of the noise. As he neared the front of the house, he saw a man lying motionless on his side on the porch.

Junior ran to the man.

"My God, John. What happened to you?"

He lifted John off the porch.

John reeked of alcohol. He groaned as Junior straightened him to reduce John's increasing shaking.

Junior reached into John's pocket, retrieved the door key, and unlocked the door. After taking a few steps inside the living room, he pushed Junior aside and ran out the front door where he threw up.

John sat at the kitchen table, removed the flask, uncorked it, and turned it upside down as he put it in his mouth. It was empty. He rose and slowly walked to the cabinet, looking for another bottle.

Junior cut him off. "Look, man," Junior said, "I gotta take care of you. No more of that stuff. You getting married in a few hours."

John flailed his arms, knocking Junior's arm out of the way.

Junior grabbed John from behind, holding his chest with his powerful right arm. He backed up and forced John to sit down.

"Don't move."

As he moved away from John, he pointed his right forefinger at John as to tell him to stay put.

"You need something in your belly."

Junior fired up the wood-burning stove. Soon the water was brought to a boil. He poured the water over the grits and sat the bowl in front of John.

"Eat, dammit," Junior screamed.

John flinched at the scream. He took his first satisfying spoonful of grits. He put down the spoon and looked at Junior with apologetic eyes.

"Now finish that while I fill the tub."

Junior made several trips to the bathroom where he emptied hot water into a white galvanized iron bathtub.

"Okay, get in the tub. You smell foul, man."

John doffed his coat, followed by his shirt, then pants. Each piece of clothing lay wherever he threw it. Finally naked, he put his right leg in the tub and quickly yanked it from the water as it was too hot.

"Just get in, or I'll throw you in."

John finally spoke his first words. "Wait," John protested, "I've got sensitive feet."

Junior looked at John's feet; the discoloration was evident. "What happened to your toes?"

"I got frostbite in Birmingham."

"What happened?"

"Tell you later."

John tested the water again a few minutes later. This time it met his satisfaction.

"Where's the soap?" Junior asked.

John pointed to a small cabinet on the floor. As Junior bent down to open the cabinet door, he tasted gossamer cobwebs. He pursed his lips to blow out the cobwebs and opened the cabinet to retrieve a bag of powered almond soap; he poured a heavy dose in the tub. He yanked a cotton wash cloth from the towel rack and began to scrub John's back. John raised his right arm high, and Junior scrubbed John's axillary area. John raised his left arm high, and Junior scrubbed again. He tossed the washcloth in the tub and said, "Okay, hurry up, you on your own now."

Within a few minutes he stood. Junior threw him a towel. After drying off, he wrapped the towel around his waist. He had reached his full height of six feet, two inches tall. He had added more pounds to his slightly muscular frame.

At twenty-three years old, there was no need to shave; he didn't have much facial hair, or much body hair for that matter. He brushed his wavy hair with a coarse swine bristle comb.

He placed his right hand about six inches from his mouth and exhaled, letting out a burst of warm moist air. He took a dollop of charcoal tooth powder from the tin container sitting on a stand next to the sink and placed it in his mouth. Mixed with his saliva, the powder turned into a sticky paste. He used his tongue to distribute the paste throughout his mouth, then brushed his teeth with his wooden horsehair bristle toothbrush.

The clock was ticking. Less than one hour to go. John looked at the wedding clothes he'd laid out the day before. Everything was still there. He threw the towel on the chair in the corner of the bedroom, then walked over to his bed and donned his cotton union underwear. He tugged on the gusset to make sure he had breathing room in the groin area.

Fifteen minutes later, John walked out of his bedroom, looking like a soigné bridegroom. He made a mental check to make sure he had not forgotten anything. He put his finger in the air as if to say wait. He ran to the bedroom and retrieved his overcoat. All was now in order.

Looking at John, Junior said, "It's a miracle how you cleaned up. Now, let's go."

As he patted Junior on the shoulder, John quipped, "Can I at least enjoy these last few minutes of freedom?"

As they walked alongside each other, John was thankful for Junior. He knew he should not have drunk to excess, but it was his way of dealing with demons that had continued to haunt him; he just thought the alcohol would excise them from his mind.

He had come close to missing out on his wedding, for which he figured Tilla would never forgive him, and for that matter neither would Fannie and his mother.

31

LATE DECEMBER 1899

Ever since John assumed the operational duties of running *The Messenger* three years earlier, he spent less and less time at home with Tilla and their three children, Theo, Bessie, and Eunice. His income from *The Messenger* and his farm was just enough to keep a lid on Tilla's emotional need for him to spend more time with the family. She knew what it was like for her father to dote on her, and she expected her husband to deliver the same to their children. She knew that she and the children were competing for John's time, but she'd give it a while longer before she'd consider saying something.

John had provided her with a nice house. They lived in a Folk Victorian home that had a charming pastiche. Built on a native limestone foundation, the house had a southeast corner turret, fish scale shingles, and a distinct attic dormer. The home had four bedrooms, a large living room and dining room, a modest-sized kitchen, and a bathroom, which had a toilet, sink, and tub with running water.

At twenty-three, she was content with her life. She was keeping her part of the conjugal relationship. She dedicated herself to studiously attending to managing the house and taking care of the children while John ran his businesses.

The Messenger, a weekly newspaper, was a hit in the colored community from the beginning. Women liked it because it contained information about marriages, deaths, society stories, sales prices. Men liked it because they relied upon it as a source of news, rather than getting the news from a local newspaper that was run by whites, who had little to no interest in running stories that Negroes cared about. And it was not afraid to tackle issues that hit the colored community hard. John knew that even with the amendments to the Constitution abolishing slavery and giving equal rights to all citizens, the South was determined to rebuild the opprobrious monument to white superiority. *The Messenger* would act on the inertia of a culture that acted as though manumission was nothing more than an abstract notion.

John's inspiration for some of the articles in his paper drew from his experience in Richmond and as an itinerant before settling in Mount Hope. He knew that Douglas, his best friend who had shepherded him from Richmond to Birmingham, left Richmond because he wasn't going to get a fair trial for accidentally bumping into a white girl. And Birmingham taught him that the word of a colored man could not be counted on to use as testimony in court against a white man.

John lit the fuse that would sear the hearts of many whites when he gave the go-ahead for Jethro Dawkins, his eristic reporter, to run a story about how the "vile anti-miscegenation laws" were just another piece of legislation designed to "let colored men know that they best keep their mitts off white women." Jethro rejected the self-effacement of many in the colored community, and he used John's newspaper as his bullhorn. John had approved the story because he thought that something was wrong when his white father had had his way with his mother but could act as though the rape never occurred.

It wasn't long after Jethro's volatile column appeared in *The Messenger* that it made its way into the discourse of conversation in the colored *and* white communities.

The fuse had detonated. One local white newspaper noted, "*The Messenger* is seeking to plot the destruction of the white race through miscegenation. John Davis has a lot to answer to."

No explanation offered by *The Messenger* on its position on anti-miscegenation laws could come close to mollifying angry whites who saw John Davis's paper as a threat to white Southern womanhood. An organized effort was needed to convince John he was playing with fire, that he was jeopardizing the welfare of colored folk in Lawrence County, and indeed throughout all of Alabama.

Formed ten years ago, the White Citizen's Council was part lobbying and part terror. It lobbied politicians and business interests to do things that would ensure the superior status of whites over coloreds. It terrorized Negroes whom they believed needed to be "taught a lesson." The lesson often came in the form of lynching and the burning of houses.

The Council made its decision: either John issue a retraction regarding Jethro's story or be made to "feel the pain."

John stood in the small pressroom talking to one of his pressmen when another worker told him that a "Chester White" wanted to see him. John stepped outside in the balmy December weather and saw a man dressed in a white shirt and beige pants puffing on his pipe.

"Yes, sir," John said. "What can I do for you?"

White offered no pretense. He had alabaster skin and was a middle-aged man with thick unruly brunette hair, a scruffy beard, and a pea-sized black piliferous mole just to the left side of his wry nose. Removing his pipe from his wide mouth, he said, "Look, there's no need to start trouble here in Lawrence County. This county is quiet, and we aim to keep it that way."

For the past few years, John's paper had helped him gain a wide measure of respectability in his community. He was a deacon at his church, dispensed advice to quarreling neighbors and friends, donated time and money to various progressive causes, and perhaps most importantly, some local politicians sought his support. With his climb upward, he had learned to present himself in a certain way. And indeed, the first impression one had of him was of extraordinary urbanity and poise.

He removed his jaunty hat as his mind raced to find a hint of what White meant. He found none: "Can you clue me in what you mean?" John said, with eyes wide open, begging for help.

White emitted a hearty laugh while rubbing his large belly that spilled forward and seemed more appropriate on another body. He quickly pivoted from laughter to indignation. "You damn well know what I'm talking about!"

John took a few steps away from the front entrance of the building, looking, trying to determine whether White was alone. Too many trees; others could be hiding. Best to invite White inside to talk to him in private. "Why don't you come in; we can go to my office to discuss what's on your mind," John said using his left hand to point the way inside the building.

"Ain't no need to go inside," White huffed. "You want a clue, huh?" White paused, scratched his fawn-colored beard, and edged closer to John. "How about this? We don't like what your filthy paper is doing, stirring up trouble and all. We want you ..." he said, then corrected himself, "we're telling you to write a story in that rag of yours telling your readers that you gonna retract the story about your crazy belief that black men should be permitted to marry white women."

John was now facing a bully, and looked into the bully's eyes that now were flush with rage. But John was determined at this moment to stand by what he had learned and believed. To see a man get beat by someone is one thing, but to get beat by himself would be a tragedy. "Mr. White, sir, I can't retract a story that traces its foundation to the Declaration of Independence."

White crinkled his nose and shook his head in disbelief at what he was hearing.

John pressed on: "We're entitled to our share of the Declaration of Independence. The point of the story is not about interracial marriages; it's about fair treatment of the races."

White clinched his pointy teeth and snarled, "You getting cross with me?"

"No, sir. There is a free press in this country and my paper has the right to publish that story."

White's blinkered views didn't surprise John, especially where people like White claimed ownership of the Declaration of Independence and the Constitution but didn't care to read it. But his sublime stupidity couldn't be ignored; it was built on intimidation with a powerbase.

"That don't give you no right to stir up trouble," White said.

John started to say something, but White stopped him by holding out his pudgy right hand; he had heard enough. His mouth trembled with anger from John's forward tongue. "I ain't going to stand here and argue with you. You've got two weeks to retract that story. Today's the fourteenth. I'll be back for your answer on the twenty-eighth at high noon; count on it."

As White turned to walk away, John said, "Can't do that."

White turned slowly and looked at John, who stood ramrod straight, his erect body telling White he wouldn't back down. White was nonplussed. He was used to getting his way. Like other predacious members of the Council, he expected colored folk to truckle to his demand. Refusal and obstinacy of an enemy in the past had led to dragooning by the Council.

As his blood was now beginning a slow boil, he knew a more direct threat was needed. He stroked his dewlap a few times while looking at John through eyes that matched the sneer that framed his mouth. Pulling on his braces, White said, "I suggest you think about it. It'd be a shame if something was to happen to this building and to your lovely wife."

White removed his pocket watch from his pants pocket and let it dangle from the chain attached to it. He swung it back and forth all the while saying, "Tick, tock, tick, tock. Time's awasting, boy." White spat a thick wad of tobacco juice on the ground for emphasis.

John was suddenly consumed with anger as White's words scarified him and dug into bone marrow. His usual bright mahogany-colored face was flushed red with rage: White had threatened his wife, his newspaper. He willed himself to stay calm, not play into White's slimy hands. People like White were like feral felines, desiring to catch the prey on the run, but not quite sure what to do with it when the prey didn't run. John decided not to run.

He looked into White's beady eyes, the kind that changed color from imbibing too much grain whiskey. "Mr. White," John said with as much calm he could muster, "We're free here in this country. The story we ran is a responsible one."

White was dismissive of John's comments. "I'll be back in two weeks for your answer. I just hope you have sense enough to do the right thing and not disappoint the Council. You'd be foolish to do so.

Consider your answer to be a Christmas present to the Council," he said, foreshadowing what he expected John's answer to be.

White paused, then added in a rident tone: "Oh, by the way, I'm hoping for a white Christmas."

White turned to walk away, then turn around slowly, and spat another large wad of tobacco juice on the ground. "Tick, tock, tick, tock."

32

LATE DECEMBER, 1899

Tick, tock, tick, tock—White's mocking and hectoring words—bounced violently in John's head. It had been over a week since White presented John with a ticking time bomb—retract the story in *The Messenger*, or John would risk putting his business and his wife's life in dire jeopardy. The weight of White's threatening demand was now too much to bear; it was time to tell someone, or else he'd risk his mind exploding.

"Hey, Jethro," John said while standing at the printing press wiping his hand on his ink-stained leather apron.

"Yes, boss."

John walked over to Jethro, put his right hand on Jethro's left shoulder and said, "Sit down, Jethro."

Sitting next to Jethro, John faced toward him, and his eyes locked onto Jethro's coal-colored eyes in knitted concentration. Jethro looked at John through his small-framed glasses, the kind favored by young college-educated men. His standard good looks—tall, forceful square jaw, high cheekbones, and soft chocolate-brown eyes that women loved—were somewhat derailed by a mole that was just below his widow's peak. He had something that John didn't have, a college degree, one from Atlanta University. He was an excellent researcher, and someone who knew how to let the facts drive the story.

After a few seconds of John's awkward stare, Jethro asked, "Is there something wrong?"

John gave a nearly imperceptible nod. "I haven't told anyone about this; you're the first," John said as his eyes went blank.

"Boss, you got me worried. What is it?"

"You know that story you wrote about "vile anti-miscegenation laws?"

"What about it?"

"They want us to retract that story; put something in *The Messenger* saying we don't really stand by it."

"Boss, I wrote what I believe." Feeling a need to defend himself, he added: "You told me it was okay to run that story."

John nodded to acknowledge Jethro's point.

"Boss, you have to tell me what's going on."

"Chester White stopped by here a few days ago and told me that I have to retract your story in two weeks."

"And if you don't?"

"He threatened to destroy this building and mentioned something about my 'lovely wife.'"

"Who is this Chester White?"

John wasn't finished. "He mentioned something about me not disappointing the Council. I don't know what that means."

Jethro unhooked his glasses from his large ears, removed them, and massaged his temples with his head slightly bowed. He raised his head and said defiantly, "We've got to fight back. We can't let them destroy what we're doing here in this community. Our community needs *The Messenger*. We have been victimized ever since we landed in this country. No more. We're speaking up."

John nodded, admiring Jethro's intelligence and keen insight. He knew the way out of victimhood for the colored community in Lawrence County was to cease being victims and to articulate the promise made by the Declaration of Independence and the United States Constitution. He also knew that articulation would be, as it had always been, a threat to white superiority.

As Jethro's heavy lids covered his eyes for a few seconds, he tapped into his memory bank and retrieved what he was looking for. "This Council," Jethro said, "I believe that's the White Citizen's Council. They have a lot of influence with politicians. I know they're not afraid to throw their weight around. They specialize in terrorizing colored folk. And white folk too who don't bend to their demands."

John was silent, continuing to absorb what Jethro had just told him.

"When are you going to tell Mr. White to go to hell?" Jethro said.

"If I tell him no, we've got to be prepared to deal with the consequences, especially if they're as powerful as you say."

"What does Tilla think about all of this?"

John shook his head.

"You mean she knows nothing about this?" John said nothing, so Jethro continued: "You need to tell her."

John offered an excuse. "Not yet; she's busy with the kids and taking care of the house—and helping the church with the New Year's Eve party. Tell her boss."

John stood up, as did Jethro, and John asked, "How's the New Year's Day paper coming along?"

"It's coming ... more work needs to be done."

"I want you to knock off early today. It's Christmas Eve; go home and be with your family."

Jethro returned to the unpleasant conversation about the Council. "What're you going to do about this matter?"

John deflected the question. "I'm leaving soon. I should have been at First Baptist a while ago to help with the planning on the New Year's Eve party. Tilla's probably upset that I'm not there yet."

John knew that he'd soon be forced to make an epochal decision about whether to retract the story or side with Jethro, his trusted friend and loyal reporter. But he knew he needed to hear from more voices—a lot more in short span of time.

Tick, tock, tick, tock.

Several church members had gathered at First Baptist Church to finalize the plans for the big New Year's Eve celebration. The celebration was Reverend Owen's idea, and he did most of the talking. In addition to the logistics of planning for the celebration, he told those assembled before him that they could participate in the planting of a time capsule on church property. The hole for the time capsule had already been dug and all that was needed was for the congregants to write something that when viewed one hundred years later would demonstrate how one's racial identity was no longer an issue in Lawrence County or anywhere else in Alabama and the remaining forty-four states. For those who could not write, he asked them to express their sentiment to someone who could.

"Theo, come here now," Tilla said as she sat in the church sanctuary listening to Reverend Owen.

Theo dragged his feet as he walked to his mother.

"I want you to stop running around while the pastor is talking. Now be a good boy; I've got to watch your sisters. You're five years old now. I need you to be my little man, okay?"

"Okay," Theo said with his head bowed, acknowledging the mild reprimand. He looked at his two-year-old sister, Bessie, whose eyes decried Theo's behavior. He sat next to her, and he stuck out his tongue at her. Bessie tapped Tilla on the arm and Theo quickly retracted his tongue.

"Before we depart," Reverend Owen said, "does anyone have any questions?"

Jimmy raised his hand. "Yes, Brother Jimmy."

Jimmy stood up, drawing himself to a full six feet, eight inches. He removed his callused hands from his duck-cotton overalls and threaded them in front of him, saying, "I'm going to need some men to help me haul the meat here."

"You'll get help," Reverend Owen said. "I'll see to it."

Suddenly, Reverend Owen looked at Tilla. "Where's Mr. Davis?" he asked.

She was draped in a green empire waist dress. Even with three children, Tilla maintained her hourglass shape, the same one that continued to enthrall John and male passersby. Whether it was envy or admiration, women in church and elsewhere talked about how well she managed her children, her house, and her husband. She was polite to everyone and spoke with a disarming voice. She had learned from her husband to be strong but not rude, kind but not weak, humble but not shy, and proud but not arrogant.

"He should've been here by now. I know he told me earlier that he was going to the press," Tilla said while dandling one-year-old Eunice on her lap.

Reverend Owen adjourned the meeting, telling all that he was excited about the new century and that life for colored folk would get better.

As people began to pour out of church, John walked to the front, where he saw his wife and kids. He sat next to Theo.

"How's my boy?" he said while rubbing Theo on the head.

Theo shrugged, then said, "I'm hungry."

"Your mama's going to fix you some biscuits when you get home," he said looking at Tilla, who observed John's aspect plunge to darkness; he clasped his hands, his eyes narrowed, and his head was slightly bowed.

Tilla had seen the look before, one that meant something was probably awry. Tilla stood and donned Eunice's coat. John donned Bessie's coat. Theo already had on his coat, ready to go home to eat.

"Honey, take the children home. I'll see you soon," John said.

John was anxious and needed counsel from his pastor about how to handle White. He tapped Reverend Owen on the left shoulder. Reverend Owen turned around and smiled upon seeing John, who tried to return the smile but couldn't.

"Reverend Owen, you got some time to talk?"

"What's on your mind, John?"

"I need to talk to you in private."

"Okay, son," Reverend Owen said. As their spiritual father, he called all of the male members of his church *son* regardless of age. "Let's go to my office."

John told his pastor about White's visit to the press and how he threatened the paper and Tilla. "So, I suppose you're asking me what you should do?"

John shrugged his shoulders.

"What do you know of Mr. White?" Reverend Owen asked.

"Jethro mentioned that he's with something called ..." he said pausing to recall the name. "Oh, something like the White Citizen's Council. Yeah, that's it, the White Citizen's Council."

Reverend Owen closed his eyes and nodded a few times. He looked like he was praying. He opened his eyes and looked at John, saying, "I've heard of them. First heard about them a few years ago when I attended a leadership conference for Negro ministers in Birmingham."

Reverend Owen fully understood the weight that the Council carried. "John, my son, the White Citizen's Council cannot be taken lightly. We need to gather our men colored folk here in town to discuss this matter." He paused, then added: "When did you say White wants an answer?"

"He'll be back in four days, no three days, before the church's New Year's Eve party."

Reverend Owen looked at John, recalling the first time he saw the young man in his church several years ago, when he didn't say much when asked to talk about his life. He now saw a twenty-nine-year-old man who had blossomed into a family man with children and one who was widely respected in the colored community. He stood up and walked from behind his desk to go to the front. He sat on the edge of the desk looking down as John was still seated, wondering what Reverend Owen was going to do.

"Stand up, John."

John complied.

Reverend Owen rose from the desk and walked within a foot of John. Although John was a few inches taller than Reverend Owen, John believed his minister was taller in stature. Everything about Reverend Owen exuded confidence—from his erect posture, to his soaring church orations, to his natty attire.

"Son, you've made yourself a good reputation in this community. Even some white folks respect you. I don't think you need to make a decision just yet. When White comes in three days' time, tell him you're still mulling it over."

"But Reverend Owen ..."

Reverend Owen interrupted John. "White will report back to his superiors; they'll tell him that they'll give you another day or two to reconsider."

"Then what?" John asked nervously. White was a crosspatch and his behavior seemed unpredictable.

As a minister, Reverend Owen had counseled hundreds of people and had studied their eyes. John didn't say another word to explain the pressing problem; his eyes had declared to Reverend Owen that his problem needed to be addressed urgently. The full weight of the church was needed to help John. "Let's get our men folk here in two days to discuss this. I'm going to stand by you."

"Thanks, Reverend Owen." Reverend Owen shook John's right hand while using his left hand to support John's right forearm. John figured he was going to need all the support he could get. Gale force winds were coming his way, and he would have to deal with them soon.

John finally arrived home a few hours after Tilla and the children had left church. The children were in bed, and Tilla lay in bed reading another local newspaper. John walked into his bedroom exhausted from a day full of worriment.

"We waited on you, Mr. Davis," Tilla said. She often called him Mr. Davis to let him know when she was upset about something. "You should've been here for dinner. The children wanted you to tell them a story. Did you forget that tonight is Christmas Eve?"

John looked at her and mustered a faint smile. She was even beautiful when she was mad.

John disrobed and scooted next to Tilla. "Honey, what're you doing reading the competition?" John said.

Tilla ignored him.

Now that John was in bed next to her, she could feel his warmth. She felt safe. Her anger slaked. She put down the paper and turned off the light. Although she was no longer angry, John would have to pay for his transgression. If there had been any thoughts of lovemaking, there'd be none tonight. She turned from John.

John snuggled up to Tilla, settling in a spooning position, his left arm draped across her chest. He moved her long, silky, auburn hair, exposing the nape of her neck. He stared blankly at her neck for a few seconds, then kissed her gently on his favorite spot. He thought about telling her about White, but he demurred. No need to disturb her about such weighty matters at bedtime. He'd tell her in the morning. He turned over and went to sleep.

33

LATE DECEMBER, 1899

"Where're you going?" White's wife yelled as she stood at the door with her toddler at her side. She had seen it too often; he'd leave her and the children at home while he went to some Blind Tiger or attended meetings of the White Citizen's Council where he'd rave against coloreds and curse white politicians who weren't doing enough to keep coloreds in their place. It seemed that most of the time she preferred that he'd leave, so she'd get a reprieve from his heavy hand.

White had one leg on the stirrup to his nag. He turned to his wife and said, "Shut up, woman."

"You shut up," she screamed, as though she was telling him that she was tired of the beatings. She'd have to wait for him to come home to determine whether she'd get another beating. The severity of the beatings was often commensurate with his level of intoxication.

She closed the door, looked down at her toddler son, and yelled, "Get that finger out of your mouth."

The toddler began to cry, and his face was soon dripping with rivulets of tears. "Just shut up," she said exasperatedly, while yanking her son's finger out of his mouth. She hated the way she treated her children. When her husband would beat and torment her, she'd find a way to release her roiled emotions on her children.

White's life of late was subsumed with the Council. He felt like a potentate and loved the power and sway the Council could exert over colored *and* white alike. Two things seemed to make him happy—

alcohol, usually some kind of grain whiskey, and being a member of the Council.

A few years back, White had been somewhat tolerant of coloreds. He even worked beside a couple at a local foundry. However, when he and some white workers were replaced by coloreds during a strike, he found a reason to hate coloreds even though it was his white boss who fired the strikers.

The Council met at the *Thirsty Turtle*, one of the many watering holes where they held their conclave. Allen Montgomery was the president of the Council. He was a banker, the smartest and wealthiest of the members. The members included professionals such as Montgomery, skilled craftsmen like carpenters and blacksmiths, two politicians, and itinerant workers like White.

"... twelve, thirteen, fourteen," Montgomery said counting the members of the Council as they sat in their usual spots in the back of the joint.

Just as Montgomery asked aloud where was "Chessy," White's moniker, White opened the door and stumbled in. He had started drinking at home before the meeting. White made fifteen, and all were present. Although the Council had fifteen official members, there were dozens of auxiliary members who stood ready to assist the Council when needed. White had once been an auxiliary member; he told people that he earned his "commission to be on the Council by killing a Black man."

Montgomery opened the meeting for business. He was from England. His father was a wealthy merchant in England who supported the Confederacy during the Civil War. While his father seemed more interested in investing in the side of whomever he thought would win the War, the son was more interested in seeing to it that the races were kept separate.

Some members of the Council were concerned that under Montgomery's leadership, the Council was failing to keep coloreds from advancing too much in Lawrence County. To the Council, factory jobs belonged to whites; Negroes should not be permitted to hold any position that could impact the lives of whites. And most of all, the racial purity had to be maintained. It didn't matter that many

Negroes were the offspring of a white male, especially when coloreds were considered property under the United States Constitution. To keep the race pure, the Council had lobbied state lawmakers to pass a law making interracial marriages illegal in Alabama.

The article in *The Messenger* about Alabama's "vile anti-miscegenation law" had caused consternation among Council members. The Council agreed that the article was a direct attack on white Southern womanhood. Action was needed.

After addressing a few small matters, Montgomery asked White to report on the "John Davis matter."

White gulped a shot of Jim Beam whiskey and began to speak. "That Davis got a mouth on him. Don't like him one bit. I let him know that he had to retract the story," White said with a whiskey-soaked mouth.

"What'd he say?" Montgomery asked.

"He said he won't do it," White said while pouring another shot of whiskey into his shot glass.

"How much time did you give him to retract the story?" another member asked.

"Two weeks," White told him.

"When does his time expire?" Montgomery asked.

"Three days," White said. "What if he sticks by what he's saying, what'd we do?"

Montgomery advised patience for now, but thought that a little reminder of some sort could cajole John into making the right decision. "You may want to let him know that we're not playing around. Consider paying him a visit before the deadline. Perhaps give John Davis a little Christmas present. If he continues to refuse to budge, I'll consider that an affront to this Council, to the great white American way," Montgomery said with steely resolve.

White stayed at the *Thirsty Turtle* after all the Council members had left. Six ounces of 120 proof whiskey sat in front of him. He picked it up and swallowed the inebriant without even a slight shudder. He forced himself to ponder what he could do to get John to retract the story. If he failed, he knew that he'd be kicked out of the Council. And if he were forced to leave the Council, he knew his life would soon be in shambles. His wife and children would surely feel his frustrations.

It was late; time to go home. He stood up and teetered, realizing that it was not easy to stand straight, like a newborn fawn struggling to keep his balance after standing just after birth.

As he stumbled toward the bar on his way out, the owner stopped him by grabbing his left arm. "Sit right there, Chessy," the owner said pointing to a small table near the bar. "I'll make a fresh pot of your favorite coffee."

Although White was too soused to understand what was said to him, he had been through the routine many times before, and knew that when the owner grabbed his arm as he would leave the bar, he was supposed to sit down, just like a trained dog obeying a command. White took a few sips of his coffee before he plunked his head down on the table and quickly started to snore.

About an hour later the owner shook White's right shoulder. White slowly raised his head, which now seemed too heavy for his body. "I'm done cleaning now. I'm closing up," the owner said to White.

White scratched his head and shook it a few times as though he was trying to shake off any remnants of inebriation. As the owner's face came into focus, White realized it was time to go. "You're a good man," White said to the owner with slightly slurred speech, which was caused by fatigue or perhaps a reminder that he was not yet totally sober.

"You gonna be all right, Chessy?"

"Yeah, thanks for the coffee."

The owner nodded.

As White sat atop his nag on the way home, Montgomery's words came to him—*to give John Davis a little Christmas present*. Membership in the Council meant everything to him, and he just couldn't fail it, fail Montgomery. To him, his commission to the Council was more valuable than being a member of the Confederate Fifth Alabama Calvary Regiment.

34

LATE DECEMBER, 1899

Tilla raised her head from her pillow, trying to gauge the timbre of the cry. Two of her children were crying: Eunice's cry overpowered Bessie's. They were not familiar cries to Tilla, ones indicating hunger or even some kind of agitation. The decibel levels ratcheted up; they were wailing.

"John, wake up," she said while rocking him on his right shoulder.

John grumbled. "What is it?" He was annoyed after being awakened so early after just going to bed.

"The kids are crying."

"They'll settle down," John offered, hoping to be able to quickly return to his peaceful repose.

John had always been a heavy sleeper, which Tilla didn't necessarily mind even though it was she who got up in the middle of night to tend the children when they cried. She had something John didn't: breasts to sate the nighttime hunger of her children. The children also preferred Tilla's soft touch and words to settle them. John just didn't have Tilla's touch, her well-honed motherly skills, the right unction that a young child needed in the middle of the night.

The screaming continued and didn't quite seem right to Tilla. The screams seemed laden with fright. Tilla wondered whether her children were too young to have nightmares. Normally she'd check on them, but she wanted John to carry the load that night.

Now that he was awake, John couldn't ignore the screams any longer. Tilla demanded that John check on the children. John thought it was one more punishment being meted out for him coming home so late last night.

He scooted to the edge of their bed where he came to a momentary rest, hoping the cries would cease. He rubbed his eyes with the back of his right hand, stood slowly, and toddled blindly to the closet door where he retrieved his housecoat from the hook on the inside of the closet door.

As he walked out of his bedroom and into the hall, he felt a tinge of cold air. As he neared his girls' bedroom, cold air rushed over him. He turned on the light and saw Theo holding Eunice in bed, trying to comfort his younger sister. The bedroom window was shattered. He walked slowly toward the window, apprehensive with each step. A large rock sat about a foot from Eunice's bed.

His heart sank as it began to beat with odd little jerks. His children could have been killed. He turned around and saw Tilla standing in the doorway, sobbing heavily.

He looked into her pained eyes for a few seconds, all the while resisting the urge to look away. Finally, he said, "Honey, I don't know what happened."

Tilla said nothing.

"Let's take the kids to the living room," John said.

John picked up Bessie and Tilla picked up Eunice. "Let's go," John said looking down at Theo as they headed to the living room.

"Stay right here, away from any windows," John said to Tilla. "I'm going to see what I can find out."

John put on gray woolen pants and a heavy shirt and black brogans. He retrieved his Winchester rifle from the closet and opened a dresser drawer where he grabbed a box of rifle cartridges. He spied the kerosene lantern by the door and ignited it with Lucifer matches.

He walked tentatively out of the back door; he was scared, but had a young family to protect. He walked around the perimeter of the house, noticing nothing except roving raccoons and stridulating insects. The moonlight lit the sky. Suddenly, he saw a shadowy figure in the distance near large elm trees. He held up the lantern to aid his vision. The figure didn't move. He then saw another shadowy figure.

As one figure was turned sideways, John saw an extended belly; he thought perhaps he was looking at a pregnant woman but dismissed that notion. The body structure of the figure seemed too big to be a woman. The shadowy figures turned and faced John, who couldn't see any facial features but felt the sting of their eyes. Suddenly, John shook as if he were under the influence of a galvanic shock. He figured they saw him because they had to see the kerosene lantern that shone like a beacon guiding a ship to shore. But John didn't care. They had to know that he was going to protect his family and his property at any cost. He raised his rifle and pointed it at the shadowy figures; they didn't move.

The two shadowy figures walked away as though they wanted to tell John that they had delivered their message. As John returned to his house, he thought about whether he had actually seen a pregnant woman, for if he did, she was a rather large woman. He didn't know for sure but thought that it was White's spill-over belly.

John boarded the window at sunrise, needing to stay busy. He had to buy time, so he could mull over what he'd tell Tilla.

Tilla had set her jaw and was quiet as she made breakfast. She wanted John to say something first. She wondered what John meant when he said he didn't know what happened when he looked at her as she stood in the doorway sobbing. Her mind would not let it go. She then convinced herself that she sensed something was wrong last night, when John came home late, missing Christmas Eve with the children. She even sensed something was wrong when John was in bed with her. His touch just didn't seem right to her. There was something about his visage; a story encased inside his eyes, but one she couldn't quite discern.

The children had already eaten breakfast. Only one plate was on the cherry-wood kitchen table. John walked into the kitchen, looked down at his plate of grits, biscuits, and ham. Tilla watched him sit down; he pretended not to see her tall frame. He buried his head in his food, his face just a few inches from his plate. He ate two biscuits before feeling Tilla's penetrating glare, which forced him to look up. He could take the silence no more.

He looked at her and thought about asking her to pour him some coffee. But he had to say something about what he knew. She was hurting too much. She was a part of the team, and he knew she felt left out, like the left hand not knowing what the right hand was doing. Tilla was the right hand that stayed home to run the house, to feed John and the children, to clothe, clean, bathe, and nurture the children, and on it went. She had become the biddable wife: whatever John asked of her, she did with rare complaint.

"I think I know what happened last night," John said, breaking the deafening silence. The large rock on the floor near Eunice's bed entered his mind, and a vein in his temple twitched. He breathed deeply and readied himself to spill what he knew.

Tilla stood resting on the counter looking at John, refusing to offer him any refuge. He had to just say it. "Last night, I saw two people near the elm trees near our back yard. I think one of them may be the devil that through the rock through the window."

The forlorn look remained on her face. Even her long curly lashes couldn't conceal the pain in her eyes.

"Tilla," he said softly, "sit down." She sat reluctantly. He grabbed her right hand and caressed it. "I'm so, so sorry."

He told her about White.

35

LATE DECEMBER, 1899

The church, like most Negro churches in the South, was a spiritual haven and community center that addressed moral, economic, and social problems facing Negroes. So it was natural for dozens of men to gather in the sanctuary of Reverend Owen's First Baptist Church to discuss putting together a unified position on how John should respond to White's demand for a retraction.

Reverend Owen facilitated the meeting. They needed a plan to avoid an improvident response to White's threat. He stood at the altar and called the meeting to order. "Thank you for coming. I see word has spread about how we need to help Brother John with his situation." He corrected himself, saying, "I mean our situation."

"That's right, our situation," someone shouted to acknowledge and invoke a kind of esprit de corps among the assembled men.

John sat in the front pew next to Jethro. Reverend Owen looked at John and asked him to tell the men what had transpired.

Most of the men in the church had been threatened and belittled one way or another by a white person. The men listened with rapt attention as John told them about White. White's demand for a retraction and the accompanying threats of violence were unsettling, indicated by scattered paroxysms of guttural sounds. But they were outraged and emitted a loud collective gasp when John told them about the shattered window in his house.

The men were clamoring to ask questions. Jimmy stood and looked directly at John. "You mean you got to give an answer to this white man in two days?" Jimmy asked.

John nodded, saying, "That's when he's expected back."

"What are you going to tell him?" Jimmy said.

Reverend Owen interjected: "That's why we're here now, to decide how to handle this unfortunate matter."

The men needed a full understanding of why Jethro wrote the article. John asked Jethro to explain.

Many of the men nodded in unison as Jethro told them whites should stop treating coloreds like "second class citizens." To Jethro, a law forbidding interracial marriages or a law allowing a colored man to be arrested for vagrancy was just another way of using the law as a cudgel to slam the soul of colored folks in Alabama.

After about an hour of questions, Reverend Owen said, "We've been going at this for a while. Let's wrap this up."

The issue of righteousness had been vetted enough. "We're going to put this matter to a vote on what we think John should do," Reverend Owen said. "But before we do," he said waving for John to join him at the altar, "I want y'all to know I support John for standing up for what's right. John didn't ask for this fight. It came to him. This man White is our enemy; he's the devil. He's not attacking John for what John's doing. Oh, no," he said, waving his right hand in the air, "he's attacking John because of who he is."

"What you mean, Reverend?" a bespectacled slender man near the back shouted.

"You see, he wants to sow discord in John's heart; make John feel it's not worth it to fight back. Then the rest of us would feel that way. It's like a disease that spreads. We catch what John gets."

"That's just what they want," another man said.

"Precisely," Reverend Owen said, pointing to the man.

"If we fight back, we gonna die. More of them with guns I suspect," the bespectacled man said.

"But if we don't fight back, we die anyway," Jimmy said, pointing to his heart.

Reverend Owen removed his waist watch from his fob and noticed the hour. "Let's put this to a vote. By show of hands, how many say John tell White that he's not going to retract the story in *The Messenger?*"

With his right hand raised high in the air, a man shouted, "Tell White to go to hell."

Reverend Owen shouted *Amen* at the near unanimous vote.

While John knew he wouldn't tell White *to go to hell*, he'd try to remain equanimous in telling him that *The Messenger* wasn't going to retract the story.

"What'll we do when they come with rifles after John stands his ground?" the bespectacled man asked.

"We match them with rifles," a man said in a husky voice.

"What do you mean?" Reverend Owen asked.

Reverend Owen didn't recognize the man. "Stand up and tell us your name, would you?"

"I'm Otis Jefferson," the tall, burly man said. His height and weight matched his baritone voice. "Jimmy told me about this meeting. Glad I could make it."

Reverend Owen looked in Jimmy's direction and nodded to thank him for recruiting men for the cause.

Jefferson raised his arms as though he was holding a rifle. "I'm talking about our right of self-defense," he said.

"Go on," Reverend Owen said.

"I am Twenty-Fifth Infantry Regiment," he said, a gleam in his eyes.

"What's that?" someone asked.

"Colored men like me fought for this country over there in Cuba over a year ago in that war with Spain. We was foot soldiers," Otis told the assembled men.

Jethro knew something about colored men serving in the War. Ever ready to showcase his knowledge, he asked Otis: "Are you one of them buffalo soldiers?"

"That's what they say," Otis said while rubbing a large, raised scar on the backside of his left hand. "You see this scar?" he said, holding up his left hand. "I got this fighting in the battle of San Juan Hill. I got scars all over my body. I'll take some more if need be," he said to applause.

After the applause subsided, he continued, letting them know he could procure weapons: "I got some trapdoor rifles and other arms we can use. I can get a hold of other weapons if need be. Some of my infantry buddies can help."

"Sounds like we got the makings of the Lawrence County Colored Brigade," Reverend Owen said. He paused, then bestowed his blessing on Otis, adding, "Otis, make that Colonel Jefferson, will command the brigade."

Given Otis's military experience and his access to weapons and his former infantry buddies, it was quickly decided he would be in charge of leading the Lawrence County Colored Brigade to defend John and the press office.

They devised a plan for several armed men to be stationed in the press office and to conceal themselves in woody areas surrounding the grounds of the press office when White would come for John's answer. Two or three men would act as sentries, ready to sound the alarm if White brought company.

The church represented the community, so John knew he had their backing. But even so, he knew he stood alone; the weight of it all seemed too much for his broad shoulders. He was the target, not anyone else. This kind of fight was new to him.

Championing the ancient Anglo-Saxon right of self-defense to protect himself, his family, and his property, seemed reasonable. But there was one problem: John and the colored community were not Anglo-Saxon. White and the Council had perfected the art of using intimidation, of getting their way. John found himself thrown into White's well-used cauldron and had grave concerns that the brigade could act as a deus ex machina and save the day.

36

LATE DECEMBER, 1899

One day remained before White had said he would come for John's answer.

John didn't sleep well, tossing and turning most of the night. Much needed to be done before he could give his attention to White. With pressing work issues on his mind, he arose at dawn and decided he'd go to the press office to finish printing the rest of the New Year's Day edition of *The Messenger*.

He went to his barn and looked at his favorite horse, an appaloosa. Just as he reached for the reins to the horse, he decided against it. He had given Jethro and the other workers the day off to spend time with their families on Christmas Day and the day after. His appaloosa would also get the day off. The sting of the early morning chill hung in the air. He quickly put out fodder for his horse and other animals and hurried to the press office on foot.

As he inserted the key into the door of the press office, he paused, wondering whether he'd be strong enough to confront White. A sudden gust of wind rocked his body, impelling him to turn the key. He quickly walked to the furnace and tossed in a bucket of coal. While he rubbed his hands in front of the furnace, feeling the heat that his body begged for, an image of White popped into his head, and he shivered as his body warmed from the furnace.

He turned and looked in the corner of the office. Four hundred copies of the New Year's Day edition of *The Messenger* sat of the floor.

He picked up a copy and sat down; he looked at the paper, but he was unable to focus. White's words—*tick, tock, tick, tock*—entered his head. *I'll be here at high noon* followed. He shook his head to try to dislodge any image of White from his mind. It worked. A smile lit his face as he looked at his paper and the once-blurred words came into focus. He was proud of the special New Year's Day edition. The headline—HELLO TWENTIETH CENTURY—in twenty-four-point type was Tilla's idea.

The lead story discussed the gains that *The Messenger* wanted to see Negroes make in the new century. He jumped to the last paragraph of the article.

> Colored people intend to cash their promissory notes for all the sacrifices we have made from the moment we first set foot in this country to where we are now. We intend to claim our rightful share of freedom and fully participate in American commerce of service and industry. A new era is upon us, and we will seize the moment.

White's image returned just as John finished the article. John shook his head again to dislodge the ghastly image. It didn't work. He walked to the press and turned it on to crank out the last one hundred copies of the New Year's Day edition.

The last copy was finished an hour later. A few delivery men were scheduled to deliver the paper tomorrow morning to the usual places—businesses and homes of the people who could afford to pay five cents per paper.

John sat down and put his head in his hands, hoping the matter with White was just a bad dream. He reached down into his shirt and pulled out the rust-colored locket his mother had given him twelve years ago on the night he left Richmond. It was an amulet of sorts; he later believed it, along with prayer, were responsible for his successful journey to Mount Hope. Just as he was about to open it, a sudden wave of melancholy rushed over him, and he began to cry. He spit out the salty tears as they reached his mouth.

Cacophonous sounds of bells ringing loudly and cannons being shot now wracked his head, and his body absorbed vibrations from irritating shards of noise. His hands trembled and his heart raced. He sat paralyzingly still in the chair, his eyes wide open, hoping the harsh sounds he heard were a figment of his imagination.

It was not his imagination. Over the sound of his racing heart, he heard a rat-a-tat-tat; it couldn't be ignored. He put on his woolen coat and retrieved his revolver from a desk drawer. His arms and legs tingled with gooseflesh. He shook his limbs and gumshoed toward the door, careful to stay close to the wall and away from the front of the door. There were no windows to look out of to see who was filling him with fear.

He was not ready to face White. His mind was not right. He needed to see his family to gain strength before he could face down White and all the evil things that came with him. The Lawrence County Colored Brigade was not due to arrive until tomorrow morning. He wondered whether White knew about the brigade. He shuddered while thinking that anyone at church could have betrayed him.

Despite his concerns, he yelled, "Who is it?" while holding his revolver tightly.

"Open up, Boss," the man yelled. "It's cold out here."

John had forgotten that one of his delivery men was due to pick up *The Messenger* for delivery.

"Are you alone?" John yelled.

"Yes, Boss. Like I said, it's cold out here."

John opened the door slowly until he could see the face of his delivery man. "Get in here," John said, grabbing the man by the right arm and yanking him inside.

The man removed his hood from his head. He saw John's trembling hand holding the revolver. "What's wrong?" he asked.

John didn't have the strength to talk much now. "I forgot that you were coming to get the paper today. You know where they are."

"You alright?" the delivery man asked.

John nodded.

He just wanted to go home to hug his wife and children. "I'm going home. Lock up when you're finished."

"Hey, Boss," the delivery man said.

John looked at him, his eyes vacuous, his soul in retreat.

"Me and my wife and kids looking forward to the New Year's Eve party at the church."

John nodded and felt that he'd disappoint his delivery man if he told him there might not be a party. Many in the Lawrence County colored community were counting on it. Despite the help of the church, though, John felt alone in going up against a beast that excelled in instilling fear in people.

A few hours later, Theo sat on a sofa in the living room and watched his father polish and look over his Winchester rifle to make sure it was in fine fettle. John looked at Theo periodically but said nothing.

The silence was shattered when Tilla said, "John, you and Theo come on to the kitchen and eat dinner."

John sat down in his usual end spot, and Theo sat next to him. Theo remained quiet as he looked at his father. John returned the look and saw worry in his boy's eyes, as though he felt something was awry with the Davis household.

Noticing two plates filled with pork chops, snap peas, carrots, and mashed potatoes on the table, John said, "Tilla, I want you to sit down and eat with us."

"Oh, honey, I've been nibbling all along. I want to make sure I'm taking care of my two favorite men right now."

"Mama, I ain't no man," Theo said.

Tilla looked at Theo and smiled. At five years old, Theo had the markers of future handsomeness: an elegant nose, his father's hazel eyes, and the kind of cheek dimples that people liked to poke a finger in. "You're my man," she responded.

Theo looked at John. "Papa, am I a man?"

"You heard what your mama said."

"Yes, Papa. I'm a man."

John tore into his food and asked Tilla for a second helping. As she refilled his plate, she said, "Honey, you're eating like this is your last meal."

Tilla's words bore through John's heart. He ate two spoonfuls of mashed potatoes. Theo was still working on his pork chop. "Theo,"

John said, "go check on your sisters. If they're alright, I want you to go to your room, okay?"

"Yes, Papa."

"Honey, I'm done here," John said using his head to point to his food.

"What's the matter, John? I can tell something's wrong."

His belly was full, but his eyes were empty. "I wish I could talk to my mama right now. She'd tell me what to do."

Tilla dipped her head as she'd done whenever John talked like that about his mother. John had come to learn that she felt she was competing with her on matters of grave importance, but John had assured her it wasn't so.

It had been over twelve achingly long years since that night he left his mother in Richmond. He wanted to hear advice from her, for her to tell him he would make it through the troubled waters, for her to sing a hymn letting him know that God would usher him safely to shore.

Tilla's core was stronger that John's. Where he needed to talk to his mother to gain her counsel, Tilla could rely on the same core as Ann—innate wisdom and fortitude. She couldn't depend on counsel from her parents. Her mother Fannie had died a few years ago, supposedly from the bite of a black widow, and her father Pony had been murdered a few years back.

Tilla knew the confrontation with White was brewing and drew nigh. John had told her about the vote at church, but he had taken her vote for granted. The loss of her parents and her sister's disappearance years ago weighed on her. So the thoughts of her young family losing a husband and father tormented her day and night. She tried to keep her roiling emotions to herself, reluctant to say something lest John ask. But every once in a while, she'd make a roundabout comment how it would all be so easy for her husband to issue a retraction; how John was hefting the heavy burdens of the colored community. But because John had showed so much courage in the face of the maelstrom that he was facing, she sucked it up and decided to do her uxorial duty and support her man no matter what.

Indeed, in a moment of reflection a day or so ago, she had told John that she would stand behind him. "*Behind* me?" John said with a smile and quick laugh.

She started to ask John the meaning of the laugh but stopped because the meaning had become clear. Tilla returned the smile and said, "You know what I mean," as she gave him a love tap on the arm.

Things were serious now, and John needed his mind to be in the right place. "Tilla, come with me to the living room," John said.

"But the kitchen's a mess. I need to clean it."

John helped her clean the table. He put the scraps in a large bucket outside for the hogs while she washed the dishes.

As he returned to the house, he saw Tilla at the sink scrubbing the last plate. John stood a few feet away peering at his wife, hoping she'd understand what he was about to tell her.

John's tired eyes widened, begging for her attention. "Okay, okay, I'm coming," Tilla said.

She sat next to John on the settee. He took in a heavy sigh and let it out slowly. His mind was a tumult of heavy waves and strong currents, crashing up against the walls of his head, having nowhere to go, making him feel dizzy. He sighed again.

Tilla saw distress in his eyes and reacted like she'd do to comfort one of her children; she'd touch them, caress them, knowing that her hands had a palliative effect. She extended her hands and massaged John's temples. It worked. The dizziness soon vanished.

He opened his eyes, and they landed on Tilla's heavy eyebrows. Then the rest of her face came into view. Her long nose and large round eyes gave her face immediate authority. Her full, sensually curved lips and deep dimples gave her an arresting natural expression. He wondered what she'd do if he didn't survive tomorrow.

John picked up her left hand and began to stroke her hand and forearm. Her skin was still as soft as when he first touched her nearly seven years ago. "You and the kids are going to stay with Junior and Goldie tonight," John said.

Tilla recoiled as though John's words punched her in the stomach. She recovered, expostulating, "There's no need for us to leave this house tonight." She paused, then added with a wan smile: "We'll go there tomorrow morning before you go to the press."

She was often better at reading life's imperatives than he, but he decided to take complete control, at least as best he could. "Listen to me," he said looking at her sienna-colored, moist lips, afraid to look her in her eyes for fear of what he might see, eyes now sunken in stone. "Junior says it's okay. Now I want you to pack what you need to pack." He stiffened his posture and forced himself to look Tilla in her eyes, large eyes that had dazzled him for so many years, were now losing a bit of luster with each word he spoke. "I'm going to take my family to Junior's. Now hurry up, I want to do this before it gets too dark," he said as his voice began to crack.

She closed her eyes to overrule her remonstrating heart.

Tilla finished packing. She gathered the children in the living room at John's request. "Thank you, honey," he said.

Tilla gave a faint nod, pursed her lips, and held her tongue for the nonce.

"Theo, my little man, you're going to stay with Cousin Junior tonight. Now I want you to take care of your mama and sisters while you're gone. You hear me?"

"Yes, Papa."

Just several more hours before he was scheduled to face White. Otis and his brigade would set up at eight o'clock in the morning to be ready in case White made an early arrival. John was content that his family was with Junior. His heart had grown obdurate; he needed to face down the Council's men, led by White.

He retrieved his Winchester rifle that hung in the closet. A drawer in the closet contained his socks and rifle cartridges. He removed the cartridges and placed the rifle on the bed and the cartridges on the walnut chest of drawers that had once belonged to Tilla's father. He blindly rubbed the surface of the chest of drawers, then opened the top drawer, unsure of what he was looking for. As he closed the drawer, he saw a sliver of silver underneath a pile of old clothes.

It had been twelve years since he held them so tightly. He had risked his life for them; they had caused him to flee from Richmond. Without the flasks, he told himself, there would be no Tilla and no children. He thought of Monsieur Billingsly asking about them in Sloss Furnace in Birmingham. He didn't know what was going to happen tomorrow, but he wished he had told Tilla about the flasks. He had his family, and the flasks just didn't seem to matter anymore. He put the flasks back where he found them.

His mind turned to a large hand-drawn portrait of his mother he had commissioned last year. He did his best to recall the picture he took of his mother using just his memory. He ambled into the living room and went to the back and adjusted the catawampus portrait. The color portrait was an oil on canvas painting of his mother that hung high on the eggshell-colored wall. John was proud of the location he selected for the picture of his mother. It gave visual height and historical depth to the house.

His bond with his mother was infrangible; he relied on it to give him strength and sustenance to face difficult situations. He looked at the picture. Ann looked down at John with the same soft eyes he remembered twelve years ago. She wore her favorite tignon. The smile was as wide as John could make it, almost too big for her face. And of course, the front gap teeth were present.

In a moment of lamentation, he said, "Mama, I'm sorry I had to leave you. There's so much I need to tell you. I just couldn't tell you what happened that night I came home with that rifle. I told you old man Wilkerson gave it to me. Not so, Mama. Please forgive me. All you knew was what I told you, that I had to leave because I couldn't take being in Richmond anymore. Truth is, Mama, I didn't kill Madame Billingsly. She tripped and fell down the steps. But I was mad at her. She didn't like me.

I saw when you looked at the hole in my pants. I was so happy you didn't ask me about it. Truth is, I tore a hole in my pants climbing out of a window in Billingsly's shed. I used a sledgehammer to break into Billingsly's cabinet. I took something that didn't belong to me. Wait one moment, Mama."

John walked to his bedroom and retrieved the flasks.

"You see these," he said holding them up to the picture. "This is what I took that night. I took them because I heard Billingsly say there was something valuable in the cabinet in his office. I never figured out what this is," he said pointing to the engravings on the flask. "No need to, I guess.

"Oh, Mama, you won't believe this. I saw Billingsly about six years ago in Birmingham. He asked me about something valuable that was taken from him. I didn't answer. He threatened to kill me, but he almost lost his own life when he nearly fell into the furnace. I saved his life by pulling him out. I couldn't tell if he was thankful. Seems these whiskey flasks have been nothing but trouble for me.

"Soon after seeing Mr. Billingsly, I packed up to move to Mount Hope, the place you told me to go to look for Cousin Riley. I didn't find him because he was dead, but I found his son Junior.

I wish you could see my beautiful wife, Tilla, and my children. Mama, I run a weekly newspaper now. Seems it's caused me some trouble."

He recounted the situation with White and the Council. "What should I do?" he asked his mother.

As he waited for his mother's answer, he heard a loud thumping sound at is front door.

He heard someone yell, "John Davis." His heart began to race again just like it did early in the day when he was at the press office. The same heavy fear had returned. Bile rose up his esophagus, something that hadn't happened for a while.

37

LATE DECEMBER, 1899

Goldie had made a remarkable transformation. Just a few years ago, she was part of the underworld, selling her body to help pay the rent for her and her mother. With the help of Reverend Owen, the former prostitute didn't allow her experiences to become her existence; she succeeded in claiming victory over her past. She was now the wife of her man, and the mother of four kids.

Tilla and Goldie sat at a table in Goldie's modest-sized kitchen snapping string beans in preparation for the New Year's Eve party. Tilla's mind was elsewhere.

"What's eating you?" Goldie asked. "It's that damn cracker man ... White. Don't you worry, our menfolk will handle it."

Tilla nodded, then uttered words in a manner that didn't betray what followed: "Yes, they will," she said softly while snapping a band of string beans.

The conversation sagged into silence. After of few more minutes of silence, except for the children romping in the background, Goldie stood up, saying, "Stand up, Tilla."

Goldie hugged her tightly. She released her hold on Tilla and stood back to look at her. "You gotta put some meat on them bones," Goldie said as though she were comparing Tilla's loins to the chine of an animal.

Tilla defended herself; she stood akimbo, accentuating her hips. "My man seems to like these bones," she said, surprising herself by laughing, a distraction from thinking about John and White.

Goldie was always thick in stature, but even so, she had curves. She had the type of body that if she ate just one or two more biscuits than usual, she'd pack on the pounds. Her face was rounder, her backside bigger, and the curves were no longer noticeable. But she was happy. She took care of the kids, her mother, and her man.

"How do you do it?" Tilla asked after they sat back down to snap more string beans.

"Do what?"

"You've got four young children; your mother is staying with you. You work on the farm. You volunteer at church. Don't you ever get tired?"

"I'm doing no more than you, girl. You're the talk at church; the women and men talk about you in a good way. They say you're doing something right. And that's true."

Because Goldie had been complaisant with Junior, tending to his many needs, he reciprocated in the bedroom. "It's the bedroom. My man keeps me satisfied," she said as a paean to Junior's lovemaking skills. "He knows his way around this," she said, causing her hands to cascade down her body.

Tilla leaned toward Goldie and whispered, "How often do you do it?"

"Two to three times a day," she said. "It used to be more before the last youngin' came along."

Tilla could no longer hold it in. The day of reckoning was only several hours away. She began to mewl.

"What's wrong, dear?" Goldie asked.

"I don't want to lose John," she said, sobbing softly. "John's going to tell White he's standing by *that* story," she said, allowing a larger degree of ambivalence about the story to play in her head. I don't know how it's going to end."

There was no ambiguity by Goldie or practically anyone else in the Negro community. Some things were worth fighting for. "Your husband's a courageous man, standing by for what he believes. That's not easy. He's right, though. The white man's got to know colored people's fed up with being stomped on."

"But why does my husband have to be the one to take a stand?" she said through a sniffle.

"Someone's got to do it. God's appointed him to do it."

"Even though I had mixed feelings, I came to believe that John is doing the right thing. I support what he's doing. It's just as the time gets closer, I have to fight not to lose my nerve."

Tilla stood up and walked to the edge of the living room where she saw Bessie asleep on a large pillow wrapped in a blanket. Lillie was holding her youngest grandchild, rocking her to sleep. Tilla felt safe knowing there were two men from the Lawrence County Brigade guarding the house. But she sensed she would have felt safer if Junior was at home. She turned around and returned to the kitchen. Goldie had started peeling sweet potatoes.

"Where's your husband?" Tilla asked.

"He said he was going somewhere to take care of some business."

"At this hour?"

"See, honey," Goldie said, "I don't ask questions unless I have to. Some things I just don't need to know. It's better that way."

"You're sure?" Tilla asked.

Goldie took slight offense. "Look, honey," Goldie said with authority, "my man ain't no bedswerver. He gets all he needs from me."

Point taken and Tilla let out a well-timed yawn. "Whew, I'm getting tired. I better put the kids to bed."

The sound of a heavy knock on the door coursed through Tilla; she flinched and her heart pounded. Goldie responded to Tilla's reaction: "Honey, it's okay; it's just the men guarding the house. It's cold out there. They knock before allowing themselves in. They've been staying warm with the fire they got going. They just checking on us."

Goldie resumed snapping string beans, and Tilla followed. She picked up where she left off before the knock on the door and lectured Tilla about the duties of a good wife.

38

LATE DECEMBER, 1899

John sat on the sofa in the living room with his eyes closed as he mentally unpacked his crate of dire problems. Closing on thirty years old, he stood at the precipice looking into an abyss of roiling oceanic waters. A brighter future lay off in the distance, but it was just too far to see. He just hoped that he'd be able to get off the sinking ship and use a pinnace to get to shore. But for now, perhaps he'd fight gallantly, ending with his young life extinguished, and his wife and fatherless children would know that he died giving hope to them and the small colored community in Lawrence County. He'd die with dignity and self-respect.

He rose from the sofa and walked to the marital bedroom to read a note he had composed to Tilla on his old but reliable Remington typewriter.

> Dearest Tilla:
>
> It is with a heavy heart that I write to you, my wife and mother of my children. By the time you read this note, I will have left this world and gone skyward. I beg of you to tell our children one day that their father died fighting for what he believed in, freedom for the Negro community. I took a stand. Maybe someday they will be in a position to take a stand for something they believe in.
>
> Please know that I have the most profound love for you. I would have retracted the story if you had asked me to.

But you loved me so that you knew I would have lost my soul if I had done so.

Everything I own is yours. You will find some money I withdrew from the bank under the loose floorboard in Theo's bedroom.

I'm likely to die at the hands of the White Citizen's Council. The law probably won't do much, but let them know anyway.

You're a young woman. Find a good man and marry him. He'll probably want you to have more kids. Oblige him.

Don't despair. I've moved on to a better place. Maybe I'll see you again someday.

Your loving husband,

John Moses Davis

Satisfied with the letter, he put it under Tilla's pillow.

John's eyes shot open upon hearing a loud knock at the front door. As his heart raced mightily, he took deep breaths to slow it down. His heart slowed after a few seconds, but another loud knock sent it racing again.

He scurried to his bedroom to retrieve his Winchester rifle. He walked through the back door with his rifle in hand. He crept along the house with measured steps until he reached the front. Cold air blew out from the person's nostrils, but it was too dark for John to tell who was at his door.

He lifted the rifle in place. The sleek knurled butt of the rifle felt alive as though he was touching a water moccasin. "Hold it right there," John said calmly while aiming the rifle at the hooded head of someone who could do him harm.

"Don't move," he said as the person seemed ready to look in John's direction. John was ready to shoot if he detected the slightest furtive movement.

"What business do you have with me?" John said.

"I suppose you don't want to shoot me, fool. It's me, Junior, your cousin."

John stood down, put down his rifle, relieved that he hadn't confronted White, his tormentor, the man who had his mind and body tied in knots. "Boy, you almost got yourself killed. What are you doing here?" John asked. "You're supposed to be at your house with … Oh, my God. Is something wrong? Is my family okay?" John asked.

"Everybody's okay," Junior said slowly and reassuringly.

"Then what're you doing here at this hour?"

Junior inserted his left thumb and middle forefinger in his mouth and belted out a piercing whistle. "Just watch, over there," Junior said pointing.

Colonel Jefferson emerged from the darkness holding a kerosene lantern while sitting atop a golden-colored palomino. Others followed him on horseback and on foot. Soon all, except for the two who were at Junior's house performing guard duty, were before John. John hung his head low and closed his eyes. He opened his eyes and realized he wasn't dreaming. The argus-eyed Lawrence County Colored Brigade was at his service.

"Thank you," John said, quietly nodding his head.

"Everyone will be in place tomorrow morning by eight o'clock," Colonel Jefferson told John. He then saluted John.

Colonel Jefferson maneuvered his steed to face the men under his command. "All right men, we've got a big day facing us tomorrow. Now go home, have some fun time with the wife, and eat a good breakfast in the morning."

The brigade broke formation and disappeared into the darkness.

John and Junior walked into the kitchen and sat down. "Everyone's fine at my house," Junior said to John as he lit the tobacco in his corn pipe. "Colonel Jefferson's got two men guarding the house."

John was thankful for the meeting at First Baptist Church that Reverend Owen had facilitated. And in this moment, he was thankful for the donations that poured in to help the brigade. They and their horses would need to be fed.

John felt somewhat relieved, like one feels when only a few leaks of many from a leaking roof have been plugged. Ever since White delivered his threat to John two weeks ago, John found it impossible to relax; he was spending too much time thinking about dying and leaving behind a young wife and children. He was spiraling into a mess of depression. And Tilla and the children sometimes felt the short end of his temper.

"I'm staying with you tonight. You and me will go to the press together in the morning. And when White comes knocking, don't worry, I'll be right *behind* you," Junior said laughing.

John didn't offer any emotion. "Junior, walk with me," John said, leading him to the back of the living room.

John pointed to the large drawing of his mother and said, "That's my mama."

"Boy, I know who that is. I remember when you first hung it up."

"That woman is responsible for who I am today."

"You think I can meet her someday?"

"Maybe someday I'll find my way back to Richmond," John said, knowing he'd likely never see her again. "I remember the night I left her. I told her I had to leave Richmond. Never told her the real reason."

"How old were you when you left?" Junior asked.

"Seventeen. She didn't ask too many questions. She knew I had to leave. She told me to go to Mount Hope to find Cousin Riley. I'll never forget that. It took me three years to get here. But I made it."

John turned to face Junior who was still looking at the picture, focusing on the widest smile he'd ever seen anyone wear. "I took the Davis name in honor of you and your pa," John said.

"I know that," Junior said. "Tilla told Goldie about it."

"I sure wished I could have met your pa," John said.

"You remember when you had me looking down the barrel of your rifle when I met you for the first time at your pa's house?" John asked.

Junior laughed. "Yeah, I remember, and I remember just an hour ago you pointed a rifle at me."

A slight chuckle tumbled out of John. Turning slightly more serious, he said, "I'll never forget that day. That damn mutt of yours was ready to tear me apart. I think I peed in my pants thinking of what that dog wanted to do to me."

"Oh, that's Sadie being Sadie. She meant no harm," Junior said.

John returned his attention to the picture of his mother. "If Mama hadn't told me about Mount Hope, there'd be no Tilla for me, no Davis children. I wouldn't know you."

The conversation was too morose for Junior, and he didn't want to hear much more of it. He tried to change the subject. "When're we going fishing?"

Not a good time to change the subject. John was looking at his potential demise at twenty-nine. "I don't know if I'm going to survive tomorrow. But I need to tell you this: I want to thank you and your pa for what you've done for me," John said, hugging Junior.

John was going to stand up and fight for something, like he recalled his mother doing when he was a ten-year-old boy in Richmond.

It was a sunny mid-October 1880 morning in East Richmond, a good day to walk to church, to feel the soft sun rays on the skin, to come together at church to renew bonds with God, to find out about who's pregnant, who died, the best place to hunt possum, the best place to buy feed for the cattle, to hear the latest gossip.

"Good Sunday morning to all of you. I want to thank y'all for coming; the Lord thanks you for coming," Jeremiah Greene said to fifty or so colored men and women, and a scattering of children who were crammed into his small red brick church to hear him talk about whether the colored people of East Richmond should vote in the upcoming election. He was a bookish-looking, forty-year-old little man with pecan-colored skin, spectacles that covered his deep-set, penetrating, chocolate-brown eyes, a thick black mustache and short coarse black hair. His uncle, who later became a professor at Hampton Institute, taught him to read the Bible at an early age, and even then he knew he was destined to become a minister.

Jeremiah stood at the altar for all to see their stylishly attired pastor. He wore a black frock coat, a black waist coat, contrasting gray trousers, a freshly ironed white cotton shirt, a black floppy tie, and black-laced Oxford shoes. Everyone settled in and waited for Jeremiah to give the invocation. After three minutes of invoking the Lord's name, thanking the Lord for freeing the slaves and setting them on the road to freedom, John, who sat next to Ann in the first row of pews, became restless and slid down the pew, nearly falling onto the floor. Ann pinched his right ear, causing him to grimace while she covered his mouth with her left hand to stifle any sounds of pain. "Amen," the congregants said in unison after Jeremiah finished.

"The Lord says change is coming. I believe it. He's giving us the power to change things around here. We now have the Fifteenth Amendment to the Constitution. We're free to vote; had that right for several years now. As citizens of this country, we got to vote," he said, panning his flock with even measure. "How many of you believe the Lord can change things, to make a way out of no way?" he asked looking at Ann, who raised her right hand and nodded approvingly. Nearly everyone raised their hands, including most of the children, who followed the lead of the adults.

"Close your eyes, brothers and sisters. Now imagine a better life—one for you, your children, your grandchildren. Imagine a life where the colored people will be given the same equal opportunities as white people. Some of us may not live long enough to see the fruits of this new day, but our children and grandchildren will see it someday. We need to continue to chip away at the ugly walls of hatred. One day those walls will come tumbling down like the walls of Jericho."

Jeremiah was schooled in politics; he'd enmeshed himself in it to find candidates who courted the Negro vote. "The Republicans have the hammer and chisel to help us knock down those walls, to pave a road to a better life. The Democrats just want to turn the clock back. Ain't no turning the clock back, ain't no stopping us now. The Republicans, people like Billy Mahone, offer us hope and inspiration," he said before he was interrupted.

"Our best hope, Pastor, is the Lord," someone shouted from the rear. A few people said "amen" in unison. John recalled that even though his mother remained silent, her eyes gave evidence that she hung onto every word as she held him to keep his fidgety body settled.

"You can never go wrong with the Lord on your side," Jeremiah said, trying to resume control over his flock.

"I've been studying the candidates for this upcoming election. Got a chance to see Billy Mahone speak; even shook his hand. I say we help get Billy Mahone elected as our senator from Virginia."

"Ain't no white man's going to help us," a thirty-three-year-old, tall heavyset farmer with sun-beaten swarthy skin in denim overalls shouted in a plummy voice.

Jeremiah told his flock that he heard Mahone promise to work to break the power of wealth and established privilege, to promote public schools, to help the colored folk break loose from the ravages of slavery, all of which rang melodiously in Jeremiah's ears. He was a white politician whom Jeremiah could trust, whom his flock should trust.

"I don't believe what that white man say. He ain't interested in us. I say let's go back to Africa," a raspy voiced farmer said, standing up looking around trying to exhort people to support his position.

Even with the Fifteenth Amendment being the law of the land by 1870 allowing Negroes to vote, the seeds of the political maelstrom that threatened the promise of Reconstruction were firmly sowed long ago, and no piece of paper containing a few words that altered the Constitution was going to easily wash away the deeply rooted seeds of racial separation.

"Why don't you tell 'em what happened to Denmark Vesey and Nat ... can't recall his last name?" the raspy voiced farmer said indignantly, surprising Jeremiah. "The white man killed 'em for trying to free our people."

"But we free now, no more slavery," Ann said crisply as she looked at John and nodded.

"Don't matter what a piece of paper says," the heavyset sodbuster said in a rejoinder. The sodbuster stood up and moved to the aisle for all to see, revealing the earthen color of the land he worked that was caked on the bib and knees of his cotton duck overalls. His face was lined with hard work and bitterness. "Reverend, tell 'em what happened when the white man killed over one hundred Negroes down there in Colfax, Louisiana, a few years ago. We free then, but they slaughtered 'em like cornered possums. Even a blind man couldn't miss they was so cornered. I just want to live to see another day. My wife's eight months pregnant; gone be our fourth child. Got to be there for them kids. Leave the politics to them white folks," he said, continuing his jeremiad.

By now all eyes were focused on the farmer, whose physical presence drowned out those near him. Jeremiah had seen the farmer a few times but had never learned his name. "What's your name, brother?" Jeremiah asked, pointing to him.

"Willie l. Wright," he said resuming his seat.

"Right, right my foot. He ain't right about nothing. His name's *Really Wrong*," Lucy said, evoking a risible response from the audience. Lucy didn't know her true age, but most people thought that she was at least ninety-five years old. Her black, cherry-colored face folded in on itself like a pug, which she used to her delight to scare young children, especially when her mouth was agape, revealing a few teeth that seemed to hang on by sheer will.

Willie thought that he had been mocked by Lucy, just as he had several times before in his life because of his imposing physical mien. His plump lips were tense and began to vibrate with anger, his large nostrils flared, and his thick body shook as if it was ready to explode like a volcano with too much pressure from gases within molten rock. It was happening to him again, but this time in church where he could find no refuge.

Jeremiah acted quickly with his usual calm, well versed in interceding in verbal salvos launched by sparring parishioners. "Sister Lucy, his first name is Willie, not Really, he said in raised voice slowly sounding out the difference in pronunciation. His last name is Wright," he said spelling it. "I think Brother Willie said his middle initial is l."

Adept at seeing both sides of an argument, Jeremiah used this well-honed technique to make members of his flock feel special, like they belong, even in a world that was not all that welcoming to them. "Brother Willie's right about something. The white man has killed us over our God-given right to be free. And like Brother Willie said, even after we got the paper telling us we're free, didn't stop what happened down there in Colfax."

Ann's eyes enlarged to the size of a fawn's, and her face registered a look of concern, one where she was afraid to look around the corner for fear of what she might encounter. "Jeremiah, tell us what we need to know. We can't go into this blind."

"Okay, Sister Ann," who by now had released her vice-like grip on John's throbbing hand.

Jeremiah went on to say: "Ever since we come to this country in shackles on filthy ships, we just wanted to be free. The history books record that we took action to be free. Everything seems to be fine if there is no agitation, no talk about us Negroes just wanting freedom.

"Some of you probably heard of Denmark Vesey. He bought his freedom and became a free man. He didn't like slavery and conjured up the idea of overthrowing that wicked institution. They found and killed him before he could even get started. Word spread that what happened to Denmark could easily happen to other Negroes. Negroes were scared and terrified of what happened to Denmark; they thought the same could happen to them. But people can only take so much suffering before something happens again."

The flock listened with rapt attention and even the children seemed to sense the gravity and weight of Jeremiah's words.

"How many of you heard of Nat Turner?" Jeremiah asked.

Three people raised their hands, including Willie and Lucy.

"Nat was from Virginia, where we live. In 1831, I think it was, Nat and a band of brothers led some kind of rebellion by going house to house freeing Negroes and killing the slave owners."

Lucy raised her hand to be recognized. "Yes, Sister Lucy," Jeremiah said politely.

"I shole wished he'd stopped by my massa's house," Lucy said to gales of laughter. Even Willie managed a slight grin.

Jeremiah appreciated the levity that fractured his homily. But he had to continue on to make his point. He stretched out both arms waving them up and down slowly to quiet the laughter. Lucy, a surprisingly spry nonagenarian, stood up to face the parishioners, took a deep breath, saying "Shhh," loudly for all to hear.

"Thank you, Sister Lucy." She nodded, thanking him for acknowledging her help, which she considered was the least she could do for causing the laughter.

"Sister Ann and Brother Willie made a point. You need to know the rest." Ann leaned slightly forward as to try to absorb Jeremiah's revelatory words. "After the white man caught Nat, they strung him up and hanged him. They cut him up, and gutted him like a trout you gut from the James River. Gave his body parts to white folks as souvenirs. The white men then killed a lot of Negroes in turn, they say to teach us a lesson."

"Tell them about what happened in Colfax along that river," Willie shouted, believing the more Jeremiah spoke, the more people would side against him.

Jeremiah acknowledged Willie's point. "It happened on Easter Sunday seven years ago. They call it the Colfax Massacre. It took place down there in Colfax, Louisiana. Willie's right about the slaughter. The white man killed over one hundred Negroes who did nothing more than defend the rights of colored and white elected Republicans."

Willie stood up again, interjecting before Jeremiah could continue. "Them colored folk down there in Colfax supposedly waiting for the federal troops to come help. No help coming. Just like no help coming to us. Them Negroes down South had a chance to be with their families, but they gone way before they time. I say we put it to a vote whether we vote in this here election."

Ann slowly turned around to face the altar after Willie finished speaking. She closed her eyes and thought of the promise of the years to come. She remembered the heady days of Reconstruction. With federal boots on the ground, scattered throughout the South, the promise of Reconstruction allowed Ann to believe, to hope, that freedom and better days lay ahead. She was happy to receive food rations, clothing, anything, from the Freedmen's Bureau—established by the federal government to help freed former slaves—that improved her miserable lot in life. When she learned that the Fifteenth Amendment gave colored men the right to vote, she raised her hem and did a dance that was unfamiliar even to her.

Even as the programs that were put in place to help Ann and other coloreds began to evaporate, she still continued to believe in a better tomorrow for Negroes, especially with God on her side.

"Ain't your right to put nothing to a vote," Ann said while standing to face Willie, who was several rows away from her, but given his towering presence, he might as well have been standing next to her. "Our men got the right to vote, and if they want to vote, let 'em." Ann sat down with a satisfied feeling that for the first time in her life, she was taking a stand for something. She looked at John as though she hoped that he'd remember that one day he'd need to stand for something.

"Maybe Willie's right. The federal troops left here a few years ago. We ain't got their protection no more," said a middle-aged man in the second row dressed in a brown sack suit.

John looked at the man in the brown sack suit, believing that the timbre of his voice rang familiar. "Mama, who's that man?"

"Mr. Abbott." John's eyes begged for more information. "Last year he helped you with reading, writing, and 'rithmetic. He say my boy smart; say you got *talent*." John wasn't sure what talent meant, but figured it was something good because it was just a few words away from *smart*.

Jeremiah knew that the nation had been torn apart by a bitter four-year war. But his side won, and the victor deserved some long overdue spoils. He'd read about coloreds from Mississippi being elected to serve in Congress as Republicans, and he'd wanted the same thing for Virginia. But even with the election of Republicans who were more likely to champion the cause of Negroes, and with the Fifteenth Amendment cemented in the Constitution, Jeremiah knew that Negroes had to keep voting to have any way of affecting change. He believed that they had come too far, fought too hard to give up.

Although he knew there could be no turning back, he had a feeling that events had been moving inexorably in the wrong direction. Jeremiah's optimism of a brighter day for colored folks grew dimmer with the presidential election of 1876.

When both Democrats and Republicans claimed victory following the election, the nation was faced with a Constitutional crisis. A Faustian bargain broke the logjam. To win the election, Republican presidential candidate Rutherford B. Hayes agreed to remove federal troops that were propping up Republican state governments in the South. The Democrats accepted this agreement, along with a few others, allowing Hayes to become president. Even with this ominous development, Jeremiah believed that Negroes had to forge ahead. As a minister, he felt it was his obligation to continue to beat the drum of justice.

"I'm a citizen of this country and I'm going to vote," Jeremiah said while checking the time by looking at his watch chain attached to his waistcoat. "I'd prithee for my church to be with me on this. Brother Willie, just know that because we haven't been receiving much, that don't mean it ain't pouring. It's pouring some now, and it's going to pour a whole lot later, but we must be persistent, like Job was persistent in weathering all of the difficulties in his life. Someday the rain's going to wash away all this misery. And even if the plans to vote are ruined somehow, just know that God triumphs over ruined plans."

Reversing his position, Mr. Abbott stood and said, "I'm with the pastor on this."

"Me, too," said someone from the rear.

Soon the congregants stood and roared their approval by clapping. Jeremiah looked in Willie's direction, hoping he'd reverse course and see the benefits of voting. Jeremiah's logic and emollient words and tone couldn't sway Willie, who gave a faint dismissive wave of his beefy right hand to acknowledge that his argument to stay away from the polls burst with as much force as when he made it.

On a cold and windy November morning, Jeremiah and his flock of dedicated colored men and women, along with some children, trudged five miles through mud washed out by recent rains to get to the polls. They formed a tight bunch on their way to the polls as a way to show their solidarity and to encircle the children to protect them from the wind and cold. Although they were prepared for violence, they encountered none, just some craven taunts—"What you boys know about voting" or "Haven't you coons learned a lesson."

Willie didn't vote, refusing to loosen his grip on his beliefs about the perils of voting for colored folk.

John thought about Ann taking him to listen to Jeremiah when he was ten years old. He'd hope that any lesson from that time would give him the fortitude he'd need to confront White.

The day of reckoning had finally come for John to confront White. The brigade was in place at eight o'clock. The early morning balmy temperature in the high fifties made setting up outside tolerable. Most of the brigade stationed outside played the card game *Brag* to pass time. At seven thirty, Colonel Jefferson ordered his men to man their stations.

High noon and no sign of White.

"You suppose he's not coming?" Junior asked, looking at his watch that registered five minutes of noon.

John wished it were so, but knew it was just of matter of time. *Tick, tock, tick, tock,* rang in his head.

A brigade infantry man guarding the perimeter spotted White and his cavalry coming out of the woods about a mile away from the press office. He quickly alerted Colonel Jefferson that White was on his way.

White and his retinue had arrived at the bonfire with the timber stacked high, and he was the match.

He dismounted his nag and quickly ran his right hand through his hair to try to tame it. He moved confidently to the door and knocked hard three times.

John's heart began to race. He knew his heartbeat needed to slow down before engaging White. Three more knocks. His heartbeat was now at a manageable level. Five brigade members wielding rifles—three on the first floor and Junior and another on the second floor—were prepared for battle.

"Yes, Mr. White," John said. "What can I do for you?"

White needed a victory, a feather in his cap to show the Council that he caused John to write a retraction in *The Messenger*. He would try to sway John with kindness, something that ran counterintuitive to every fiber in his body, never a reason to be pleasant to a Negro.

He spoke to John with thinly disguised contempt. "Good day," White said pausing as he stumbled over his next words, "Mr. Davis."

"Good day to you, sir," John responded.

"How're your wife and kids?" White asked.

John's heart skipped a beat. He wondered what White and the Council knew about his family.

"We're okay, all things considered," John said hoping his family was indeed okay.

"Well, looks like we didn't have a white Christmas," White said offering a concession while still trying to gauge whether John would tell him the story was going to be retracted.

"Indeed, we didn't."

John's strident answer was a blowback to White. But White tried again, offering an excess of paltering words. Yet he gained no traction as he worked hard—harder than he wanted or expected—to wring a retraction from John. John was standing toe to toe with White, refusing to make White's job easy.

One of the men in White's cavalry became bilious and impatient with John's obstinacy. "That's enough talking to that troublemaker," the man said. "Just tell us that you're going to retract the story in that rag of yours."

No more wheedling. All pretense was over. "You heard the man," White said. "What's it going to be?"

John looked at the men in White's posse, thinking of Tilla and his children, the note to Tilla he placed under her pillow. He looked into White's hostile, wintry gray eyes, then tensed his body to summon every nerve within his being to help him with the words that were about to come out of his mouth. "Mr. White, I will not retract the story."

White started to say something, but John interrupted him and blurted, "Sir, you need not waste your time trying to persuade me otherwise." Though John's mind immediately teetered on regret, he willed his exterior to remain calm.

White's face grew red with annoyance and anger. It was as if John's words lacerated White's body like a whip used on slaves. It was a full-frontal assault that hit White hard. As he walked toward John, he saw the locket dangling from John's neck. He moved closer and stared at it. John had forgotten to put it inside his shirt. White, quicker on the draw, yanked it from John's neck as John tried to prevent a piece of his soul being ripped from him. All John could do was grab air. John moved toward White but stopped suddenly upon hearing the cocking of a rifle. After White fidgeted with it for a few seconds, the locket popped open. White tossed it to the ground and stomped on it with his size-ten brogan. It shattered, and John's mother's hair was gone.

A spectral image of his nemesis, Madame Billingsly, appeared, and his chest pounded with an irate heart, the same heart that had been cosseted by the locket for so many years. But there was an opportunity he could seize. Where Laura Billingsly had given him rage, White gave him hope, hope that whether he survived, the colored community of Lawrence County would see better days ahead through his actions. And he'd have Jeremiah, Reverend Owen, Douglas, Tilla, and of course his mother, and many more to thank for the opportunity.

White then turned slightly and nodded to one of his men on horseback. The man dismounted his horse and lit a torch, and White smiled at John as the man walked toward the press office. White's blood was in full boil. "Now," White said looking angrily at John, "I think you can be persuaded."

John felt the heat from the torch as the man put it two feet in front of John's face. With a stiffened spine and nerves still on high alert, he refused to move.

White turned and nodded to another man on horseback. The man jumped off his horse and threw a rock through the window on the first floor.

John saw his life passing in front of him; his eyes glistened as he did his best to contain his dread. He stood still like a statue, seemingly not a whit afraid.

"The next step," White said, "is your building will go up in flames. With all that paper and kerosene stuff in there, this building will burn for days, and your destruction will be seen from miles away. Now, this is your last chance. You better say you retracting that story."

The statue felt White's icy words but continued to gainsay him. The statue didn't quail or move, except for the glistening eyes that followed the man as he reached back to toss the torch through the shattered window.

"Chessy," someone yelled, "look what we got here." All eyes turned to one of White's men who held Tilla's right arm tightly. "The wench was hiding behind them bushes," the man said pointing.

The armor fell off the statue. John's heart sank. "Tilla," he mumbled. "Why did you come," he mouthed.

White ambled to Tilla, who wore a long overcoat. He stroked her cheek with the back of his left hand. "You sure enough a pretty girl." He grabbed her jaw with his right hand and squeezed hard.

She shook his grip loose and said, "My husband hasn't done anything to you...."

White turned slightly away, then suddenly turned back and slapped Tilla with the back of his right hand. She fell to the ground.

John took a step in her direction, but the rifles aimed at him stopped him in his tracks.

"You and your husband about to feel the power of the Council."

Horse hooves were heard coming from the back of the press building. The leader of the brigade vanguard rode his horse to the fore of the other horses. He sat gallantly atop his palomino, accoutered in the uniform he wore in the Spanish-American War. "Hold it right there," Colonel Jefferson shouted to the man wielding the torch. "I wouldn't do that if I was you." He looked in White's direction and said, "Let Mrs. Davis go."

White's eyes shot a bewildered look. "Get out here, boy, all of you," White shouted as he looked at the retinue of seven other men of the Lawrence County Colored Brigade surrounding Colonel Jefferson on horseback. "This don't concern you. I suggest you leave now or you will be killed." White walked to his nag and retrieved his rifle. "If you don't leave now, I'll shoot you right between the eyes," White said pointing his rifle at Colonel Jefferson's eyes.

Colonel Jefferson's men formed a solid phalanx, and they were ready to act. "Sir, you're surrounded. The perimeter is secure. You cannot escape. I respectfully request that you leave. You trespassing on private property," Colonel Jefferson said with sang-froid, hoping White or his men wouldn't make any daft movements. "You shoot anyone of us, none of your men make it out of here alive."

Tilla broke loose from her captor's grip and ran to John, who put his arms around her.

The men in White's company trained their rifles on John and Tilla.

White wiped the sweat from his brow; his body began to tremble. He had miscalculated, failing to anticipate that John would act to protect himself and his property. The bravado that came with being a member of the Council was failing him. He became timorous, and his brain was now addled with turmoil like honeybees finding out the queen bee is dead. He was descending into a spiraling state of confusion. The thought of being kicked out of the Council entered his mind if he failed.

Suddenly, he dropped his rifle and walked over to the front door where John stood. White removed his pistol from his holster and put it to John's head. Tilla remained at her husband's side. The little bit of light in White's eyes began to extinguish slowly. His failure to convince John to retract the story would make him a failure to the Council, and he'd be mocked by whites. He needed to act.

There they all stood, each side sure of the tableau of American justice that should prevail: White's defiant dismissal of the Thirteenth, Fourteenth, and Fifteenth Amendments to the United States Constitution abolishing slavery, granting coloreds the right to vote, and making Negroes *equal* to whites, or John's belief that these amendments served to fortify a document that once bent toward slavery.

Another set of clopping hooves disrupted the showdown. He was instantly recognized, not by his large belly and bulbous nose, but by the large badge he wore on his overcoat. The sheriff broke from the team of horses carrying his deputies. He rode to within ten feet of White and John and Tilla.

The sheriff had received a tip about the potential showdown at *The Messenger* when someone had told him that a gun battle could erupt at John's press office.

"At ease, men," the sheriff said trying to bring order to the standoff. "I want everyone to drop their weapons."

All failed to heed his command.

"Now!" the sheriff yelled. A mingy amount of spittle had begun to pool at the corners of his mouth. "I am the law in this county. If my command is not obeyed, I'll have all of you arrested."

All dropped their weapons or put them away, except for White, who just put his revolver to the side of his leg. "Chessy," the sheriff said, "drop it." White was known to the law, having been arrested several times for disorderly conduct, mostly due to being intoxicated. White wanted to crawl inside of a whiskey bottle, but reality intruded. He was center stage, and he'd have to find a way out.

Colonel Jefferson was usually calm even in the face of danger, but he grew increasingly fidgety in his seat. White had failed to obey the sheriff's lawful command. He had to be ready to act to try to save John's life. He loosened his holster and readied his revolver, anticipating the need to shoot White, which came in a split second as White raised his gun to shoot John in the head.

It was over in a second. White, John, and Tilla fell to the ground, all bloodied.

Colonel Jefferson's crack shot hit the revolver White had pointed at John's head, but it was too late.

John was dazed; he unfolded himself and got up slowly from the ground. He helped Tilla get up, then looked at the unmistakable blood that was splattered about. White's head had exploded like a rotten pumpkin tossed from a roof. John's heart was still racing, and he was breathing with celerity.

The sheriff addressed White's men. "You boys go home now. Someone'll need to tell his wife." I'll get someone to get Chessy's body.

He turned his steed and addressed the Lawrence County Colored Brigade. "You bucks not the law. I am. Now get the hell out of here."

As John and Tilla walked through the doorway of the press office, the sheriff yelled: "Hey, John, if I was you, I'd be very careful what I write from now on. The law might not be around next time."

The Council asked for an investigation, but the sheriff had little appetite for one. White had exposed himself to danger even in the face of the law—it was like he was spitting in the face of the sheriff by failing to heed his command to drop his weapon.

John and Tilla now went home and ate supper alone. Very few words were spoken. Retrieval of the kids from Junior's house would only cloud matters. They needed time together to feel each other's presence and to quietly try to make sense of what happened earlier in the day. Questions that filled John's head about how and why Tilla risked her life could perhaps surface in time, but not now. He knew Tilla meant everything to him; she had risked her own life to be with him.

After supper, they walked into the bedroom together holding hands. Each doffed their clothes and put on nightclothes, then went to their sides of the bed. Tilla leaned back slowly and her head came to a rest on her pillow. "Tilla," John said, "could you get me a glass of water?"

She nodded.

As she exited the bedroom, John lifted Tilla's pillow and quickly retrieved his farewell letter he had written to her. He folded it two times and put it the pocket of his pants that were in the closet.

Tilla handed him the glass of water. He took a swill. "Thanks, honey."

He turned off the light. They faced each other and breathed each other's scents. Tilla wrapped her temple hair around her ears, then kissed John on the mouth. After she let go, John gave her a deeper kiss. She turned around, and John moved her hair and kissed her on his favorite spot. He settled in a spooning position and held her.

39

DECEMBER 31, 1899

Although it was John's idea to have a New Year's Eve party at First Baptist Church, he was conflicted about ringing in the new year with a celebration as he had just survived a showdown with White. But Tilla had made the choice for him, telling him that he had to go to the celebration, that he couldn't let down the church.

It was Tilla who wanted, indeed needed, to go to the party to celebrate John's victory, the victory for the colored people of Lawrence County. The original idea of celebrating the new year slid behind celebrating Lawrence County's new hero. And even if no one knew but her, Tilla wanted to claim rights to a part of the John's success. She was his ballast that kept him sailing.

They arrived at church at eight o'clock. As they approached the large oak double door to the church, John and Tilla stopped on the landing and listened to the revelry going on inside the church. John raised his head and said a brief prayer. The church, the kinetic center of life in the colored community, came through for him, and he thanked the church members who stood by him.

After he lowered his head, Tilla looked at him and said, "We're heading into a new century. In a few hours, it will be nineteen hundred. I didn't know how it was going to turn out with White. I don't know what I would have done if I had lost you. I don't know if I could have gone on."

John's eyes glistened as he fought back tears. He thought of the letter he wrote Tilla and was relieved that he had removed it from under her pillow. He blinked and one tear finally dropped, landing on the ridge of his right high cheekbone.

"Look at my handsome husband," Tilla said with a mesmeric smile, revealing teeth as white as a wedding cake. "I'm so proud of you. You stood by what you believed to be right." She knew how and when to praise her husband. She continued to put a song in John's heart and a rhythm in his step. She wasn't necessarily keeping count when she praised and supported her husband, but she expected a corresponding return somewhere down the line.

John looked at Tilla; she looked resplendent cap-a-pie, from her touring hat that was a confection of red and black feathers, to her five-strap, jade suede two-inch Cuban heel shoes. "You don't look so bad yourself," John said.

She stepped backward and looked John over one more time before they'd go into the church to join the celebration. It was John's night; he was the cynosure and everything had to be right.

His starched white bib shirt was not fully tucked into his Edgewood charcoal, herringbone red-and-black pinstripe pants. She inserted her right hand down his pants and pulled on the shirt to straighten it.

"Hey, watch it," John said as she moved her hand up and down his trousers to obtain the perfect fit. "We can turn around and go home. The kids are away," he said, smiling with an aspect in his eyes that could make Tilla melt.

But not now. "No, sir," she said, returning the smile, looking at him with come-hither eyes. "We're going to have a good time in this church."

John reached for the door. "Wait," Tilla said.

She reached over to him and adjusted his pert striped waterfall tie. She looked at John's clothes; everything was in place. He looked gallant enough for her. "Can we please go in now?" John asked.

"In a moment," she said. She moistened her right thumb and stroked his right eyebrow to tame a few strands that stuck out. "There," she said, proclaiming that her work on him was done. "Now we can go in." She went first, lilting her way in.

"Good evening, Mr. and Mrs. Davis," someone said as they entered the church. "Go get something to eat."

"Good evening," John said while removing his black Homburg hat.

As they walked into the church's refectory, they could taste the food as the air was thick with the aroma from collards, cornbread, ham, turkey, cow peas....

"Happy New Year, Mr. and Mrs. Davis," Reverend Owen said to John and Tilla at the door to the refectory. "Son, I'd like to talk to you," he said looking at John.

"Baby, go over there to be with Junior and Goldie. I'll be right over," John said.

Because the lighting in the refectory was dim, Tilla could not tell where he was pointing. Tilla squinted and finally saw Goldie. "Oh, I see them," she said.

Reverend Owen looked at John. "You're looking mighty dapper, son."

"These old rags?" John said.

"Listen, son. Colonel Jefferson said there could be trouble tonight. Seems like some folks may not be ready to let it go," Reverend Owen said.

"Let what go?" John asked.

"What happened to White and all."

"We acted in self-defense. White came within a whisker of killing me."

Colonel Jefferson has a few men looking out for us tonight. I've asked the Lord to protect us. I don't want you to worry, but I thought I should tell you."

"Thanks, Reverend Owen," John said as he patted Reverend Owen on the shoulder.

Reverend Owen looked at John and emitted a sober smile. "You know, John," Reverend Owen said, "a wise man once said that fortune is not for the faint-hearted. Thank you."

John sat down next to Tilla. "Honey, this is your plate," Tilla said pointing to it.

"Boy, you better dig into that food," Junior said. "If you don't, I will."

"Don't worry about me," John said, "this food won't be here long."

Junior had cleaned his plate and was not quite sated. "Darling," he said, looking at Goldie, "go get Papa some more black-eyed peas and collards."

"Anything for my baby," Goldie said.

As she sashayed from the table to please her husband, Junior yelled, "And I want some more cornbread."

John had difficulty eating his dinner as he was waylaid with people streaming to him to thank him for taking a stand against White and the Council. John had illuminated the hearts and minds of the colored community for standing up to White and was now basking in the phosphorescence of being a celebrity.

Reverend Owen noticed the disruption and asked the crowd to let John enjoy his meal. But no sooner had he finished eating, the stream started again. Jimmy was the first in line. "John, Tilla, this here is my woman. Soon to be my wife. Tell 'em your name," Jimmy said.

"Elizabeth."

"Do you go to our church?" Tilla asked.

"No, my papa's a minister at another church. That's where I go."

"Thanks for what you done for us," Jimmy said. "I'm glad I was part of that brigade. Made me feel good; made me feel like I am somebody."

Others clamored to talk to John. People from the Colored Farmers' Alliance brought a smile to his face. He shook hands with all those who approached him. Even with a throbbing hand, he gave no indication his hand hurt.

"Listen, my brothers and sisters." Reverend Owen shouted. He raised his arms in the air and moved them slowly down as a signal for the pianist to stop playing as the witching hour was upon them. "Five minutes before midnight. Five minutes before a new century arrives. We're going to start counting down at ten seconds."

He suddenly remembered the time capsule. "I want to thank you for writing something for our time capsule. We won't be here in a hundred years when it is opened, but let's pray that the Negro race will be truly free by then and that there be no more such thing as racial superiority." Up until this point, the Negro had been in some kind of bondage; whether it was being an afterthought as a second class citizen before slavery firmly took hold or after slavery, that bondage had begun to fray a bit after the passage of the amendments to the United States Constitution during Reconstruction. The bondage grew tighter, though, after Reconstruction. "Two hundred and eighty-one years of being treated as an inferior people by our white brothers must come to an end."

The pianist at the Newby and Evans upright started up again, playing "Maple Leaf Rag," a ragtime favorite. Junior, the supreme archon of dance, instantly recognized his favorite ragtime tune, grabbed Goldie's arm forcing her out of her seat, and swung her around; they then settled into doing their favorite dance, the slow drag. As the tune neared its end, he grabbed Goldie tightly around the chest, kissing her with an open mouth, and she squeezed his back side, both now oblivious to their environment.

Reverend Owen removed his waist watch from his trousers. Less than a minute to go. He raised his hand signaling for the crowd to listen. "Attention, attention," he shouted. "I want everybody to stand. When I start counting, count with me."

Tilla held John's left hand tightly.

"Ready for this new century?" Junior said to Goldie.

She kissed him, fiercely and lingeringly. She released his lips, saying, "What do you think?"

Reverend Owen: "Ten, nine ..." Everyone joined him and they counted the rest in unison. "... three, two, one."

"Happy New Year!" they all shouted.

John's heart skipped a long beat, his eyes widened. He put his arm around Tilla's waist, squeezing her tight, unsure how to react to the peal of rifle and gun shots he heard from outside.

Fear emanated from John's visage, and Junior noticed it. He knew it was just some roisterers outside partaking in a jamboree. "It's okay, boy; just some of us shooting in the air to mark the new year."

Council President Allen Montgomery had been charged and convicted of bribing three elected officials within six months after White's collapse in front of *The Messenger*. With his initial time spent preparing for his defense, he neglected the Council's business, and the Council soon went out of business. Some in the colored community talked of John's showdown with White as causing the collapse.

Within five years after the New Year's celebration that ushered in the new century, John sold *The Messenger* and was out of the newspaper business. While the colored community continued to show its appreciation of John's militant stand against the Council, the marvels of celebrity that surrounded him five years ago had faded. He was still a deacon at his church, he still dispensed advice to neighbors, and on occasion, he'd talk to a politician about offering his support. He figured he'd miss attending conferences on journalistic standards, meeting colored journalists from other states. But because he needed to spend more time with his growing family, he was satisfied to leave the newspaper behind. Time had come for him to do something else.

40
SPRING, 1910

The beatings had become routine, but the one she received last night hurt the most. She'd give anything for the beatings to stop. If she tattled, she'd be responsible for shuttering the business, and her pittance of pay would vanish. Perhaps she'd go elsewhere for business, a place where there would be no beatings, or fewer of them.

As she neared the general store, each step was heavier than the next, but not because of the throbbing pain in her ribs and the pain of battered eyes. She wasn't much of a tattler, but perhaps it was time for her tormentor to feel her pain. Her nerves were as tight as the fists that had pelted her body. But that was good because that way she knew they were in place, and she'd continue to the store.

Only fifty feet to the steps of the store. Her nerves were still in place, and she fought hard to keep them there even though her steps became heavier.

She saw shelves of food items and dry goods through two large plate glass windows. The rocking chair to the left of the front door moved. She stopped in her tracks. A tabby jumped from the chair and strolled across the front door. A sign of life, but none yet detected through the windows.

The sign on the door said, OPEN.

She pulled open the door and toddled in. She panned left to right and didn't see anyone. As she moved slightly to the right, she saw a man's back behind the counter. She cleared her throat, and the man turned around and looked at her. He diverted his eyes from her as he attended to a customer who had placed a sack of flour on the counter.

The customer said, "Thank you, Mr. Davis," and left.

She edged closer to the counter and raised her head slowly. "Oh, my God." The carmine bruises to her eyes clashed with her skin that was the color of corn. "Who did that to you?"

She grimaced deeply and touched her rib cage. She spoke slowly and haltingly, as if each word was a monumental effort. "I got a beating last night."

"Can I get you some Postum?" John asked.

"Okay."

John poured the Postum in a noggin and handed it to her.

Her hand trembled, and John held his hands under the noggin until she had control of it. She took her first sip and quickly spit it out.

"Careful there, it's hot."

She blew short breaths into the noggin, then took another sip. As tears began to stream from her battered eyes, she sniffled, and she put the noggin on the counter. John handed her a tissue, and she dabbed the skin beneath her eyes.

A nerve from the bundle of nerves popped loose. "I think I better leave." She turned and faced the door.

"Wait," John said. "Tell me what happened."

Although John had lost his trim shape, he looked several years younger than forty. He wiped his hands on his white apron. He moved quickly from behind the counter and stopped within two feet of the woman.

The bruises were even more pronounced up close; they looked like someone had painted them on her face. He moved closer and held her face with his right hand as his eyes moved across her face pocked with acne, inspecting the damage. He lowered her lower lip; a few teeth were missing. He raised her upper lip, none were missing.

"Here," John said pointing to the chair, "sit down." John hung up the closed sign on the door and pulled down the shade, hoping she'd feel more comfortable.

John handed her a handkerchief and, as soothingly as he could, said, "Now, tell me what happened."

She dabbed her eyes with the handkerchief. A minute later she whispered, "Baker beat me."

"Who is Baker?"

"He'll kill me if ..."

"If what? You tell me."

"I can't."

John was exasperated. "Then why are you here?"

She recoiled slightly from John's tone and unballed the handkerchief to dab her eyes again. But John's sympathy had worn thin. "Go on home, Miss.... Tell your mother and father what happened to you."

"My name's Barbara."

A slight opening, but not good enough. "Barbara, I need to open up my store. I may be losing money talking to you. We've been at this for a while now."

She nodded. "Okay, Mr. Davis, it's like this. Baker pay you rent to live in that house on your property."

John shook his head. "Mr. Payne is in that house; he pays me rent."

Barbara shook her head.

"Describe this Baker?"

"What do you mean?"

"What's his age?"

"Maybe your age, thirty or so."

"It's been awhile since I've held that number."

"What else can you tell me about him?"

"Black mustache. A little darker than you. His walk a little funny. Like a duck."

The walk gave him away. She had indeed described Albert Payne, John's tenant.

"So Baker did this to you?"

She nodded. "Yeah, and some of his friends."

"This Baker is Mr. Payne. How'd he get tagged with Baker?"

It was a nickname. "They say he know how to bake pies. He made me the best blueberry pie ever. You didn't know?"

"No, I didn't. Apparently, there're lots of things I don't know about him. I want you to come to my house this evening. We'll talk more. Stop by my house tonight."

She nodded.

Barbara told John and Tilla all about what Payne was doing in the house. John's rental was being used as a bordello. Payne accused Barbara of cheating him out of *his* money for a liaison she had with a customer. He had beaten her before using the same excuse.

John saw no need to go inside his rental. Payne had proven himself to be a good tenant. The rent was paid on time, and Payne he didn't complain about anything. He never gave John an excuse to evict him. Seemed like it was the perfect setup.

Tilla wrapped her arms around Barbara and said, "Thanks for telling us this. You sure you got a place to go?"

She nodded.

Tilla handed her a bag of pastries.

She stood straight and had talked more confidently than she did earlier in the day. Her bundle of nerves had loosened and had settled to a more comfortable plateau. "Yes, Miss Tilla. Thanks for the bag."

"You're welcome, honey."

She looked at John and Tilla and said, "Bye."

Tilla's children were always uppermost in her mind. A bordello was in her backyard right under her nose, and she had missed it. Something had to be done.

"John, we have six children now, ages one to fifteen. We don't need this mess around us," she said as they lay in bed. "We should have used the money you made from the sale of *The Messenger* and moved from this place."

John could forgive Tilla for not thinking clearly. He knew how she felt about the children. "Where do you propose we go?" John asked as she brushed her long auburn hair, giving attention to each delicate strand.

Tilla wanted to be in a big city, something Roscoe had promised her—to live in a *real* city. "Anywhere but here," she said. "Don't you want to be in a bigger city?"

"Where're we going?" He punctuated the air with his right forefinger and said, "This right here is home, right here in Mount Hope. I say we raise our children in this town. It's the people who make the town. It's the people who bring life to the town. The Davis name is a good brand name here. People know us. We got a store here. We got this house, the rental. Lots of people, colored and white, would like to have our house. We're lucky enough to have land to grow crops. We got cattle, chickens, pigs. Got a couple of mares, a dobbin, and a Morgan. No other place better for colored folk. You're interested in the big city? Moulton's across the way. How about Birmingham? Sheffield? Crime is everywhere you look. Less of it here."

John stopped for Tilla to say something. Her only riposte was having her arms folded across her chest. But that was a good sign for John. Her voice—her lyrical instrument—was at rest. He had scored solid points where Tilla was often ahead.

He had to protect his family. "I've got to clean up this mess in my backyard. I've got to find out for sure if Barbara was straight with me. I can't accuse Mr. Payne of something without proof. I'll need evidence. I'll get Jimmy to go over there one night. He'll ask for Barbara, and ask how much. If what Barbara told me is true, I got to move him out. Hate to lose the money, but I can't have my children surrounded by that filth. Theo will go with me. The boy is fifteen now. I reckon he's old enough now to know about the wretched things that go on in this world."

Tilla wanted off the subject she had broached. It was like starting a fight with no plan on how to win it. She had missed her period, and she knew the answer. Even at thirty-four, this pregnancy was easy to catch, just like the others. She laid her head on John's chest; her right hand rested against his belly. "John, ..." she said, "we're going to have another baby."

John stroked, rubbed, and scratched her head as on cue, just like he did when his dog rolled over on his back, expecting a belly rub. "That'll be seven, he said. "You want a boy or girl?"

"She turned the question on him. "What do you want?"

"Doesn't matter. Just another mouth to feed."

She listened to John's heart beat against his chest, wondering if John's heart was as pure as the day she fell in love with him. She raised her head and used her right hand to lift up off his chest. She tilted her head left, then right, looking at John as though she was staring at a stranger, a person's heartbeat perhaps she no longer recognized. "Who is this man sharing this bed with me?"

"My name is John Moses Davis, father of Tilla Davis's six children, soon to be seven," he said.

She huffed: "Well, act like it. Don't say our child's just another mouth to feed. They're precious gifts from the Lord." She then turned on her heels and walked to the kitchen to start cleaning.

John learned that Barbara had told it straight about Payne.

Payne told Jimmy that Barbara was *unavailable*, but he could have someone else. "Stop by tomorrow 'round nine o'clock, and I'll take care of you."

"Where's the room we use?" Jimmy asked.

"Anywhere you want upstairs," Payne told him.

"Can I see for myself?" Jimmy asked.

"Not now, it's busy up there." Varing pitches of erotic screams were heard coming from the second floor.

"Come by tomorrow," Payne said impatiently, ready to close the door.

As Jimmy stepped down off the dimly lit porch, two women sashayed in his direction. The portly of the two women peered at Jimmy, saying in a raspy voice, "You want some?"

Jimmy had heard many sermons from Reverend Owen about vices such as prostitution. The good word was everything to him. He gave a terse answer, "No!"

Tilla wiped her brow after she put the scrub brush into the soapy bucket in the kitchen. She sat on her knees, momentarily wondering how John would confront Payne. She reached in the bucket to retrieve the scrub brush and resumed scrubbing the poplar wood kitchen floor. With six children, it was a never-ending battle to keep it clean.

Maggie ran across the wet kitchen floor and slid and fell, hitting her head on the icebox. "Maggie Mae," Tilla said, "you see Mama's working. Now you and Pearl take that play outside, unless you want to help. Take Claude with you. He wants to play."

Maggie was at the age where she was confused whether or not to cry. The bump on her head stung; her heart told her to cry, but her mind prevailed. She was a big girl now and needed to show it.

Maggie rubbed her head trying to make the sting go away. "Maggie Mae, start stepping."

"But Mama, it's hot out there."

"You heard me. Go on," she said, looking at the girls to make sure their dresses where suitable to play in.

Tilla knew that their day would come when they would get their assigned chores. But they still had age on their side: Maggie was eight and Pearl six. Thirteen-year-old Bessie and twelve-year-old Eunice had already begun their distaff tasks of cooking, cleaning, and ironing, and whatever else Tilla demanded. When not working in the field or attending school, Theo helped his father in the store.

Maggie, Pearl, and Claude played tag with Kathleen, the young white neighborhood friend, under a canopy of hackberry trees. Pearl spotted John turning the corner on his way home. She smiled and said, "Look, Daddy's home."

Maggie and Pearl ran to John and grabbed him by the waist.

"How're my girls?" John said as he wiped his brow with the back of his right hand.

"It's hot out here, Pa. Mama made us come out here to play," Maggie said.

"You do what your mama say, you hear me?"

John looked over by the hackberry trees and saw Claude and Kathleen sitting up against one of the trees.

Claude wore a cotton shirt and tweed knee-length pants. His stockings had fallen to his ankles. Kathleen's original orange-colored dress was faded. The black soutache trim on the dress was nearly gone, and the little that remained barely hung on. Any form the dress had was long gone. She had dark gamine eyes, and her naturally ruddy cheeks were splotched with dirt caked on her face.

Looking into four-year-old Claude's blithesome eyes, John said, "Hi, son."

"Hi, Pa," Claude burbled.

"Son, pull up you stockings."

"Yes, Pa."

"Kathleen, how's your father doing?" John asked while noticing that every time he saw her she wore the same tattered dress.

Kathleen's father was off work due to a mishap at work. He had shattered his radius in his right arm when he fell on the job. Ever since her father's injury, John worried about the family. He gave them vegetables from his field to help a hapless man and his family who had become mendicants. With her large blue eyes, Kathleen looked at John, seeming to ask him to adopt her. She was losing her way, not quite sure where she fit into a society that was confusing to her. She and her family counted on favors from the Davis family, yet society had defined her and her family as being superior to the colored people.

"He's okay, I guess.. After a pause, she then said, "Mama say can we have some onion blades? We really like them, Mr. John.

"I'll get you some before you leave." He reached into his pocket and said, "I've got some candy for you kids." He threw the candy in the air and the kids scrambled to fetch the pieces scattered on the dirt road.

As John walked to the house, the thought of his girls becoming Payne's victims caused him to stop and shudder. He needed to act.

41

SPRING, 1910

"Theo, wake up," John said, "we're going to pay Mr. Payne a visit." Theo was a heavy sleeper like his father. "Theo," he said tapping him on the shoulder as he lay in a deep sleep, "wake up."

Theo groaned, turned on his side, and saw a figure standing at his bedside. He rubbed his eyes, wondering whether he was dreaming. His father's brown fustian trousers came into focus, then his father's mahogany face, as his eyes drifted upward in an effort to understand why his peaceful sleep had just been punctuated. "Pa, it's early in the morning."

"That's the time to catch him—in the act. We talked about this yesterday. Now hurry up and get dressed. And be quiet. Don't wake up the rest of the family."

They strode toward the rental. The sun was pushing itself up in the sky. The early morning temperature gave a hint of the hot day that lie ahead. "Okay, son, go put your rifle behind the tree like I told you. And hurry back."

John checked to make sure his revolver was in place in the holster. He closed the jacket to his brown sack suit to hide the gun.

"Okay, let's go knock on the door," John said.

John knocked three times. No sounds could be heard coming from the house. It was quiet except for the early morning relaxing sounds of a few songbirds.

John looked at Theo, who was an inch taller than he. "Son, you're taller than me; when did you pass your pa?" John said.

Theo shrugged his shoulders.

John knocked again. Nothing.

John said in a firm voice, "Mr. Payne, it's John Davis. I need to talk to you."

Theo looked at John. "You suppose he's not home, Pa?"

"Could be, son, but I'm not leaving here till I find out."

John knocked again. Nothing. John removed the door key from his pants pocket and inserted it in the keyhole. "I know this is the key to this door." He turned it back and forth several times. "It's not working. He changed the lock. I *own* this house. He's in a heap of trouble."

"Looks like we gotta break in, Pa."

"You're right, son." John removed the revolver from his holster and cocked it, holding it tightly in his right hand. "Step back, son." John kicked the door with his right foot. It gave a little. The next kick caused the door to fling open. "Quick, go get your rifle."

The stench was quick to assault their olfactory nerves. Theo opened the living room window to remove the fug, but it wasn't likely to do any good as the air outside was still and misty. They looked at the dice and playing cards on the gambling table in the living room. Open bottles of whiskey were strewn on the floor. John walked to the kitchen. Theo didn't follow; he was sidetracked by pictures of naked woman plastered on the living room wall.

Payne was sitting in a chair slumped over the kitchen table. John grabbed the back of his shirt to raise his head. The front of his white pullover shirt was soaked in blood. John could see the entry wound. He was shot in the chest. John shook his head in disgust and slowly lowered Payne's head back to the table.

John walked out of the kitchen and looked at Theo who was still gawking at the pictures. He wondered whether his fifteen-year-old son had ever seen a naked woman. It was too much to consider, and he quickly purged the thought from his mind. "Son," John said breaking Theo's concentration, "Mr. Payne's dead. Someone shot him. Nothing good can come out of what he was doing. You remember that."

Theo nodded.

"I'm going to look around some more down here; you see what's upstairs," John said.

"Anybody here?" Theo said as he opened one of the bedroom doors. He saw an unmade bed and a whiskey bottle on the nightstand.

He turned the knob to another bedroom door, but the door didn't open; the door was jammed. He bore into the door with his right shoulder using enough force to cause the door to fling open. He immediately saw a girl under a thin bed sheet. She began to tremble at the sight of Theo's rifle. As Theo started to say something, he noticed that her eyes darted about like a bird looking for a safe place to land. Her eyes settled on a closet. Theo put his left index finger to his mouth, telling the girl not to make any noise. Theo held the rifle in his right hand as he opened the door with his left hand.

As Theo turned around, a man leaped from behind the chest of drawers and rushed Theo, knocking the rifle to the floor. The man, at least thirty pounds heavier than Theo, had Theo pinned on the floor. Theo was a scrappy lad and had prided himself on his pugilistic skills, but this was a fight where there were no rules. Theo grabbed him tightly around the waist to limit the man's ability to throw punches. But the man broke Theo's clutch and punched Theo in the mouth. Theo yelled and covered his face with his hand to deter more damaged to the face. The man began to punch Theo in the ribs.

"Let my son go or I'll kill you right where you are," John said, pointing his revolver at the man's head.

The naked man stood up, revealing a dumpy frame and thick arms that seemed designed to lift heavy objects and that would be useful in a brawl. Theo slid a few feet where he came to a rest against the wall; he felt his puffy upper lip and spit out blood.

"Get over there," John said still pointing his revolver at the man. "Where're your clothes?"

The man pointed to a pile of togs near the foot of the bed. John grabbed the man's pants and shirt, and searched them for any kind of weapon. John threw the clothes at the man and said, "Put them on." The man stood still with eyes that exuded fear. "Now!" John screamed at the man.

With a slightly calmer voice, John said to the girl, "I guess this is your dress," as he held up the dress for the her to see.

She nodded.

"Here," John said tossing it to the girl. The girl looked about Bessie's age. "How old are you?" John asked.

"Fourteen."

John looked at the man. "What about you? How old are you?"

"Thirty-eight."

John was incredulous; the grayish-black hair and deeply wrinkled forehead made him seem older. But John saw no need to quibble with the man about his age. "I own this place. Get the hell out of here."

The man bounced down the steps with John behind him holding his rifle. As the man reached the front door, John said, "Hold it right there. Mr. Payne is dead. Do you know anything about that?"

"No."

"Go now. Don't come this way again," John said.

John turned around and saw the girl in her tattered dress traipsing down the steps. "Where's my son?" he asked her. "He's right there," she said softly and pointed to the hallway on the second floor.

"I'm coming, Pa."

"What's your name?" John asked the girl.

"Hanna."

Hanna's vacuous eyes looked like those of a person who hadn't eaten for days, like something emanating from a barren soul. She was afraid. "Hanna, you're a pretty girl," John said. She smiled a smile which seemed too womanly and sly for a young girl. John continued: "You shouldn't be involved in this mess. You go to church?"

She shook her head.

"There are people who can help you. I want you to find your way to First Baptist. People there will help you. You hear?" John said, hoping she'd seek the church's help to keep her off the road to perdition.

She nodded.

"You got a place to go?" John asked.

She nodded again.

"Go on," John said.

John looked at Theo's puffy upper lip and was glad he got there in time to prevent more harm to Theo. "Let's get you home and fixed up. Your mama's going to be upset."

Theo felt his lip, then tugged on an incisor, wondering whether it would stay in its socket.

John closed the front door. "Son, we're gonna need to get this house in repair to rent again. We need the money. Your mama's going to have another baby."

42
SPRING, 1910

John had risen early, in part to beat the stifling heat that was sure to be ushered in in a few hours, and in part for feeling guilty for not having sown some of his crops two weeks ago. It was early May, and all of Alabama was already experiencing a heat wave.

As he turned over the soil with his hoe, his mind was also turning over: He thought about the need to spend more time with his children. He thought he'd work less hours as a grocer than he did running *The Messenger*. Tilla helped him with the bookkeeping in between keeping close watch on her growing brood of children. But he was still coming home late from work and rising early to open up for business. He had a few helpers here and there, but they didn't last long.

Before he knew it, the sun had shot up and reached its peak in the cloudless sky. He had tilled the soil for several hours without respite, but was content that he had settled things in his mind.

Bessie ambled to her father, who was deep in the field working. "Pa, Mama said to give you this glass of water."

Bessie was a blur to John, his vision clouded by the sweat in his eyes. He removed his wide-brimmed straw hat and retrieved a sweat rag from the back of his overalls and wiped his brow of the sweat that was stinging his eyes. He blinked a few times and his vision was restored, so much so that he could now see the thick haze blanketing his field. Bessie had her father's high cheekbones and her grandmother Fannie's freckled skin. "How's my baby girl?"

She was thirteen years old and had begun to sprout breasts. "Pa, Mama said for you to drink this water."

He took the tall glass of chilled water and gulped it down like the parched man he was. "Thanks, baby girl. That hit the spot."

Looking at Bessie, he knew he'd need to spend more time at home to be with his growing brood. Tilla had done a wonderful job with them, teaching them to read, write, and do math. But she couldn't do the things John could do—pick them up, wrestle with them, and do more in their lives as a father. He knew how it felt to not have a father. An absent father, he thought, was not good. He'd soon sell his store and return to a life of farming. It was going to be hard work, especially as he got older, but at least he'd spend more time with the kids—at least that was the plan. He'd use the money from the sale of the store and spend some on the farm, the family, and invest some.

"Some man's at the house asking Mama questions; Mama needs you," Bessie said.

"Let's go see who it is," John said as they loped to the house.

Tilla stood in the parlor talking to the census enumerator. John and Bessie walked into the parlor, happy to be out of the searing heat. "Oh, honey, this is ..."

"Paschal Leigh," the man said finishing Tilla's sentence. "He wants to ask us some questions," she continued.

"How can I help you?" John said, looking at the thick ream of paper the enumerator was carrying.

"Well, I'm here on behalf of the government. I'm to take the census of residents here in Mount Hope. Just need to ask you folks a few questions."

"All right, let's go to the living room." Mr. Leigh followed John to the living room, going through the kitchen first. "Have a seat. Can we get you anything?"

"No," Mr. Leigh said while his eyes drifted up to the oversized drawing of John's mother on the wall.

"Oh, that's my mother. She was a good woman," John said as to realize that she was probably dead. "Everything I have in this world is because of her," he said, "and this woman here," he added, looking at his wife, who emitted a smilet.

"Where were you born, John?" Mr. Leigh asked.

"Richmond." Mr. Leigh wrote it down and paused. "That's Virginia," John added.

"I know where it is," Mr. Leigh said smartly.

"How about this lady right here on the wall—where was she born?"

"Don't know. Wish I did."

"How about you?" the enumerator said, looking at Tilla.

"I was born right here in Mount Hope. Same for my ma and pa."

"Tell me the names and ages of your children."

"Tilla, you better tell him that. I'll get it mixed up."

"Let's see. Theo is fifteen, Bessie is thirteen, Eunice is eleven, Maggie is eight, Pearl is six, Claude is four, and Willie is eight months."

"Do you own or rent?" the enumerator asked next.

"Own," John said proudly.

"What's your occupation?" the enumerator asked.

"Well, I'm a grocer now, soon to be a former grocer. I'm going back to farming full-time. Need to spend more time with my wife and children."

Tilla arched her thick eyebrows, and the surface of her eyes expanded beyond their usual large size. She had asked John for years to spend more time with the children, and she had finally gotten the answer she had long yearned for.

After having all of his questions answered, Mr. Leigh stood and shook John's hand and thanked him for participating in the census. "We need more colored folk like you, Mr. Davis," he said.

Recognizing the slight, John extended his hand to shake hands with Mr. Leigh again. John squeezed Mr. Leigh's right hand tight and looked him in his small eyes and said, "And we need more white people like you to take the time to talk to colored folk."

When John released his grip, Mr. Leigh shook his right hand as to bring life back to it. "That's quite a grip you got there."

43
JUNE, 1917

It was two o'clock in the afternoon, but the stygian sky had plunged daylight to darkness. Lightning streaked across the sky as it glowed in a springtime thunderhead, giving an indication that the sky would soon pour out a heavy rain. John, Junior, and Jimmy quickened their step as the first raindrops fell. Jimmy held open the door to the pool hall and he followed John and Junior into the place where they liked to go on Saturdays to play billiards.

Although they were met with a mingled aroma of liquor and smoke, it was the unusual frenetic buzz that seemed out of place, one that resembled Nikolay Rimsky-Korsakov's "Flight of the Bumble Bee." The conversations were fast-paced as though the speaker had reason to say something quickly before he'd be interrupted.

It quickly became clear to John, Junior, and Jimmy what the buzz was about. The winds of war had been blowing across the country for some time, and even the little hamlet of Mount Hope had caught the war contagion. The winds had been fueled by talk that Congress would soon declare war against Germany for the war that was raging in Europe.

The usual mix of people—the serious pool players like them, those looking for social interaction, and those looking to get an early start on their way to inebriation, were present. Junior caught sight of an open pool table and tapped Jimmy and John on the arm, beckoning them to join him. John told Jimmy to go first as John was more interested in the buzz.

"Don't worry, Johnny boy," Junior said as he stroked his stick as though he were smoothing out the mane on a dog, "you're next after I beat Jimbo."

Jimmy fought back. "You going down today," Jimmy said, sounding plucky. He bent his large frame over the table and broke the balls, befitting of a man who possessed great strength. After the balls settled, three of them had fallen into separate pockets, and the rest had come to a stop on the baize, causing him to look at Junior with a deeply furrowed brow as if to say the game would be over soon.

Several conversations were going on, all about the war, at the same time. As John looked around the tatty poolhall to decide which conversation he'd join, an elderly colored man with half a right ear recognized John, and said, "Ain't that right, John?"

"Nate, you haven't been right since I've known you," John said as he walked over to Nate and playfully massaged his upper back.

"John," a lanky, slender-faced man who was a regular patron of the pool hall said, "what you think about this here war coming?"

Because John hesitated slightly, the void was quickly filled. "They talking about our colored boys going over to Europe to fight ... for freedom, they say. We get freedom here first, then we go fight," said a bushy, gray-haired, seventy-year-old man. "My grandson talking about going overseas to fight. I'm gonna talk to my son about it; my grandson ain't going nowhere near where they fighting." Thunder roared from the sky as he pounded the table to emphasize his point.

Someone chuckled and said to the bushy, gray-haired man, "God must be listening to you."

The slender-faced man decided to give John another chance; he knew that John had a son who was draft-eligible. Looking at John seated next to him, he said to him, "Man, don't you got a son in the age to be drafted for the war?"

John had mixed feelings about the war. He believed in his country, but his country still didn't believe in him as a colored man. He knew that things had gotten a little better for colored folks for a few years after the Civil War, but many of those gains were reversed, causing John to write in *The Messenger* several years ago that "freedom for colored folk was chimerical." His country would do the right thing, he believed, if it witnessed colored soldiers fighting for it. Since he was too old to fight, he'd fight vicariously through Theo.

"We're going to make them give us our freedom by fighting in the war," he had told Tilla a few days ago.

He rehashed what he had told Tilla. "I want my boy to fight for his country. Besides, it'll do him good; he can stand a little growing up." He paused briefly, and quickly began to expostulate: "We're going to make this country give us our rights; we're equal citizens. When they see colored men fighting for the country, they have no choice but to honor us. You'll see."

The bushy, gray-haired man met John's optimism head on by dismissing it: "Equality may be a right, but I says no power on this planet can make it a fact."

"Look," John said, "W. E. B. DuBois is for it. I side with him and other Negro leaders on this issue. I just can't see how this county can deny us our freedom if we die for it."

After swilling the last of his whiskey, the bushy, gray-haired man said, "The white man ain't going to give us no rights, no matter how much we fight for this country."

Cicero, a pool hall habitué, lifted his large head and suddenly awoke from his besotted state. His right eyelid drooped down to cover the missing eye he lost in a brawl a few years back. He interjected: "Yeah, that's right. The white man has stepped all over us ever since we landed in this country. We best go back to Africa."

"What country in Africa?" John asked rhetorically. He took a quick puff on his pipe and continued: "Africa is not your home now; it's a strange land to us. We're here now and we got to stay and fight for what belongs to us. That's what I say."

About an hour after Junior and Jimmy began their match, Junior was on the verge of winning his first game. He had one ball left and Jimmy had one. Junior realized he needed to clip his ball ever so slightly to get it to go in the side pocket. He looked at Jimmy and nodded. The shot was foozled and he cursed; the cue ball lined up nicely for Jimmy to end the game.

Jimmy shouted over the still-buzzing conversations several feet away, "Hey, John."

John caught Jimmy's baritone voice, stood up and looked at Jimmy, who sported a wide grin on a weathered face.

"Our boy Junior's about to go down three times in a row."

Jimmy steadied his stick, then struck the cue ball into the eight ball, which went in the corner pocket off a bank just liked he called, and solidifying his status of a complete pool player, the best in Mount Hope.

Junior had had enough. He extended both arms and flicked his hands as if to acknowledge he'd been beaten and had to surrender. He walked over to John's table and joined the still-buzzing conversation about the war. Jimmy took on another player.

Junior had shaken off his defeat by Jimmy and thrust himself into the debate. Never shy of obtruding his opinions on others, he said, "No need for us to go fight in that war. Otis Jefferson fought in that war over there in Cuba or Puerto Rico; I know it was one of them places. Thousands of colored men like Otis fought for this country; that don't mean squat to the white man. And y'all know I'm telling it like it is."

The thunderstorm had passed, and the sun reappeared in the sky. More patrons flooded into the pool hall and the war debate rolled on like a train with no brakes. Everybody had an opinion.

John looked at his pocket watch. He had been at the pool hall for four hours; it was time to leave. Dinner would be waiting for him at home, and he needed time to prepare his thoughts about what he'd say in Sunday school the next day. He stood up and waited for Jimmy to turn his way, and when he did, John waved. Jimmy nodded. John then said to Junior, "I'll catch up with you later."

With the door handle in his right hand, John turned around and looked at the table he'd just left; the heated war debate roiled on. Junior was right in the middle of it.

44
JUNE 1917

A zephyr rolled over John as he sat in a rocking chair on his front porch, puffing on his pipe with his eyes closed. By the yap he heard, he knew the postal carrier would be at his house in about a minute.

The mixed-breed beagle yapped at John's feet, and John's eyes snapped open. He bent forward and rubbed the dog on the head.

"John, how you be today?" the postal carrier said.

"Howdy, Mr. Weems," John said to the postal carrier. John had been in a contemplative mood about the war. "Now that war's been declared on Germany by the government, I've been thinking about my oldest boy and whether he's going to be drafted."

"I've been delivering draft notices for the past week. Looks like you can stop wondering." Mr. Weems handed John a bundle of mail; the one from the government was on top.

"Talk to you later, John."

"Good day, Mr. Weems."

Mr. Weems pivoted and walked down the three steps to the ground. The yapper continued on his route with Mr. Weems, keeping him company as he often did when Mr. Weems would first round the corner to start his deliveries. But before he continued with Mr. Weems, the yapper turned and yapped at John as if to say goodbye.

John looked at the envelope from the *United States Government*. He shook it mindlessly, contemplating whether to open it. But he quickly settled in his mind, since it was Theo's mail, Theo had to be the one to open it.

"Tilla," John yelled.

After a few seconds, she appeared at the door.

"Sit here, sweetheart," John said, pointing to the rocking chair next to him.

Tilla wiped her hands on her apron and sat next to John.

"Where's Theo?"

"I don't know where he is. He's twenty-two years old now; he's a grown man. He's not checking in with me when he comes and goes."

He had stopped checking in when he started slumming with his buddies. And when he wasn't slumming, he found time to take up boxing, dreaming of being the next Jack Johnson, known as the Galveston Giant, former boxing heavyweight champion. He wanted the women just like Jack had.

"Now watch where're you going," Tilla said to Willie, who darted to the door to go outside and resume playing. "Wait," Tilla yelled. "Come here and let Mama kiss you." She kissed him on his cheek, and he resumed his sprint to the front door.

Peace and quiet resumed in the house. Bessie and Eunice were married with children and living several blocks from John and Tilla. Willie, Claude, and Charlie were outside playing, and Maggie and Pearl were at Junior and Goldie's house, playing with their two youngest daughters. "Honey, I want to talk to you," John said. "Let's talk in the living room."

After fifteen years, Ann's picture still adorned the back wall in the living room. Tilla or one of her girls kept it clean. The living room walls were mottled and needed a fresh coat of paint. The furniture had been purchased when John made good money working at *The Messenger*. The sofa and couches were now dated and the wear and tear were now evident from extreme use by their boys bouncing on them. Tilla didn't complain; after all, she was happy to see John spending more time at home with her and their children.

They sat on the settee, where they often found themselves when discussing a serious family matter. At forty-six years old, John looked like he did at the turn of the century, except that he'd grown sideburns, and there was slight evidence of bags under his eyes. Eight kids had had an effect on Tilla's body. Her pulchritudinous looks of so many years had begun to vanish. Her radiant smile and high cheekbones were still present, but her middle more resembled a bee's waist than the wasp-like waist she had maintained for so many years. And even her backside, the same backside that Goldie said needed more meat about seventeen years ago, was more padded. Her togs had changed, too; they were no longer modern and sassy. Money and fabric were needed for the children. While John maintained his raven hair, Tilla's auburn hair now had a few strands of gray. But even with her slowly fading looks, she still was capable of turning the heads of men.

"This was delivered today," John said showing Tilla the white envelope that had Theo's name on it.

She knew what it was. "John, you know how I feel about this. I don't want Theo going to war. He might never come back."

"Ma, Pa," Theo said as he entered the house through the front door.

"We're in the living room, son," John said.

His handsomeness as a boy never dissipated as he went through his teenage years into his adult years. He was rangy and muscular at six feet, three inches tall, and had wavy brown hair, pearlescent hazel eyes, his mother's slender nose, father's full lips, and blemish-free tawny skin. "Sit down, son," John said.

He sat on a couch a few feet away from John and Tilla.

"Son, this has your name on it. It's from the United States Government," John said. He waved the envelope for Theo to retrieve it.

Theo sliced open the envelope with his right index finger. Although he knew what was inside, he hesitated before removing the contents.

There it was in black-and-white: Lawrence County men between the ages of twenty-one and thirty years of age had finally received their notices when to register for the draft. The notice directed Theo to register at the Sixth Precinct in Mount Hope on June 5, 1917.

"What does it say?" Tilla asked.

Theo hesitated with his answer as his head moved as in the direction of words written by the federal government. "They want me to fight in the war. I need to register with the draft board by June fifth."

"What're you going to do, son?" John asked.

"I don't know, Pa," he said expressing feelings of anxiety. He added: "I reckon I gotta register."

"We know that, Theo, but what we want to know is what do you want to do?" John asked.

Theo looked at Tilla and felt her heavy heart; he quickly turned his eyes to John. "They say we're going to be shipped off to France. Never left the country before."

"Son, there're a lot of colored men going to be drafted. If they see what we're doing for this country, the government will make it right for us," John said.

What better way to hasten the day that would cause the sclerotic system of bigotry to collapse in on itself than having colored men fight for their country, John thought. He paused, then added, "They just have to make it right," he said, with abundant doubt in his head but with plenty of hope in his heart.

It was the same fin de siècle hope and optimism that he held onto at the end of the nineteenth century, notwithstanding the darkness that had crowded colored life, which was woven into the fabric on Alabama's Constitution of 1901. Even though the new Constitution outlawed interracial marriage and imposed stringent suffrage restrictions on coloreds, Theo's generation would make a difference, he thought.

The light that had been filtering in through the drawn curtain began to fade. But the gathering darkness outside did little to dissipate the heat that had built up over the course of the day. While John continued to wax philosophically about the war, Tilla stood and turned on a small lamp next to the settee. She picked up a folded newspaper and began to fan herself as she looked at Theo massaging his goatee.

Theo was contemplating his navel. War was raging in Europe. He could possibly be with some of his buddies overseas. He'd get away from his parents' carping about his libertine behavior. He'd have an income, a place to live. The thought of boxing in the army could be a possibility. Change could be a good thing, he concluded. It was settled. "Pa, Ma, looks like I'm going to war."

"How many days before you register?" Tilla asked.

Theo looked away from Tilla as he counted the days in his head. "Eight."

"What did they tell you when you went to the precinct to register?" John asked Theo as they sat on the front porch in rocking chairs.

"They're shipping me to New York in two weeks," Theo said.

"Me, you, and Junior are going hunting tomorrow," John said. "We got some things to talk about."

"Okay, Pa."

"You going to need a good night's sleep. The roosters will wake us up," John said. "Junior will be here waiting on us."

Theo didn't get much sleep; his mind was jammed with thoughts about the war over in Europe, and what he would be asked to do. He wondered whether he'd come out of it alive. He arose before the rooster's cock-a-doodle-doo, dressed hurriedly, and walked to the kitchen where he saw John and Junior sipping coffee. "Good morning, Pa, Uncle Junior."

"Good morning," they said in unison.

It was time to start their early morning hunt. "Everything's ready," Junior said.

Two of Junior's steeds were hitched to a dray as Theo loaded it with hunting accoutrement. Theo hopped on the camion and John and Junior rode the horses. Theo lie supine on the camion and rested his head on strands of hay he used as a pillow. The ride was too bumpy to fall asleep. He wanted to think of anything but the war and his impending departure, but he found himself thinking about where he left off before he arose just a short while ago.

After about a twenty-minute ride, they reached the part of the woods where fowl and whitetail deer were known to be found.

Junior tied the reins to an elm tree and placed feed bags over the horses' snouts.

Theo retrieved the three Winchester rifles from a box on the dray. He gave one each to John and Junior.

John looked at one of the rifles. "Theo, this is your rifle. You need to claim ownership of your weapon, son."

"How do you know this one's mine?"

"Look here," John said, pointing to Theo's name that he had etched into the surface of the barrel.

"Do y'all have your knives and cartridges?"

John and Theo nodded.

"We're hunting deer and any kind of fowl," Junior said. "Let's go."

After about twenty minutes of walking and looking for a target, they found themselves deep in the carpeted woods. There was no sight or sound of any animal except for a few dogs sniffing for food. They sat down to rest against a large rock in the canopied woods. John took out his carving knife from his haversack and began to whittle on a thick tree branch. Junior practiced his troat calls, an effort to attract deer.

It sounded funny to Theo. "Hey, Uncle Junior, what are you doing?"

"What do you do when you want the attention of a young lady?" he asked rhetorically. "You whistle at her. You may dress a certain way. You talk to her. Well, I'm talking to the deer."

"But they're not listening," John said laughing.

"Look," Theo said softly, pointing to a whitetail buck about fifty yards away.

John pointed to a tall maple tree a few feet away. They crept from the rock to the tree. Theo was to get the first shot.

"Easy and steady," Junior said. "Don't shoot until you're ready."

The bullet hit the buck in the flank, felling it. Theo moved toward the deer.

"Wait, son," John said. The deer seemed to be sending out a distress call to other deer. "You hear that?"

After ten minutes, the buck took his last breath. "All right, son, go claim your prize. It's your catch."

John and Junior stayed near the tree.

Theo stood at the side of the carcass and kicked it just to make sure it was dead. Theo was impressed by the buck's huge rack. It was too big to transport to the dray; they'd have to carve the meat on the spot.

As Theo turned and looked at John and Junior, a doe appeared quickly and stood within three feet of Theo, ready to mete out revenge on the person who felled her stag. Theo had placed his rife on the ground.

John moved closer to the cauldron to intercede on Theo's behalf. Theo was frozen with fear; all he could manage was to raise and wave his arms to make himself look bigger to the revenge-seeking doe. Before John or Junior could reload their rifles to shoot, the doe raised off her hind legs and began to kick at Theo as though she was a prizefighter in a boxing ring.

With his rifle reloaded, John fired off a shot that whistled past Theo's left ear and hit the doe in the belly. The doe limped away and collapsed a few feet away. Junior fired another shot into the doe just in case she possessed a phoenix-like ability.

Theo was bleeding from the head, mouth, nose, and arm; he was dazed, unsure of what had just happened. He needed attention.

"Can you walk, son?"

"I think so," Theo said groggily.

He felt woozy. "Put one arm around my shoulder and the other arm on Junior."

They walked slowly to the large rock where Theo sat. "We gotta get you home. You know your mama's going to be upset," John said.

45
JUNE, 1917

Three days remained before Theo was set to go to New York. His injuries from tussling with the doe in the woods a few days ago were well on their way to healing. He had been hanging out with some of his buddies who were also going to New York. John and Tilla understood that he needed to spend the time as he saw fit to get ready for the war.

But John and Tilla had to take care of the rest of the family. Dinner time drew nigh, and Tilla ordered Maggie to corral her siblings.

It was Pearl's turn to watch Charlie; they came in the house together.

"Where's Claude and Willie? I didn't see them outside, Mama," Maggie said.

"Willie has a fever. I put him to bed to rest. See if Claude is in his bedroom."

"No, Mama, just Willie's in the bedroom."

"Maybe he's at Aunt Goldie's. Run over there, Maggie, and see if he's there."

"Pearl, you set the table," Tilla said.

Pearl counted the number of plates needed on her fingers. "Let see: Me, Maggie, Claude, Willie, Charlie, Ma, and Pa. That's seven."

"No plate is necessary for Willie; I gave him some chicken soup an hour ago. Your pa is tending to business across town. So how many plates do you need?" Tilla asked.

"Five."

She filled each plate according to how much a particular person would eat. Three-year-old Charlie received the smallest portion.

Maggie returned huffing and puffing, the result of running home.

Tilla looked at Maggie, who had long hair that was a shade darker than Tilla's auburn hair. At fifteen, she was as tall as Tilla and had inherited her mother's high cheekbones, Indian red skin, and intellectual curiosity. "He wasn't at Auntie Goldie's house. I even stopped by Kathleen's house to see if he was playing with her brother. He wasn't there either."

Tilla's face registered a look of mild concern. "Maggie, you see to it that everyone is fed. I'm going outside to look for Claude."

Her first stop was at Goldie's house. Like Maggie reported, Claude hadn't been there. Same for Kathleen's house. She walked several blocks looking for him calling his name. He knew what time dinner was usually served. He was eleven years old and too old to get a spanking, but she'd leave it up to John to mete out his punishment.

She returned home an hour later, where she saw John at the kitchen table reading a newspaper. "John, I've been out looking for Claude. Have you seen him?"

"Pearl told me. And no, I haven't seen the boy."

"Wonder where he could be?" Tilla queried.

John shrugged his shoulders. "It's getting dark," John said. "He best be making his way home now or he's in trouble."

The sun had set two hours ago; still no sign of Claude. John and Tilla sat up in bed wondering where Claude could be. John had set a gas lamp on the front porch hoping it would serve as Claude's beacon to get home. They couldn't do anything else for the nonce, but they hoped he'd knock on the door while they slept.

Tilla tossed and turned through the night, not knowing whether she was dreaming that Claude hadn't returned home. Although she had been fully awake for an hour or so, she got out of bed just before dawn to go look for Claude. As she walked out of the front door, she quickly pivoted and decided to check his bedroom. She opened the door; a few pants and shirts were folded lying on the floor. She bent down and looked her the bed. No Claude. She then called out his name several times as she had done so many times. Tears trickled down her sullen face and she used a cloth to dry the tears. Standing in the doorway to her bedroom, she took a few steps to her bed and collapsed from the pain of not knowing the whereabouts of her son.

The day had finally come for Theo and other Lawrence County men to ship out by rail to New York to get ready for the war. Theo was looking for an escape from the doldrums and lazy days of summer in Mount Hope; France beckoned, and he looked forward to befriending the French, especially the young *fils*, assuming he'd ever get cross the Atlantic and get there.

Tilla and the rest of her family went to the train station to see Theo off to New York. The station was bustling with excitement about the new adventure the men of Lawrence County were about to embark upon. Their country had called them to duty and they had responded.

Tilla was lachrymose, and had been so ever since she learned of Claude's disappearance. Her eyes seem to grow more forlorn as each hour passed without word from Claude. Her temper grew short—John and the children knew to use words and a voice that would mollify her in some way.

But her soul was abrading, and her mind and heart were tormented. It had been three days and there was no sign of Claude. Her torment had increased as each hour elapsed to the countdown to Theo's departure. John had told her not to think of it, but she had no control over her mind, which wandered to family members who left her too soon—her father who was murdered, her mother who died of a spider bite at age forty, her fourteen-year-old sister Caroline who was never found. Claude was still missing. The thought of losing Theo in a charnel region somewhere in Europe was too much for her to bear. She sat impassibly on a bench, barely moving, and unaware of the hoopla in the station, hoping God would release her from her nightmare.

A sergeant barked out the names of those whose turn it was to board the train, last name, then first. "Wallace, Gregory; Taylor, Jessie; Bean, Paul; Jackson, Burdette; Davis, Theo...."

Theo stepped on the stool with his right foot and the left landed on the floor on the train. In a few months' time, he'd be on his way to

France to help make the world safe for democracy. He turned around and saw his family waving. With his mouth agape with excitement, he waved in turn. But his mouth closed when he saw his poor mother who had her head buried in her husband's chest. Upon hearing the train's piercing whistle, she unglued her head from John's chest and looked in Theo's direction. Her eyes had the look of a soldier who has a thousand-yard stare after he has been in heavy combat involving great casualties.

"Bye, Theo," four-year-old Charlie burbled.

Tilla heard Charlie's excitement and emitted a thin keening sound.

46
SPRING, 1920

As the wind rustled against his dilapidated two-story shed, George, who was Lawrence County's best blacksmith, worked to put the finishing touch on a wrought iron gate that a wealthy insurance executive ordered for his antebellum home. Robert, his whiskey-swilling octogenarian friend, lumbered into the shed, exhausted after fighting the fierce March wind.

Noticing that George rubbed his hands together to warm them up, Robert handed a silver flask filled with whiskey to George and said, "That should warm you up."

While clutching the flask, George said, "When did you start drinking?" He paused, then added, "Never mind, probably when you woke up."

Robert assented with a couple of nods.

George felt the engraving on the flask, mindlessly looked at it briefly, and then took a long pull on the whiskey. "This some good stuff. Where'd you get it?" George said while evincing the strong taste of the whiskey by grimacing, revealing yellow-stained teeth that matched the color of his skin.

"Secret recipe," Robert muttered.

"I heard you. It won't be secret for long after I beat it out of you."

"You try and I cut your throat with this here rusty knife," Robert said, holding up the knife in a trembling hand.

"I was kidding, old man."

"You'd be wise not to mess with this old man." George rolled his eyes at Robert, who was a waif and bent over from age. He had a pair of coal eyes that were the only external signs of a crafty mind within. And he combined a defiantly idiosyncratic temperament with a universal approachability. Robert knew where people's skeletons lie in town, and George liked imbibing all the gossip George served him.

George looked at the engraving on the flask again, a bit more carefully. "Looks like a man with a missing arm. What do the letters mean?"

"Don't know. Wondered that myself."

"You mean Uncle Remus don't know?" George asked, mocking him.

Robert was slapped with the Uncle Remus moniker because he loved to tell stories. George loved to hear Robert's parodies of slave plantation life. He particularly liked hearing Robert's story about how Old Man Buchanan shot his wife in the rear end while she was bending down to retrieve something in the field. The way Robert told it, Buchanan mistook her rear end for a sow's. Old Man Buchanan blamed the mistake on his failing vision. "It was such a wide target, I just knew I couldn't miss," Buchanan told Robert. "Buchanan's old lady made him sleep in the barn with the pigs for a week."

George moved the flask toward and away from his eyes to find the right distance to see the engraving. "It's hard to make out. I see a letter *A*." He squinted to refocus his eyes. "That look like *U* or *O*." He turned the flask over and said, "Now I can see these letters, *TB*."

"What does *TB* mean?" George asked.

"Don't know. This flask been with me for at least five years. Never really paid it no mind. I found it outside the shed one day. I just liked what I keep inside."

"Got any tobacca, Uncle Remus?"

"Only the best: Prince Albert."

"I need some for my pipe," George said.

Robert removed a large packet of tobacco from his vest pocket. He scraped a dollop onto a nearby table.

"I need more than that," George said.

"People in hell want ice water," Robert countered.

Robert relented and scraped some more tobacco on the table. George packed his pipe with the tobacco, lit it a few times, then blew a smoke circle.

With his corncob pipe dangling from his mouth, George mumbled, "What you say wrong with Miss Tilla? She ain't been the same for a long time."

"Yeah, you right," Robert acknowledged. "Some say she ain't forgiven herself for what happened to her boy, Claude."

"What happened?" George asked.

"Ever since Claude disappeared, Tilla ain't been right. Every so often, she'll walk miles around town looking for him, calling his name. One day she walked too far, got lost, and did not return home for a day. A passerby found her sleeping outside of a barn. He gave her something to eat and helped her get home. Some say Claude had consumption and just passed out in a field somewhere. Some say he met his doom by looking cross at a white woman."

"He was just a boy," George said.

"Don't matter. It's 1920, we still ain't free. May never be free," Robert said.

"What do John and the kids think?" George asked.

"Don't know the answer to that one."

"Want some more of this here whiskey?" Robert asked.

"I really shouldn't be drinking this hooch; doctor say it ain't too good for my condition."

"The doctor don't know about my secret recipe," Robert exclaimed proudly. "I guess I'm about eighty-five. Whiskey's got something to do with it."

It was weighing on George's mind. He needed help. "Robert, my woman's pregnant. She can't go to no hospital around here. The midwife we once used moved; don't know where. You know everybody. Who'd you recommend?"

"I'll take a look at her," Robert said chuckling.

"You won't go near my woman, dirty old man."

"Unless she got something no other woman got, I ain't interested. I've seen plenty trim. I got twenty kids," he vaunted.

"Yeah, by twenty different women," George replied.

"You want my help, Robert?"

George's silence indicated his assent. "Then watch your mouth." He paused, then added: "They call her Minnie P. She can be found in Birmingham. She may can do it. Make sure the price is right."

47

SPRING, 1920

A wan shaft of sunbeams broke through the darkness, slowly spreading soft rays through the bedroom. John opened his right eye first, then his left. He opened his mouth wide like a yawning hippopotamus and closed it just as slowly as he had opened it. Tilla was asleep, and he moved quietly to the bathroom.

It was Independence Day and he had promised Tilla that he'd take her and the children to Bessie's house for a fish fry. But he had work to do first. And he did it. By the time the sun had reached its peak in the sky, John had plowed a half-acre of land for a second planting of vegetables, slopped the pigs, put out fodder for his two dobbins and two mules, and milked Clara, his dairy cow.

It was one o'clock, two hours before John would take Tilla and the kids to Bessie's house. He sat in his favorite rocking chair, eating flummery and biscuits. Just as he stood up to return his dishes to the kitchen, he heard Theo yell, "Hey, Pops."

John put the dishes on his chair and looked at his son. He hadn't seen Theo in weeks and hugged him tightly for several seconds. Theo returned the affection by putting his arms around his father. John released his embrace first. John took a step back and looked over Theo. His pearlescent hazel eyes had an air of confidence that was unsettling to John.

"Come on in, son; say hello to your mama and the kids."

As John grabbed the screen door, Theo put his right hand on John's left arm. "Wait, I need to talk to you."

"What is it, son?"

"I need to borrow your revolver."

John was silent.

"Say something, Pa."

John said nothing.

Outwardly, John struck a nonchalant pose, which irked Theo, whose face was now as sour as an unripe pippin. "Look, Pa," Theo said, "I see the way you look at me. You want me to be what you want me to be."

"Son, it's not that simple."

"It is that simple. Can I borrow your gun? Just tell me."

"I just want the best for you, son. You survived the war in France, and it would be a shame if you didn't survive back home. I don't like the life you're living. I hear things."

"You hear things?" Theo said with a twisted look on his face. "Ain't you supposed to love me no matter what, right?"

John believed Theo was gaming him and dismissed Theo's words as folderol. He was tired of Theo's excuses; an adult life of neglect and contempt didn't cut it with John. "Son, I do love you. Please know that. I've been thinking. I'd like for you to help me with the farm. I have all this land; we work it together, raise and sell the crops ... With your help, we can bring in more money. It'll be good for you."

Theo had seen an eye-popping cultural change in France. He shook his head slowly and said, "I'm not working on no farm, not after I've seen gay Paree."

Although some colored soldiers fought under the command of the United States, most fought under the command of the French government. While Theo never saw the front line in the war—he did support work like building railroads, latrines, and serving as a mess man—he, like the rest of the colored soldiers, was treated like a hero in France.

The French thanked the colored soldiers for their efforts on and off the field. Theo had gone to many nightclubs in cities like Montmartre where he found the color of his skin to be an asset. He tasted French wines, mingled with French women, and enjoyed the jazz music being played in the nightclubs. It was the 369th Infantry

Band from New York that brought the jazz germ to France, and the French were swept up in the rollicking melodies.

For the war efforts of the colored soldiers, one French newspaper said, "Posterity will be indebted to you with gratitude." Another newspaper referred to the colored soldiers as *les enfants perdus*, which the soldiers were happy to accept. Theo was swept up in the marvels of being a colored soldier in France. But the reality was that a rolling wave of hope from the Western front was met with a rising tide of fear and intolerance in the country that had sent the colored soldiers to fight in France. Nonetheless, when he returned home, Theo wanted to live the exciting life he had witnessed in France. He was trying to live that life, but things were moving too slowly for him. He had seen what other young men in Lawrence County were doing—from partying to wearing fashionable attire. He wanted what they had, even if he had no reputable income or way to obtain it.

John shook his head at the way Theo talked. John had prided himself on using standard English language; he and Tilla had taught the children not to use double negatives and especially not to use *ain't*. John looked at his son again and wondered who was standing in front of him. He told himself that Theo had a Davis soul, but that his son's mind was still fixated on slumming.

John thought that Theo had been searching for an individual identity before he was shipped to France. But it was apparent that nothing had changed: Theo was slumming before the war, and he was doing it after the war. Theo needed a new direction in life. "What are you, twenty-five? I'm twice your age. The fact of the matter is I'm going to need some help with the farm, and I'm offering it to my oldest child."

Theo shook his head in disappointment and said, "Goodbye, Pa."

"Son, you never told me why you need the revolver."

He thought for a second of telling his father that a man threatened his life, accusing Theo of talking to his woman. Instead, Theo said nothing.

Theo sat in a booth in a barbecue joint, still sore about the conversation he'd had with his father two weeks ago. Although the danger had passed and he no longer needed to borrow John's gun, he felt a widening gulf between himself and his father. He finished tearing a piece of meat from a rib bone and pushed the plate away. Perhaps his father was right, he thought. He had no steady work. He made some money here and there by washing dishes, running errands for local businessmen, selling goods he had stolen. Ever since he returned home from the war, the good life he sought continued to elude him.

He stood up and walked to the back of the rib joint to say goodbye to Joe, the owner.

"Ain't that right, chief," Theo heard a man say.

Theo continued his walk to the back of the joint. "Chief, I'm talking to you."

He turned and looked to his left and saw a nattily attired man sitting in a booth between two colored women. "Come here, boy," the man said.

As Theo closed in on the man's booth, the man said, "I said, ain't that right."

Theo didn't know how to respond, other than just nod.

"Why the long face, chief?"

The man eyed Theo's green fustian pants, black brogan boots, and white linen shirt. "You can stand some new duds," the man said.

Theo looked at the young women on either side of the man. Each wore a strawberry-colored straw hat with picot ribbons. The woman to the man's right had cream-colored skin, and the one to his left had deep-chocolate skin. The man's skin color was somewhere in the middle of his companions, whose bosoms were high and stood at attention as though they were held up by racks. He turned his attention back to the man and said, "I reckon you're right."

"I'm Charlie Capstone," the man said. "They call me Cappie."

"Nice to meet you, Mr. Capstone," Theo said.

"Where you working?" Capstone asked.

Theo shook his head.

Capstone elbowed the young woman to his left and lifted his head upward. She scooted out of her seat to allow Capstone to stand up. Capstone drew himself up to all five foot, three inches. He wore French-style pointy shoes, high-waisted trousers, a long black jacket, and a green fedora embellished with an egret's plume. Two shiny rings adorned fingers on his right hand and three shiny ones were on the fingers of his left hand. Capstone blew smoke from his Cuban cigar in Theo's face.

"Here, take a puff?" Capstone said using his pudgy fingers to extend the Cuban cigar to Theo. Theo hesitated. Capstone stabbed the air with it, saying, "Go on, boy, it's from Havana; it's some good stuff."

Theo took two slow drags. "Yeah, Mr. Capstone, it is."

"Call me Cappie."

Theo continued to look at Capstone's attire. "Cappie," Theo said, "You're a sharp dresser." Pointing to Capstone's shoes, Theo said, "I saw shoes like that in France."

"I see a man who knows taste," Capstone said while extinguishing his Cuban cigar with the bottom of his right shoe.

Theo chuckled.

Capstone removed a small comb from his pocket and combed his walrus-sized, brindled mustache. He turned to look at his two bosomy escorts and winked. He then moved his head toward the front entrance for Theo to follow him. Capstone shifted his fedora to block the sun's rays from his eyes. Theo squinted as he listened to Capstone offer him a job in his numbers business.

"Numbers?" Theo asked.

"Yeah, numbers. I need someone to run my numbers for me. Tell you what; meet me tomorrow in the shed located on the corner of Moulton and Leaves. Be there after sunset. I'll be there with my boys."

Theo looked down and found his eyes drifting to Capstone's shiny black shoes. He looked up and squinted and saw the face of a man who was used to getting his way.

Theo wanted a hat like Capstone's. "I'll be there."

Capstone lumbered his wide body over to his 1919 burnished black Model T. He stepped inside and waited for his driver to start the car by turning the hand crank on the front of the vehicle. After hearing the engine roar, the driver walked over to the right side of the car and held open the door as Capstone's two female companions joined him in the back seat.

Theo watched them leave, then went back inside the joint to talk to Joe. Before Theo could say anything, Joe said, "I saw you talking to Cappie. Stay away from him. I hear things working in this joint."

"Don't worry about me, Joe. I'll be all right."

48

SPRING, 1920

Theo walked with a pep in his step as he closed in on the building at Moulton and Leaves. He had seen Capstone's lifestyle and wanted to be suffused in it. He stopped at the front door and looked himself over. If he wanted the job, he figured he had to dress the part. The brown derby that his father had given him was cocked slightly to the left. The crease in his tan trousers was so sharp it could draw blood. And the matching jacket fit nicely over his torso.

No answer. He knocked again. No answer. Hearing a footfall, he turned and saw a large rotund man coming toward him. The man peered at Theo, causing Theo to say, "I'm here to see Cappie."

The man said nothing. Theo stood back as the man opened the door and walked in. Theo didn't move. "You coming?" the man asked.

Theo nodded.

"Follow me," the rotund man said.

Theo followed at a distance. The rotund man's skin was the color of the inside of a strawberry shortcake; he was at least a half a foot taller than Theo, and he moved like a bull walrus on land.

The shed was dilpidated, and boards were missing from the one of the walls. Wrought iron rested against a dividing wall. An anvil and other blacksmith tools sat on a table.

The rotund man approached a sliding wood door and rapped it. Someone from the other side of the door slid it open, and the rotund man walked in, followed by Theo.

The air was redolent of beer, whiskey, and smoke. As a patch of smoke cleared, Theo saw Capstone sitting at a desk near the back wall. He looked around the spartan room, starting at his left where he saw the two minx women he'd seen at the rib joint; they looked at Theo and teased him with their eyes, looking at him like he was a steak dinner. To his right were three of Capstone's associates, each wearing suits and sitting on bales of hay, peering at Theo.

While writing something on paper, Capstone said, "I said at sunset. Where you been?"

Theo recalled that as he spoke to Capstone just outside the entrance to Joe's rib joint the day he met him, Capstone had said *after sunset*. But because Theo felt his skin tingle from Capstone's menacing voice, he dared not gainsay the man who'd provide him with income. He felt it best to apologize. "Sorry I'm late, boss."

Capstone stood up, adjusting the foulard around his beefy neck. He moved from behind the desk and looked at Theo, who was about fifteen feet away.

The suite was once a stable for horses, but Capstone had it converted for his personal use. The only sign of human occupation was the desk and three chairs. Light passed through from a window up high. When darkness fell, kerosene lanterns were used to shine light on Capstone's illicit activities.

Capstone stuffed his ubiquitous Cuban cigar in his mouth and picked some fluff from the sleeve of his burgundy suit jacket. Satisfied that the fluff had been removed, he extended his short arms to Theo. "Theo, my boy, welcome to the executive suite. Come to Papa."

Theo removed his derby and did as commanded. He bent down to allow Capstone to wrap his arms around him. After the embrace, Capstone said, "How you been, boy?"

"Been doing good, Cappie."

Capstone returned to his seat and propped his stubby legs on the desk. "Ready to start collecting? Can you do that for me, my dear boy?" Capstone said.

"What's that?" Theo asked.

Capstone looked at Pad, the bull walrus who had escorted Theo inside the shed. Capstone nodded at Pad, which cued Pad to tell Theo his job assignment. Pad said, "Every Wednesday and Friday, your job is to collect numbers from bookies at different locations. Got that?"

Theo was silent.

"This boy here's dumb, Cappie. Want me to make him talk?"

Capstone hired Pad because Pad was useful in helping Capstone get his money. Pad had worked in a prison mining camp for two years because he was convicted of failing to pay a debt. Coming out of the pestilent mining camp, he had found his way north where he met Capstone. He had become hardened and angry, just what Capstone desired in a man to help him with his business.

"Give him a chance," Capstone said.

Pad grabbed Theo's left elbow and ushered him to a corner of the executive room to explain the rules. Pad ended the conversation, saying to Theo, "Don't let Cappie down."

"See you Saturday," Pad told Theo. "Don't be late."

Theo nodded and headed for the exit. As one of Capstone's associates began to slide open the door, Pad said, "You gonna need a piece."

"Why?" Theo asked.

Pad pulled out a silver whiskey flask, removed the top, and took a swill. As he put the top back on the flask, Pad said, "It's for your protection, and you gonna need it to enforce payments. Shallow receipts won't look good around here."

After Theo left, Capstone looked at his men and asked, "Think he'll do right by me?" He didn't wait for an answer. He removed a pistol from the desk drawer and stroked the barrel.

Capstone looked at Pad who was swilling whiskey. "Come here," Capstone instructed Pad.

"Yeah, boss."

"Let me see that bottle or whatever it is."

Pad hesitated. "I don't want your cheap whiskey," Capstone added.

He handed the flask to Capstone. Looking at the engraving on it, Capstone said, "Where'd you get this?"

He told Capstone how he had found Robert, the busybody that most town folk knew, dead on the floor. "This shiny bottle was in his vest pocket; I took it."

Capstone shook his head. "I liked the old man," Pad said. "After I bought this place from George, he made me promise that Robert could come to the shed every morning for an hour and drink his whiskey. I guess he did that even after George moved to Atlanta."

Still looking at the flask, Capstone asked Pad, "Do you know the meaning of all this?"

"No."

49
SPRING, 1920

John dropped his pocketknife and emitted a painful sigh. He rubbed his right thumb over this left index finger in an effort to staunch the bleeding. Money, a brown and white beagle, sat next to John on the porch, barked, and looked at John as if to ask if he would be all right. "Yeah, boy, I'm fine." A few minutes later, John picked up the knife and resumed whittling a figurine for Tilla's cocktail table.

"Hey, John," Junior called out as he sat on a swayback.

John waved. "Morning, Junior."

Junior dismounted the swayback and tied her to a nearby black gum tree. He favored his left leg as he walked to greet John on the porch. Age had also caught up with him in other ways. The taut, muscular body he once had as a young man was gone. If any stomach muscles still existed, they were now covered by a thick sheath of fat. Hair that was once a lustrous black was now mostly gray. Although he was just a few years older than John, he now looked a decade older.

"That gout still bothering you?" John asked.

Junior leaned on the wood railing that surrounded the front porch. "I guess it's gout," he said. "Doctor told me to lay off the whiskey. Maybe I'll try it to see if it works."

John raised his right brow and said, "Man, you're going to do what?"

The point was taken and Junior didn't respond.

He looked at John as he carved legs on the figurine. He then asked, "You ready?"

"For what?"

"We supposed to go shoot some pool today, remember? Jimmy's probably already there."

"Oh, shoot. I forgot all about that. I'll pass this time around. I'll go the next time around."

"Okay," he said. "How's Tilla?"

"She has her good days, her bad days. But I have to say that she's not crying over Claude as much as she used to. She's now worried about Theo."

"How's the boy doing?"

John shook his head to tell Junior he didn't want to answer the question. Better not to say anything than to open his mouth and risk losing control of his tongue, he thought.

As Junior turned and began to limp to his swayback, John said, "Why're you still using that old nag?"

He laughed and said, "My daughters keep me broke."

Tilla, having just finished cleaning the kitchen, opened the screen door just as Junior finished mounting his swayback. She yelled, "Morning, Junior."

"Morning, Tilla," he shot back.

She handed John a tall glass of freshly made lemonade. Holding the glass up high, he moved it around to make the lemon seeds swirl. With the lemonade still churning, he held back his head, opened his mouth, and drained the glass. "Thanks, sweetheart. "

"Want some more?" Tilla asked.

"No, dear."

"John," she said.

John looked at her waiting to ask a question.

"Oh, nothing."

"Spill it, honey. What's on your mind?"

"You know I worry about Theo. He's running around with those hoodlums. I wish he'd go to church. Reverend Owen would be glad to have him."

John nodded to signal he commiserated with her.

"How's Maggie?" John asked.

"Still got the blues. She really wants to get married."

"Where is she now?"

"Folding clothes in the back yard."

"Where's Pearl?"

"Over Goldie's."

"What about Willie and Charlie?"

"In the back."

John looked at Money and said, "Money, go to the back and fetch Maggie."

Tilla was always amused when John talked to Money. "That dog can't understand you."

"You hear that, boy; she thinks you're dumb. Now go fetch Maggie."

Money stood up and leaned back as he stretched. After shaking his body a few times, he jumped from the porch to the ground. "Go on," John said.

"How's this?" John asked as he showed the figurine to Tilla.

She stood up and kissed him on the cheek. "It's splendid, dear."

Money tugged on Maggie's apron.

"What is it, Money?" Maggie asked.

Money continued to tug.

Maggie tossed a shirt in a basket, and Money released his grip as Maggie followed him.

Money barked, and John looked to the left and saw Maggie in tow. "Maggie," John said, "come here, darling."

"Yes, Pa."

John pointed with his head for Maggie to sit in the chair next to him. She removed a folded newspaper from her apron and tossed it on the floor. She swept her blue chiffon dress under her as she sat down.

At eighteen, Maggie was a handsome woman, powerfully built. She was naturally smart, and she carried herself with a quiet intellect that would be her hallmark. She had long reddish-brown hair, skin the color of cornsilk, and Prussian blue eyes. Her small waist tapered to hips that were slightly out of proportion to her waist. She believed that she wasn't supposed to work; she was to have babies and support a husband just like her mother.

"Your mama's worried about you," John said. "Now tell your pa what's wrong."

Maggie hesitated at first but after a little prodding from John, she told him that she wanted to find a man and get married and start a family.

"There some good men in church," John said.

No response from Maggie. As John searched for what to say next, he thought of Theo, the *bad penny* in the family. Theo knew lots of people and perhaps knew of a potential suitor for Maggie. "I'll ask Theo."

Maggie's eyes shot to John to register a concern about meeting someone Theo knew. "It's all right, darling. Theo may know someone who meets your standards."

"And exactly what are my standards, Pa?"

"Well, we'll find out, darling."

Tilla opened the screen door and said, "Maggie, go check on Willie and Charlie." Maggie rose and did as instructed.

"I'll be back in an hour or so," Tilla said to John.

"Where are you off to?"

She did it once a month as best she could. "You should know by now."

"To look for Claude?"

She nodded.

"Why do you still look for that boy? It's been about three years since he …" John stopped in mid-sentence, allowing the rest of the sentence to perish.

She looked at John and said: "Just like a baby cub knows his mother's call, my boy knows my call. He'll come." Tilla then walked out the front door to search for Claude. Money, now under the low-slung porch, heard a footfall on the steps and slithered out from under the porch. He whimpered until John gave him the go-ahead to tag along with Tilla.

"Tilla," John said, "you best use this hat." She turned around and retrieved John's oversized straw hat.

—⚬—

A loud shot rang out and Tilla's heart began to race as she sat under a mulberry tree surrounded by a meadow. She chewed quickly to finish off two mulberries already in her mouth. Just as Tilla's heart settled, another shot rang out.

She whispered to Money, "You hear that?"

Money looked at Tilla as she stood and began to walk in the direction the shots came from. She wiped her hands on her apron and straightened the back of her dress where she felt moisture. She turned her head to the right as she tugged on her dress to bring the moist spot into view. The back of her lisle cotton dress was stained with mulberry juice.

She looked in the direction of several trees about eighty feet away. She heard conversation coming from the direction of the trees and quickly hid beyond a knoll. After hearing no more talk, she peeked over the knoll; she saw a tall man wearing a white hat exit a building ensconced in the trees. The man appeared to be dressed in a suit. A woman ran up to the man and began to argue with him. The woman tried to slap him, but the man pushed her aside and she fell to the ground. The man's hat fell to the ground while tussling with the woman.

Money barked one time, and Tilla's heart raced. She saw the man reach into his jacket and retrieve what she thought was a gun. The man picked up his hat, brushed it off while walking, and looked in the direction of the barking dog. Tilla ducked behind the knoll. "Money," Tilla said quietly. She had lost sight of him. "Money," she whispered again. Her heart began to pound, fearing Money would spoil her cover. "Money, I need you," she whispered. Money clawed dirt over his droppings in a tussock and ran to Tilla, who let out a big sigh of relief. Tilla looked over the knoll and saw no one. They scurried home.

Money ran to John and jumped in his lap. "Where's Tilla?" he asked as he rubbed Money's head.

A minute later, Tilla climbed the porch steps. She doffed the straw hat and handed it to John. As Tilla moved onto the porch, the red mulberry stains on her dress came into John's view. "What's that on your dress?"

"Mulberries stains."
"Where did you go?"
"We just went looking for Claude."
Tilla's eyes looked vacant. John asked, "Is something wrong?"
"No."
Her answers were too laconic for John.

John looked at Money and said, "What's wrong with Mama? You can tell me." Tilla grew a slight smile as John talked to Money.

"I heard gunshots near Moulton and Leaves."

"Did you see something?"

"Just a man coming out some kind of an old building wearing a white hat. A woman was with him."

"Are you alright?"

She nodded.

"Honey, you look tired. Go wash up and change that dress."

50
SUMMER, 1922

Capstone was in a foul mood. His receipts had been diminishing for months, and he wanted to make sure that others heard about it. Theo, a few collectors and bookies, Pad, and a few of Capstone's associates convened in the executive suite for a lecture about Capstone's money problem.

Capstone stood behind his desk, looked at all the men in his suite with inimical eyes, and said, "Somebody's been skimming money from me."

Silence.

He opened the desk drawer and plunked his pistol on the top of the desk. "No one's leaving here till I get my answer," Capstone said.

"Boss, no one's stealing from you. They know better than that," Pad said.

"Shut up!" Capstone snapped at Pad. "I'll do the talking."

A cordlike vein popped up on Pad's right temple and his body swelled beyond its normal gargantuan size.

Capstone observed Pad's vein and knuckled it with his left hand. Pad stood still as Capstone walked over to one of the collectors. The collector wore a beige slouch suit and a brown derby. He smelled of whiskey and was a head taller than Capstone. Capstone brushed off a few pieces of fluff on the collector's lapel and looked the collector in eyes that tasted fear and said, "You doing right by me?"

"Yeah, man. I got sense not to do nothing like that."

Capstone reached up and caressed the collector's cheek with his right hand. He nodded to signal that he believed the collector.

A few others had passed the test, and they were told to leave. Capstone came to his next subject, Theo. Theo wore a two-piece suit that was the color of a mason's brick. Capstone unbuttoned Theo's jacket and looked at the double lining. "Nice suit, Theo. You got some nice threads. Assuming you didn't steal it, it must of cost you a nice penny."

Theo remained calm and uneffusive.

Capstone applied more pressure. "I hear your girl's pregnant. You gonna need money for the baby."

Theo felt a knot in his stomach.

Capstone's teeth were clenched and his nose crinkled. There had been a crimp in his velvet earnings. "You been stealing from me, pretty boy?"

"No, Cappie. I wouldn't do that."

Capstone gave his head a quarter turn, then drew his right arm back and hit Theo in the jaw. Theo grabbed his jaw with his left hand, and Capstone kneed him in the groin. Theo fell to the floor. Capstone walked over to his desk and picked up his pistol. He returned to Theo and said, "Open up, pretty boy."

With his eyes closed, Theo shook his head sideways in protest. Capstone struck Theo on the right temple with the butt of the pistol and shouted, "I said open your mouth!"

Capstone shoved the gun in Theo's mouth. "Now, you wanna tell me the truth."

Theo mumbled as best he could with the pistol in his mouth. Capstone said, "Speak up, pretty boy. Papa can't hear you."

As he straightened Theo's jacket, he ordered two of his bookies to fill a large barrel with water. Looking at Theo, Capstone said, "Come here, pretty boy."

Theo's feet were anchored to the floor.

Capstone nodded in the direction of two men; they forced Theo from his mooring and dragged him to Capstone. "You know what this is?"

Theo knew the answer, as did most colored men. They had either seen it used in a prison camp or heard of it being used. It was a form of water torture. "This is the truth teller. It's for waywards like you."

Theo pivoted quickly and ran toward the door, but his escape was blocked by three men. Capstone said, "Don't do that again!"

"No need to put him in the barrel, Cappie," Pad said.

Capstone snapped, "Shut up! I run things around here."

Three men picked up Theo and plunged him headfirst into the barrel. After a long twenty seconds, Theo began to flail his arms and kick his legs. Capstone nodded, and the men pulled Theo from the barrel. "Let this be a lesson to all of you; steal from me...."

Handing one of the men a piece of twine, Capstone said, "Tie his hands behind his back." With Theo's hands now tied behind his back, Capstone added, "Now put him back in there." The same three men picked up Theo and plunged him headfirst back into the water.

Theo kicked his legs, but after fifteen seconds, all vigor had disappeared. Twenty seconds after Theo had stopped moving, Capstone ordered his men to remove him from the barrel.

Theo lay on the ground supine, motionless. Pad lumbered over to Theo and stood him up. As his body was limp, Pad readjusted his position and squeezed Theo's diaphragm with his muscular arms. No sign of life from Theo.

Pad gently placed Theo on the floor face down.

After a minute, Capstone said, "Get him out of here. Bury him somewhere."

As he was being picked up, Theo began to cough. "Theo, you alive," Pad said with a sigh of relief.

Capstone muttered gruffly, "This damn fool won't die."

He hurried to Theo to bring his life to a quick end. Looking at Theo's limp body, he removed his pistol from his jacket and pulled the trigger.

It jammed. He cursed and shook the pistol. He aimed it at Theo's head.

A shot rang out.

Blood oozed out of the back of Capstone's head.

Theo sat up and looked at Pad, who was holding the gun that cut down Capstone.

Pad had grown sick of the way Capstone was slapping him around, the way Capstone laughed when calling him stupid or an idiot. What especially irked him was that Capstone made Pad get on his knees and clean his shoes. Through it all, though, Pad had remained the loyal lieutenant; he needed the money. That day he felt trapped and cornered like a feral cat—he couldn't take it anymore, and he availed himself of the opportunity to bring his misery to an end. It helped that other of Capstone's flunkies hated Capstone but just suffered in silence.

"Here," Pad said handing Theo his whiskey flask.

Theo took two swigs and said, "Man, you saved my life." He handed the flask back to Pad, who put the top on it.

Handing it back to Theo, Pad said, "You keep it. You gonna need it to deaden the pain you in."

Two weeks after his near-death experience, Theo went to see John and Tilla. He arrived at nine-thirty just as they walked out of the door on their way to church with the kids.

"Theo, my baby," Tilla said. "What a surprise to see you."

Theo hugged Tilla, then looked at John and said, "Hi, Pops."

"Hi, son. We're on our way to church. You can come with us, you know. Reverend Owen would like that."

Church wasn't for Theo. He knew people were aware of his dissolute lifestyle, and he didn't want to be around people who'd snicker around him. "Maybe some other time."

"Won't you join us for dinner?" Tilla said. "I'll have your brothers and sisters come over."

"Okay, Ma, I'll be back here later on."

"Be here by five," Tilla said.

As Theo was leaving, John shouted, "Theo." Theo turned around, and John said, "I love you, son."

—⁂—

Tilla barked out instructions. "Maggie, Pearl, get supper started." She looked at her watch. "Theo's going to be here in an hour or so. Fix some pork chops, cow peas, poke weed, mashed potatoes. Pearl, any more sweet potato pies left in the closet?"

Pearl nodded.

"How about Coca-Cola?" Tilla asked.

"Yep," said Pearl.

"Charlie, do whatever your sisters tell you."

"They can't boss me," Charlie said while hitting Pearl.

"Boy, come here," John said with eyes that shot fear into Charlie. "Do you want me to spank your bottom?"

He shook his body and head.

"Then you do what your mama tells you."

Charlie looked at Money ambling across the kitchen floor. "Pa, when you going teach me to hunt with Money?" Charlie asked.

"Money's retired now."

"What's retired?"

"He's too hold to hunt. He can't run fast enough to chase and catch dinner."

"Oh, okay." Curious about Money's name, Charlie asked, "How did he get that name anyway?"

John told him about a bet he made a few years ago with a man who lived a block away. He and Clarence bet each other that one of them could grow the biggest watermelon. The loser would give whatever amount of money he wanted to the winner. John's melon weighed fifty-three pounds; Clarence's weighed one pound less. When John went to Clarence's house to collect his money, Clarence gave him Money and told him that Money would help put food on the table.

It was five o'clock and Theo walked into the kitchen. He was on time; it was his first respectful showing. He wore a tasteful black suit, a sober red tie, and a white fedora hat.

"Theo, my baby," Tilla said.

"Hi, Mama." He walked over to Tilla, who was sitting at the kitchen table, and kissed her on the cheek.

John walked into the kitchen and said, "Son, glad you could make it."

"Hey, Pops."

Theo turned to Maggie and said, "Hey, Sis. You look good."

"Thank you," Maggie said.

Willie and Charlie walked in the living room. Theo hugged his little brothers.

"Where's Pearl?" Theo asked.

She had finished her cooking assignment and was in the back yard playing jacks with Kathleen. "She's in the back," Maggie said.

After dinner, John asked Theo to join him for a talk in the living room. Theo sat across from John. "How are you doing, son?"

Theo's jaw was still sore from Capstone's blow, but he overlooked it. "Can't complain."

"Good, son. You're the one who determines whether there's something to complain about. Treat yourself as you want to be treated, and you'll do fine."

As the conversation began to dwindle after twenty minutes, John told him he loved him and wanted him to find his rightful place in the world.

As John left the room, Theo took off his jacket. As he began to lay it over the arm rest, he felt the whiskey flask; he removed it, uncorked it, and took a long pull. He was asleep within a minute.

Tilla tapped Theo on the leg. "Theo, Theo."

He felt groggy. "Ma, what time is it?"

"Nine."

He sat up on the sofa and said, "Nine, I need to go."

"Okay, son. Come back any time."

He put on his jacket, kissed Tilla, and left.

An hour after Theo left, Tilla sat on the edge of the bed and combed her hair, making sure to give careful attention to the ends. John sat up in bed, reading the newspaper. Tilla put the brush on the chiffonier and climbed into bed.

"John," Tilla said.

"Yes."

"Oh, nothing."

"You sure."

She decided to say it. "I've seen a hat like that before."

"What're you talking about?"

"The hat Theo wore here today."

"I gave him that hat and a few others."

"When?"

"I don't know. I think it was after he returned from the war."

Tilla's mind was still a little unsettled with John's answer, but she thought perhaps she'd forget all about it in the morning. She reached over to the nightstand and extinguished the light, and she and John fell asleep.

51
FALL, 1922

Tilla had cried ever since they were told that Eunice, their second oldest daughter, wouldn't survive her third pregnancy. She had kept vigil with Eunice and her husband for the past week. John had stopped by periodically to see his ailing daughter and to comfort Tilla.

The first week in October had brought sunny skies and mild temperatures to Mount Hope, and John worked as much as he could on the farm to ensure a nice harvest in anticipation of the annual Thanksgiving Day dinner he and Tilla hosted. A few roosters crowed, and Tilla opened her tired eyes. It was Sunday, a day different from the cycle of rising, fixing breakfast, and staying with Eunice until nightfall. Maggie and Pearl fixed dinner for John and took plenty to Tilla and others who were at Eunice's bedside.

After a breakfast of grits, sausage, and biscuits, John and Tilla left home and walked three blocks to Eunice's house. They were dressed for church. John was turned out in black wool pants, a matching jacket, a crisp white shirt, black Oxford shoes, and a black derby, one of his many hats he had collected over the years from his favorite milliner. Tilla's attire was more colorful. She wore a dress Theo gave her last Christmas: a floral-patterned drop waist chiffon dress that had velvet appliqués and small beads near the hem. Her hair was coiled in a chignon and was covered by a red cloche that belonged to Maggie.

The front door was open and John and Tilla went inside. The body heat from the number of people inside deadened the air. People were scattered in the kitchen and living room. John removed his jacket, and he and Tilla walked upstairs and into the bedroom shared by Eunice and Ernest.

Two windows in the bedroom were wide open. But little air came in. Eunice depended on two or three people to fan her with newspaper or cardboard. Tilla descried a cloth next to a bowl of water. She dipped it in the water, twisted the cloth to wring out some of the water, and then tapped her daughter's forehead with it. With some effort, Eunice opened her eyes as Tilla looked at Eunice's ashen face. Eunice's lips quivered as they moved; Tilla recognized the strain and put an upright left forefinger to her mouth to tell Eunice not to talk.

John tapped Tilla on the arm to tell her they needed to head to church. Tilla walked out of the bedroom followed by John. Tilla said, "I can't leave my baby now. You see the way she looks."

But Tilla quickly changed her mind. Reverend Owen's son had been murdered, and John and Tilla needed to be there to support him. And if they found a way to ask for an intercessory prayer for Eunice, they'd ask.

John stuck his head in the doorway and fingered for Ernest to see him. "Tilla's a wreck. Are you okay if we go on to church? We'll be back soon."

"Pops, come whenever you can."

John wondered about the last doctor's visit. "Did the doctor come yesterday?"

Ernest's mother had worked for Dr. Fennell, cleaning his house. Ernest called in a favor, and Dr. Fennell agreed to see Eunice. "Yeah, he was here yesterday morning for a short time. He said Eunice's got a pretty bad infection." He paused, adding: "He said it don't look good."

"Ernest, let me talk to you in private," John said.

They moved away from Tilla. John continued: "This may not be my place to say, ... but I understand you have an opportunity to send your wife to the hospital."

Ernest's eyes clashed with John's eyes. He needed to be polite to his father-in-law. "People are telling me she can get into the hospital because she can pass for white." Pointing to his dark skin, he added, "What them folks at the hospital gonna say when a colored man go to visit his wife?" Ernest looked at John, daring him to say that he didn't have to go. John knew the trap had been set; he just nodded and rubbed Ernest on the shoulder.

"We'll be back, Ernest. Maggie and Pearl will bring dinner."

Church service was over. Reverend Owen had talked about the wicked person who had killed his son. And he prayed for Eunice's recovery. But Tilla didn't feel much lifted by his sermon. Her heart remained sunken, and she began to feel lonely, the way she felt when Claude didn't return home.

John and Tilla were next in line to shake Reverend Owen's hand. As the congregant in front of them moved on, they took a step forward. Reverend Owen leaned forward and Tilla extended her left cheek. He shook John's hand.

John spoke first. "We're so sorry about your boy."

Tilla interjected: "It's a shame the way he died; a shot to the head and all."

"Where was he found?" John asked.

"Sheriff said his body was found in the field near Moulton and Leaves. He also said he was involved in the numbers business; said something about how they had an eye on him."

John turned around and saw a few people waiting in line. He inched forward, but Reverend Owen moved to block his path. He had one more thing to say. Looking at both John and Tilla with a wide smile, he said, "I remember the day I married you. It was on a Wednesday; January 10, 1894, as I recall." Tilla showed a glint of a warming emotion by smiling. She was always amazed at how well Reverend Owen could recall dates. "I just want to say thank you Deacon John and Sister Tilla. I'm going to continue to ask the good Lord to take care of Eunice. And I ask you to pray for me."

Maggie sat on the front Porch in John's rocking chair, reading a magazine. "Hi, baby," Tilla said as she and John walked up the porch steps.

"That's my girl, always reading something," John said.

"Ma, Pa, I've been thinking. There's this lady they call the Medicine Woman from Birmingham; she delivers babies. She was featured in the paper a while back. She's supposed to be real good. I say call on her; nothing to lose at this point."

After discussing it with Ernest, he agreed to allow Minnie Pearl Walker, a well-known midwife that some called the Medicine Woman, to attend to his ailing wife. She needed help, and he wasn't going to turn it down. She was at Eunice's bedside within thirty-six hours after receiving the telegram.

Eunice's health continued to decline. Bedsores now bothered her. While she slept, she gained a reprieve from the pain in her back. The window was open to provide ventilation.

Tilla and Ernest gave Minnie Pearl a run-down of Eunice's health. Minnie Pearl nodded and felt her forehead. "A bit warm."

Minnie Pearl reached into her worn valise and pulled out knit bone. She placed a poultice of it under Eunice as Ernest and Tilla rolled her over.

"What's that for?" Ernest asked.

"It will help reduce her back pain and help with the bedsores," Minnie Pearl said.

The knit bone seemed to work. Eunice had stopped wincing and moving in bed.

Eunice awoke an hour before dawn. Minnie Pearl remained at Eunice's side, sitting in a rocking chair. "Ernest. Ernest, you there?" Eunice said.

"Your husband is sleeping on the couch," Minnie Pearl said.

Eunice turned her head to follow the direction of the unfamiliar voice. "Who are you?"

"Minnie Pearl Walker's my name."

Eunice heard the answer but saw no one. She struggled to sit up in bed to turn on the light on the nightstand.

Minnie Pearl leaped up and moved toward the light. "Let me do that."

Eunice looked at Minnie Pearl standing over her. She wore a blue boudoir cap that covered her hair. Her dress was a drab gray and fell to the floor. Her skin was the color of dark chocolate. Two of her bottom teeth were missing. Her eyes were soft and gentle.

Minnie Pearl saw the puzzled look on Eunice's face. "It's okay, dear. Your husband said it's okay. I'm going to deliver your baby."

"Where're you from?" Eunice asked.

Minnie Pearl was happy that Eunice was talking, perhaps a sign that she was gaining strength. "Birmingham, I live in Birmingham." Minnie Pearl felt Eunice's forehead. She felt satisfied and nodded.

Eunice felt the life inside her move. She touched her stomach. A few seconds later, a parturient pang came along, and Eunice laid her hands on her stomach again.

Minnie Pearl continued to talk to Eunice to gauge her strength. Eunice's face was no longer ashen. Minnie Pearl felt hopeful. She lifted the cover and looked between Eunice's legs. Eunice winced. The contractions were starting.

Minnie Pearl offered an optimistic note: "When this baby's born, you take care of him. Watch over all your children." Eunice grimaced as though she had just hit her thumb with a hammer while pounding a nail.

Eunice managed a slight smile.

Time dragged on. It was six-thirty, and the house was still quiet except for the conversation in Eunice's bedroom. Eunice grimaced and moaned with more birthing pangs. "I'm here, darling," Minnie Pearl said as she held Eunice's hand.

Ten seconds later, Eunice said, "I think the baby's coming," with labored breath, ready for the baby to be pushed out into the world. Minnie Pearl lifted Eunice's blanket, observed what she had seen countless times when birth was near. She timed the contractions. They were ninety seconds apart. She reached in her medicine bag and pulled out several pieces of trillium. The roots had been boiled in milk.

"Open your mouth," Minnie Pearl said. She placed the trillium on the right side of Eunice's mouth.

"Don't bite or chew it," Minnie Pearl said.

"What's it supposed to do?" Eunice mumbled.

"It's going to help with your childbirth," Minnie Pearl said. Eunice spit out the trillium and let out a loud scream, waking Ernest. Ernest ran to Eunice where he saw Minnie Pearl caressing Eunice's left hand.

"Is she okay?" Ernest asked.

"The baby's coming soon," Minnie Pearl said.

Eunice's face was twisted with pain, but he was happy to see her face had life in it.

As the time for delivery drew nigh, Minnie Pearl gave instructions to Eunice. "If you feel the need to push, resist it. Your contractions are still a bit too far apart for you to push. Save your energy for now. Look at me." Eunice turned her head and looked. "I want you to pant like a dog, like this," Minnie Pearl said demonstrating. "Do it." Eunice did it and Minnie Pearl said, "Good girl." After a few seconds, Minnie Pearl told her she could stop panting. "Now take deep breaths."

Minnie Pearl returned to the rocking chair, and Ernest sat on the edge of the bed, holding his wife's hand.

It was the loudest scream yet. "Okay, honey, do you feel the need to push?"

"Yes, real bad."

"I'm going to start counting to time your contractions; each count represents one second," Minnie Pearl said.

After a count of eighty, Eunice screamed again. "Do you feel like pushing?" Minnie Pearl asked.

"Yes!"

"Don't. I'm going to start counting again." The next scream came after twenty-five seconds. Minnie Pearl walked to the foot of the bed and lifted Eunice's blanket and looked for signs that delivery was near.

"Keep your legs apart. Breathe slowly. Okay, now push. Give it all you got."

Minnie Pearl saw the crown of the baby's head. She placed her hand under the baby's head, careful not to pull it, but to support the neck. "You're doing good. Keep pushing." The baby's right shoulder came out next. Minnie Pearl continued to support the baby's neck. The baby then turned left, allowing the left shoulder to come out.

The baby slid out effortlessly and began crying immediately. She stroked the baby's nose downward several times to remove mucous and amniotic fluid. She then wrapped the baby in a towel and placed the baby on Eunice's chest, hoping the baby would begin to breastfeed.

The baby boy did not show an interest in breastfeeding. Minnie Pearl reached into her gripsack and retrieved a set of shoestrings. As she grasped the umbilical cord, the placenta flushed out. She then used a shoestring to tie the umbilical cord at four inches from the baby's navel. She used another shoestring to tie the umbilical cord at eight inches from the baby's navel. After an hour, she cut the cord with a sterile knife.

And after about another hour, the baby latched onto a nipple.

"I'm gonna stay here a little longer; make sure the baby and mother will be okay." She handed Ernest a few sassafras leaves. "I want you to put these in boiling water. She'll need this to drink."

"What's it for?"

Minnie Pearl had used it many times as a midwife and believed it helped. "It will help with her recover and keep bad things away."

John and Tilla arrived within a couple of hours after the baby was born. Both lent effusive praise of gratitude to the medicine woman Maggie had recommended. "I don't know what you did, but you worked a miracle," Tilla said.

"Ah, thank the man up high," Minnie Pearl said.

By one o'clock, the house began to fill with well-wishers. Minnie Pearl was satisfied that mother and baby would survive. She had to return to her children in Birmingham.

John, Tilla, and Minnie Pearl sat on the porch as they waited on her ride to the train station to take her home. John handed Minnie Pearl an envelope.

"What's this?"

"It's for your services."

"Ernest already paid me." She extended the envelope to John.

"No, you take this," Tilla demanded. "You saved our daughter's life."

John stood up and shook his left leg to wring out the soreness in his knee. He went inside the house.

Minnie Pearl reached in her gripsack and retrieved knit bone. She handed it to Tilla and said, "Give this to John. It should help his knee feel better. Just use it to make tea."

Tilla was curious about the contents of the gripsack. "What else is in there?"

"Oh, a bunch of things." She pulled out a small jar.

Looking at the jar, Tilla said, "What's that?"

"Mucuna leaves." "What do they do?" Before Minnie Pearl could answer, Tilla said, "Let me guess; make tea with it."

Minnie Pearl smiled and nodded.

"But what's it for?"

"If you having a problem in bed, you and your husband drink it two hours before going to bed. Your husband may not fall asleep *before* he drops on the bed." Tilla guffawed.

"Excuse me," Minnie Pearl said. She stood up and walked off the porch.

"Where're you going?"

"To look for Kirby."

"Who is Kirby?"

Minnie Pearl told Tilla about Kirby's disappearance when he was ten. Tilla's eyes moistened. She told Minnie Pearl about Claude.

While waiting on Minnie Pearl's ride, they walked a mile, calling the names of their lost boys.

52
FALL, 1923

The number of occupants in the Davis household had decreased by one. Pearl married in the spring and moved with her husband to Colbert County. Three children remained: 20-year-old Maggie, 12-year-old Willie and 9-year-old Charlie. When not doing chores around the house, or tending to her small garden in the back of the house, Maggie spent her time working at the colored library and babysitting for a wealthy white couple. The boys continued to help John on the farm by feeding the animals, milking Clara, grooming the remaining mule and two dobbins, sowing the land for crops, and harvesting it all.

John and Tilla sat on their front porch as they did when most chores had been extinguished. He whittled a figurine, and Tilla started knitting a sweater.

Maggie walked up the steps returning from her job at the library. "Hi, Ma, Pa."

"Hello, sweetheart," John said.

It was Tilla's turn. "Hi, baby."

John and Tilla looked at each other as to determine who would say it first. Tilla figured John had a softer touch, and he broke the silence. "Sit down, Maggie."

She stooped and sat on the porch, both feet resting on the step.

"We're worried about you, sweetheart."

She knew what he meant. She told him that there were a few boys whom she met at the library, but they seemed more interested in her body than the books. Maggie convinced herself if they showed an interest in the books first, then she'd possibly show an interest.

"Maggie, dear," Tilla said as she put down her knitting project, "is there some great reason why you're saving yourself?"

"Ma, I'm not saving myself."

Tilla looked at Maggie askance. "Your sisters have mentioned your name to some men, but you've not shown an interest. There are young men at First Baptist. You're not going to find a perfect man."

"I know, I know. I'll do better."

A reprieve for Maggie arrived. Charlie chased Willie out the front door. "Hey," John shouted, "settle down."

Willie lifted his head back and drank from a whiskey flask.

"What is that!" Tilla said. She extended her right hand. "Let me see that."

Willie handed it to her and said, "It's just water."

She poured out the contents. "I don't care what it is. You have no business with this. Where did you get it?"

"Me and Charlie were playing on the couch; it was under the cushion."

Tilla stood up and opened the door. "You boys go to your room. Now! Maggie, please excuse yourself."

John saw Tilla's question coming and said, "It's not mine. Let me see it."

Tilla handed it to John. He thumbed the engravings on the flask and shook his head. It was one of the flasks that he'd stolen from the Billingslys thirty-six years ago in Richmond. He searched his brain to figure out how it got under the sofa cushion. It came to him. "Honey, remember way back when Theo slept on the sofa?"

"Yeah, what about it?"

"We talked for a good while. I didn't say anything, but I could tell he had been drinking. I'm wondering if he had this flask, and it fell out of his pocket somehow."

"There's one way to find out."

John stood up and said, "I'll be right back."

Money heard John's footfall and scampered to him. John opened a closet in his tool shed and removed a metal box. He opened the box and pulled out a string-tied burlap bag. Money watched as John removed a whiskey flask from the burlap bag. As he held up both flasks, he thought about the night Madame Billingsly tumbled down the stairs and died. He thought about his mother, not knowing whether anyone told her that he stole the flasks.

He returned to the porch, holding both flasks. John wore a contrite look. "Honey, I need to tell you something."

"Go on."

He told her that he stole the flasks from the Billingslys, and why he stole them. He added: "I guess the clues to the supposed fortune are on these flasks."

"You never told me about all this."

"Didn't really see a need to. Guess I'd been too embarrassed."

"Why didn't you go back to Richmond? You had the clues."

"I met someone."

"Who?"

"You."

John had looked at the flasks and the engravings many times when on his long trek to Mount Hope. But each look would cause his mind to swirl, and headaches often ensued. So, he hung onto the flasks as far as he knew, but because of the torment they caused him, he decided to no longer look at the engravings.

But now it was time to look at them again. He felt a skosh of bile rising; he swallowed saliva, and it was gone. Looking at the front of one flask, John looked at the letters *LGB* in the bottom right corner. A sketch of a lady using one hand to cover her breasts and her long hair to cover her genitalia was in the center. A tree was engraved on the opposite side the of the flask; *Empress* was engraved on the vertical part of the tree with *Ag 6'* just under the tree. *With all our love, Edward and Marie* was engraved at the bottom.

John turned his attention to the other flask. The front contained the letters *TB* in the bottom right corner. A man with curly hair from the waist up was in the center; his right forearm resting on the top of his head and part of the left arm missing. Turning it over, John saw a tree with *Oak* engraved on the vertical part of the tree with *Au 6'* just under the tree. *With all our love, Edward and Marie* was engraved at the bottom.

"Does it make sense now?" Tilla asked.

"No, can't say that it does. They're supposed to be worth something. That's what Monsieur Billingsly said in 1887."

"Do you want to say something, or do you want me to say something to Theo about the whiskey flask?"

John needed to have a man-to-man talk with his son. "I'll talk to him," he said.

While still upset that Theo may have left the whiskey flask buried under the sofa cushion, she had another concern about Theo. She thought about the gunfire she heard and the man wearing a white hat at Moulton and Leaves. "I know where I saw that white hat Theo wears," Tilla said.

"Oh, Lord, Tilla. What is it?"

Tilla asserted herself. "I saw that same white hat the day I heard that gunshot that appeared to come from that barn that Robert used to own."

"There is more than one of those hats," John said.

"But how many hats like that are stained with red clay on the back of the hat?"

"What're you saying, Tilla?"

"I'm saying Theo was in that barn when that shot was fired."

"What does that mean?"

"I'm betting he knows something... He may know what happened to Reverend Owen's son."

—⚜—

Theo had done his best to shed his libertine behavior. His wife's insistence that he hold a steady job, coupled with his desire to please his parents, helped him do it. Although he didn't give up drinking, he stopped hanging out at the juke joint where bad things happened that he sometimes found himself in the middle of. Besides, because of his job at the foundry, there was no time to slum it.

With a week off work, he drove his car to his parents' house. He had something to prove. He alighted from his car and walked toward the house where he saw John moiling the soil in inhospitable weather. John moved slower now; it was as if his bones and joints had begun to protest the years of work they had endured for so long.

"Pa," Theo yelled.

John doffed his straw hat, wiped his brow, and squinted at Theo to ease the pain of the salty sweat. "Hey, son."

"Pop, you look like you need some help out here."

"The boys have been helping." John turned and saw Charlie chasing Willie in the cornfield. Laughing, he said, "Maybe I do need some help."

Theo was dressed to help; he wore the overalls that he wore when working in the foundry. "What can I do?" Theo asked.

Not much work needed to be done. John was mostly finished. Looking into Theo's indulgent eyes, John knew he couldn't turn down Theo's offer. "I asked the boys to take some bales of hay out of the barn; they still haven't done it."

"I'm on it, Pop. Anything else?"

John began to temporize, trying to find the right time to talk to him about the whiskey flask. "Just do that for now. I'll think of something else."

An hour later, John and Theo found themselves on the front porch, rocking in chairs and sipping lemonade Tilla had made. Theo had noticed that Tilla had a sad countenance when he saw her. "Something wrong with Ma?"

"Not that I know of, son."

A few seconds later, Tilla opened the door and handed John a bag, as if he needed a reminder of what he needed to say to Theo. She returned to the kitchen.

John held his glass up high and swirled his lemonade, watching the seeds spin. He finished it off and removed a whiskey flask from the bag. "Son, Willie found this under the sofa cushion in the living room. Have you seen this?"

Theo extended his hand, and John handed it to him. He looked at it and said, "I saw one like it; this one has a naked lady on it. The one I remember had a man on it."

John removed the other whiskey flask and handed it to Theo. "Is this it?"

"Yeah, Pa," Theo said, "where did you get this?"

"Like I said, Willie found it under the sofa cushion. Any idea how it got there?"

Theo scratched his head then said, "I think I know what happened. It must of fell out of my jacket pocket when I fell asleep on the sofa. You know, I wondered what happened to it."

John was thankful that Theo had come clean. But the obvious question had to be asked: "Where did you get it, son?"

The night Capstone nearly killed him surfaced in his mind. "Pad gave it to me." He wasn't sure if he let the answer slip out, but he was sure more sinuous questions were on the way. Please don't ask who Pad is, he said to himself.

"Who is Pad?"

He had told the truth once already, so he decided to stay on that path. "He was in the numbers business."

"Go on."

He could not bring himself to mention what Capstone had done to him. John could tell Tilla. He had to veer off truth's path somewhat. "I was in a fight and got hit in the jaw. He told me to drink some whiskey to help with the pain; told me to keep this flask."

"Do you know where Pad got the flask?"

"No, I have no idea."

"Thanks, son. You've been a big help."

Theo was curious why John had the two flasks. "Do they belong to you, Pa?"

"You come over next Sunday for dinner after church, and I'll tell you."

"Okay."

John could see and feel that Theo was trying to make things right with him and Tilla. "Thanks, son."

"For what?"

"I love you, son. I appreciate what you've done for Maggie. She met this man, William McKinley, at the library. She's been going out with him."

"He's a good guy." Pops.

"I sure hopes he likes to read. You know your sister."

Theo smiled and said, "I think she got it from her newspaper father. Where is Maggie?"

"She may be in the back reading or tending to your mother's garden."

She sat in a chair on the back porch reading. "Hey, sis," Theo yelled. "How's Mack been treating you?"

"Real nice. Thanks, Theo."

"Listen, sis," Theo said, "something's been eating at me, and I need to tell someone, or I'm gonna burst wide open."

Maggie put down her magazine and looked at Theo. "I'm listening."

"You must promise not to tell anyone. I need time to figure out how to handle it."

She nodded.

"I know who shot Christopher."

"You mean Reverend Owen's son?"

"Yeah. You see, I used to work for this man, Capstone. He was the lead numbers man in town. I think he came to believe that Chris was skimming money from him. Don't know if it was true, but Capstone said it was. He called a meeting at that shed that Robert used to own, the one near Moulton and Leaves."

"You were at this meeting?"

"Yeah, I was there. Anyway, Capstone shot Chris as a warning to the rest of us."

"Why didn't you tell anyone about this, Theo?"

"That's just it, I didn't know what to do. I was scared; still scared."

"That's a lot to digest, Theo."

"I know. Remember your promise to me."

Maggie nodded.

"I'm going to say bye to Ma now," Theo said.

Tilla moved quickly away from the kitchen window to the living room. She sat on the settee and began to cry after overhearing Theo's conversation with Maggie on the back porch. It all made sense to her now. It was Theo who wore the white hat coming out of the shed, just like she had feared. The gunshot she heard came from the shed.

"Ma," Theo yelled, as he walked in the house. "Ma," he repeated.

Tilla wiped her tears with the back of her right hand, stood up, grabbed a dust cloth and said, "Here I am, Theo." She smiled, but she couldn't hide her moist red eyes.

"What's wrong, Ma?"

"Oh, you know how I worry about the family. But it's nothing the Lord can't fix. How have you been, son?"

"Doing good, Ma. The wife and kids are doing good, too. The job is hard work, but it something that's steady." He brushed away a tuft of hair that had fallen over Tilla's brow and said, "Ma, you sure you okay?"

"Your mama's going to be okay."

Theo hugged her tightly, kissed her on the cheek. "Pa invited me over for dinner this coming Sunday. Said something about he's going to tell me about the flasks."

"We want the whole family over. There's a lot we're going to talk about."

After Sunday dinner, the children gathered in the living room, and John began to discuss the days of yore. He started with his precious mother. After talking for twenty minutes or so, he pointed to Anne's portrait and said, "That's why I had this commissioned years ago."

"Why does she have that funny-looking smile?" Willie asked.

John explained and Willie asked, "She smiled like that?"

"That's what I recall, son."

"Pa, why did you leave Richmond?" Bessie asked.

He told them about how he hated Madame Billingsly, how she died, and why he stole the flasks. "But I let the hate go a long time ago."

Tilla held the flasks and said, "These are the flasks." She handed them to Pearl first, saying, "Y'all look at these."

As the flasks were passed from sibling to sibling, Eunice asked, looking at John, "Do you know what the clues are?"

About five years ago, when money had grown a little tight, John had taken the flasks to have them appraised by a man he met at Moulton and Leaves. He thought they were sterling silver but wanted to be sure. The appraiser told him the flasks were indeed made of sterling silver, and they were worth a "decent grip." When John asked about the letters on the flasks, the appraiser told John that AU means gold and AG means silver on the periodic table. John thanked the appraiser and put the flasks in the bag. While walking home, a dog gave chase, and John dropped the bag.

He had carried his gun with him just in case the appraiser or anyone else tried to take the flasks from him. John tossed the bag aside and stood and pointed the gun at the dog, who, upon seeing the gun, turned around to look for other quarry. John picked up the bag and returned home, where he stored it in his shed. He didn't care about the flasks and didn't even look inside the bag when he stored the bag in the shed. It happened again—the flasks were causing more trouble, this time in the form of a menacing dog.

"Yes, I know something about them. I'm guessing *TB* stands for Tyrone Billingsly and *LGB* is for his wife."

He didn't tell the children or Tilla that he had the flasks appraised, and that the flasks could perhaps draw a decent sum, and that gold and silver could be located on the Billingsly's property. He didn't want anyone to try to push him in the direction of selling the flasks or making an effort to steal gold and silver that rightfully belonged to Billingsly. He was in possession of stolen property—God saved him once and he wasn't going to chance it again.

"What are you going to do with the flasks?" Tilla asked.

"I don't know. But they're not mine."

"Pop, you ever try to go back to find your mother?" Charlie asked.

"No, son. Before I met your mama, I met Cousin Riley in Mount Hope. I had to stay to learn more about him."

"Who's Cousin Riley?" Charlie asked.

"Well, son, he's Junior, your Uncle Riley." John then explained how he met Cousin Riley while trying to fulfill his mother's wish by finding Cousin Riley's father.

John later added: "And when I met your mama and we had you and you ..." he said pointing at his children. "I had to take care of my family."

Maggie put down her pencil and notepad and asked, "Pa, why did it take you so long to make it to Mount Hope?"

After explaining the places he stayed, the people he met, the times he nearly lost his life, Maggie said, "Pa, we heard that you had a problem with a white man who threatened you about some article in the newspaper."

The article was sitting in his lap. "That's right, it was all over this article. You kids can read the article yourselves." He went on to explain the confrontation with Chester White and how it ended.

While holding the flasks, Charlie asked, "Pa, can I have these?"

"I haven't decided what I'm going to do with them."

"Mama," Charlie said, "can we hear about your family?"

"Next time, baby."

53

FALL, 1928

John and Tilla sat on the front porch in their rocking chairs shaded from the noonday sun. John swirled his lemonade, and Tilla knitted a sweater.

Fourteen-year-old Charlie, the lone remaining child at home, walked out the front door and said, "I'm going to Fred's house. Be back for supper."

"Wait," Tilla said. Charlie turned around, and Tilla looked up at him. She saw John's mahogany skin color and her narrow nose in him. The thought of Claude surfaced in her mind. She reached for his hand, and he put his hand in hers. "I love you, baby. Supper will be ready when you get back."

Tilla released her grip and Charlie pivoted and ran off the porch.

A small block of wood sat on the floor next to John. He finished his drink, picked up the block of wood, and removed his carving knife from his shirt pocket.

"What are you making now?" Tilla asked.

Looking at the wood with an artisan's eye, he said, "Something inside is begging to be set free." He started hewing, something he started ever since Kelly taught him to make frog gigs in Greenville, South Carolina. About ten minutes later, Tilla shattered the silence, saying, "I wonder how Minnie Pearl is doing."

"Who?"

"The medicine woman from Birmingham who saved Eunice's life and delivered her baby."

John nodded.

"Where're you going?" John asked Tilla as she rose from her chair.

As she had done too many times to count, she was set to go hither and thither to search for her missing boy. With time, she began to recover her soul that had been rended by Claude's disappearance. She didn't know Claude's whereabouts, but the good Lord did. She asked the Lord to take good care of Claude, and having received promise from the Lord that Charlie was safe with him, her soul began to repair itself, like a starfish grows another leg after losing one. She'd continue to look for Claude, though, just in case the good Lord made him available to her.

She knew that John could never feel the depths of her pain; only a mother could. Someone like Ann, who surely felt it when she lost her husband when he was sold to another slave owner; when her twin eight-year-old daughters died of disease; and when John left home at seventeen. Someone like Fannie, who lost her fourteen-year-old daughter. Someone like Minnie Pearl, who lost her ten-year-old son.

"I'm going to look for Claude." She put her knitting project on the chair and took her first steps on her ritual journey.

John stopped her in her tracks. She turned and faced him. They hadn't talked about it for over twenty-eight years. "Tilla, you remember the time capsule we buried on church property?"

"Yes, darling. What about it?"

"You never told me what you wrote."

"That's because we made a promise back then that whatever we wrote would remain a secret until someone dug it up." Until then, her note would be between her and God.

Tilla turned and walked down the steps.

Money crawled to John and looked at him with a rueful roll of his rheumy eyes, seeking permission to go with Tilla.

"Go ahead, you old hound."

With creaky legs, Money leaped onto John's lap, licked his face with slobbering chops, and trotted to catch up with Tilla.

A half hour later, the clouds gathered and blocked the sun.

Weems's yapper caught John's attention. Mr. Weems was on his way with the mail.

"How you doing, John?" Mr. Weems asked.

"No use complaining, Mr. Weems."

Weems removed a bundle of mail and handed it to John. He told John that two letters did not contain his address, but because the letters were sent to the post office, and they contained John's name and city, Weems told someone at the post office he knew John and would deliver the letters to him.

"The missus okay?"

"Yes, she's fine."

The yapper barked as to tell Mr. Weems it was time to move on. "Okay, boy."

"How long the dog been following you?"

"Oh, I don't know. A while, I suppose. Don't know what I'd do without him."

Another yap, and Weems nodded to John and left as the first rain drops appeared.

John shuffled through the mail and stopped at the sight of the name Edgar Billingsly from Richmond in the sender's corner. His stomach knotted, and bile rose to the back of his mouth. He took a swill of lemonade, and the bilious taste went away. He thought of his narrow escape from Billingsly at Sloss Furnace many years ago and wondered whether he was still alive. If not, perhaps another Billingsly wanted the flasks. He'd gladly hand them over and finally receive absolution.

He carefully ripped off a slender piece of the right side of the envelope. Holding the envelope to his mouth, he blew into it, inflating it, and with a slight shake the letter fell into his lap.

> Dear John,
>
> I trust this missive will find you. It's time that we meet. Mama once mentioned that you might be in Mount Hope, Alabama. She trusted that you'd make it there someday. She doesn't remember too much now. She stays with Jenette and me and the kids.

The more he read, the heavier the letter felt. He looked away, and his hands fell to his lap. He picked up the letter, and tears trickled from his eyes when he read that a man named Herbert was Edgar's father, and that Ann told him that Herbert had been shot and killed when Edgar was a toddler.

John's mind slowed to absorb that he had a brother, a brother who was a college professor. John immediately harkened back to Atlanta University where Dean Fairbanks offered John the opportunity to attend the university. He wondered what his life would have been like if he had. There'd be no Tilla, who was everything to him.

He'd take Tilla with him to meet his precious mother. Junior would go, too. There'd be much to talk about even if she didn't talk. He'd do all the talking; he'd tell her that he never gave up hope that he'd see her again. He'd tell her that he was on his way to see her in 1893, but news that Tilla was carrying his first child derailed his plans. He'd tell her about his large family, his newspaper business, the general store, her grandchildren.

The smile on John's face vanished as he looked at the sender's address on the next envelope. The name was unfamiliar: Erich Gottschalk from Birmingham, Alabama.

This time it had to be about the flasks; it just had to be. He swallowed hard, forcing the bile back down his throat. He picked up his glass of lemonade and finished it. The brackish taste quickly disappeared.

He wasn't as gentle with this envelope. He ripped it open and immediately started reading the letter. As he lip-read the letter, he wondered how the sender had found him. He folded the letter and put in back in the envelope, contemplating what and when he'd tell Tilla.

He picked up his project and resumed carving. But the letter gnawed at him, and he removed it from the envelope again.

He read aloud a passage from the letter as though to convince himself it was real:

> Before she passed away, Mother (Gretchen Gottschalk) told me that you are my father. I am a physician living in Birmingham. My twin brother lives in Cullman. I would like to meet you some day. My kids have been asking about their grandfather.

In the space of a few minutes, he had gained a brother and two sons. He could handle the discovery of his brother, a saint who had given him concrete information about his mother. Two more children was something else.

Money barked a few times to announce he was on his way home with Tilla. Always eager to return to John, he was several paces ahead.

John stood and walked to edge of the porch. He looked up; the gray skies frowned. He put the mail in his pants pocket and sat down. Money dropped to John's feet.

Thirty seconds later, Tilla picked up her knitting project and sat down.

As she had said on countless returns from her search, the refrain was the same: "No sign of Claude."

"Tilla."

"Yes, Darling."

The sky's frown intensified; a thunderclap roared and shook the house. Tilla rose quickly and placed her right hand over her heart. John popped up from his seat. As they got up to go inside, a strong wind blew over their rocking chairs. Money took shelter under the porch.

Tilla stepped inside first. John quickly closed the door and looked out the window. Their chairs were floating in the air. He turned around, reached for Tilla's right hand, and kissed it. Gazing into her tranquil eyes, he said soberly, "I've got some news to tell you."

The End.

ACKNOWLEDGMENTS

My gratitude to those whose knowledge, faith, wisdom, kindness, and patience helped *Lost Souls Recovered* come alive: Darryl Atwell, Heidi Ashley, Lovie Debnam, and Hayley McClaren.

ABOUT THE AUTHOR

As an amateur genealogist and certified family historian, Eric Walker was impelled to write his debut novel *Lost Souls Recovered* when he discovered the richness of family stories through research of historical documents and those told to him by relatives.

As he read historical documents and talked to relatives, he'd envision a way to bring to life in fiction form many of his ancestors who lived a hardscrabble life and who worked to overcome hardship. He believed the written word could unlock doors as well as the imagination and unite our spirit through our visions. He is working on a second novel involving land loss in the early post-Reconstruction era. He is a lawyer and lives in Ohio.

Follow Eric:

twitter.com/sennachietyme
tiktok.com/@sennachietyme
instagram.com/sennachietyme
facebook.com/sennachietyme